Glenn activated his _____ _____ ____. "Mission control. It may have been foolish, but Rick's out. I'm starting my extraction now. Wish me luck." Glenn turned over on his back and reached up to shift the frame out of his way. A white glow enveloped his left arm. Someone screamed over the comm. As he gasped for breath, he realized it came from him.

He scooted on his butt, half crawling, half dragging himself out from under the wreckage by pulling with his legs and right arm. He needed to let go of the spar he was holding with his left hand. He tried and heard a new alarm—suit integrity. The fabric of the spacesuit had melted onto the hot metal, pulling his hand away had torn it open.

At least the temperature is dropping.

There was a boulder directly ahead, part of the frame was resting on it, and there was just enough gap for him to roll over and crawl out. More red lights appeared in his display, and he heard an ominous cracking and popping from behind him—just before his oxygen tank blew up and drove him feet-first into the boulder.

BAEN BOOKS
by ROBERT E. HAMPSON

The Moon and the Desert

Stellaris: People of the Stars
edited with Les Johnson

The Founder Effect
edited with Sandra L. Medlock

To purchase these titles in e-book form,
please go to www.baen.com.

THE MOON AND THE DESERT

ROBERT E. HAMPSON

THE MOON AND THE DESERT

This is a work of fiction. All the characters and events portrayed in this book are fictional, and any resemblance to real people or incidents is purely coincidental.

Copyright © 2023 by Robert E. Hampson

A Baen Books Original

Baen Publishing Enterprises
P.O. Box 1403
Riverdale, NY 10471
www.baen.com

ISBN: 978-1-9821-9336-2

Cover art by Dominic Harman

First printing, March 2023
First mass market printing, April 2024

Distributed by Simon & Schuster
1230 Avenue of the Americas
New York, NY 10020

Library of Congress Control Number: 2022056101

Printed in the United States of America

10 9 8 7 6 5 4 3 2 1

DEDICATION

To Ruann—the love of my life and protector of my writing time. You're that special person who truly knows who I am.

To Mom—my first fan, first reader, and finder of typos. Thanks for staying up and watching all of these shows with me.

To Dad—my hero and role model. I wish you could have seen this one. We miss you, deeply.

To Sandra—my sometime coauthor, sometime coeditor, and always copyeditor. You make it all look good.

To Sam Deadwyler—my mentor for a fantastic career in research—including the first glimmer of bionics.

To the strong and resilient people of Lahaina, Maui, Hawaii—may you arise stronger, faster, better!

...and to Rick Boatright—alpha reader and technical watchdog. A good friend, and great conversationalist. You're gone much too soon; you would have loved this one.

PROLOGUE

Oh, this is well and truly going to suck, Glenn Armstrong Shepard thought to himself as he started toward the crashed Dragonfly trainer. "Mission Control, this is the Monitoring Medical Observer," he commed. "Pilot Morykwas is trapped underneath the Dragonfly. I'm closest. I'm going in to pull him out."

"Negative, MMO, that's a highly dangerous situation right now," came the response.

"His vitals went through the roof. Blood pressure increased, respiration and heart rate were elevated. I *told* you all of that. *He* knew he was losing control, and *I* knew he was losing control. It was obvious to anyone watching his vitals, so don't tell me you couldn't see it."

Glenn could see Rick Morykwas trapped underneath the struts and spars of the test vehicle. It was a simulator for the Mars flyer. It was much too fragile to operate on Earth, so they trained on the Moon. The problem was that with *no* atmosphere and less than half the gravity of Mars, it was unstable as hell. Rick was trapped and Glenn was the closest of the Moonbase support team.

"I'm going to have to crawl under there to get him out." Glenn knelt down to make his way under the wreckage. He immediately saw his spacesuit's temperature indicator begin to rise.

"MMO, you can't crawl in there; you'll rip your suit. We can't risk two people."

"Easy for you to say, CAPCOM, you're sitting in an air-conditioned room in Tucson. He's at risk of burning up."

A new voice came on the line. "CAPCOM, lockout the rebroadcast and make sure this is a closed channel. Nothing goes out. MMO, this is FLIGHT. Don't risk yourself; this isn't your job."

"Like hell it's not." Glenn respected the Flight Director, but that simply was not an order he could follow.

There were spars in the way, and a white glow further down the metal rod. He could feel the heat through his gloved hand—through insulation and into the interior of his suit. The stakes had just risen drastically. "FLIGHT, the hydrazine tank has ruptured. We have a fire *in vacuum*. That means the oxidizer tank has ruptured as well."

"That's why you need to stay out of there, MMO. There's no point in risking yourself. You'll never see the flame!"

Glenn knew it was already too late for that warning. His left hand was tingling, and it was starting to sting. On the other hand, he wasn't sure if the flame had gotten to Rick yet. At least . . . he couldn't see any white spots near the upside-down cockpit.

"Hang on Rick, it's Glenn. I'll pull you out of there."

"Glenn, it's hot. Something is blocking my legs. I'm trapped."

"One of the spars has your legs pinned. I'm going to try to lift it up. See if you can slither out." Glenn crawled up under the wing root and pushed up on hands and knees to put some upward pressure on the frame of the Dragonfly. As his backpack touched the frame, alarms went off in his helmet display. The heat of a fire couldn't spread in vacuum, but it could certainly be conducted through the metallic frame of the trainer.

Glenn ignored the warnings and vowed to get this over as quickly as possible. He reached for Rick to help him out, but the pilot was facing away from him. He grabbed the rescue handle on the other man's life-support backpack. Carry straps and handles had proven their worth for soldiers and emergency workers on Earth, and they were now standard equipment off-Earth as well.

As he started to pull, Rick screamed—the leg of his spacesuit had that same white hot glow Glenn had seen earlier. The hydrazine flame was right there, and he'd have to pull Rick through it.

The problem was, he didn't have enough leverage.

Glenn inched forward, closer to the fire, and grabbed the rescue handle with both hands. More red lights showed on his helmet display. A squirt of warm water came from his drinking tube—the heat was beginning to affect his own life-support. A sharp tug got the pilot away from the invisible flame. Free of restriction, Rick turned over and started to crawl out from under the wreckage.

"Mission Control, Rick is loose, he's climbing out."

"MMO, FLIGHT. I told you to get out of there. I don't want to risk both of you. Especially not the chief medical officer for the mission."

"FLIGHT, you assholes knew this was happening. I told you that his vitals indicated he was in trouble, and you told me—and I quote—'stay in my lane.' If Rick dies, it's on you. If I die, I'm coming back to haunt you and make sure you never get another night's sleep. Now shut the hell up and let me do my job."

Rick rapped on Glenn's helmet as he crawled past. The frame shifted as he passed, and Glenn could feel additional pressure on his back. To get himself out from under it, he'd have to flip over and scoot out on his back. The air in his suit had gotten warm. He nudged the airflow valve with his chin and was rewarded with even warmer air. It tasted strange, too, sort of sickly sweet . . .

Crap. The coolant system ruptured. That's propylene glycol! He noticed how raspy his voice had become when he next activated the comm. "Mission control. It may have been foolish, but Rick's out. I'm starting my extraction now. Wish me luck." Glenn turned over on his back and reached up to shift the frame out of his way. A white glow enveloped his left arm. Someone screamed over the comm. As he gasped for breath, he realized it came from him.

He scooted on his butt, half crawling, half dragging himself out from under the wreckage by pulling with his legs and right arm. He needed to let go of the spar he was holding with his left hand. He tried and heard a new alarm—suit integrity. The fabric of the suit had melted onto the hot metal, pulling his hand away had torn it open.

At least the temperature is dropping.

There was a boulder directly ahead, part of the frame was resting on it, and there was just enough gap for him to roll over and crawl out. More red lights appeared in his display, and he heard an ominous cracking and popping from behind him—just before his oxygen tank blew up and drove him feet-first into the boulder.

PART 1
RESURRECTION

CHAPTER 1:
The Moon and the Desert

George J @spacefan
> Any news on the astronaut injured on the
> Moon?

USSF Public Information Office
@SpaceForceOfficial
> @spacefan, US Space Force is unable to
> comment at this time.
> Please see our website for the latest
> news and exciting opportunities in the
> Space Force!
>
> ChirpChat, January 2039

Glenn Armstrong Shepard drifted in and out of consciousness. He really had no way of knowing if he was dreaming or actually seeing and hearing his surroundings. He saw white—white walls, white ceiling, people moving around him, all in white. There was a strange lack of depth to it all.

9

The next moment he was watching the Dragonfly crash. The trainer reminded him of a Wright Flyer—a biplane with a fuselage of tubing and wire, just ... longer, with wings three times the size of the Earth-bound original and reaction-control rockets for training on the Moon. This one *had* to be a dream; he was the *pilot*.

He watched himself struggling to control the unstable trainer. The right wing of the Dragonfly began to lift, so he corrected the tilt by firing the control thruster on the left wing. The burn was too long. Instead of coming level, the left wing rose even higher than the right had. The nose was starting to lift as well.

It was surreal, how he was both watching the imminent crash, and part of it at the same time. He vaguely heard Mission Control telling him to "stay in his lane."

"He's going to lose it," he heard himself saying into the dedicated channel to Mission Control. "How the hell is he supposed to fly this in Mars's atmosphere if he can't hold it steady in vacuum with half the gees?"

"Pilot. You need to eject." He heard his own voice coming over the comm.

"I ... can ... control ..." he grunted through gritted teeth.

He heard himself scream, and everything faded to black.

Glenn was drifting, his viewpoint changing as he directed his attention to his surroundings. There was a female doctor preparing an operating room. She was dressed from head to toe in a white isolation garment. He couldn't see features, but he felt he knew this person.

Female. Tall and thin, mid-forties, long brown hair, pale skin like most of the people on Moonbase who ignored the mandatory hour-a-day "grow lights" which substituted for sunlight. He couldn't see any of that, but her voice triggered memories.

He *knew* her.

"L.I.S.T.E.R., we need to set the bay for hyperbaric oxygen, with pressure at twenty-two PSI and oh-two at thirty percent. In preparation, we need a Level One hard decon. Double check the pressure seals right now, give me hard vac and two-hundred thousand lux UV B and C sterilization for ten minutes, then prep for hyperbaric conditions."

An artificial voice replied. "Acknowledged, Dr. Barbier. Closing shutters and pumping down to hard seal." The thick transplas portholes into the procedure room darkened, and there was a thrum of air pumps. "Decontamination commencing." The pumps stopped, and the faintest glow of light was visible through the darkened ports. After ten minutes, the glow reduced and there was a slight hiss of air. "Argon purge commencing."

Hyperbaric therapy was common in the treatment of decompression sickness and "the bends"—caused by air bubbles in the blood—and had been in use since divers first ventured into the deep ocean. It was also useful as a follow-up for astronauts whose spacesuits lost pressure; however, as a medical treatment, it had risks. High pressure oxygen should be the perfect healing environment; unfortunately, too long an exposure would cause seizures. The counter argument was that pure oxygen would speed the healing process and could prevent the need for amputating badly damaged limbs.

Yvette waited for the rescue crew to bring her one-time colleague, friend, and former lover into the sickbay facility on Moonbase. The reports had mentioned burns and a crush injury, and complications from those injuries involved heightened risk of infection and lack of blood flow to the affected limbs and even organs—especially in the reduced pressure environment of the lunar surface suits. Thus, she'd elected to sterilize the medical bay by exposing it to vacuum. It was easy enough to do on the Moon, easier still in this location right on the edge of Moonbase's pressure dome. Once her patient arrived, the increased pressure and oxygen concentration would force oh-two directly into his tissues no matter how badly damaged the circulation. She would need to balance the atmospheric pressure to gain the maximum benefit of oxygen penetration to his damaged tissues and keep her patient stable until she could figure out the extent of his injuries.

The visitor standing in the hatch to the med bay had two stars on his collar, but the doctor was just too tired to care about his rank. Besides, she was a civilian. There wasn't too much he could do to her if he decided she was insubordinate.

"How is he, Doctor?" the two-star asked.

"He's a tough SOB, General." Yvette Barbier stripped off an outer set of gloves, then pulled down her mask and face shield to rub at her eyes. There was a lot of blood— on her scrubs, gloves, mask, and hair net, but the shield had protected her face and the wisps of blonde hair on her forehead. "There's no way he should be alive, and frankly, I'm not sure that he *should* remain so from the point of view of the Hippocratic Oath. Keeping him alive may well cause more harm than good. Both legs are crushed below the knees. One leg has a fracture above the knee while the other has a partial fracture—what we call a 'green-stick break.' His entire left side is burned. Even if he keeps the arm, the healing from that is tricky, and he'll probably lose it to circulatory failure. The heat damage is severe, even on top of the burns."

"So. Bad, then."

Yvette looked up and stared angrily at the commander of the Space Force contingent at Moonbase. "General, he was breathing superheated steam mixed with glycol. The only thing that saved him was when his suit vented—but then he was in low pressure. At this point, I don't even know if he can breathe without a ventilator." She sighed and slumped in her chair. "It would be a mercy to just turn it off. I checked for a DNR, but I don't see one in his file."

A Do Not Resuscitate, or DNR, order was common among active Space Force members. The theory was that anything in space that didn't kill you instantly might as well have done so anyway.

"Oh, he's got an advanced directive, alright. You're not going to like it, though."

"Why?"

"It reads simply, 'Rebuild me. Bionics if necessary.' It goes on to say that as long as heart, lungs and brain are functioning, he volunteers for prosthetic augmentation."

Yvette was shocked. "Is that even possible?"

"We can rebuild him; we have the technology. He even offered a trust fund to pay for it."

"Oh, God." Yvette closed her eyes and whispered, "God, how I wish you didn't."

Glenn was awake this time. At least, he thought he was. The room still had the flat, two-dimensional effect, and it extended to sounds as well. Things seemed . . . flat and muffled, but he was pretty sure he was actually there this time and not floating around.

Yvette had done something to turn off the nerve impulses which carried pain. He still had a vague sensation of his body—he could feel the temperature-regulating fabric relieving the heat from his burned skin, there was air movement on the right side of his face, but his whole left side felt dull, flattened. He knew he was talking with Yvette, but the first part of the conversation was a blur.

Oh, right. "I can't do it, Glenn. There's too much risk," she'd told him.

"Amputation will stabilize me until they can get me back groundside. You know wounds don't drain properly in low gee," Glenn countered. His voice was raspy and barely more than a whisper; frankly, it was amazing he could talk and be understood with the bandages covering his face. The hyperbaric oxygen had prevented more damage from the burns, but his airway had already suffered from inhaling heated contaminants. "Waiting only risks gangrene and losing the rest of the legs. It will make fitting a prosthetic that much tougher."

"Stop it! You know I can't do that. You've always

known." Yvette turned away with tears in her eyes. "Why couldn't you have had a DNR like a sensible person? You can't live like this. I can't stand to watch you die by inches. I won't do it."

"So, you want me to die just like . . . well, I'd snap my fingers, except, you know . . . the bandages," he growled.

"NO! I don't want you to die, but I can't watch you live in agony. You think you're okay now, but that's just the nerve interrupter. When that gets turned off, it will be either a life of drug addiction or pain."

"There are other possibilities."

"That's what you said, but there's a less than five percent possibility that it will work."

"I know a doctor. Martin Spruce. His technique pushes that up to fifty percent."

"For your legs, sure. But your arm? You're probably going to lose that. Your skin, your face, not to mention eye and ear, are so badly damaged that you have to keep pushing that probability until your luck runs out."

"I have to try."

"Listen to yourself! You can't even talk above a whisper from the inhalation burns. I took an oath to 'First, do no harm.'" She let out a sob. "Letting you live like this is more harm than my conscience can bear. I'm taking myself off your case."

"Fine then. Call Dr. Spruce. Get him up here, or get me down there. I'll have to go back down to Earth anyway, so might as well get me prepped and on my way, then you'll never have to deal with me again."

"I know," Yvette sobbed.

※ ※ ※

Yvette was sitting at a workstation just outside the intensive care module. The monitors said he was asleep, recovering from anesthesia. Through the observation window she could see him lying on the treatment table, unmoving. A white drape didn't quite cover his body, but was held suspended so that it didn't touch the burned skin while still providing protection and a token amount of modesty. Drainage tubes connected to the stumps of his legs and left arm were connected to pumps to compensate for the lack of gravity-induced drainage.

She turned away from the window and picked up her tablet to leave, when multiple alarms went off. She looked back through the window and saw Glenn tense up and start to convulse. By the time she could get through the isolation door into the room—ignoring her own protective garments—he lay very still. The heart monitor showed a wiggling line instead of regular—or even irregular—heartbeats.

"L.I.S.T.E.R. Code Blue!" she shouted. Convulsions meant she'd made a mistake and the high-pressure oxygen was affecting his brain. Seizures were often caused by brain swelling, and the effect on his heart meant the swelling had affected the brainstem. She would have to act fast—faster than assistance could arrive.

The heart monitor was connected to an automated defibrillator. Electric shock would overcome fibrillation—uncoordinated "vibration" of the heart muscle—and hopefully restore a semblance of a heartbeat. The problem was that she needed to do other things: administer drugs to reduce swelling, reduce the strain on the heart, check his breathing, blood pressure, electrolytes and more. However, if the AD fired while she was touching Glenn, the transmitted shock could cause burns at best, or at worst, stop her own heart. This would have to be timed carefully.

Her heart told her she was doing the right thing, even if her medical training said otherwise.

When he eventually awoke, she would need to be elsewhere, and once he left for Earth, he would be gone. But for now, she would do everything she could for him, even if he would never know.

CHAPTER 2:
Broken Doll

Waldo J. @MagickInk
Who *wouldn't* want to live in space and
not have to worry about gravity or body
weight?

ChirpChat, June 2039

Time passed, and the dreams—or at least the accompanying
lucid periods—seemed more frequent. There were more
doctors and nurses. The outline under the sheet took shape,
and Glenn could see *through* the covering to metal frames,
wires, gears, and fibers in the shape of human limbs. At one
point, the images gained more color, more shape, and for a
brief time he seemed to have regained his vision, hearing,
and . . . sense of smell. The latter was unfortunate, because
now he smelled all of the odors of a hospital—antiseptic,
blood, burnt skin and hot electronics.

Glenn woke up.

He tried to move and found that he couldn't.

※ ※ ※

"So how am I supposed to learn to use these things if I can barely lift them?" Glenn was sitting up in bed—if one could actually call it a bed. They had transferred him overnight into a device that was more supporting framework than mattress. It was not quite as wide as the hospital bed and had hinges and articulations at all of the same points as his new—and old—limbs. He wasn't exactly strapped into the frame, but he could see that there were fittings for straps and clamps.

Doctor Martin Spruce smiled. He was a relatively short, brown-haired man in his late fifties. Every time Glenn saw him, he seemed to be holding a mug of coffee. He seemed to prefer a strong, bitter brew, but diluted it with heavy cream—the evidence for the latter being the hint of cream on Marty's graying mustache. One would think that the high caffeine intake and the fact that Marty never seemed to stop moving would mean that he was thin and wiry, but the surgeon was comfortably thick around the middle, more like a wrestler than a runner.

Marty led the team supervising the "extensive rebuild" as Glenn called it. "Well, we don't expect you to be able to use them right away. Your brain needs to learn what signals to use, and the processing chips in your arm and legs need to learn what signals to read." He gestured to the framework. "This frame will support your weight as you re-learn how to walk. It's also your new bed until you develop the strength and coordination to move yourself around even lying flat. We didn't spend all of this time and money putting you back together just to give you bedsores, Shep."

Glenn understood that last point perfectly well—especially the point about bedsores. Before the prosthetics were fitted, he'd been like a worm on a sidewalk, capable of rolling and squirming, but not much else. Even that small amount of movement had been sufficient to prevent the kinds of skin ulcers and pressure injuries suffered by patients confined to bed for too long without moving. Now that he had the additional weight of the prosthetics, though, his ability to move his body around was greatly diminished, and he risked developing lesions where the constant pressure compressed the skin and muscle, causing permanent bruises and eventual bleeding and open sores.

"I'm a little curious why you haven't sent me back to Moonbase or one of the stations. Now that wound drainage is not an issue, I would think that lower gravity would be an advantage."

"Not a chance, Shep," Marty answered. "You need to learn to work against full gravity. If I let you get by with just a fraction, you won't relearn normal reflexes. Besides, we learned a few lessons about orbital rehab with Asimov Station."

Glenn's expression darkened. The privately owned station had been popular with celebrities and the extremely wealthy—many of whom thought rules were for others. Advertising emphasized health benefits, and a clinic had been set up for those rich patients who could afford the multimillion-dollar price tag to escape Earth's gravity. Patients and celebrities alike had proved unable to care for themselves in an emergency and lives were lost, including a doctor who'd been helping a rich, elderly patient get to an escape pod after the station suffered emergency decompression.

He'd been Glenn's best friend from medical school.

"Yeah. Got it," Glenn said, gruffly.

He tried to lift first his legs, then his left arm. He could move the leg stumps, but the prosthetics were just so much dead weight. "Huh. Speaking of reflexes, you said that the arm is completely controlled, and the legs partially controlled by electrodes on the motor cortex of my brain. I know that those regions of the brain send the actual movement commands to my muscles ... but there has to be more to it than that. What about reflexes? Balance? Precise position adjustments?"

"Hah! I knew you'd pick up on that." Marty nodded. "You're right, if we were able to completely control the prosthetics by reading the remaining leg and arm nerve impulses, you'd have the benefit of spinal reflexes and your cerebellum smoothing out all of your movements. With only motor cortex control, you'd have a tendency to lurch and jerk at the start and stop of each movement. Unfortunately, we only have a partial nerve interface for the legs, and none for the arm."

"So how did you fix that? You can't fool me; I see that grin on your face. You came up with something clever."

"Uh huh, you're too smart for your own good. Well, we gave you a computerized implant hooked up to all of the synthetic muscles and touch sensors. It contains a machine-learning algorithm which will learn how to smooth out the motion of the prosthetics just like your natural limbs. Combined with neuroplasticity—the ability of your own brain to learn how to operate it—it should give you the ability to move your new legs and arm just the same as your original equipment."

"Wait, a learning machine...you put an Artificial Intelligence inside me to operate my limbs? I mean, I can see using an AI for robots, but these are *my* legs and arms. What's to keep the AI from deciding to rebel and do things on its own? Besides, how big is this computer you stuck inside me?"

"Actually, it's about half the size of your phone."

Glenn looked at the one-inch square plaque on a strap around his right wrist and raised his eyebrows at Marty, who laughed at the expression.

"It's a quantum computer, just like the sensors in your brain aren't really electrodes, but SQUIDS—Superconducting Quantum Interference Devices. They work off of the electromagnetic signals your neurons give off. Much longer lasting and greater sensitivity than wire electrodes detecting voltage changes."

"So, not just room temperature, but body-temperature superconductors, advanced computers, AI...what am I? A meat shell for a walking computer?"

"I hate to break it to you, Shep, but that ship has already sailed," Marty intoned in a solemn voice.

"Always with the Navy metaphors, Marty. How about a Space Force saying for once? Maybe like 'that rocket has already launched.'" He paused for a moment; his face screwed up in concentration. "Wait...you put SQUIDS inside me? Dang, you really are trying to corrupt me, putting SQUIDS in a Space Force officer!"

"Well, they *were* developed with a Navy grant," Marty retorted.

"Typical," said Glenn, as he laid back on the frame and thought about the implications of being equipped with devices that operated on light, magnetics and quantum tunneling. "They're never going to let me into a secured facility again, are they?"

The framework had the advantage of closing around his body so that he could be rotated securely without having to move himself. Glenn knew that he should be in terrible pain from all of the muscle and connective tissue that had to be moved around to replace his shattered femurs with titanium bone all the way up to the hip socket, not to mention attaching a complete arm to the shoulder socket. Somehow, the doctors managed to block the nerve impulses, reducing pain to manageable levels while still allowing him to be conscious. That method, however, left him barely able to move on his own, hence the need for the rotating frame to allow him to alter sleeping position.

Marty had shown him how to give voice commands to the bed control so that he wasn't at the mercy of calling for doctors and nurses when he wanted to turn over. Unfortunately, the more time he spent in the bed, the more impatient he became to start working with his prosthetics. This led to a bit of—experimentation on his part.

"Bed. Sit up." Glenn was staring at the ceiling, watching the shadows formed as the sun rose outside his hospital room.

"Please specify angle." The synthetic voice was pleasant—he'd tried several variations, settling on a female voice with a vaguely Australian accent. The voice reminded him of a charge nurse he'd worked with named Matilda.

"Bed, please respond to keyword 'Matilda' for all commands."

"Acknowledged. This unit will listen for the voice tag 'Matilda' to activate voice control functions."

Good, that was easy, he thought, just as the computerized voice repeated the previous request.

"Awaiting input for the command 'sit up.' Please specify bed angle."

"Seventy degrees, Matilda." He was tired of the perpetual reclining position of hospital beds. It was time to Sit. Up.

"Warning, postural adjustment in excess of fifty degrees is not advised."

"Shut up, Matilda, just adjust the bed." It was unfair. After all, he'd volunteered for this. He was just getting so impatient.

"Acknowledged. Adjusting posture." The head of the frame began to move upward. As it did, he felt increasing pressure on his midsection.

"Stop," he gasped.

"Acknowledged. Head elevation fifty-two degrees."

"Okay, Matilda. I won't doubt you again." He stopped and caught his breath; it felt as if his diaphragm was all crunched up.

Ah. Of course, it is. My hips are at totally the wrong angle. Sitting in a chair is not the same as lying in a bed.

"Matilda, can my feet be lowered?"

"Affirmative. Please specify leg angle and pelvic tilt."

"Um, okay, how about legs twenty-five degrees down and tilt my hips up by fifteen degrees."

"Acknowledged." The bed moved again as his feet

were lowered and his hips raised just enough to be comfortable.

Okay, I can work with this. Glenn looked around the room. There was a vid screen on the wall, and a keyboard on a small desk in the corner of the room. He hadn't watched vidcasts in several months, but then again, he'd been in a medically induced coma off-and-on during that time. Later he might ask the nurse to place the keyboard closer, but not now. He might need a voice transcription module, though, since he was going to be typing one-handed, and it was certain he wouldn't be using gesture-based controls for a while.

There was a mirror off to one side. It was fairly close to the door, but he might be able to catch a glimpse of himself if the angle was right. Marty had showed him the X-rays of his bones and the new prosthetics, but he had yet to see what they actually *looked* like.

"Matilda, can the bed be moved?"

"Affirmative, I am allowed to adjust position if converted to exo mode."

"Wait, exo mode? As in exoskeleton? Marty didn't say anything about that. Matilda, what is exo mode?"

"Anytime the legs exceed negative forty-five degrees, this frame converts to a full support exoskeleton. You will need to be passively restrained to the frame for exo mode."

"Can I move around the room?"

"Affirmative."

"Bonzer, mate, strap me in and let's take this tinnie out for some tucker."

"Query, command not parsed."

"Matilda, activate the passive restraints and exo mode.

Set leg angle to negative seventy-five degrees and head angle to positive eighty degrees."

"Acknowledged. Pelvic tilt will be automatically adjusted to forty-five degrees to maintain comfort. Please remain still as passive restraints are placed."

The bed frame began to move at the outside of his vision. First, eight bands curved up and over—four to each leg, two above and two below the knee. The supports clicked into place and tightened down to secure each leg. He couldn't feel the restraints, but he could tell they were snug. Next, three wider curved bars arced over his hips, waist, and chest. The inner surface appeared to be some form of airbag, as they each inflated to secure him to the frame. The hip restraint was tight, but not uncomfortable. The waist and chest restraints were cushioning, but not tight. He could still move slightly from side to side. Surprisingly, restraints similar to those on his legs enveloped his left arm, but not his right.

Oh right, can't move that one yet.

Once the restraints were in place, the frame adjusted again, bringing several hinged rods up from underneath the bed to fully enclose his torso from the armpits down. When he was completely surrounded, his legs tilted down and his head up. He felt something move under the fingers of his right hand—it turned out to be a small joystick. He tapped it briefly and felt the bed roll slightly across the floor.

Oh yeah, I think I'm going to like this.

He didn't dare try any major movements with the joystick, so he just tapped it briefly until he was oriented in front of the mirror.

Oh. Oh my.

He appeared to be wearing a one-piece undergarment serving as both briefs and T-shirt. He could see tubes coming out of one leg hole. Probably his Foley. He couldn't really feel anything down there because of the nerve block, so they would have had him catheterized. That led him to another thought...

Does everything still work down there?

His face was puffy and red. Two tubes led out of one side of his nose. His scalp had been completely shaved, and a bit of stubble was growing back in. He could see numerous small scars on the right side and a rectangular area near the top of his head was slightly raised with a puffy rim.

His left eye and ear were covered with bandages. From what Marty had told him, the retinal and cochlear implants were in place, but not yet ready for him to use. The plan was for the stem-cell-seeded ear and eyelid grafts to finish growing, first. Scientists had been growing skin in the lab, even 3-D printing it, for more than twenty-five years. He knew from the start that he could regain form. The challenge was regaining function.

That's what the prosthetics were for.

His undergarment had a short sleeve on the right, but ended at the collarbone on the left. There was puffy, reddish-brown skin right up to where the arm should emerge from the shoulder, but instead of skin, there was a plastic shell, gleaming metal artificial bone and many fine fibers and tubes forming his new arm. The upper arm was bare for now, allowing him to see the mechanism, but from the elbow to fingers was covered with a material that certainly looked like flesh from his angle.

Not . . . bad.

He tried to flex his fingers but nothing happened. He couldn't feel any sensation from the arm, but his body was telling him it was there. The shoulder felt like it had the appropriate weight hanging from it, it just felt . . . numb, as if it was wrapped in cotton.

Unlike his arm, which eventually had to be amputated all the way up to the shoulder, the docs had been able to save his legs about halfway down to the knees. The flesh of his upper thighs was also reddish-brown, except for many fine, longitudinal scars, which were a pale red. They'd had plenty of time to heal from the bone replacement and skin closure. Like his shoulder, there was a clear plastic shell over the junction of natural and artificial limbs, so he could see a metal rod, thicker than the one in his upper arm, sticking out of each stump. He knew that each artificial femur extended all the way to the hip joint, as it was easier to simply replace shattered bones with the same material used in his artificial limbs than to attempt to bind fragments back together into something that could support the prosthetics. The artificial bones ended in sockets, and attached below those were prosthetic legs. As with his arm, the upper sections were exposed, but from the knee down was covered in synthetic skin. There were even dark curly hairs on the shins.

The docs were a long way from being finished with him, and he still had to learn how to use it all, but Jack Steele and Martin Caidin would be proud.

He'd become a cyborg . . . a bionic man; the first human to be reconstructed so thoroughly with the intent of getting back to work and fulfilling his life's goals.

CHAPTER 3:
The Ghost of Jack Steele

Tammy D @SMagnolia
Hey, guys, I need a definition. What's a 'portmanteau?'

Jack E. @Steelyeyed
@SMagnolia, a portmanteau is a combination of two words, with a meaning that combines both. Example: Biologic + electronic = bionic.

ChirpChat, November 2039

"No, Aunt Sally, I don't think I'll be there for Thanksgiving."

. . .

"Yes, I understand that it's Uncle Hugh's eightieth birthday, too."

. . .

"I appreciate that you have wheelchair ramps and wide doorways, but Doc Spruce was adamant. They're still worried about infection."

. . .

"That's right. Stick a slice of Hoop's cake in the freezer and keep it for me."

. . .

"I love you too, hon. I'll come visit you as soon as they let me."

. . .

"Same here, Momma. You take care."

Glenn sighed. His aunt worried over him so much, but then she'd taken him in when his mother, Rosemarie, died during his freshman year in High School. He'd been in fifth grade when his mother remarried, but his step-father, Vernell Hairston, never really connected with him, and was even more at a loss how to handle this extremely intelligent—and now extremely sullen—teenager. It was only through visits with Glenn's Aunt Sally and Uncle Hugh that he had even learned much about his father. Sally's brother Roland had been an Air Force officer. All he'd gotten out of his mother was that his father had cheated Death too many times, and Death won in the end.

Aunt Sally told different stories and filled in many of the gaps in his memories of his father. Sally and her husband still lived in the house where she and Roland had grown up, and his father's old room became Glenn's after Rosemarie's death. Sally and Hugh had a daughter who'd grown up and moved away, so they funneled all their love to their grieving nephew and eventually rekindled his passion for science, math, and all things space-related. Rosemarie Shepard Hairston might have been his mom, but it was Aunt Sally who had comforted him and filled the void left by tragedy. She had earned the label of "Momma."

Never one to take "no" for an answer, Sally insisted on

visiting him, even though she'd have to travel from Virginia to Texas to do it. Marty was worried about infection, the therapists were worried about his mental state, and the San Antonio Military Medical Center, where he was being treated, was worried over security and the possibility of adverse publicity. What had happened to Glenn was not well known; Mars Mission Control— MMC or "double-M"—had reported only that he had been injured during a lunar training accident. There was the very real fear of protests and sensationalism if some of the more . . . graphic . . . pictures of his injuries came out. Glenn finally convinced Marty that the sister of a U.S. Air Force officer and wife of a Royal Air Force officer was unlikely to leak pictures to the media, so Marty browbeat the hospital into submission—as long as she maintained the isolation protocol.

Glenn was not having a good day. He'd been complaining that Marty and the team of doctors and technicians had gone to so much trouble to fit him with bionics, but hadn't turned them on yet.

So last week, they had.

The sensory feedback had been intense; it felt like half his body was on fire. Sensory nerves which had been either unstimulated or pain-blocked for months now had input and the combination of sensations was simply too much. The motor nerves weren't much better, and he'd thrashed about as if having a seizure.

Marty said it would get better and allowed the techs to keep the bionics turned on at regular power for an hour. By that time Glenn had screamed himself hoarse and broken everything within reach—including the exoskeleton. The bionics were turned off, and the neural engineers would have to rethink their protocol for activating the artificial limbs and organs.

Yesterday morning Marty had announced that he was reluctant to turn on the eye and ear prosthetics given the events of a week ago, but that he'd turn on the arm and legs at low power for the upcoming visit. That had been yesterday, and it still hurt, but was—barely—tolerable. Moreover, since Glenn needed to get used to the sensation, the bionics were left turned on overnight.

Glenn hadn't slept at all, and the pain made him irritable. He lashed out at Marty, the techs, and the nurses. He'd even tried to throw his meal tray at the young lady from food services...

...and that was when Aunt Sally walked in.

"Glenn Armstrong Shepard! You behave! I raised you better than that!"

"Yes, ma'am!" The change in Glenn was immediate. Gone was the forty-year-old angry man; in his place was the orphaned fifteen-year-old who'd finally found a loving home with his aunt.

"You apologize, young man!" Aunt Sally was the kindest, gentlest soul one could ever meet, but there was steel in her voice.

"I'm sorry, Miss Neville. I've not been feeling well and it got the better of me," Glenn sheepishly told the food services orderly. "I apologize and we'll get this cleaned up ourselves."

"Sure, okay," the girl mumbled and quickly left the room.

"That's better, Glennie," Sally said. "Now, how are you going to clean that up? You're in there, and I'm stuck outside this glass. I feel like all of those movies where the mother visits her son in prison, and has to talk to him on a phone while watching him through a bullet-proof window."

"Well, I'm not handcuffed to a table, so there's that."

Sally grinned, ruefully. "Yes, but maybe you should be after that shameful display. You be careful; I'll smack you on the back of your head. You know better than to act out like that."

"Yes, Momma, but it *hurts* so bad."

"You told me you volunteered for this."

"I know, it's just . . . I didn't think it would take this long. They don't even have everything turned on, let alone turned all the way up—and it hurts when they do."

"Give it time, Glennie. You have plenty of time."

"Do I? The Mars Three expedition leaves in a year. I don't have time to spend months in recovery gaining only an inch at a time."

"You don't have to go, you know."

"Yes, Momma. Yes, I do. It's what I trained for. It's what I've dreamed of."

"Really? It seems to me that young Glennie Shepard only wanted to be a doctor."

"Flight surgeon, Momma."

"How well did that work out for you? Playing hero on the Moon?"

"I just did what anyone else on the crew would have done."

"Nope, I'm not buying that. I know that being an

astronaut was your father's dream and you're honoring that with your own career, but you went into a fire to rescue a patient. That's not an astronaut . . . that's a *doctor*."

"It's still nothing special."

"Yes, it is, your Uncle Hoop said so—and he should know." When he was very young, Glenn had trouble understanding his uncle Hugh Pritchard's Welsh accent, and had first called him "Hoo Pitcher" and then shortened it to "Hoop" or "Hoops."

"Yeah, he told me about the doctor who rushed in when his ejector seat malfunctioned." Glenn became wistful for a moment. "Maybe . . ."

"Right. Now, that's settled. I need to give him a report. I can still see the junctions for your legs. Are they going to cover that?"

"Eventually. The skin has to finish healing, then a polymer filler and a combination of synthetic and stem-cell grafted skin will cover the rest."

"The arm looks good, although the skin looks darker than the rest of you—more like your mother."

"Well, I've been out of natural sunlight for a while. Once I can get some sun, the skin color should match up."

"Okay, I can understand that. Now, what's wrong with your ear? You look like Hoop's cousin Donny did after a lifetime of boxing."

"You mean cauliflower ear? Well, it's kind of like that. Every time a surgeon reattaches an amputation, or performs a transplant, they have to worry about getting the blood vessels and lymph ducts right. With tissue engineering, the vessels don't even necessarily line up properly. Blood vessels leak, clots form, and the next thing you know it's all swollen from accumulated blood and fluids and the doc starts talking about attaching leeches to drain the blood." Glenn glared through the glass, past his aunt to Doctor Spruce, who had been hanging back at the nurses' station.

"If only someone would invent nanomachines that could seal leaks and break up blood clots," said Marty in a deadpan voice without even looking up from his computer screen.

"Yeah, you get right on that, Doc," Glenn retorted. Marty just grinned. "Anyway, Doc tells me that the circulation is good, it's just draining slow. It should resolve in another couple of weeks." Glenn leaned back, put his right hand behind his head and rubbed the palm back and forth a couple of times over the short stubble of his hair. "Anyway, the skin seems to be doing okay, still feels a bit numb, but it *does* have feeling."

"So, you said they haven't turned everything on full power, yet, right?" Sally pointed toward his face, although it wasn't clear if she was indicating the swollen ear or the patch over his left eye.

"Well, my bionic legs and arm are working, as you can see." Glenn shifted a bit in his exoskeleton, moved his legs slightly and wiggled his fingers. "The electrodes are in place for eye and ear, but the interface has to be trained. Legs and arm first."

"Bionic, you say . . . I've heard that term before."

"Well, you know how you and Hoop taught me all about the space program and the Sixties? All of the important firsts—like Alan Shepard and John Glenn and Neil Armstrong's 'One small step . . .'? Well, this one starts in 1960 with an Air Force doctor named Jack Steele. He coined the term 'bionic' to mean bio-like or life-like, although it's also supposed to be short for biological electronics. Steele and colleagues also proposed that bionics and biomechanical enhancements would be essential for humans in space . . ."

The conversation would have gone on for hours if Marty hadn't come over and interrupted. "That's good for now, this brat needs rest. I'm going to turn up the nerve blocker, induce some delta rhythms, and *make* him sleep. Miz Pritchard, you're welcome to come back, and as soon as we can drop the isolation, bring your husband as well.

"As for you, Mister Grumpy, nighty-night." Marty reached out and touched a control beside the door.

"Night, Momma . . ." Glenn slurred as he faded off into induced sleep.

"How's he really doing, Doctor?" Sally asked Doctor Spruce as she watched her nephew's features relax.

"Glenn? Superb. He's beating the odds every day."

"Really? I didn't get that impression when I walked in."

"That's just post-trauma adaptation—what they used to call PTSD. We now know it's really the brain trying to reconcile an expectation that everything will be the same as before the accident, with the reality that everything has changed."

"Post-trauma . . . PTA. He's been a pain in the ass?"

Marty laughed. "Yeah, a bit, but that's depression, too. He's doing well, but it's not fast enough for him. He's going to be seeing one of my colleagues—a doc that specializes in people with PTA and chronic illness. Used to be a pediatric psychiatrist, now he treats wounded veterans."

"He treated kids? That's ... somehow appropriate."

"Yup. I thought so, too. Anyway, Nik—that's Doctor Pillarisetty—should be a lot of help, and I predict that Glenn will progress much faster once he's got his head on straight."

"It's going to hurt, Hoops. Hell, it already does, but then you know all about that." Hugh and Sally Pritchard had driven down to San Antonio and were staying with some of Hoop's Air Force friends. They'd been allowed to visit in person once the chief immunologist had relented and allowed Glenn to have in-person visits. The doctor had wanted to keep Glenn in isolation until the last of the grafts and therapy were completed, but Glenn was of no mood to comply. The compromise was masks, gowns, and gloves ... and transferring Hoop to a hospital wheelchair instead of his custom-built powered chair.

"I know, Glennie, I can see it in the corner of your eyes. You look like I felt after my ejection seat fired." His uncle was a Royal Air Force officer who'd been a liaison to the U.S. Air Force. A training mission had him seated at the navigator station on an old B-52 American bomber. The position was below the pilot, which meant that the only way to eject was down or to the side. An onboard fire caused his seat to eject while the aircraft was on the ground. Hoop had to be pulled out of the wreckage, but was able to walk—well, limp—away from the accident. Over time the injury had led to chronic pain and weakness; spinal implants would have helped keep him out of a wheelchair, but the deterioration was simply too much after forty years.

"Physical therapy is a bitch. Not the walking part so much as the flexibility exercises. I have to do yoga to prevent my new skin grafts from stiffening." Unlike old-style grafts, Glenn's burns had been sprayed with a solution of nutrients and stem cells—cells from his own body that had been "de-differentiated" so that they could become just about any adult-type of tissue. "I should be happy that I could regrow my own normal skin without scarring. For that matter, it's good that they could make stem cells from me, instead of giving me skin that was too dark or too pale. My ear was grown from the same stuff, but they make me stretch, bend, flex—they even have a machine that presses on my skin, then releases, to make sure it stays soft."

"So, how's the walking?" Hoop had asked the question every time they'd talked, whether by phone or through the glass.

"I really thought that attaching the legs directly to titanium bones would be better. After all, I'm not rubbing the skin of my stumps raw in the socket of a peg-leg, but all it did was transfer the pressure to my hip joints." Glenn lay back in the hospital bed with a sigh of relief. He still used the exoskeleton, but that morning's four-hour therapy session had him taking about half of his body weight on his new legs, and even half was a strain.

"Hah! Maybe I should get myself an exo like yours, then I could whip your ass in therapy, challenge you to a race and then beat you at it." At eighty, Hoop didn't lack for enthusiasm. If anyone understood what Glenn was going through, it was Hoop.

The thought made Glenn smile. "Yes, and then you can

terrorize the nurses on this floor for me." He paused a moment. "Well, maybe not Lacey, she's pretty nice, but you might want to teach Marty a thing or two about bedside manner."

"Hey! I heard that!" Hoop and Glenn both laughed. Doc was never far when there were visitors. Something about making sure he didn't overdo it.

"Momma, you've been pretty quiet." Sally reached out but then she realized she had reached for his left hand, and recoiled slightly. Glenn moved the artificial digits enough to catch her fingers and pull her hand back. He didn't have a lot of strength, but he was rapidly relearning hand and wrist control. "No, I mean it. I can read the calendar off of the nurse's tablet even though the chief head shrinker thinks it's a bad idea. I know what day it is."

"We just didn't think you should be by yourself today. We can't help it when you're on a mission, but lying here?"

"Yeah, well, I try not to think too much of February first. I know Mom loved me, and I know she loved Dad even if she did her best to bury the memories."

"That was just pain and grief, Glennie," Hoop said.

"I know, Hoop." Glenn leaned back in the bed. "She held on the best she could. I just couldn't she believe died to the minute, hour, day, and month the same as Dad. Do you think she knew?"

"The pain was *bad*, hon. Rosie was heavily medicated. You were there, as was Vernell." Glenn grimaced at his aunt's mention of Rosemarie's second husband, but Sally continued. "It was better that way."

"It's funny, you calling her Rosie. That's what Dad

called her; she wouldn't let Vernell call her that. He finally settled on 'Em.' She tried so hard to bury it all. She buried him, then worked so hard to eliminate every memory, even the fact that Dad actually survived the damned grenade that day." He reached for the cup of water at his right side, took a sip and swallowed with an audible gulp. "Did you know he looked just like me? I mean, me after my accident. He tackled the bank robber and landed on top of him, so the bastard took the worst of it, but the grenade shredded Dad's legs and left arm. His face was exposed and he took a piece of shrapnel in the left side of his face, peeled the skin from just under his left eye all the way past his ear. Even with that, he lived three more days."

"I knew."

"I know you did. And I know she made you promise. Mom told me all of it in the week after she got the letter from the oncologist." He took a deep breath, and raised his left arm toward his head, but only made it halfway. He let it fall back toward the bed. There was a hint of wetness in the corner of his right eye. "I think she knew, Momma. I read that letter—the docs gave her six weeks to six months. Instead, she had three weeks. Eight fifty-nine a.m., Saturday, February first. Nine years to the exact minute from when she turned off Dad's life support.

"Twenty-six years ago, today."

The three sat in silence for several minutes. There were the usual clicks and whirs of the ever-present intravenous infusion pump, as well as distant tones and announcements over the hospital public address system. It was a solemn moment, and Glenn was glad that neither of the others felt a need to speak. He knew he couldn't. The tears he felt on his right cheek, and the lump in his throat said it all.

He could feel Sally squeeze his hand. There wasn't much feeling there, although the electrodes to provide sensory feedback to the brain were in place and active. There was still so much to do to train his brain to work with the new inputs and outputs, that his doctors and therapists were not ready to simply turn everything on at full intensity.

He wiggled his fingers a little and felt the slight pressure back from his aunt.

"The skin—it's a little cool. I expected it to be either hot or cold. It feels..." She was at a loss for a moment as she searched for the right adjective. "...not rubbery, but kind of like..."

Sally stopped. Her eyes went wide. Her face turned a very bright red.

Hoop just laughed; the tension of the last few moments seemed to lift.

"Yeah, Momma. It's SymSkyn, the stuff they developed for 'living dolls.' I wanted them to just spray it with skin culture, but Marty said there was no way skin could survive without a whole network of blood and lymph vessels." Glenn could feel the heat rising in his own face at the thought.

"Our boy, the sex toy," Hoop said.

From the nursing station they could hear Marty coughing.

"Not to look at me, yet. The grafts are still puffy and my hair is just starting to grow."

"You're telling me, I haven't seen peach fuzz like that since I taught you to shave, buddy."

"It's the new skin cells. It's coming in jet black with no trace of the gray and white speckles that have crept in over the last ten years."

"Just like it was when you were sixteen." Hoop reached up a hand and touched Glenn's cheek. "Soft, too. Just like a teen."

Glenn was startled. He had *felt* that! Not only was the skin maturing, as shown by the fine hairs, the nerves were becoming fully functional.

"Yeah, the problem is, up until now, my beard has been salt-and-pepper. If I decide to grow it out, I may have to dye it."

"Or just get yourself covered with more of this SymSkyn, then you'll truly be a sex toy—the new Glenn Shepard doll!"

Aunt Sally turned red. "Hugh Nigel Pritchard!" she exclaimed, and slapped him on the shoulder. Hoop began to cough, and her expression turned to concern.

"As long as all his parts work," Hoop managed between coughs.

Once it became obvious that the coughing was from holding back laughter, and not the slap, she turned stern again and alternated her glare between the two . . . boys.

Glenn laughed until tears streamed once again from his good eye. There was a faint sensation under the patch over his left eye, but he knew that it was too soon to hope for tears. Still, it felt good to laugh. Dredging up those memories had been a bit too melancholy.

The laughter led to coughing and then yelps of pain as

his chest muscles spasmed. Marty looked up in concern, and he must have triggered an alarm, because the nurse practitioner—her name tag read "L. Charon"—bustled in, took control of Hoop's wheel chair and shooed Sally out of the room.

Glenn managed a hoarse, "Goodbye, love you, see you next week!" before Marty came in and closed the door.

"Actually, I'm kind of glad you did that. Too long in bed leads to shallow breathing, and shallow breathing leads to pneumonia." He placed a hand behind Glenn's back and helped him lean forward slightly. "Laughter is good for you. Love, grief, and joy. It helps remind us all that you're still just human."

"And a little bit more, Doc?"

"And a little bit more, Shep."

CHAPTER 4:
Ohm Wasn't Built in a Day

Mars Exploration Consortium
  @TheRealMarsX
  MarsX is pleased to announce that Doctor
  Yvette Barbier has joined the third Mars
  expedition as Chief Medical Officer.
George J @spacefan
  @TheRealMarsX, so, what happened to
  the previous doc?
                          ChirpChat, March 2040

The first month of rehabilitation involved working up to the ability to put full weight on his new limbs and relied heavily on the exo-bed that Glenn seemed determined to turn into his personal racing vehicle. Marty threatened to take it away the day he came onto the floor to find Glenn zipping down the hallway beating one of the other patients to the nursing station—wheelchair versus exoskeleton.

"Hey, Marty! Jakob here wants me to join the wheelchair basketball league. I bet him that I had the better lay-up and he said I needed to prove it."

"No, no, no. You are *not* going to ruin everything I went through putting you back together just to put a ball through a hoop. Not to mention what DARPA is going to say about you using their multi-million-dollar exoskeleton to play Horse."

Marty's reference to the one-on-one basketball challenge made Glenn chuckle. Finding humor had been getting easier as he healed. Visits, especially by Hoop, helped; his uncle had a dry wit, combined with a love of wordplay, that had shaped his own sense of humor.

"No, wait, didn't you say this was a Navy project? They had that Academy grad...whatshisname..." Glenn paused a moment, and unconsciously raised his left hand to rub the close-cropped hair on his scalp. He then pulled his hand back and raised his forefinger. "Oh yeah! Robinson. Later played pro-ball here in San Antonio, but before that he played basketball at the Olympics while still a serving officer. Just tell them we're upholding a grand tradition."

Marty just shook his head. "No. trust me. You do *not* want them sending you the bill."

"Hey, guys, get moving, I'm about to lap you!" Another patient in a wheelchair had just rounded the corner behind Glenn and Jakob and was heading their way. The newcomer had dark brown skin, extremely short black hair, and his features showed ancestry from the Indian subcontinent. He also had very broad shoulders and well-developed arm muscles.

"Um, Nik..." Glenn began as the man skidded to a halt next to him.

Marty looked on in shock. "Doctor Pillarisetty, *what the hell are you doing?*"

The psychiatrist's face was the perfect picture of innocence. "Just some morale building!"

"Is *this* what you consider professional bedside manner?"

"Well, actually, I consider it *chair*-side manner, but... yes." The look on Nik's face discouraged any further argument from the surgeon.

"Yeah, you should have seen him last week," Jakob added. "He was wearing a Batman cape and mask. While visiting the pediatric orthopedics floor."

"It really is good for morale, Marty. When Batman comes into the physical-therapy gym using crutches—and it's obvious that he actually *needs those crutches*, the kids tend to stop complaining and work hard on their therapy." Glenn could see the anger drain from Marty's face and posture. After all, he'd been responsible for hiring the psychiatrist. The decision had been heavily influenced by his ability to relate to his patients.

"Okay, but you're still not playing basketball in the exoframe. You can use a chair like everyone else."

The second phase of rehab was spent getting Glenn used to the weight and sensation of his new limbs. The bionic interface had been set as close as possible to normal human levels of force and feedback. He could *feel* with his fingers and feet. He was still learning to translate the position sensation into balance, which was made more difficult by the fact that the new limbs were not an exact size and weight match to the flesh and blood he'd lost.

Technology had advanced considerably from levers and springs for leg prosthetics and hooks and clamps for his arm. Instead, his new limbs worked much more like bone and muscle, except that the bone was made of ultralight alloys and the muscles of electrically reactive polymers. Those materials would still have been considerably heavier than human limbs if not for the latest process used to make the "skin" of the *Ares Percheron*, the ship that would be taking Glenn and his fellow explorers to Mars in a few more months.

Materials scientists had long touted the benefits of nanocomposites, in which sub-micron sized particles of silicon carbide ceramic were suspended in alloys of lightweight metals such as magnesium, aluminum or beryllium, but those materials did not always hold up to conditions inside the human body. This was in addition to the disadvantages conferred by other base metal properties such electrical and thermal properties, including flammability. By comparison, titanium, the metal of choice for artificial joints and implants—or worse yet, surgical stainless steel—seemed leaden and cumbersome, ill-suited to creating artificial limbs. In order for a limb to pass as human, it needed to be lightweight, have a full-range of motion, and still be strong enough to withstand the forces necessary to mimic human muscles. To overcome these limitations, Glenn's new magnesium nanocomposite bones were wrapped with graphene—single layer sheets of carbon molecules that were incredibly strong, light, and nonreactive with the body. His joints were formed of carbon-fiber and more graphene, and the small "bones" in the hands and feet were simply tubes of graphene filled with a ceramic "foam."

The structural elements of his limbs mimicked the biological arrangements of bones and cartilage as closely as possible, given that the purpose was to provide the same flexibility and dexterity as flesh-and-blood. Likewise, the bionic "muscles" needed to mimic the function and attachment of biological muscles. Sheets of electrostatic polymer membranes—EPMs—were wrapped, folded, rolled, and bundled into cords and fibers that contracted and flexed when the correct voltage and amperage were applied. When Glenn learned how his bionic muscle operated, he made the expected joke about how "resistance was futile." Marty just ignored him, but Dr. Nik responded by attempting a yoga pose and simply intoned, "ohm."

His new limbs were light, flexible, and had few moving parts. In fact, the only physically rotating or sliding joints were the magnetic bearings at the elbow and knees, and magnetic couplings at wrist and ankles. There were no wires, no blood, and very little fluid for lubrication. All communication between brain and "muscles" used short range wireless communication. It was meant to facilitate maintenance, repair, and even upgrades, by making components detachable and replaceable.

There was only one problem.

Glenn *loved* practical jokes.

Once Glenn could walk with support, he graduated to a new physical therapy class with other patients at the hospital. It was affiliated with the San Antonio Military Medical Center, but the advanced rehabilitation facility was at a different location within the city. This facility was also on a military base, with many soldiers present learning to use their new prosthetics—although none as advanced or extensive as Glenn's.

As with soldiers the world over, their humor was often crude, and their language salty. Occasionally a therapist from "outside the culture" would complain, prompting the hospital to require mandatory "sensitivity training." The course was designed primarily for the hospital workers, but the Physical Therapy unit insisted that everyone—patients, therapists, and doctors—attend the video lecture.

"Health care providers have an obligation to provide a welcoming environment to our patients . . ." The speaker's voice might have been tolerable if it had been softer, smoother, or less nasal. Instead, her voice seemed strained and pinched. It was no wonder, though, since her face looked strained and pinched as well—at least until she turned to glare through the video link at the people in the classroom.

There were twenty-two people in a conference room designed for twenty. However, twelve patients in wheelchairs took up most of the space, and the eight therapists, plus Nik and Marty, had to stand next to the walls in order to see the screen. The speaker controlled a camera that could focus on anyone with a question, and one corner of the screen echoed her view of the classroom. Currently it was focused on Jakob, who had made a rude comment earlier and earned a glare from the speaker.

"When a doctor or nurse looks at a patient and feels disgust, it shows on their face. No patient wants to experience a healthcare provider who doesn't want to see the patient..." As she droned on, Glenn realized that neither her pinched voice nor her pinched expression was the most annoying thing about her. No, the most annoying thing was that she "clicked." It had to be some movement of the soft palate against the back of her throat, or perhaps the tongue against the roof of the mouth. Either way, she couldn't talk without clicking. "Providers <click> need to train themselves <click> to <click> look neutrally at patients even though <click> they feel disgust."

Oh, dear God make it stop, he thought. It wasn't bad enough that she was a horrible speaker, but the fact that, in theoretically training employees to avoid prejudice, she was showing that very prejudice in herself.

That led to a new thought. A delicious thought. A very...evil...thought.

After yesterday's PT session, his bionic hand had refused to flex one of the fingers. Marty was not amused when Glenn demonstrated that all of the digits could flex and curl except for the middle one. He'd called in one of the engineers, who'd needed to physically detach the hand to inspect it. The technician worked for twenty minutes at a small bedside table on his detached hand. He poked and prodded...

...and instructed Glenn to move it...

...on the table...

...completely disconnected.

So, Glenn tuned out the speaker and engaged his plan. There was a pressure point on the wrist which released the magnetic bearing. The main power supply was further up the limb, but capacitors in the hand would suffice for now. He disconnected his hand and laid it palm down on the table in front of him.

He then commanded the fingers to press down, curl, and retract. Sure enough, the hand moved about half an inch. He repeated the command and caused the hand to gradually work its way across the table in front of eleven soldiers whose rough sense of humor was the *only* thing getting them through rehabilitation.

The first snort came from one of the physical therapists. Then a lieutenant clenched his artificial hands and was practically *vibrating* with suppressed laughter. A grizzled sergeant major let out a guffaw, then the whole room broke up into laughter.

Glenn snuck a glance to the side to see Marty, eyes wide, a look of shock on his face. Nik, resting on his crutches, had one hand over his mouth and tears streaming from his eyes.

"*WHOSE HAND IS THAT?*" Miz Click shouted from the screen. The remote-controlled camera panned the room. Glenn held up his left arm, minus the hand. "*MISTER SHEPARD,* <click> *THAT IS NOT FUNNY!*"

"I thought it was, and so did everyone else," Glenn replied softly, but with a hint of defiance.

"Stop that <*click*> this instant!"

Glenn pictured pushing up with the thumb and forefinger, and curling the other fingers. The disembodied hand flipped over, and he relaxed the fingers so that it laid there...limp...palm up.

For a moment.

Then the fingers began to fold down toward the palm, except for the middle finger, which remained pointing straight out.

Miz Click turned red, blustered briefly, and then cut the video connection.

The whole room burst into laughter and applause. Several of the other patients wheeled over to slap him on the back. Marty just came and stood over him and glared.

"Um, Marty, I think we still have that flex problem in joint two of digit three," Glenn said, innocently.

"We're going to have a problem with her."

"Not really—did you notice her look of disgust when she saw us? The way her lip curled when she was describing prejudice against the amputees?" Nik said. His comments elicited nods from several of the therapists. "This was her punishment from HR. Human Resources knows she's the worst offender regarding prejudice against the disabled. They made her teach this, and their purpose *was* to teach us something—just not what *she* was presenting. It was meant to teach us what *real* prejudice looks like. Besides, if she complains, send her to me." Nik leaned back on his crutches, linked his hands, turned them palm out and cracked his knuckles.

"If you say so." Marty turned back to Glenn. "And since you're such a wise-ass, Shep, I'm turning you up to one hundred percent tomorrow. Full strength, and full sensation." He managed an evil grin and rubbed his hands together. "This should be fun."

CHAPTER 5:
Nightmares and Daymares

George J @spacefan
  What is Space Force hiding? Did he die?
USSF Public Information Office
  @SpaceForceOfficial
  @spacefan, US Space Force is unable to
  comment at this time.
  Please see our website for the latest
  news and exciting opportunities in the
  Space Force!
George J @spacefan
  @SpaceForceOfficial, pretty much what I
  expected. Who runs your Chirp feed? A
  mynah bird?
                    ChirpChat, September 2040

The nightmares came often, with the frequency varying as his recovery progressed. Each time, Glenn woke up sweating and thrashing around. Several times, he damaged pieces of the bed. The first time it happened, Marty threatened to turn the gain back down on the prosthetics, but Glenn talked him out of it. It was his problem; he would solve it.

This time, Glenn opened his eyes and blinked away water. "Which one was it?" Doctor Nik Pillarisetty was sitting in his wheelchair beside Glenn's bed. "The crash? Sickbay? Asimov Incident? The one where everybody kept eating all the shrimp off the buffet and you didn't get any?"

"I haven't had that last one in quite a while. I'd almost forgotten it. Thank you so much for reminding me." Glenn always woke up grumpy when the nightmares interrupted his sleep. Nik just ignored it. "Hey, why is my face wet?"

"New therapy technique." Nik was holding a squirt gun in his lap.

"You *shot* me with that thing?"

"Naw, just a little squirt." Nik reached around to the pouch on the back of his chair and pulled out a garish green and orange object which looked like a weapon from science fiction. "But, if you act up, I'll just soak you."

"Oh, nice bedside manner, Doc. That's sure to lower my stress levels."

"Hey, it works." Nik gave a mischievous grin that told Glenn that the psychiatrist would not hesitate to use the high-volume water gun on him. "Okay, based on the fact that you're just grouchy and not trying to bite my head off, I'd say it was the Dragonfly crash. I can understand that one—you were there. My Hindu ancestors would be very interested in the other one. I've checked out the details and you're one hundred percent accurate, but there is *no way* for you to recall events from the operating room so accurately. You were unconscious, in a medically induced coma."

"No, no, I remember waking up and talking with Yvette. I don't remember seeing the other events, but the convulsions? The cardiac arrest? It's so vivid in the dream."

"Right. The part where you watched yourself die. There's no way for you to know any of that. I've interviewed you countless times when you've woken up screaming—and you've had the details correct every time."

"You're saying I died and was watching?"

"No, I'm saying that the human mind is complex, and contains mysteries we may never solve."

"Hey, you're the head-shrinker—should you be talking like that?"

"Shows what you know. All good head shrinkers should question existence. It's how we deal with the worst in our field. Besides, I'm Hindu. We have a spiritual and mystical streak."

"And I'm Baptist. We believe in . . . potlucks and bake sales."

". . . and not dancing."

"No, we got over that. The point is—I believe in miracles. After all, I *am* one. But *practical* miracles that result from someone's hard work. It's like luck. Luck is what you get when you put in the time and effort. Out-of-body experiences, astral projection? Nope. No way."

"Remind me to introduce you to a physicist I know.

He's also a science fiction author and thinks that the 'mind' is a phenomenon of quantum physics—that all neural events are due to quantum functions."

"He's never met a neuroscientist, has he?"

"He did...once. The guy gave him a pretty long lecture on why he was wrong—as far as the examples he used, then told him that overall, he was probably right."

"So—quantum physics? That's something I can't wrap *my* mind around."

"Congratulations. You're sane."

"I think I liked your other explanation, better. The Hindu one."

"So do I. Okay, now let's work on post-trauma adaptation." Nik held up the smaller of the two squirt guns. "Close your eyes." *<squirt>* "You're watching the trainer fall to the lunar regolith." *<squirt>* "Tell me what you see..."

"Tell me, Nik, why do you do this?" Glenn was back in the hospital bed, trying to relax his hip and chest muscles, and debating whether to call a nurse to administer the pain blocker. It had been a grueling day of physical therapy, still just passive movement of the muscles around the attachments for his bionics, and Nik had been beside him for most of it.

"I used to work with kids who had serious injuries and chronic illnesses. I trained in emergency medicine and psychiatry, and it was the most obvious application of psychiatry to trauma. The kids were great, and I related well to them, but the department leadership always wanted me to basically work for free."

"Wait . . . what? They didn't pay you?"

"Oh, they paid standard entry-level salaries. I developed a bunch of new programs—I was *good* with the kids—and those programs resulted in new treatments and more patients. The problem was that the department chair always took credit and the promotion boards never saw any reason to promote me or increase my pay."

"I hope this place pays you better, but what's with the jump from peds to adults?"

"Look at yourselves. Wounded soldiers are no different than children . . . hell, half the guys on this floor aren't even twenty-one. The attitude and sense of humor is certainly the same, *Mister Shepard!*" Nik pitched his voice into a high range, pinched his nose to get a nasal sound, and *clicked* just like the HR briefer.

That elicited a laugh, and then a wince of pain from Glenn.

"You okay, Shep?" Nik looked concerned.

"Mostly just sore." After a few deep breaths, he continued. "Not all of the problems are the same, though."

"You'd be surprised."

This dream was . . . frankly, embarrassing. Yvette figured prominently, and like many of his dreams involving her, they were arguing. The two of them had been quite passionate when they were in residency together—both in their arguments and in their lovemaking.

That was part of the problem, and the setting of this nightmare. They'd just made love, and Glenn had asked Yvette why she was so willing to forego birth control.

When she told him that it wasn't possible for her to get pregnant because of a hysterectomy, his first reaction was concern over what had warranted such drastic surgery at her age. When she revealed that if she ended up in space, then she didn't want kids, his concern had turned to anger.

"What right do you have to deny your partner children?" he'd screamed.

"What right do *you* have to dictate what I do with my body?" she retorted. "Once again, you're trying to tell me what to do!"

It was one of the arguments they'd never resolved, and the dream left him feeling . . . odd.

He woke up, and for once, Nik wasn't sitting by his bed with his water pistol. Probably because Glenn could see daylight through the small window in his room. Nik's vigils were usually at night.

The odd sensation continued. He couldn't quite place it until he went to pull the thin sheet aside to try to sit up and noticed it was tented over his legs.

Oh.

That.

It was the worst possible time for a nurse to enter the room. So, of course, that's exactly what happened.

"Good morning, Shep!" Nurse Cudde greeted him, then stopped abruptly as her attention was drawn . . . lower. "Oh! Good for you. Doctor Nik's notes said it was about time for that. The day staff has been rooting for you."

"Um, you have?" Glenn's voice squeaked as he tried to sit up to cover for his involuntary reflex. There were only two problems with that idea. First, he needed to reach across with his right arm to grab a bar and pull himself upright. The motion caused the sheet to dislodge, fully exposing him. The feeling of tightness increased. The second problem was that the nurse was just so . . . cute. Blonde, with full hips and bust, and a thin waist; she looked a lot like a girl he'd dated in college.

"Ooh," she exclaimed. "Do you need help with that? I can call a therapist for you, but I was about to give you a bath, and I'm perfectly willing to help out."

"What!" he almost shouted. "No!"

"It's okay, we're used to it. Major trauma causes all sorts of sexual dysfunction—even more so for the wounded veterans we get here. There's counselors and specialized therapists, but we're all trained in the basic techniques." Her expression had gone through several changes, from surprised, to happy, to proud. "*I* have gone through *advanced* training!"

"Um . . . well . . . thanks, but please, just page Nik."

She pouted, but went back to the nursing station to update his medical record and put in a call to the psychiatrist.

Glenn was eating his lunch when he heard the tapping of Nik's crutches in the hallway. The psychiatrist rounded the corner into his room, settled his weight, leaned forward, and leered at him.

"I hear you exposed yourself to Nurse Cuddly this morning."

"It wasn't like that; it was an accident. A dream."

"Oh ho! You're having *those* dreams now. No wonder she was so happy, she won the pool."

"You *bet* on me? On—that?"

"Not money, that would be unethical. Cuddly gets to pick the break-room music for the next week. She likes country—not the classics—the bad 'K-Pop meets Willie Nelson' kind. On the other hand, it helps us keep a sense of perspective. Patients are just problems and probabilities."

"You don't believe that."

"True, and for that matter, I haven't quite figured why I like you. It obviously isn't your sense of humor, Shep. So, did she help you out?"

"No! I'm nearly twice her age."

"Nurse *Cuddly*, remember?"

"Yeah. I know." Nik cocked an eyebrow at him, and Glenn responded, "I *know*! I was just too embarrassed."

"You're going to have to figure it out. Most of the guys—and the women, too—have dysfunction and issues with body image. You're lucky, Shep. You're well on your way to looking like a recruiting poster, but the problem isn't going to go away. You don't *want* it to go away."

"But I could have hurt her!"

"Ah hah! So, *there's* the problem." Nik shifted his weight and set his right crutch to the side, reached behind his back, and pulled out the water pistol.

<Squirt>

CHAPTER 6:
Setbacks

Mars Exploration Consortium
@TheRealMarsX
Mars Three is en route to Elysium
Planitia. Humanity's first permanent base
on Mars is now underway.
ChirpChat, January 2041

Glenn had been looking forward to the day that the strength and feedback for his bionic limbs were turned up to full power, but it had been something of a letdown. Granted, he was still effectively learning to *use* them to stand and walk, or to reach and hold. He had hoped that full power would mean instant freedom from the exoskeleton and the assistive device he used to grab items on his left side.

Oh, he was certainly out of the exo, but it wasn't freedom. On that point he had been terribly mistaken.

"Lift your leg. Lift . . . lift . . . lift it up. Okay then, slide it forward. No. Forward." The physical therapist was patient, but Glenn had been trying this movement for the past thirty minutes.

"I'm trying, but every time I attempt to lift, it goes to the side. I can slide it, but I can't seem to take a damned step." Glenn, however, was growing extremely impatient.

"Okay, let's try something different. Relax. Just let yourself hang."

Glenn was suspended by a harness that went between the legs, around his waist and chest, and under the armpits. Normally, a leg amputee would stand between parallel bars and support their weight on their arms. That was not yet possible, although he and Marty had discussed whether he needed to build up arm strength before leg strength.

"Relax? Okay, I'll try." He closed his eyes and let himself go limp, hanging in the harness as if hanging from a parachute.

"Okay, eyes closed? Good. Now imagine swinging your leg out in an exaggerated kick. Like an exaggerated march or a soccer kick." The therapist's voice was now coming from across the room, and there was a tapping sound, like a keyboard or touch screen.

Glenn imagined kicking his leg and felt the telltale tingling sensation that accompanied programming of reflexes and coordination in his bionic co-processor. Control of the artificial muscles came from signals picked up from nerves that *should* have been connected to his biological muscles, as well as electrodes in the part of the brain that controlled leg movement. Unfortunately, walking involved much more than simply commanding muscles to contract. Various parts of the brain—including the cerebellum, brainstem and spinal cord—provided coordination and reflexes to turn lurches into smooth movement.

The reflex co-processor did the same thing, but it had to be taught. When the therapist had him relax and think about swinging his leg, Glenn's brain provided the commands, and the processor learned the differences between the intent and actual movement.

"Okay, keep your eyes closed. Now think about lifting your leg and moving forward. Good. Swing the leg and plant your foot. Lean forward a bit. Now the other foot. Good.

"Open your eyes." The therapist was back by his side, and Glenn could see that he'd made two steps forward. "Think you can try that with eyes open?"

"You mean *eye*, singular." Glenn's tone was a bit harsh.

"Perhaps, but just like your legs, you have to keep the brain thinking about operating normally."

"Normal?" Glenn started to wave his hand to gesture around the room, but the moment his hand left the railing, he wobbled, and would have fallen if not for the suspension harness. "Just turn the stuff on and let me do this for myself," he snapped.

"They *are* turned on, Shep." Marty's voice came from behind him. The therapist looked up in surprise, and must have received a nonverbal command, because he went back to his console and entered several commands. The harness began to lower him toward the floor, but Glenn felt something under his backside, then Marty pulled him into a sitting position on a chair.

"You say that, but I've got one eye, one ear, I lose my

balance, I can't hold a glass in my left hand without dropping it, and I can't walk!"

Glenn turned to stare at his doctor, who in turn reached out and removed the ear patch and ripped the bandage off of the left side of his head.

"Ouch!"

"Oh, good, something works. Your facial nerves have regenerated just fine." There was a dark note of sarcasm in Marty's voice. "Makes sense, since you're a touchy son of a bitch. Well, I have news for you, buddy. When I said one hundred percent, I meant it. Everything is turned on and functioning."

"I can't see anything! I can't hear anything!"

"Whine, whine, whine. Tell me, flyboy, how do you tell the difference between a pilot and a jet engine? Well, they both whine, but at least the engine is going somewhere!" He put his hands on his hips and glared back. "So, what are you going to *do* about it?"

"*I can't walk!* You assured me I'd be able to do this by now."

"Are you really trying? I saw your legs move when you had your eyes closed and weren't thinking so much."

"I tried! Just like I took off the patch this morning and tried to see. Nothing! You failed." Glenn broke down in sobs. "I failed."

"Ah, so that's what it is. The Mars mission." Marty placed a hand on Glenn's shoulder and let him take the time to work through the emotions.

"I asked them. They had two launch windows, now, and in six months. I petitioned to be allowed back on the team. In six months, I would have been ready."

"I'm not so sure."

Glenn looked back and glared at him again. Both eyes were focused, distinguishable only by the faintest reflection in the iris of the left eye. "I can do this."

"Physically? Yes. Psychologically? You've got a massive chip on your shoulder. What's that about?"

"Yvette." He practically spat the name. "She stole my mission. By leaving now, they have to take her instead of waiting for me."

"I'm not sure you're being fair to her. She didn't want the mission. I didn't talk to her, but the Space Force general—Boatright—did, and he said she turned it down."

"Oh, she's always done this—didn't want the emergency medicine fellowship, but the moment I applied for it, there she was, and got it. She said she didn't want Chief Resident, but got that, too. Eventually we shared it, but she had better ratings from the attendings than I did despite the fact that I consistently outscored her. We always argued over patient care and cases. She even accused me of trying to push her aside and take over. She left the Force to be a civilian space contractor, and immediately broke up with me because I didn't follow her."

"Back up. You said you were fighting and she accused you of undermining her."

"Yes, but lovers fight, and make up, and fight, and make up again. At the time we thought that was all it was. But she left the military, yet somehow ended up back on the Moon as Medical Officer."

"Well, Moonbase *is* a civilian posting, these days."

"Uh huh, sure. How many civilian CMOs have they had in the past ten years?"

"One. But then, they've only had two other CMOs, and you were one of them."

"Sure. Okay, fine. She took the job, though. Probably jumped at it the moment it was offered."

"Not quite. They asked her three times before she said yes."

"Yeah, that's her pattern. Anyway, that's when I realized that her career has been driven by competition with me. And spite. So don't tell me that wanting to turn off my ventilator was her way of wanting me to live."

"I wouldn't say that . . ."

"Don't tell me she had my best interests at heart, either, Marty. She didn't want to call you in. She didn't want to stabilize me to get me back to Earth. Back when we were residents at Petersen AFB, a young airman came into the ER late on a Saturday night. He'd been in a car crash. The impact pulverized the bone in one leg. I argued for amputation of the leg due to the multiple fractures, bone fragments and damage to blood vessels. Yvette wanted to use hyperbaric therapy, and argued that they could save the leg if they could keep the tissues oxygenated. I countered that the shattered bones could not be adequately repaired and the young man would be confined to a wheelchair. With a prosthetic, he could return to work as an aircraft mechanic. She disagreed; the man's military career was over. She sneered at me—was I recommending that they amputate the man's fractured ribs and cracked jaw as well?"

"You can think what you want about her motivations,

but she reacted instinctively and saved your life back then. She was conflicted. Her heart told her one thing, but her medical training told her another. Even *that* was in conflict—end your pain, or save your life? When I first saw you, I was amazed at how well she'd stabilized you for transport. She personally convinced Space Force to get that experimental SFX shuttle up there to get you back down to the ground in minimum time and no transfers. She wasn't your personal physician anymore, but she cared enough to give you the best possible chance."

"She's going to Mars. In my place. *Especially* because it's my place."

"Yes, she is, because you're not ready. Your time will come."

"No. It won't. Read this."

Glenn handed the envelope over to Marty, and the doctor pulled the official stationery out and started to read. "... heroic rescue ... risk of life ... severe injuries ... Purple Heart ... Wow, you've been awarded a Silver Star!"

"Keep reading, Doc."

"Coast Guard Gold Lifesaving Medal? Yeah, that fits. Morykwas was Guard, and he's alive because of you."

"Nope. That's not it. Besides, that's a civilian medal. It should be a clue."

"... promotion to full colonel ... needs of the service ... potential contribution to the mission ..." Marty looked up in shock. "They're retiring you? General Boatright promised me that you would just be on standby reserve until you recovered. What is this?"

"It gets better ... or ... something."

"*Psychologically unfit for duty!* What the hell? Is this Pillarisetty's doing?"

"Actually, no. There was a medical competency hearing, and his was the lone dissenting voice. A board made up of headshrinkers and flight docs from the Space Force, Air Force, and Navy held a kangaroo court and drummed me out of the Service."

"Why wasn't *I* consulted?" Marty asked. "I'm the one who knows your whole progress, not a bunch of people who've never even *met* you."

"They were all military docs. Nik was included only because he's considered Veteran's Administration hospital staff." Glenn's voice was filled with resignation. "Notice who else signed it. She's back in uniform, at least as a reservist. It's confirmation bias in action. We're trying to make a point here, but their minds are—and in particular, her mind is—already made up."

"I'm sorry, Shep." Marty put the letter back in the envelope and put it on a bedside table. He walked over and put his hand on Glenn's shoulder. "I know how much this meant to you, showing people that they shouldn't be afraid of the risks inherent in space exploration. I admit that I thought going to Mars as anything other than a proof-of-concept demonstration was a long shot, but you'd think that after what's been invested in you, they'd at least see it through."

Marty sat down on the edge of the bed and stayed silent for a while in sympathy with his patient ... and friend. A few moments later, he had a thought.

"Wait ... does this mean they're not going to pay for any of this?"

The anxiety on Marty's face made Glenn snort. Laughter was still out of the question, but there was a small bit of humor in the doctor's expression. "No, they're still paying—at least the part my trust fund didn't cover. General Boatright insisted on that part."

"Oh, good, because you're expensive, Shep."

"Six million dollars?" It referred to a popular TV show from almost seventy years ago. It was also the amount he'd drawn from the trust fund account created from his father's and mother's insurance policies and supplemented over the years by his aunt and uncle, not to mention capable financial advisors.

"Oh, you are so, so far beyond that, my friend."

They lapsed back into silence for several more minutes before Glenn spoke again. "Marty? Let's prove them wrong."

"Yes," Dr. Martin Spruce replied. "Let's do exactly that!"

CHAPTER 7:
The Doll Factory

※

Scott K @Kman549
> Y'all already know I'm a neuro nerd, but did anyone else see the article in Rehabilitation Journal? The new neural control prosthetics are *amazing*!

DARPA @YesDARPA
> @Kman549, if you think that's amazing, wait until you see what's coming next!
> ChirpChat, March 2041

Despite numerous setbacks, and Glenn's occasionally bleak attitude, the therapy had progressed well—he was walking, albeit with the assistance of a cane for stability, and could even use that cane with his artificial arm.

Dr. Pillarisetty thought the issues with vision and hearing were psychological, and had been working with him to train himself to see and hear again. Even though the interfaces were perfectly functional, they were not a perfect match to purely biological connections. The human brain could be trained to use the new inputs, but the patient had to *want* to do so. Many hours of counseling with Nik—one of the few people who would not be swayed by Glenn's self-pity—were beginning to pay off.

"We're going to have to put you under for the next one," Marty had said. "We're going to do an exploratory procedure to see why your vision and hearing aren't working right. The engineers think it's a power connection since that's the only thing that would account for malfunctions in both. The power distribution built into your bionic processor is reading normal, but they want to check that, too." Privately, Marty thought there was substance to the idea that the malfunction was all in Glenn's mind, but the test instruments indicated that at least with the visual prosthetic, the signals were simply not reaching the brain.

"But that's not what you think, is it? Nik thinks it's a mental block."

"I'm not sure what to think. Dr. Pillarisetty is not one hundred percent certain about the psychosomatic issues, and as I said, the bioengineers want us to check some things."

Glenn sat quietly for a few minutes. "How will you be able to tell if it's working and I'm just ignoring it?"

"Well, I wouldn't say you're ignoring the implants." After a moment, Marty said "Wait, I have an idea," and left the room. He returned a few minutes later with a portable EEG machine.

After fitting the electrode cap over Glenn's head, the two of them watched the multiple horizontal lines trace from left to right on the screen. Marty had him put a patch on his left eye, and then flashed a light in his right eye multiple times.

"Okay, now see here, this is the point where the light flashes occurred." Marty pointed to a spot at the left of the screen. "To the right is an average of all of the flashes. You can see the regular bumps to the left as the visual information passes through the various neural pathways to get to your visual cortex. Now the left eye."

Glenn moved the patch to his right eye. All he could see was gray nothingness, not even the random flashes he normally got when his eyelids were closed.

"Okay, take the patch off and look. I flashed the light ten times and you never reacted." Sure enough, the traces on the screen showed only random fluctuations instead of the regular peaks and troughs of the visual signal processing. "Now the hearing."

He handed Glenn a set of headphones, and for the next few minutes he listened to clicks and beeps or different pitches. When they were finished, Marty showed him a screen comparing the signals recorded as each ear was tested.

"See, here with the right ear you have the clicks, the low and the high frequency beeps. You can tell the difference in the two frequencies by the spacing of the peaks. Now on the left you get some of the appropriate bumps for the clicks and beeps, but not the rest of the information. We think a signal's getting in, but you're just not decoding it properly."

"This procedure will fix that?"

"If it's connectivity, yes."

"And if not?"

"We cross that bridge when we come to it." Marty started coiling up the wires from the EEG machine. "Now let's get this off of you. The nurse will be in here in a few minutes to shave your head for surgery."

"Again."

"Yes, again. I don't know why you're complaining, Shep. You have a full head of hair, yet you wear it in a buzz-cut, and run your hand through it like a brush all the time. Your left hand, I might remind you." Marty cocked an eyebrow at him, then rapped a knuckle against his own bald head and ruffled the fringe of hair at the sides.

"Yeah, well, it feels funny now when it's completely shaved."

"Sucks to be you, doesn't it?"

"Right there," the surgeon said, pointing to the magnified view of Glenn's left eye.

"Scar tissue?" asked Marty. The two stood off to the side while another surgeon and technologist worked on the auditory prosthetic.

"Not necessarily. It *looks* like gliosis—but that doesn't usually happen in the eye. All neurons are surrounded by glial cells. They provide metabolic and structural support and even provide protection where they form the blood-brain barrier. It's not uncommon to see glial cells encapsulate a recording electrode. However, this doesn't look like encapsulation and I'm not seeing individual cells." The surgeon spoke a command to the viewer and it zoomed in on the membrane covering the electrode grid resting on Glenn's retina.

"That looks fibrous. Just like scar tissue. So, what's the difference?"

"Yes, that's what it looks like, but scar tissue like that doesn't normally grow in a neural environment. Gliosis might occur if the cells grow too much, but what this looks like is the sort of posterior capsule opacity we sometimes see after a cataract lens replacement. This can't be exactly the same, because we completely removed the lens and its capsule to implant the camera system. However, in those cases, cells just like the ones lining the interior of the eye itself start to grow in the capsule where the natural lens used to be. On the other hand, we certainly disturbed the interior of the ocular space enough to cause some sort of overgrowth."

"Ok, I can understand that. It's a natural body defense mechanism, then. What do we do about it, and why doesn't this happen with other implant patients?"

"Well, we can burn the cells off with an ocular surgery laser. Out of deference to your electronics, we have to do it through an incision on the side instead of going in through the lens. As for why? How long did you wait to have him start using it?"

"He had an extensive rebuild, and the first time we turned everything on, he was overloaded. After that, I didn't want him to have to adjust to everything at once. I waited for the incisions to heal, and then he was struggling with arm and legs, so we waited some more."

"Two months? Three? Four?"

"Um . . . we tried it again at six months . . . and it's been about a year since the last surgical procedure. Why?"

"We see gliosis and scarring around purely passive,

record-only electrodes. The small amount of current going through a stimulating electrode usually works to minimize overgrowth. He wasn't fully activating the system, and it allowed the membrane to grow."

"So, long term, it should be okay as long as he uses the implant?"

"It should, and we can treat it if it does. That all presumes that he *doesn't* actually have a psychological block, like the ear."

"Actually, he doesn't have a purely psychological block there, either," came a voice from the other side of the surgical table.

Marty turned to address the other surgeon who was looking at a scan of Glenn's brainstem. "What do you see?"

"This, right here." He indicated a dark spot on the scan right where the spinal cord began to swell into the medulla oblongata. "There was a clot right here above the cochlear nucleus. Now don't worry, it's just a spot of necrotic tissue putting pressure on the nucleus and affecting the signals from the cochlea itself. I'm going to laser ablate the mass, hopefully that will relieve the pressure. Otherwise, you're going to have to go with a surface electrode directly on the auditory cortex."

"Okay, Dan. Go ahead, once Adrian finishes in the eye. Then we'll see what Glenn can tell us after he wakes up."

It wasn't that simple or that fast. The technology team insisted on doing more tests while they had direct access to the implants, but after twelve hours in surgery and another four in recovery, Marty sat quietly in the darkened room as Glenn slowly opened his eyes.

"Damn, but that's bright!" Glenn said, then flinched at the sound of his own voice.

Marty reached out and touched a control on his tablet. "I've turned down your low-light sensitivity for now," he whispered.

"You don't need to shout," Glenn said in a quiet voice.

"Ah, I take it I can turn down the audio sensitivity as well." He touched another control, and then commanded the room lights to return to normal illumination. "There, how's that?"

"Wow," was all Glenn said for a moment. After several minutes just looking around the room, he continued. "It seems to be getting less sensitive. The room was much too bright at first, but it's better now. If I look at something for a few moments, it becomes clearer."

"That's the active feedback system in the visual sensors. Now that everything is working, the camera that replaced your iris activates electrodes that directly stimulate your retina. However, there's a processing chip to help you sort through the light levels, distance vision and focus. That's what you just experienced."

"And my hearing?"

"More pre-processing there. Cochlear electrodes are 'known tech' but we gave you a lot more selective attention and filtering, and built all of that into the outer part of the ear when we rebuilt the cartilage and skin."

"Clearly, you fixed the problems. What were they?"

"You had cells growing between the electrode and retina, and pressure on the cochlear nerve. We fixed that without having to do much surgery. The rest of the time was just making sure the electronics were okay."

Glenn looked up at Marty and smiled—something that had been rare these past few weeks. "So, now the rest of me works. What's going to keep it from happening again, though?"

Marty sighed. "Well, actually, it's my fault. The membrane in your eye grew because I waited too long to let you try to use vision. The hearing issue was from not looking at the whole pathway; we found the remains of a clot and were able to remove it. I can't guarantee that you won't have more problems, but I *can* guarantee that it won't take so long to find the problem as long as you are using sight and sound every day."

Marty sat in silence for a moment, and Glenn began to worry that there was bad news his doctor was reluctant to share. "Spit it out, Marty. You've got bad news. It can't be too bad because you fixed everything else."

"It's not bad—not to me, and not for you. It's more a matter of it being in your medical record."

"What's so bad about something in my record. Space Force retired me, so it's not like they're recertifying me as a pilot."

"It's more complicated." Marty paused then blurted out the next bit, "You have a cooling problem, so we put in an Ell-Vad."

"As in L-V-A-D? A Left Ventricular Assist Device? I have an artificial heart pump?"

"Not so much for your heart. The bionics generate heat. Your body has plenty of ways to get rid of waste heat, as do the arm and leg components, but where any of that is in contact with your biology, you pick up additional heat. The solution is to boost blood and lymph circulation. We used an LVAD pump, but it's not supporting the left ventricle of your heart, it's lower down and connected to the lymph circulation."

"But . . . my medical record now shows that I have what amounts to an artificial heart."

"Right. Air Force and Space Force fitness regulations have been pretty lenient with respect to artificial limbs, but heart surgery? Even something as benign as boosting lymph circulation could block your flight status."

"Oh, hell, Marty. I'm half machine as it is, and they already retired me. We'll just have to cross that bridge when we come to it. We could even argue that the LVAD improves my gee-tolerance!"

"That's true, I hadn't thought of it that way. Alright, then." Marty got up and headed for the door, then turned with a sly smile. "Get some rest and sleep off the anesthetics. Tomorrow we have to go over the radio, recording and remote systems."

"What are you doing, trying to turn me into some sort of spy?"

"No, not at all, but we still want to get you back into space, LVAD or not. These functions are specifically for that purpose."

"As you just said, presuming they let me go."

"They will. You and I just need to make sure Command sees it. It's time to get you out of the hospital and back to work. You're going to be officially discharged soon. General Boatright is trying to get you attached to the civilian Space Program, and he's arguing that you should rejoin astronaut training to show them what you can do. The question is whether you'll go to Astronaut Basic in

Houston at Johnson Space Center, or MarsX crew training in Tucson."

"Well, okay. Just so I don't have to go back to Spacer Basic, again."

"What, you don't like twenty-mile ruck marches? Didn't you get the memo? You're never going to have trouble with *those* again," Marty laughed as he exited the room.

CHAPTER 8:
More than Human

Beth L @SpaceNewsNetwork
Hey folks, did you see this? US Space
Force today announced new opportunities
in physiology, pharmacology,
neuroscience, rehabilitation medicine and
tissue engineering. It's for that new Office
of Scientific Integration we've heard
about.

George J @SpaceFan
@SpaceNewsNetwork, new opportunities,
sure, but you realize @USSFActual still
haven't told us what happened to the
astronaut injured on the Moon.

ChirpChat, May 2041

"Nik, dude, an *orange track suit*? What is this, the
Seventies?" Glenn looked more closely at the outfit he'd
just been handed. "Polyester? Damn it, it's going to be

hot. It's May and San Antonio is already in the nineties. In Virginia we don't do nineties until the depth of summer."

"Hey, the orange tracksuit is traditional, and that's the only one I could find, Shep."

"Uh huh. Right. You have an odd taste in retro TV shows for a psychiatrist."

"Ah, but you know it's from an old TV show, which means you've seen it, too."

"Okay, you've got me there. In my defense, it seemed relevant."

"Yeah, well, you're not him. Keep that in mind."

"Yes, Doctor."

Nik mimicked Glenn, "Yes, Doctor." He continued in a normal voice, "No, I'm telling you as a friend. You can push yourself a *little* but don't overdo it, smartass. Now get in there. Marty's waiting for you and the physical terrorists have tests to run."

For the next eight hours, the physical therapy team put Glenn on a treadmill, then an indoor track. They had him doing squats, jumps, and lunges. Following today's physical tests of his legs, there would be additional days of testing for his arm, eye, and ear. By the end of the day, he was tired and sore.

The results were . . . interesting. There was a common misconception that fully integrated bio-electric prosthetics would convey abilities that were well above the normal human ability range. Much to his chagrin, Glenn had even believed it, but the results showed that he was not a superhuman—although his abilities were considerably improved from the average human.

For example, in 2008, and again in 2012 and 2016, Jamaican runner Usain Bolt had shocked the world with his winning times in the Olympic one-hundred- and two-hundred-meter sprints. He already held a world record in the one-hundred-meter sprint prior to his Olympic debut. In his day, he was called the "World's Fastest Man," with sprint speeds of over twenty-three miles per hour.

During the same time period, Oscar Pistorius reached a record speed of twenty miles per hour on spring-like "running blade" prosthetics. Glenn thought that surely, he would be able to surpass Bolt's and Pistorius' speeds given the nanocomposite "bones" and bioelectric "muscles" in his new legs. Hell, he might even manage sixty miles per hour, like the character from the old TV show Nik joked about. Thus, it came as quite a disappointment that Glenn's top speed on both treadmill and open track rarely exceeded twenty-one miles per hour.

One of the testing staff was a runner and trainer who had worked with athletes competing in World Championship and Olympic trials. Keith Miller had even run in the Boston Marathon and consistently placed in the top three for his age group in other races. Now retired from competition, he consulted with runners and trainers alike. Marty had brought him in to work with his prize—and stubborn—pupil.

"You know there's many reasons why you aren't going to beat record sprint times, right?" Keith was massaging Glenn's upper thighs to help prevent cramps from the rigorous testing. "You aren't starting from the 'spring' starting position that gives a runner that extra burst of distance, you haven't been training for this, and frankly, you don't have the cardiovascular conditioning that allows you to focus all of your energy into the sprint."

"Yeah, I get that," Glenn grunted as Keith dug a thumb into a particularly tight spot on the iliotibial band. "It's just that my legs don't rely on blood, oxygen, glucose, or any of those cardiovascular components. For the parts that do, I've got a booster pump."

"Oh, really? Well, for one, your prosthetics are still attached to flesh, blood, and bone. Your knees and lower legs are artificial, but they still have to interact with muscle at your hips. Like this one—" Keith dug his other thumb into Glenn's hip, right between gluteus maximus and gluteus medius.

"Ow!"

Unfazed by Glenn's reaction, Keith continued, "For another, I want you to start doing planks, and there's a core crunch you can work on. Your abdominal muscles are important to endurance, and frankly, you're getting a little flabby around the middle."

"Hey!" Glenn protested as Keith slapped him lightly on the stomach with the back of a hand. "I'm not fat. The extra poundage is all machinery."

"So you say, but there's a fair amount of jiggle in that belly. If you're going to go back into space, you need to tighten your core to compensate for positive and negative g-forces. It will allow you to pull more gees, especially since you *don't* have all of the extra cardiovascular plumbing to worry about."

The massage was finished, and it was time for Glenn to transfer to the "chiller" to reduce swelling in his purely biological muscles. It looked like a regular bed, but with a hard top cover that encased the whole body except for his head. While the prosthetics were rated for low temperature, the heat-absorbing clamshell would work overtime trying to chill the continually heat-producing bionics. Usually, Keith just helped him disengage the magnetic couplings in the arm and legs and lay them on a table to the side of the chiller.

Not today.

"We're going to work on your emergency moves. Take off your left leg, and stand up. You're going to hop over to the chiller, then seat yourself, and lay down."

"Hop? You want me to not only balance, but hop?"

"Exactly. You never know when you might have to move yourself around with damaged bionics. Accident or on purpose, you need to be self-sufficient."

"Um, okay." Glenn took off his left leg and tried to stand. He had to catch himself with his hands several times, but he was finally able to keep his balance.

Keith moved up beside him. "Now, I'm going to be right here, but what I want you to do is think about a pogo stick. The co-processor for your bionics works as much on movement *intention* as on the movement signals from your motor cortex."

"I got that, *Torquemada*, it's a different part of the brain. Premotor cortex, Brodman's Area 6."

Keith grinned at the reference to history's infamous torturer. It was a running joke between them. "Your co-processor will handle balance. Now. Hop."

Glenn waited until he felt settled, then flexed his knee and made a small lurch forward.

Keith put an arm in front of him to stop him from

toppling forward, but surprisingly, Glenn felt the artificial muscles in his ankles make the adjustments to maintain his position. He waved off the offered arm, and hopped again.

This time it was easier, and with growing confidence, he hopped the remaining three feet to the chiller table.

"Great. Good work. Tomorrow we do it again, then you'll do the left leg, then repeat without your arm."

"Gee thanks, Keith. You'll make me into a one-armed hopping bandit."

"The scourge of Dodge City, Shep."

Once Glenn was in the chiller, Keith pulled over his tablet and began reading the results of the tests. Marty and Nik entered the room and Keith handed over the tablet to share the results with everyone. "Okay, so you aren't the world's fastest human on the one-hundred- and two-hundred-meter sprints," Marty began. "You managed right around twenty point six miles per hour, which is awfully close to the record for the four-hundred-meter. The thing is, you maintained between nineteen and twenty miles per hour for almost two hours on the treadmill. Did you realize that?"

"Actually, no. Is that good?"

"It's fantastic. World record speeds drop down to fifteen miles per hour at any distance over a mile. You ran a marathon in an hour-and-a-half, and you were fifty percent faster than record pace."

"So, I'm a tortoise, not a hare."

"That's well, actually, that's not a bad analogy," Nik said in agreement as Marty held the tablet out for him to scroll down through the results. He looked up at Marty and nodded as he handed the tablet back.

"Keith says your cardiovascular performance was pretty good. Both leg and core muscles use a *lot* of oxygen and glucose during a run, but not having to completely supply your legs meant that your heart rate never exceeded one-forty beats per minute, and your blood oxygen saturation stayed around ninety-four percent. That's without the LVAD ever kicking in. There were a few rhythm irregularities and dips in pulse-ox that could be smoothed out with it turned on continuously, so we'll look into that. You did extremely well."

"Yup, slow and steady wins the race."

"Twenty miles an hour for nearly two hours isn't slow."

"No, but I'm not going to be outracing a speeding bullet or leaping over tall buildings."

"Well, to start with, you look terrible in spandex, Shep. Superhero costumes are my schtick, anyway," Nik admonished. "Still, your performance was certainly more than human."

"More than human?" Glenn said. "I'm not sure how I feel about that. I'm still working on getting back to *human*."

The following days involved tests for his arm: weight lifting ability, speed, and precision of motion. Despite being right-handed, Glenn was pleased to learn that he could now lift deadlift hundred-pound weights one handed, throw a baseball at speeds up to one hundred twenty-five miles per hour, and throw a shot-put a distance of one hundred feet with his left hand.

In the weightlifting tests, Glenn excelled at any task that emphasized leg and lower back strength such as squats, deadlifts, pulls, carries, and drags. As long as he could manage most of the effort with his artificial leg muscles, he could lift and carry near world-record weights of up to a thousand pounds. Dragging, pulling, or carrying heavy weight was all handled by his prosthetics, much like the endurance run on the first day.

More tests of arms and legs ensued. In cycling, Glenn was able to reach a top speed of nearly one hundred miles per hour, about twenty percent faster than the prior unassisted human record of eighty-three point three miles per hour. More importantly, he could maintain forty miles per hour for more than two hours, and in one test, didn't vary by more than five percent for six hours. Those numbers were more than double the prior endurance and distance records by unaugmented humans.

Keith said it was because those efforts could be accomplished almost exclusively by the bionics with minimal involvement of mere flesh and bone. Such comments were usually followed by a physical therapy session that almost hurt worse than the physical exertion. Deep tissue massage relieved the strain and tightness around his hips and thighs, but left the muscles feeling bruised and sore. His ribs also ached, considering the amount of oxygen he'd been taking in to supply the rest of his body during the exertion.

His high jump height was more than ten feet, and his long jump over forty feet—all more than twenty-five percent better than the current world records. Keith had a particular way of digging his thumbs into the intercostal muscles that Glenn swore resulted in him levitating off the table. The therapist said it was good for him, and at least he wasn't suffering from shin splints, plantar fasciitis, or lower back pain. In all, the patient should suck it up and remember that he volunteered for this.

Another day was devoted to sensitivity and acuity of his bionic eye and ear. The ultimate test was being placed in a lightless room configured to dampen sound and eliminate all noise. It was a huge facility the size of several large aircraft hangars and used for environmental testing. Glenn was instructed to disable his bionics, then was blindfolded, hooded, and spun repeatedly to confuse his sense of position and direction. He was then placed in the center of the room and instructed to activate his bionics and find the exit despite a complete absence of sight and sound.

To make things even more difficult, for each test, the room—and his body—were pre-conditioned to temperatures ranging from minus ten to one hundred twenty-five degrees Fahrenheit. The first time, Glenn walked out of the facility in seven and a half minutes. By the third test he was exiting in just over thirty seconds. Marty, Nik, and the testing team were quite pleased.

On the evening after the final test, Marty and Nik visited Glenn in his quarters. "One more day with us here and then transfer. The general did it; you're headed to Houston for two weeks, and then the Mars Terrain Simulator in Hawaii," Marty informed him.

"Well hooray for sunshine and tropical breezes."

"You know it's *cold* on top of the volcano, right?" Nik asked.

"Well, sure, but the last time I trained there I got to stay in Lahaina for a week after we came down." MTSH utilized the ten-thousand-foot-elevation Haleakalā volcanic crater on the island of Maui to simulate the dry rocky conditions found on Mars. Additional facilities took similar advantage of other volcanic features on the big island of Hawaii, such as the Hawaiian Island Simulated Long-Orbit and Planetary Exploration habitat located inside a dormant volcanic cinder cone near the summit of Mauna Kea. The location was used to test low-pressure and arid environments, and to simulate the isolation of a long interplanetary voyage. The rocky walls and floors of the Halemaumau and Kilauea Iki craters at Hawaii Volcanos National Park were used to test all-terrain rovers, EVA suits and autonomous exploration vehicles for both lunar and Mars use.

Marty cleared his throat. "Well, don't be expecting to do much sunbathing. The skin on your legs and arm isn't going to match any skin color changes. The DoD isn't going to pay for an all-new covering of SymSkyn just so you can look like a tabloid star."

"I bet he does it, anyway," added Nik.

Glenn just raised an eyebrow at the light-skinned surgeon and dark-skinned psychiatrist. "Well, when I stand between the two of you, we look like an ad for copier toner. If I'm two-tone, we'll just call it a bad photo edit."

"Anyway, that's not why I'm here," Marty said, as a technician entered the room pushing a cart carrying the exoskeleton Glenn used early in his recovery. "Remember this old piece of iron? Higher-Up suggested one more test, so we're going to run that now."

"With this? What's left to test?"

"Ian, here, is from tech division, and he suggested we see if we can give you those superpowers you wanted. You'll do an abbreviated version of the run, jump, and lift tests in the exo."

"O—kay, I'll guess that will be interesting. Can the exo handle the stress?"

"Oh, most certainly. It was built to protect you, and we always had the servos turned down so that you wouldn't hurt yourself."

Nik tossed Glenn a shirt. It was a long-sleeved exercise T-shirt, designed to be form-fitting and maintain his temperature while wicking away perspiration. It was bright blue, with a red-outlined yellow diamond on the front. In the center it had a large letter "D."

"Umm, 'D'? Isn't it supposed to have an 'S'?"

"Well, the letter was supposedly some translation of 'House of El.' I had them change it to a 'D' for 'House of Dumbass.'" Nik grinned and opened his white coat to reveal a black shirt with yellow shield and a bat outline. "I've got my mask and cape to cheer you on."

"Oh. How thoughtful!" Glenn replied as he threw the shirt back at the psychiatrist.

The test went even better than the "unassisted" feats of the past week. Using the exoskeleton to balance bionic ability with flesh-and-blood limitations, he was able to maintain a thirty mile per hour run with sprint speeds up to forty-five. In all other events, including jumping and weight lifting, he nearly doubled his previous record, but sacrificed some reaction time under a full load.

"Well, that tells us something," Marty began the review with Glenn, Nik, and Ian. "The intelligent controller we developed for the bionics will control servos as naturally as they control his limbs. In fact, during the final run, we turned off the force-feedback loop and let the exo operate strictly on the limb-control signals. Aside from the communications tether, Glenn could probably operate the exo without even being in it."

"So how do we test it?" Glenn asked. "I've been sitting here trying to command that thing to move, and it just sits there."

"We can't, at least not with your current configuration," Ian spoke up. "See, we designed all of your bionics to talk to each other on a proprietary short-range wireless network so that we didn't have to have physical wiring connecting all of your prosthetic bits."

"For that, I am eternally grateful," said Glenn sardonically. "Especially the part where you call them 'bits.'"

"Hey, to an engineer, *all* bio stuff is just fiddly bits," Ian countered.

"Yeah, as I said...We all know that I can still control my bionics when they are disconnected, so there's communication between my brain and the...bits."

"Yeah, I've seen your stunt, and frankly, if we had used some of the original designs, you would have been able to link everything up with Wi-Fi. The first guy to have a prosthetic mount grafted directly to the bone of his upper arm, used to disconnect his forearm at the elbow and shake hands with people. It was the highlight of his demonstrations. Unfortunately, his hand wasn't really strong enough to move on its own, and the wireless interface could only be used for about an hour, twice a day. On the other hand—so to speak—the wireless had a range of several feet. We took a different approach with your prosthetics, though. You have a Q-processor in your hip to handle communication and coordination, and it's directly—and quite exclusively—entangled with the transceivers in your legs and arm."

"Wait, what? I know about the computer, what do you mean by 'entangled'?"

"Quantum entanglement, Sir." Ian looked to Marty and received a nod in return. He then walked over to the digital whiteboard in the conference room, pulled a control stylus out of an inner pocket of his retro-style white lab coat, and began to draw on the board. Dark lines appeared wherever he touched the surface with the stylus, and the image was graphically interpreted into circuits and diagrams on the computer displays in front of each place at the conference table. "Quantum theory told us that photons could be created in pairs, and that any force acting on one of the pair, would affect the other, no matter how far apart they were. Quantum computers basically operate with light—photons—instead of electrons and electrical impulses, so if we used entangled photons, we could essentially send signals back and forth between the controller and the various sensors and actuators with no delay and no distance limitations."

"Oh . . . that's right. I seem to remember Marty saying something about SQUIDs. Okay, got it. It's quantum, don't try to understand, just accept."

"Yeah, not quite *that* simple, once we learned how to

entangle more than just photons, but that's the essence of it."

"Hah!" exclaimed Nik. "If you ever find yourself actually *understanding* quantum physics, you have to roll for sanity check."

Glenn looked over at the psychiatrist. "I've read *that* book, too, Nik." He then turned back to Ian. "So, what you're saying is that my controller and bionics are 'entangled' but you can't do that with the exo."

"Actually, Shep, we could do it, we just haven't. The current exoskeleton can operate purely on a force-feedback basis, just like the ones the Army developed for soldiers to wear on mission. For this test, though, we plugged the exo into the bionic control circuits for your legs and arm. The limb control signals went directly to the servos, which is how we know you can control it directly; we just don't have a version of the exoskeleton that incorporates the Q-processors directly."

Glenn looked at Marty, then Ian. The satisfied look on the technician's face told him everything he needed to know.

"You're planning on it, though, aren't you?" Glenn asked.

Ian began to speak, but Marty responded first.

"Basically yes. Your processor can be keyed with many more quantum links than you could possibly use, and this test suggests it would be worth it. The processor is deep in your left hip, but there's a way to give you a port under the skin of your abdomen. Docs have been using them for years for drug delivery, dialysis, gastric bands, and anything else that needs a sterile access point inside the body—a short needle through the skin and into the silicone bubble, then thread a connection probe through the needle into the port. We need to implant the port tomorrow; it's a minor procedure with local anesthetic. Ian's team will rebuild the exo with its own Q-processors, and provide the linkage keys. It should be ready for you by the time you get to MTSH."

"Oh good, more toys to play with and tropical beauties, too!" Glenn started to rub his head, then stopped himself, and rubbed his hands together. He grinned at Nik. "Isn't that what the doctor ordered, Nik?"

"Hey! Save some for the brave doctor that put your head back together. For that matter, save some for Marty. He needs to get out, too."

Marty just shook his head and sighed. "Oh, do grow up, you two."

CHAPTER 9:
Less than Superhuman

❋

USSF Office of Scientific Integration
@OSIGenBoatright
> Colonel Glenn Shepard has recovered
> from injuries sustained during a training
> mission on the Moon. He will be leading
> one of our medical advancement and
> integration teams.
> —Major General Richard Boatwright,
> USSF/OSI

George J @SpaceFan
> Finally.

ChirpChat, June 2041

From the rehab facility in San Antonio, Glenn had to spend two weeks in Houston for in-processing as a civilian consultant to NASA and the Mars Exploration Consortium. Space Force still refused to reverse Glenn's retirement and restore him to active duty, but MarsX had been willing to let him work alongside their personnel. There was one small problem, in that he would have to undergo the full one-year astronaut candidate training program.

After in-processing, he would have a few weeks before reporting to the training center on Hawaii. Glenn was looking forward to it despite the fact that repeating the year-long training program felt like he was starting over as an astronaut recruit. On the other hand, Hawaiian volcanos were starkly beautiful, as well as excellent training sites.

He had another check-up back in San Antonio before final release to report to the training center. Glenn met with Marty to cover one more important detail. Glenn wanted to use his free month to pay a visit to Aunt Sally and Uncle Hoop. One problem, though, was that he was in Texas, and they were in Virginia. He would fly on a military jet to Hawaii, but as a retiree that option wasn't available for a personal trip. He and Marty were uncertain if he should fly in commercial airplanes; after all, it wasn't if he could walk through the security systems at an airport. As modern and unobtrusive as they'd become, he would certainly stand out on any scans. Glenn wanted to drive, but his driver's license had expired while he was on the Moon, and he'd had neither time nor opportunity to renew it yet.

There had been several inquiries at higher levels of the military and government as to whether he could—or even *should* —recertify in skills such as driving or flying. It grated on Glenn's nerves. It was almost as if he was being punished for being rebuilt with artificial parts. He'd protested to Nik and Marty that it wasn't fair; this didn't happen to people who were sick and recovered. Marty countered that it was exactly what happened to amputees with vehicle licenses.

The real insult was that there was talk of suspending his medical certifications. A message from the Virginia Medical Examination Board had arrived that morning. It argued that he was too long out of medical practice, he'd suffered severe trauma, and implied that there were concerns now that he was "almost as much machine as he was human." They hadn't taken action yet, and Marty promised that General Boatright would look into it.

It was still an insult, though.

Glenn didn't see any of his "replacement parts" as problems. He could certainly pass a vision test as part of the driving examination. If anybody wanted to test his coordination, well, the past year of rehabilitation had certainly demonstrated that he had mastered his new bionic prosthetics. He could operate anything on a vehicle, and with self-driving cars, that was unlikely to be a problem. The only real problem was that auto-drive was not going to fit what Glenn had in mind.

Glenn wanted a road trip.

"Look, it's a pretty drive, especially through the Carolinas. Hills, winding roads, lots of green. I need to get out and feel that I'm alive." Glenn was trying to convince Marty to let him drive alone. It would be nearly fifteen hundred miles to his aunt and uncle's house.

"Absolutely not," Marty replied. "We haven't put this much work into you to have a glitch occur and you drive off the side of road. I mean, I really don't think that your trust fund, the insurance companies, DARPA, the Navy, the Healthcare Advanced Research Projects Institute, and every other government agency that has had a hand in your rebuild, is going to settle for doing it a second time."

"Nothing is going to happen. I'm just driving across the country. I'll rent an auto-drive car and let it drive me most of the way. It's just that there are certain places that I love to drive." Glenn was adamant.

This was supposed to be his freedom drive.

In years past, returning prisoners of war would receive a freedom celebration upon their return from captivity. Some got a freedom flight; others got a parade. It didn't matter what the event was; it was a celebration that you were free of captivity, and your own person. This drive was important to Glenn. He needed this.

"No."

"Look, I have to go out into society. I have to go out into the world. What am I supposed to do, stay in this rehab hospital the rest of my life?"

"No, but you'll be out in public during training."

"Secured behind guarded gates or isolated on top of Mauna Kea? Nope. Not the same."

"But what if something happens?"

"That's the *point*, Marty. We need to show that I can handle it."

"I know you can handle it."

"Sure, you do. You are the one responsible for this superman shell I'm in. Clearly Space Force doesn't believe, and I'm not sure NASA and MarsX are totally convinced. We need to show *them*."

"Okay, okay, if it means that much to you. We won't

send you in a hospital van or ambulance, but you really need to take someone else with you."

"Okay, I'll take Nik."

"Nik? Why Nik?"

"Well to start with, he has a wheelchair equipped van. Even if the state is unwilling to certify me as a fully able driver, they can't deny me a handicap license. I'll take the test in a mobility chair, use hand operated controls, voice operated controls, or anything they want. Visual? Auditory? I still have one normal eye and ear. I can do everything with one hand just like any other handicapped driver. If they will accept that, then I can get a provisional license which will allow me to drive Nik's van. For that matter, Nik himself can drive if need be—but he won't have to. This is my trip."

"Will he do it?"

"I talked it over with him already. He's perfectly willing to."

"So, what you're telling me is that this is what you wanted all along. Was the rest of this argument just a way to soften me up for the real options?"

"No. Well, yes. I knew you would be reluctant to sign off on the full package, so we figured to give you an option you could accept."

"We?"

"Ah, Nik and I."

"Uh huh. As I suspected. Just how long have you two been planning this?"

"About a month."

"A month. And you're taking my psychiatrist away for how long?"

"*Your* psychiatrist? Certainly not. *My friend* will be with me for a week or so. Just long enough to get me to Virginia and stay long enough to sample Aunt Sally's home cooking."

"Your friend . . . I saw that one coming. You two are naturals. I made the right choice in hiring him for this job, but he's probably ruined now."

"Nope, not Nik. He cares for his patients, and the whole rehab unit adores him . . . docs and nurses, too!"

Marty sniffed. "Well, *I* never . . . Yes, you're right. He really is perfect for the job, and he and I both know it. Alright, approved. Just make sure you both stay in one piece. Don't add to the population, don't subtract from the population, don't end up in jail—and if you do, I'm not answering my comm."

"I'm not sure I like the looks of those clouds back there, Shep. It's pretty dark."

"At least it's in our rearview mirror, Nik. I heard the forecast—there's some nasty storms behind us, and they're headed east. Since *we're* headed east, we should still be able to outrun it."

"Okay, that's fine as long as we keep ahead of the storm. What happens when we turn north to get to Mount Airy? Should we call Mike and Cathy to tell them we're going to stop for the night and let the storms pass?"

"We should be okay. The dark clouds haven't gotten any closer in the past two hours. We only have to head north for seventy miles. It might be close, but we should be okay."

"I'm just glad you're driving, Shep. I don't know this part of the country as well as you do."

"I thought you did a fellowship in Florida. You never came up here for a glimpse of the mountains?"

"I was deep in the peninsula, not the panhandle. I never really got up into Alabama, Georgia...the Carolinas. You grew up in Virginia, so you know this region better than I do. Aside from two years in Florida, I've never been further east than the Mississippi."

"Yeah, yeah. I hear you. Y'know, I never did hear the full story of how you transitioned from that pediatric job you had before, into military rehab."

"Well, frankly, there's not a whole lot of difference." Glenn glanced to the side and Nik grinned at him. He balled up a napkin from their last stop and tossed it in Nik's direction. "My previous department wanted a program working with seriously ill kids. I built it. We treated kids with cancer, heart defects, epilepsy, depression, anxiety, you name it. I heard that some bigwig in the medical center praised the department chair for his 'innovative program.' He got a deanship; I got more hours and lousy pay."

"Okay, you've told me that part, but how did you get hooked up with Marty Spruce at SAMMC?"

"Oh, that's easy. I treated Marty's niece while she was being treated for leukemia."

"Oh, so Marty figured you could make the transition from pediatrics to injured soldiers?"

"You have to admit, the sense of humor is about the same."

"You're not wrong there." Shepard took note of the road signs for the upcoming exit. "Okay, here's our turnoff heading north. You're right, it's looking darker back there, but it's still clear ahead and above us. We should be able to make it."

"Drive on, Shep. Into—or at least, ahead of—the storm!"

"Aye, aye, cap'n!"

"Getting darker, Shep."

"We've only got another thirty miles to go. Tell me about these two friends of yours we're supposed to meet in Mount Airy? How do you know Mike and Cathy?"

"I actually met Cathy via an old bulletin board chat site. Her husband Mike's a writer who called me up for information he used in a book. He called it being a 'subject matter expert.' We've since been to a few conferences together."

"Ah. Cathy's a former girlfriend."

"Bite your tongue. On the other hand, we did have to deal with rumors. A few mutual—well, they used to be friends—tried to spread word that we were dating. We were and are just good friends. That's all."

"Okay, okay, I won't push you on girlfriends. I know you swore off them but I'm surprised you and Nurse Cuddly..."

"Bite your tongue. She's way too bubbly for me."

"What about that other nurse, Sheila? She's cute."

"Don't get me started; she's out of my league. There's no way I'm even going to be able to work up enough courage to ask her out."

"Ha, psychiatrist, heal thyself."

"Yeah, I could say the same about you, flight surgeon. Now what is it we were talking about? Oh yes, you were telling me about Yvette."

"Touché. Same here, I'd rather not talk about her."

"Not even to your therapist?"

"I thought you got enough of this when you were squirting me with water every time I had a flashback."

"That was treatment, this is therapy."

"You wouldn't let me have my own water pistol!"

"Hey! Do you know how much paperwork I had to go through to get that authorized?" Nik turned at Glenn's chuckle and shook a finger at his friend. "I'm serious! I had to get special dispensation to classify it as a therapeutic device. You were a *patient*, not a doctor. You didn't have admitting and treatment privileges there!"

"Okay, okay! I surrender. Yvette's a part of my past, and I'd rather leave it at that." He glanced over at Nik. ". . . and you're not letting me off. So sure, we were serious, even talking about getting engaged. It was while we were still in residency, but I had the flight trauma fellowships coming up, and she made it very clear that she while she wanted to go to space, she wasn't staying in the service. I planned to stay in, which meant I'd get transferred all over the place. I was willing to stick it out, despite the separations. I argued that with only one of us in the Force, it would make it easier; we wouldn't have to worry about fighting for mutual assignments. We could start a family, have kids."

"And?"

"'Not her dream,' she said. She told me she was serious about going to space, though, and she'd had an elective hysterectomy. No risk of unplanned pregnancy or genetic complications that way. So, no family, just her career. I took that as meaning that I wasn't that important to her either. If we'd stayed together, it probably would've meant the end of *my* dream."

"And there's been nobody else since then?"

"I've dated. After all, there's a certain appeal to being both a doctor and an astronaut. You might not believe this, but there's . . . well, the best word I can think of . . . is *groupies*. There was this one encounter . . . it was one of those science fiction conventions you like. Down in Georgia—lots of science stuff and an honest to God 'Space Track.' They wanted an astronaut and a doctor to talk about space medicine. They got two-in-one with me courtesy of the Public Affairs Office. They put me on a couple of panels, and those rooms were *packed*. I never would have believed a science fiction convention drew those kinds of crowds."

"Yup, I know which one you mean. I've never been to it, but there's one in California that's even bigger."

"Right. So, they put me on panels to talk about stuff like bone loss, why blood doesn't pool in zero gravity, that sort of thing. I got invited to a couple of parties in the evenings—authors, celebrities, artists, fans—folks like that. The convention assigned me a handler to make sure I got to things on time and to help me out of awkward encounters. He was a bit slow this one time— the host was out on the balcony smoking a cigar and just happened to mention that I was somewhere in the suite. BAM! Next thing I know this girl plowed through a mass of bodies trying to get to me. She practically hung all over me."

"Nice! You had a true fan!"

"I was never more uncomfortable in my life.

Fortunately, my handler worked security for the con when he wasn't shepherding me."

Nik giggled. "Shepherding Shepard and throwing himself in front of exploding bimbos. I love it, man."

"Yeah . . . no. He managed to deflect her by telling her I had an appointment with one of the directors of the convention. He and the additional security he called still had to practically peel her off of me to get me clear. As I said, I was never more uncomfortable in my life."

"Oh, the sacrifices you've made. Beautiful women throwing themselves at you and you brush them off . . . excuse me, *peel* them off."

"No, I'm not like that. Yes, I dated Yvette. We were good together and I started thinking it was going to be forever, but in the end we were incompatible. She called it quits before I did. I've dated a few women since then, but I vowed to stay away from coworkers, astronauts, or doctors. I do like intelligent girls and to take my time getting to know them, but the training schedules and astronaut duties didn't leave a lot of social time."

"So, nothing in how many years?"

"You *know* that answer. There's been nobody for the past two-and-a-half years, given that I was on the Moon for six months prior to the accident."

"Except for Nurse Cuddly."

"That . . . was a disaster. Did you know she called me a couple times? I think she really wanted to test out her therapist skills as much as to see if anything else was bionically enhanced."

"Did you take her up on it?"

"One date—if you can call it that. She came over to

Houston last week and we got together. It was supposed to be just coffee, but she clearly had other plans."

"And? Don't leave me in suspense."

"It was too much of a therapist-patient situation. I had...difficulties. She tried. Oh, how she tried. Look, she's cute, and I know she'd love to keep trying with a long-distance relationship. I've had those, and learned they don't work if you can't see each other regularly. I still haven't given up on Mars, or the Moon, and even a quarter million miles is a bit too far. Plus, I'll be essentially in isolation for the next year. Now, if there were someone really special, someone who knew me better than I knew myself—and I'd come to know her the same way—I'd be willing to give it a try. She'd have to be awfully special, though, Nik, awfully special."

"I got you, Shep. I feel the same way. I mean who wants a broken-down old head shrinker who spends his day with unruly soldiers dealing with PTA."

"There's what's-her-name."

"Put it out of your mind, Shep. Give me time. I think you're more likely to find somebody before I am."

"Hey, the wind's picked up. How much further do we have?"

"This is our exit. Mount Airy. Five miles that-a-way."

"Let's get in there and get off the road."

Glenn pulled the van into a parking spot on Main Street just ahead of the gust front that preceded the storm. Where there had once been clouds to the west, and blue skies above and to the east, there were now angry dark clouds everywhere. The wind was blowing dirt, leaves, and small bits of litter in swirls down the street.

Mike and Cathy lived half an hour away, and were driving in to meet them in the town. Fortunately, they were coming from the east, and should not be in the storm, yet. Glenn and Nik were debating whether to go inside and wait in the café, when they heard the tornado sirens.

As with any small town, the fire station was just about a block away and the sirens could be heard throughout in the city center. In addition, both their wristcomms sounded an alert; they could hear the message repeated up and down the street. A tornado had been spotted just west of town, moving east.

"Well, Nik, I guess we're going into the café. Let's see if they've got a shelter or we just find an interior hallway. We certainly can't stay out here."

"You got it. I think I'd better use my wheelchair, although . . . bring the crutches just in case."

Once Glenn helped Nik into the wheelchair, he offered to push him across the street. Nik refused. "I've got this," he said, and propelled himself across the street and into the café.

Glenn looked in the back of the van for the crutches. His eyes lit on the components of his exo-frame. He'd get the new one in Hawaii, so he'd only brought the leg braces and the components used as a wheelchair when needed. He reached for the leg braces, thinking that a little bit of extra structural support might be handy if they were going into an underground storm shelter. At that moment, the sirens went off again. Glenn closed the van door and headed inside with the braces in his hand, not realizing he'd left the crutches in the van.

The café didn't have a storm shelter, but the kitchen was at a slightly lower level than the dining area, and behind that was an oversized pantry and storage area with no windows. There were four employees and two customers in addition to Glenn and Nik, so they were all invited to take shelter in the pantry. There was a bit of an issue getting Nik's wheelchair down to the kitchen; there was a ramp for deliveries, but it was outside.

"Hey, Shep, hand me my crutches, I'll walk down and you can lift the chair."

"Um, oops. Sorry, Nik. I grabbed the wrong thing." Glenn held up the leg braces.

"Dammit, Shep, you were supposed to bring *mine*!"

"Yeah, I'm sorry. Here, I'll help you get down the steps. Just hang onto the railing and I'll grab your chair."

"Yeah, okay, that'll do. There's no sense in going back outside, the rain has started." At that moment, lightning flashed and the thunder came almost immediately. "... aaaand the lightning, too. Don't worry, I'll manage."

As the eight people got settled into the pantry, the main storm hit. The wind was loud, and raindrops struck the building with a force that could be heard all the way through the brick walls. There was a nearly continuous rumble of thunder punctuated by sharp cracks from very close strikes. Above it all was a rushing sound like a freight train. It seemed like a cliché but Nik knew the sound very well from his residency in Kansas.

He looked wide-eyed at Glenn. "That's the tornado."

At that moment, the lights went out; for several minutes, the only illumination was the near constant flash of lightning. The whole building shook and they could hear cooking utensils rattling in the kitchen. It was too loud for conversation, but they could hear the crackle of breaking glass from somewhere out in the dining area. Their ears popped from pressure decrease, and several people reacted with surprised shouts. The very fabric of the building creaked and groaned with the stress of the tornado's wind. The pressure difference and sound meant that it passed either directly overhead, or quite nearby.

The noise and shaking were over in less than five minutes. They could still hear rain, but the thunder was decreased, and took longer to sound after each lightning flash. Once the interval between flash and boom increased to more than ten seconds, they knew that the lightning strikes were at least two miles away.

They no longer heard the heavy wind.

They no longer heard the freight train sounds.

The tornado had passed.

What they did hear was car alarms, sirens...and screams.

CHAPTER 10:
. . . But What Am I?

❋

National Weather Service, Roanoke, Virginia
@NWS_ROA

Tornado Warning. NWS Roanoke is reporting a tornado one mile west of downtown Mount Airy, North Carolina. The funnel is reported to be on the ground and moving east northeast at five miles an hour . . .

ChirpChat, June 2041

"Someone's hurt." Glenn turned to the café manager. "I'm a doctor. I'll need some help in case we have to extract anyone. If you can get someone to help Nik and take his chair out to the dining room, I'll get started clearing a path."

The screams repeated, and at least one sounded quite close.

"We need to hurry."

The café manager assigned one of his servers and a customer to help Nik and also told Chuck, the short-order cook, to help Glenn. The windows in front of the café were completely blown inward. Broken glass crunched underfoot, and tables and chairs were jumbled against the wall separating the dining room from the kitchen. Glenn grabbed a chair, turned it back upright, then sat to attach his leg braces.

There was a sign in the middle of the dining room that said Polly's Treasures. Glenn vaguely thought it belonged on a shop that had been across the street. He stood and made his way to the door to look out onto the street. Their van was still there but the side was severely dented right at the sliding door. It was going take time and leverage to get that open. Fortunately, they didn't need that door other than for convenience in putting the wheelchair in. The van itself looked okay as far as the windows and other doors were concerned, but there was something sticking out of one tire—which was starting to go flat.

In front of the van was a brand-new electric auto-drive sedan from that company started by one of the MarsX investors. It was facing the wrong way, and hadn't been there when they'd entered the café. It was rolled almost completely over onto its roof and blocked the sidewalk.

The screaming came from the front seat.

The trunk of a tree protruded from the battery compartment; the car was edged up against another tree, and it was unclear if other branches were protruding into engine or passenger compartments.

They needed to work fast. Damaged batteries were usually bad news.

A young woman was in the driver's seat, hanging upside down from her seatbelt. Glenn could see a child in a car seat directly behind her. There was a pile of toys and blankets cluttering the other side of the car, and he could see a small hand sticking out of the pile. The hand was moving, and there were muffled cries coming from under the pile.

The woman was screaming, but not in pain or about herself, but about her children. "Save my babies! Save my babies! Get my babies out of here! Someone, help us!"

Glenn and the cook ran over to the car.

"Ma'am, I'm a doctor. Can you hear me?" Glenn asked the woman and received a strained "yes" and a muffled scream in response.

"Ma'am, how many people in your car?" He could see an infant, and probably one child, but getting the driver to answer was an extremely important part of a first-responder's Q&A.

"My babies!"

"How many, Ma'am."

"Two," she gasped. "Six months and three years."

"Very good. We'll get them out. Where were they sitting?"

"Russell's in the baby seat behind me. Cheryl Ann was in a booster on the other side, but she likes to slip out of the shoulder strap."

That answered that. She'd fallen out when the car turned over, and was under the pile on the other side. The hand had been joined by another, and he could see a hint of blonde hair.

The airbag had deployed and was hanging limply from

the steering yoke, so he could skip the next part of the checklist. Also, the car was electric, so he shouldn't have to worry about leaking fuel.

"Do you have any alcohol or flammable liquid in the car?"

"What? I WASN'T DRINKING!"

"Yes, Ma'am, I believe you. I just need to make sure if there is risk of fire before we pull you and your babies out."

"Oh." She tried to shift in her seat, and yelped in pain. "Get me out of here, please hurry!"

"We'll do that right now. Can you move your arms and legs? Are you stuck or trapped anywhere? Any sharp pains in your neck?"

"Yes. No. No. *Please!*"

"Right away, Ma'am. Just try to stay still."

The driver's door was stuck and the passenger door was jammed up against a tree. If need be, they could come in from the rear door once they'd extracted the infant, but he decided to apply some force to the door first. He grabbed the handle with his right hand and had no luck. He switched to his left hand, thinking to simply exert more force, but pulled the handle off of the door.

Oh, that was smart! Yeah, how am I going to get the door open now? He put his left hand on the top of his head and rubbed back and forth for a moment.

The cook was trying to get the back door open. He'd gotten it to move a bit so that at least he could reach in around the broken glass. The infant was still strapped into the car seat, which was in turn still strapped to the rear seat. If either restraint was released, the child would risk dropping onto the broken glass.

Glenn turned to the young man as he made his decision. "Take it easy, Chuck. Don't try to do that by yourself. I've got to get this lady out, so grab someone else from the café, have them undo the straps while you hold the child. Oh, and grab some towels we can use to support her neck."

Chuck ran back to get someone else to help.

Other people were filtering out into the street, so Glenn called out to the crowd, "I need a crowbar or jack handle to get this door open." The manager of the café said he had one in his car, and also sent the other server back in to grab some tools from the cleaning closet.

Glenn turned back to the driver and reassured her. "Ma'am, don't worry, we have help here and will get your baby out. I need you to shift yourself away from the door as much as possible so that I can pry it open. This is going to get a little bit messy."

Glenn looked up at a shout of dismay from the café manager—his car was currently under a tree, and the server had come back with a wooden mop.

"That won't do. Well, anything else will take too much time." He put the fingers of his left hand right at the edge of the door frame and commanded the bionic muscles to curl with as much force as they could exert. It would damage the SymSkyn outer covering, but the composite and carbon-fiber structure would punch a hand-hold right into the door. He started leaking fluid from his lacerated fingers, but it didn't matter now, he had his opening. This time when he pulled the door frame, it not only came free but separated from the hinges and flew halfway across the street. The lady screamed again in shock at seeing the sheer amount of force he'd exerted.

"Well. You don't see *that* every day." Glenn whirled at the voice behind him and saw a law enforcement officer in green slacks and tan shirt. He had a seven-pointed star on his chest and a nametag that read "Atkins."

"Ah, sorry about that. Sheriff..." Glenn paused, and the man nodded. "...Atkins."

"The kid said you needed these?" Atkins handed him the towels.

"Oh, good. Let me roll this up and brace her neck. Then, if you would work the seatbelt, I'll make sure this young lady doesn't fall." He turned back to address the trapped woman. "Hold onto the steering wheel. We're going to unbuckle you, and you'll drop down a bit. I'll catch you and help you climb out." With his damaged left hand, he reached in to grab her around the midsection while the sheriff undid the buckle.

The lady's eyes went wide when she saw his hand. "What did you do to yourself?"

"It's an artificial hand. Not a big problem. It will be okay."

"Okay... yes, if you say so."

He placed his flesh and blood hand back on the lady's shoulder. The fingers of his left hand were stiff; he'd damaged the servos yet again, but it was worth it. Marty would understand; DARPA probably wouldn't—although they should. It was a military thing, not leaving an injured person in danger. About the time he had the woman most of the way out of the car, Chuck came back to extract the infant, car seat and all.

"It's okay, ma'am, we got the baby out. He's right here. We need to get the two of you inside the café. The power's out, but at least it's out of the rain. I'm a doctor and I'll have a look at those cuts."

"But my daughter—my daughter's in there. She's on the other side."

"Yes, ma'am. She's next, we'll have to move things around to get to her, though."

The sheriff and one of the café patrons helped the woman move away from the car while Glenn took a closer look at the back seat. This was going to be tricky. A blanket and stuffed teddy bear had fallen atop the child when she slipped from her booster seat. The hand that had been sticking out from under the pile was no longer moving.

Once again, they needed to hurry. The child could suffocate. Unfortunately, that side of the car was wedged against a tree and he couldn't access the girl from here. They needed to turn the car over.

"Hey, Nik!" His friend had come out into the street to assist when Chuck and the server had returned. He motioned him over, then beckoned the sheriff to join them.

"We're going to have to turn this over. My buddy Nik has plenty of upper body strength, and I've got the lower, plus leverage, so we *might* be able to do this ourselves."

"Nope, not a chance with me in this chair, Shep. Plus, you need to brace it to keep it from rolling back. What about your Exo?"

Glenn grimaced. "Sorry. In the van, Nik. There's a great big dent in the side; I don't think that door is moving, not anytime soon. Any other suggestions?"

Atkins tilted his head. "Most of my boys are answering other calls right now, but if we can get some more volunteers from the shops, we'll do this together."

"That will work. Can we get some blankets or pillows to stuff in there so that the kid doesn't fall on any sharp edges?"

"I have throw pillows in my shop," a voice called from over his shoulder.

"How far away is it?"

"It's right here. I'm Polly."

"Oh, Polly's Treasures. I think your sign is over in the café."

"I wondered where that went. Thanks." Nik had wheeled back toward the café, and the sheriff was talking to some of the bystanders to rally additional help. The volunteers came over and lined up to push on the upper side of the car. A few maneuvered around to grab the underside, but Glenn waved them away. "Too dangerous. If you get caught, you can get hurt pretty bad." He reached down and locked his leg braces at knees and hips, then sent the mental command to lock his bionic knee joints. That way the weight would travel directly through the titanium exoskeleton and ceramic composite bones. He reached up, at first with his left hand as the weight of the car started to come over, then turned his hand to grab the edge and gently lower the car onto the ground.

"Let someone help you with that. You can't take the weight of that all by yourself," Atkins said. "That's too much; you'll hurt yourself."

Glenn slapped the leg exoframe with this right hand, then tapped his left forearm. "This is all prosthetic. I'm not shouldering all the weight by myself," Glenn assured the sheriff.

"If you say so, buddy, but we don't have a big hospital

in town. You have to go into Winston or Charlotte and the ambulances are going to be pretty well tied up. I don't want you hurting yourself, man. Not on my watch."

Not on my watch. That certainly sounds familiar, Glenn thought to himself as he began to feel the weight of the car. He shifted his stance and the strain built up across his shoulder and chest muscles. The weight of the car hung from his bionic hand and arm as long as he had a stable foundation from hips and legs. He didn't even have to support the whole weight, just to slow it down enough so that the car didn't topple, bounce or roll.

Damn that hurt. He could feel every point of attachment between artificial and natural tissue and bone. Fortunately, it was only momentary and they got the car rolled over and gently lowered to the ground.

"Pretty impressive," Atkins said. "Like I said, that's just not something you see every day. Did this . . ." He gestured vaguely at Glenn's legs. ". . . happen to you in the war?"

"Astronaut, actually. It was a trainer crash and fire."

"Well, that makes sense, I guess. I've seen some of the stuff they're doing with artificial limbs . . . but *damn,* dude!" He paused, and a funny expression came over his face. "Oh, man, you're leaking."

Glenn looked down at his legs. The cloth over his knees was wet and drops of lubricant were running down his forearm. The SymSkyn of his hand was split open and he could see some of the exposed bone and actuator structure.

Whoops, Glenn thought.

"Hey, yeah, we need to get this door propped open."

Two of the volunteers were trying to get the door open and get the child out of the now-upright car. "It keeps swinging closed and it's hard to open more than a few inches. Someone, get me a crowbar."

The child wasn't crying, and that worried Glenn. He looked around, several people had moved off, perhaps to get crowbars or jack handles, but there wasn't much time.

To hell with it—he was definitely going back in the "body and fender shop" after this. What was a little more stress on his artificial bones?

"Hang on, buddy. I'll give you something to prop the door." Glenn reached down to release the leg brace, but it wouldn't budge. Instead, he pressed the point on the side of his knee that released the magnetic gimbal. The entire lower half of his right leg—brace and all— separated at the knee and hung loose in the trouser leg. He pulled the pants leg up and removed the artificial limb. Balanced on one leg, he hopped over to the car, pulled the door with his left arm, and wedged his prosthetic leg into position. He pictured flexing his foot, and the prosthetic rotated downward at the ankle, wedging the door open. "Okay, I think you can reach in there now. That should hold."

The cook and several of the helpers stared at him with wide eyes. There was a muffled scream.

"...and I think that's my cue to exit. I will be over in the café providing medical assistance."

Glenn turned his upper body and hopped a little to get his orientation facing across the street. Well, he'd experienced worse during rehabilitation; this was exactly why Keith had had him practice hopping and maintaining balance on one bionic leg at a time. He hopped over to the café where somebody had turned the tables and the chairs back upright. He grabbed a table to steady himself, reached over, pulled out a chair and sat down.

This didn't turn out the way I thought it would. He looked at his wristcomm; there was a message on the screen from Nik's friend Cathy saying that they'd been turned back at a road blocked by a fallen tree. They were okay, though, and did they want to just meet at their place, instead?

Considering the state of the town, the van, and his own need for repairs, that probably wasn't going to happen. Neither was the visit to Sally and Hoop. Glenn hit the speed dial. "Hey Marty," he spoke into the phone once it was answered, "oh, it's been good so far but we've had a thing."

He paused to listen and sighed at Marty's tone. "Yeah, I'm going to need some help—taken a bit of damage."

After another pause, he held the comm away from his ear. Nik looked up from checking over the child that had just been rescued, and grimaced at the shouting voice that could be heard from the device.

Glenn put the comm back to his ear and spoke calmly. "Oh, no. No, I didn't start it. I was trying to help someone. I'm sure you'll be reading about the tornado in the news . . . Yes, tornado. Do tell General Boatright that I'm sorry. I didn't really mean for it to happen this way, but he should understand not letting innocents take unnecessary risks . . ."

". . . Marty, please don't yell."

". . . Yeah, okay I'll stay put."

"... sorry, no, the van is a little banged up. Tornado, remember? Okay we'll be here." Glenn hit the disconnect on his phone, put it down on the table and rubbed his eyes with his right hand.

CHAPTER 11:
Strategic Retreat

※

WSJS+ Local and National NewsStream
@yournewsnowNC
> ... amazing video from a daring rescue in Mount Airy, North Carolina. Click here for full video ...

George J @spacefan
> Hey, @SpaceForceOfficial, is that Colonel Shepard? Wow, talk about recovery!

USSF Public Information Office
@SpaceForceOfficial
> @spacefan, US Space Force is unable to comment at this time.
> Please see our website for the latest news and exciting opportunities in the Space Force!

George J @spacefan
> @SpaceForceOfficial, typical non-response. Thanks a lot.

ChirpChat, July 2041

※※※

Glenn was prepared for a dressing down, but not the fuss that came in the aftermath of the rescue. Marty was obviously upset that Glenn had injured himself. Medical scans showed muscle strain and stressed bone around the attachments to his bionics. There was minor damage to the artificial limbs themselves, aside from the damaged SymSkyn. All of that could be fixed easily with therapy and replacing a few minor parts.

What he was not prepared for was the public relations furor. He hadn't noticed, but a local news reporter had come on the scene while they were in the middle of the rescue, and there were pictures of Glenn doing his strongman-lift of the car in the local newspaper. The headline read "Astronaut Hero," but a subheading asked, "More Machine than Human?" Glenn's retirement from the Space Force was still recent and Command could still decide to throw the book at him. Despite the positive aspects of being hailed a hero, the revelation of his bionics—even though they didn't report the full extent—made Command rather nervous.

It started with interviews and briefings by the Public Affairs Office. Then it progressed to a dressing down by a general's aide supposedly from the office of the Chief of Space Operations. After that came testimony in front of closed-door sessions of the Defense Appropriations Committee, the Health Care Committee, Bio-Ethics Subcommittee, Cybersecurity Subcommittee, and a hearing on possible diversion of National Institute of Health funds. Through it all, General Boatright stood with Glenn and cautioned to let him—the general—do most of the talking. He explained that Space Force and

Congress weren't looking to punish him, just cover their own asses in case the public objected to the allocation of tax money. Finally, it was over, and Boatright told him to just keep a low profile for the near future and let the official concern and media attention blow over.

Glenn's overriding motivation throughout all of his recovery had been to get back into space. But it sounded as if that dream was in jeopardy. The upper echelon of Space Force seemed to be trying to distance themselves from media discussions of the world's first near-total bionic man. The internet had mixed opinions—"Cyborg factory" was one label seen on the conspiracy boards, while "freak show" was seen on others. "Miracle of medicine" was the best one, and the most common due to some behind-the-scenes work by friends in science fiction fandom. That still didn't change the fact that he had made the headlines. No leader liked to wake up and see, hear, or read about their organization in the morning newsfeeds.

At least they didn't cancel his training in Hawaii, although it had to be put off for a month while he underwent repairs to his bionics. As far as the military and government were concerned, keeping Glenn isolated for the next few months would allow the furor to die down.

Most of the repairs were simply cosmetic—new SymSkyn on his arm and hand, and on his right leg where it had been damaged by the emergency disconnection of his leg from the magnetic bearing. There was additional worry that he had screwed up the programming which allowed his bionics to respond to his nervous system as if they were his own flesh and blood limbs.

That last part was what took nearly a month—all of the recalibration and tests. Everything that he had been through in the month before his road trip had to be done again. He did finally get his visit with Aunt Sally and Uncle Hoop, which was good, because his uncle's health was failing. Glenn hoped he would last at least until he finished at MSTC, but was not optimistic.

"The thing is, Hoop, none of the hearings did a damn thing except allow people to make speeches. General Boatright was right, it was all about protecting their asses." Glenn and his uncle were sitting out on the screened porch at Sally and Hoop's house in Lexington, Virginia.

"Welcome back to the military, Glennie. The real question is what you think about all of it."

"Well, Boatright says it's important to show that I can do the things that matter."

"No, not the general. How do *you* feel about it?"

"Um . . ."

Hoop's right. How do I feel about it? Glenn thought to himself.

"You know? I think I proved something to myself. I'm still a man. Human. Able to go out and show people that I'm still me."

"Don't forget hero, Glennie. What you did in Mount Airy was incredible. You were strong, you took charge, you led the rescue; you treated the injured and you and your friend provided medical care for more than two hours until the emergency medical service could be freed up."

"I just did my part, Hoop. Nik was there, too."

"That's what I said, Glennie, you both provided care, but you were the leader, you were in charge."

"I rather think Sheriff Atkins was in charge, Uncle."

"Nope, you need to watch the interviews. *All* of the interviews. You were the hero that day."

It was embarrassing. He wasn't a hero. He just did what needed to be done. He was Glenn Armstrong Shepard— a boy with the twin dreams of being a doctor and going to space. He would do whatever it took—once he figured out what that was.

The transfer to Hawaii was uneventful, which was a good thing. One of the changes caused by the extra month delay was that he missed joining the timing for the next class in the MTSH. On the other hand, the Martian terrain simulation was operated by the Space Force and NASA, and Glenn was not in their good graces after the Congressional hearings. Instead, he was allowed to join civilian space training at HI-SLOPE on the Big Island of Hawaii. The Hawaiian Island Simulation Long Orbit and Planetary Exploration habitat had been built more than twenty years ago to supplement the spaceflight simulators which had been very popular in the early twenty-first century.

The first of those habitats intended to model not only isolated colonies, but closed ecosystems, was Biosphere 2, near Tucson, Arizona. From a crew perspective, it was a success, but from an ecological one, it suffered from too much humidity, improper temperature regulation, oxygen depletion and carbon dioxide fluctuation. While touted as a space colony simulator, Biosphere 2 was intended mainly as an ecological study in closed-circuit ecologies, and in those purposes, it largely succeeded.

Two more successful mission simulators were MARS-500 and HI-SEAS, the Hawaii Space Exploration Analog and Simulation. MARS-500 was a joint Russian and European simulation of a proposed five-hundred-day trip to Mars. The sealed habitat included modules meant to mimic spacecraft and landing modules, as well as living space on the planet. It was much smaller than Biosphere 2, and supported a crew of six, instead of Biosphere 2's eight. HI-SEAS was an American simulator taking advantage of the volcanic slope of Mauna Loa to practice planetary activities as well as isolation. Located above eight thousand feet of elevation, the terrain simulated the rocky soil of Mars and the Moon, and reduced atmospheric pressure and temperature meant that "simunauts" could train in spacesuits and with the same type of equipment they would use during space missions. Crews of up to eight spent four or six months at a time in simulated missions at HI-SEAS.

While MARS-500 and HI-SEAS were considered successful, the MARS-500-simulated "Mars" environment and the HI-SEAS crew habitat did not scale up to developing plans for a permanent base on Mars. In addition, there were continual worries that even five-hundred-day missions were not long enough to adequately assess the issues of rotating Marsbase crews every two-to-five years.

HI-SLOPE was built in the early twenty-first century to simulate planetary exploration missions in excess of five years. The location, high on the dormant volcano, Mauna Kea, was near the permanent astronomical telescope installations at the thirteen-thousand-foot elevation.

Astronomers and technicians could only stay at the summit for a few hours at a time. The Onizuka Center for International Astronomy had dormitories at Hale Pokahu, just above the nine-thousand-foot elevation, to allow astronomy staff to stay acclimated to the lower atmospheric pressure. Still, those facilities limited residency to two months at a time.

In contrast, HI-SLOPE was meant to be a year-round isolated facility that was entirely self-sufficient. The intent was for the habitat to be sealed up for five years, simulating a mission to the asteroids or outer solar system. It also supported a much larger crew of twenty-five to thirty people, compared to the Mars simulator crews of six to eight. The original mission had just completed three years when a viral outbreak caused the plan to be aborted prematurely. The habitat sat idle for several years until it was acquired by the Onizuka Center to expand both residential capacity and duration for the astronomers.

Since HI-SLOPE was built to emulate a spacecraft, it consisted of six two-story habitat modules surrounding a three-story core module, laid out to resemble a spaceship with a rotating ring for artificial gravity. Airlocks on each hab allowed units to be pressurized to sea level, the twelve-thousand-foot elevation of the habitat, or any pressure in between. It was later remodeled to house up to fifty persons, and the "excess" capacity was leased to civilian space training missions.

After a month of acclimation, Glenn would serve as HI-SLOPE assistant medical officer for four months. Neither MarsX nor the Space Force were quite ready to allow him to resume duties as lead flight surgeon, but they had no objection to him assisting with altitude sickness, minor cuts and scrapes, burns, or even broken limbs. For anything more serious, he still had to seek help from a certified flight surgeon.

Time at HI-SLOPE had become routine for many astronaut trainees, precisely because of the (relative) isolation and low air pressures in spacecraft and colony domes. Glenn's official duties amounted to part-time duty, so he spent the rest of his time relearning the particular protocols and procedures of civilian space missions. He was more than willing to spend the time as a "civilian" if it got him back into space. The very best part was that for six months, he didn't have to see his face on the news, read about the cyborg freak, or talk to reporters.

It was a quiet six months. In fact, for the final month at HI-SLOPE, the chief medical officer was called back to Washington. In practice—if not in actuality—Glenn was once again the head doctor of a space facility.

Now it was time for him to start working with equipment used on the Moon and Mars.

Pohakuloa Training Center was approximately four thousand feet lower in elevation than HI-SLOPE and was located in a pass, or "saddle" between the dormant volcanoes of Mauna Kea and Mauna Loa. The U.S. Army and Marine Corps used PTC for artillery practice and air-assault training. It also served as a high-elevation acclimation center for operations in mountainous terrain, which was why Space Force used it for ready access in the deep canyons and crevices of Mauna Loa that mimicked craters on the Moon and canyons such as Valle Marinaris on Mars. It was a good place to train on Mars rovers, seismic equipment, geological equipment and again, provided valuable acclimation to the dry, arid conditions of sealed space environments.

One of the things that Glenn realized that he had *not* experienced at HI-SLOPE and PTC were the common physiological reactions to lower atmospheric pressure and lower oxygen at high elevation. At such heights, atmospheric pressure was forty percent lower, and oxygen content in the air was likewise diminished. The absence of typical "altitude sickness" from low oxygen suggested that the loss of two legs and an arm had altered his body's homeostatic regulation of blood oxygen content. His circulatory system was shorter; he didn't require as much oxygen and his heart did not have to pump as hard.

So, Glenn decided to try an experiment.

Olympic athletes often lived and trained at elevations higher than that of the competition site; US Army and Air Force teams had adopted those same training techniques for special forces. Adaptation to elevation caused the circulatory system to become more efficient at transporting oxygen than at lower elevations; thus, athletes who "lived high, trained low" had the advantage of better oxygen saturation, better stamina, and better endurance at their athletic endeavors. Five months at the high elevations of HI-SLOPE and another four at PTC should give Glenn an advantage in performance at lower elevations, but he was uncertain how much of an adaptation he'd gained, given his artificial limbs. In preparation for his "experiment," Glenn started working out and running at PTC to maximize his cardiovascular fitness. At the end of his training rotation, he would go down to sea level to test himself.

After almost a year of living and exercising above eight thousand feet of elevation, his body was at its most efficient oxygen-carrying capacity. The best long-distance run he had managed during testing last year had clocked in at just short of twenty-one miles per hour, with cycling at forty miles per hour. He'd added some moderate distance runs and bike rides along the upland roads which should have served to acclimate his body to the exertion, even if he was not yet in the full heat and humidity of sea level. He would have to acclimate to the latter once he left PTC. On the other hand, he hadn't been able to do anything about swimming. He would just have to see how well the rest of his training sufficed.

The Big Island of Hawaii had long been popular for extreme sports—particularly running, cycling, and swimming. For decades, the Ironman World Championship had been held in Kailua-Kona every October. The Ironman had been a triathlon with a two-point-four-mile swim, one hundred twelve miles of cycling, and finished off with a marathon run of twenty-six point two miles—for a total of one hundred forty point six miles—exactly double the typical triathlon run throughout the world at that time. Not content to limit themselves to a mere double-triathlon, elite athletes evolved the ExtremeIron competition which used part of the original Ironman route, but increased the swim to four miles and lengthened the cycling to over one hundred fifty miles. In addition to the increased distance, the cycling component now included a four-thousand-foot change in elevation and a fifty-five-mile speed race back to Kona. The marathon component had been replaced with a fifty-mile ultra-marathon. Overall, the two-day competition was designed to test the strength and endurance of any athlete. It was the most prestigious of all distance competitions.

Glenn had never had the time to train for a triathlon, let alone one of the extreme or ultra versions. Despite his excellent physical condition, he knew there was now no hope of competing on par with the top-tier of elite athletes—he would be relegated to the "special" category of paralympic and assisted sports. Still, he had a strong desire to compare his own times on the same course with those of the most recent winners. He knew how well the bionic components performed on running, cycling, and swimming during the tests last year. Now, he wanted to see whether he could improve those times with physiological conditioning. After all, the combination might be important on the Moon or Mars.

The town of Kailua-Kona was on the western coast of the Big Island. The commercial district stretched from the main road around the island down to Kailua Bay, where the cruise ships stopped just offshore and unloaded passengers to spend their money in the quaint old shops along Ali'i Drive. The swimming phase of ExtremeIron went from Kailua Pier offshore to the cruise ship anchorage, and then inshore to a point near the distinctive Royal Sea Cliff resort, then retraced its route to the anchorage and back to the pier. The cycling phase climbed out of town to the mostly level main road through dry lava fields which ran along the entire leeward—west—coast of the island. The route started south, then turned around and branched inland and uphill toward the ranching and farming areas of the Kohala Uplands—gaining three thousand feet of elevation in about forty-five miles. From the town of Waimea, the road climbed another one thousand feet in just ten miles before descending to the northernmost town, Hawi. Many competitors changed bikes to one with a low gear ratio for the steep climb, and then changed in Hawi to yet another specialty bike for the speed-run back to Kona on the main road. The marathon extended from Kailua Pier along the main road to the resorts at Waikoloa Beach, and back.

It was time to test himself. Nik would meet him in Kona and provide support for his private race. The record for the Ironman course had been nearly eight hours; for ExtremeIron, the record was just under fifteen hours total time over two days—one hundred minutes swimming, seven-and-a-half hours cycling and six hours running. Given his individual running and cycling speed ratings from last year, he felt he could cut the time in half. Moreover, he planned to do it all in one day. On the other hand, fatigue from the combination of swimming, cycling, and running would also take a toll, so frankly, he'd be happy if he could manage to match the records of individuals who trained all their lives for the grueling course. He felt that if he could withstand the ExtremeIron, he could withstand the rigors of spaceflight and handle any test the Space Force could throw at him.

He would prove it to them. He was not just fully recovered, but faster, stronger, better than he had been before.

He wanted to get Command's attention, although he didn't figure on attracting it here. Before assignment to the Hawaiian training centers, Glenn had been told in no uncertain terms, "Keep your head down. Keep your nose clean. Do not attract attention. Do not talk to the press. Do not get yourself into any trouble or any situation that would get you noticed."

What he didn't count on, was the trouble searching him out.

The experiment started out okay, but not great, which didn't make Glenn very optimistic about challenging the performance of elite athletes.

Nik had all of his gear in an SUV he'd checked out of the motor pool at PTC. The two had worked out all of the waypoints and breaks, and Nik could also monitor his vitals and location via Glenn's waterproof wristcomm. Glenn started his four-mile swim by entering the water from the small beach across from the Royal Kona Resort on Kailua Bay, where Nik had parked the support vehicle. On race day, there would be a crowd wading out from the beach to the start buoys marking the beginning of deeper water. There would also be course-marking buoys and boats, but he didn't have those. Instead, his wristcomm sent navigation waypoints directly to the electronics of his bionic ear—including prompts to tell him when he was off course. The outbound leg to the cruise ship anchorage was the hard part. Swimming back in-shore to the turnaround point (opposite a distinctive blocky white hotel) was easier, plus he had his nav system. The datalogger would track time and distance, and sound in his ear, so that he didn't have to worry about anything other than swimming.

He was about fifty feet from the pier when his wristcomm signaled completion of the desired distance. He swam to the base of the pier, then climbed out of the water to meet Nik. Unlike a standard triathlon in which the athletes wore the same clothing for all phases, changing only their shoes, ExtremeIron phases were timed separately. Thus, athletes had time to change into comfortable—and appropriate—clothing for each phase. Glenn climbed into the back of the military utility vehicle and quickly changed clothes for the next phase.

"What was your time?" Nik asked from the front seat.

"Two hours, twenty-three minutes. Lousy time," Glenn grunted.

"Uh huh . . . and it's been how long since you swam? No pools up on the mountain, Captain Dumbass."

"Yeah, you have a point, Nik. Okay, I'll see you in a few hours."

"I'll see *you* in a few minutes. I'll be right behind you the whole way."

Little did the two of them realize that someone else was watching, and would also be right behind.

PART 2
LOVED AND LOST

CHAPTER 12:
The Chase

Richmond Times Features @JenButler
  Check out a special report from our
  Community Heroes series in the new
  three-part series on Councilman Samuel
  Garner. Learn how his efforts to revitalize
  the community are paying off—in more
  ways than one!
Yvonne A. @AlphaTeam21
  @JenButler, he did what?
                              ChirpChat, April 2042

Jennifer Butler was on vacation; one that had been forced on her by her editor and publisher. She was a journalist who specialized in interviews and human-interest stories, sometimes with an investigative edge. Her news outlet had been doing a special feature on community heroes, and she was assigned to write about a council leader responsible for reducing crime, increasing high school graduation rates, and bringing jobs to a depressed area of Richmond, Virginia. The profile was going great until she discovered that the subject of her story was maintaining two residences—complete with two wives and two sets of kids—and not enough income to account for all of his expenses. It turned out that he was receiving payoffs to underreport crimes and overreport the number of jobs provided by new companies moving into his city. There were some beneficial side effects—the additional money coming into the community paid for school and recreation center improvements, and the graduation rate was, in fact, slowly improving. Unfortunately, the jobs themselves were largely temporary, and would do more damage in the long-term than if the companies had never come to town. When she presented the story to her editor, she was told to keep it quiet until he could figure out how to handle the bombshell. To his credit, the editor pulled the profile from the special issue, and convinced the publisher to move the story of corruption and scandal to high profile and publish as its own special report.

The target of her story did not take the revelation well; he shouted his defiance even while being hauled off to jail. Soon after, Jen started receiving death threats—most likely from the criminals ultimately behind the corruption. Her publisher assured her that she still had a job, as well as paid leave, but suggested she take a long vacation well out of town . . . out of state . . . and off of the U.S. mainland.

Ever the journalist, Jen's curiosity was piqued when she noticed one—or possibly two—blacked-out SUVs repeatedly passing below her vantage point overlooking the watersports rental area at the base of Kailua pier. She was sitting at one of the many pubs and restaurants with second-floor, open-air dining rooms that looked out on Ali'i drive along the Kona waterfront, engaged in her favorite pastime of people-watching. There were the usual tourists in loose-fitting flower-print Hawaiian shirts and blouses, hotel and restaurant employees in tailored Hawaiian prints, and locals in shorts and various types of T-shirts.

The popular beaches were mostly north and south of town, and the recreational sailboats and water skimmers launched from the far side of the pier, so her attention was caught by a man walking out of the water onto a small patch of sand at the base of the pier. He walked over to a tan-colored vehicle with military plates which combined features of an SUV and a small truck. He climbed into the back of the vehicle, and emerged a few minutes later wearing cycling gear, took a bicycle out of the truck bed, and started to pedal north up the road.

Most of the people down on Ali'i drive and Kaahumalu Place were tourists, but this man didn't look like either a tourist or a local.

This guy looked familiar, and he had walked funny when he first got out of the water. He reached down and placed his hands on each side of his right thigh and seemed to squeeze. It looked like a small squirt of water came out in response. He then did the same with his left leg and seemed to walk more easily afterward.

Prosthetics? Would someone go swimming with prosthetic legs? she thought to herself.

As a specialist in writing about interesting persons, she'd once interviewed a lawyer in North Carolina who was an avid triathlete. The image of the competitive athlete was so at odds with the buttoned-down personal injury lawyer, that she'd probed for more information, and had ended up learning much more than she ever thought she wanted to know about running, cycling, swimming, and the ultimate combination of the three—the ExtremeIron race.

She'd bought binoculars for whale-watching before she'd learned that it was the wrong season, and she was not on the best island for it, anyway. The binocs were in her backpack, though, so she pulled them out and turned to focus on the intersection of Kuakini Highway and Palani Road, behind the restaurant.

There he was, making the turn north onto Kuakini for the first loop.

The tan SUV had pulled out and was following a bit behind the cyclist.

He's making good time, how fast was he going? Almost as fast as the cars!

It took about five minutes for the cyclist to return down Palani Road and turn south on Ali'i Drive. Jen's gaze lingered on the intersection for a few more minutes. A car turning at the intersection honked at another that had pulled out in front of it. That triggered a memory—there had been some sort of car accident and a picture of a man holding a car one-handed as he lowered it back to the ground.

Glenn Shepard! What was he doing on Hawaii, and why was he running the ExtremeIron course?

It was eleven miles to the southern turnaround at the town of Captain Cook. From there, he would start the climb to Waimea on State Road 180—but that was too far for her to see from here. She signaled the server for her check, paid, then hurried down to the parking lot for her rental car. There was a tiny café nestled right in between Highway 11 and 180 about six miles south of town. She remembered from her research that it was used as the first checkpoint in the ExtremeIron because it was just short of twenty miles into the race. An experienced racer would make that distance in forty-five to sixty minutes.

It took Jen almost twenty minutes to get to the café, and she was quite surprised to see cyclist and chase-car arriving less than ten minutes after her.

Forty miles an hour? I know he's supposed to have prosthetics, but how was he doing this?

That did it. She waited for a few more minutes to ensure that it wouldn't be obvious she was following. It was a good thing, too. A couple minutes later, a black SUV passed. It certainly looked like one of the ones she saw before she noticed Shepard walking out of the water. Come to think of it, there had been a black SUV heading up Highway 180 just as she arrived at the waypoint.

Security. Maybe wait a few more minutes, she thought.

It was another forty-five miles to the town of Waimea. At Shepard's current speed, he'd be there in an hour, but he'd also be climbing more than two thousand feet in elevation. She had little hope of passing two security vehicles, his chase car and Shepard himself. Not to mention, he was going about as fast as the vehicular traffic. On the other hand, if she took the Hawaii Belt Road to Kawaihae and turned east to Waimea, she could just barely make it in front of the convoy.

The ExtremeIron checkpoint in Waimea was at the elementary school; there, competitors changed to low-gear mountain bikes for the climb up the steep and winding Kohala Mountain Road. She should be able to get in position to watch the changeover—or at worst, arrive during the brief break built into the ExtremeIron course.

She arrived at the Parker Ranch Center next door to the elementary school and got out her binoculars. The tan SUV was waiting in the school parking lot. Shepard arrived a few minutes later. This was her first chance to get a look at the man up close. He was above average height; her practiced eye put him at just short of six feet. He was . . . not stocky, but . . . solid. Certainly not the lean, greyhound look of many athletes and astronauts—on the other hand, with his good looks, he could have been a poster boy for the astronaut corps. His hair was short, in a buzz cut, and she could see that the nape of the neck was uneven and there were a few tufts of longer hair. *He cuts it himself,* she thought. What she could see of hair color was black flecked with gray on the right side, and solid black on the left side.

Jen checked her watch. *Forty-two miles an hour? Uphill? How could he maintain that speed?* It had been almost two hours already, and he was showing no sign of slowing.

She watched as Shepard spoke to someone in the SUV, then switched out his road bike for one with a thick sturdy frame and knobby tires. He slapped the side of the vehicle, mounted the bike, and rode way.

The next waypoint was in the town of Hawi. It was only

twenty-five miles away, and Jen was uncertain whether she could get there in time. On the other hand, traffic was quite light, and she would . . . push it a little. She made it to Hawi in what she hoped was enough time; a black SUV was leaving town just as she arrived. She parked in front of a shop advertising ice cream, coffee, and homemade fudge to wait for any sign of Shepard and his support.

Not five minutes later, the tan SUV pulled up and parked, and a short man got out. He had slightly wavy hair that was shaved on the sides, but worn longer—and wilder—up top. His dark skin and stubble gave him a Middle Eastern or East Asian look. He had extremely broad shoulders, but was slim in the waist, like a weight lifter. His legs were straight, but he bent slightly above the waist, causing him to be slightly stooped and walk awkwardly. Her reporter instinct suggested he'd suffered a back injury.

Is this another injured astronaut? Or perhaps a fellow patient?

The man pulled a small backpack out of the back seat, followed by several water bottles glistening with condensation. He put four bottles in the pack, keeping two out.

Jen now recognized the man from the same news article about the rescue of the woman and children. That made her a bit unsure; should she attempt to contact Shepard directly or try to talk to this man first?

Given the speed at which Shepard had been traveling, she was unsurprised to see him appear less than five minutes later. He stopped next to the SUV and dismounted to change bikes. The racing bike looked like a rocket scientist had been given free rein to redesign a bicycle. It was long and low—the cyclist practically lay over the solid, disk-like wheels behind a motorcycle-like windshield. She stayed just long enough to watch the two men trade backpacks, and for Shepard to drink an entire bottle of water and reach for another. Before they completed the handover, she pulled her car out of its parking spot to head back to Kona.

Traffic on the road had been running between fifty and fifty-five miles per hour. Auto-drive cars were not common in Hawaii, and many tourists came just for the experience of being able to stop at roadside stands and scenic lookouts and enjoy the relaxed experience the locals called "island time." To this point, Shepard had been maintaining a speed—on level ground—not much slower than the cars. He would be even faster on this bike; if Jen wanted to get back to Kona ahead of him, she needed to *stay* ahead of him on the return route.

She was back on Ali'i Drive in Kona an hour later, sitting casually on a low stone wall in front of the Kona Wave Café, eating a "shave ice" and getting sweet syrup on her hand. Across the street was a kiosk selling ExtremeIron souvenirs. If Shepard was going to attempt the ultramarathon run today, the changeover should happen right here.

Sure enough, the tan SUV pulled up five minutes later. This time the man got out, pulled a pair of crutches out of the back along with a duffel bag. He came over and sat about five feet away from Jen on the same rock wall.

Was—was he suspicious?

※ ※ ※

Nik pulled up to the street in front of the Kailua Pier. There were traffic cones reserving his parking spot, courtesy of General Boatright's advance security team. He'd laughed at the thought of them running around in their black SUVs and black suits in the tropical sun, but they'd surprised him by blending in fairly well in tailored Hawaiian shirts, looking like every other resort employee in the area. They were efficient, and he was glad of their efforts in clearing the way, given the heavy vehicular traffic in the tourist town.

There was a woman across the street, brown skin—not as dark as his own, but darker than Shep. Brown hair, worn shoulder length, slight figure, she probably had to exercise a lot to keep it, too. He'd seen her before, and the "suits" reported that she'd been seen at several of the waypoints along the race course.

Before getting out of the vehicle, Nik took a picture with his wristcomm and sent it to General Boatright for an I.D. The answer came back almost immediately: *Jennifer Butler. Reporter. Low threat level; no need to drive her off—yet. Be cautious for now and call me as soon as you're back on the road—Boatright.*

He grabbed a duffel bag and went over to sit on the rock wall a few feet away from the woman. It was another fifteen minutes before Shep arrived. By Nik's timing, it was right around four hours since he'd left this exact point on his first bike. Total time since starting the ExtremeIron course was a bit over six hours.

Shep stopped his bike midway between Nik and the reporter. Nik tried to motion him closer, but Shep didn't pick up on the signal. He was preoccupied with getting disengaged from the aerodynamic shell of the speed-bike and wasn't paying too much attention—to Nik *or* the woman. He finally got off the bike and leaned it against the wall as he took the duffel from Nik and sat down to change into running shoes. "That looks like hard work," the woman said to Shep. "Hey, I've got an extra bottle of water here. It's cold, do you want one?"

Shepard eyed her uncertainly. "No problem. I'm good," he said. Nik waved his own bottle of cold water at his friend and gave her a sharp look.

Once Shep had drunk Nik's water and eaten a protein bar, he handed the bike off, and started running back the way he'd come.

As Nik started to walk the bike across to the SUV, he turned to look at the reporter. "He'll be back in about two and a half hours. Will we see you then, Ms. Butler?"

Busted.

CHAPTER 13:
Catch of the Day

Simon Q @TheExtremeIronMan
WooHoo! Personal Best. Just got the final
official time rankings for ExtremeIron2041.
I smoked *everyone* with a combined
time of fourteen hours, forty-nine minutes.
That's a record that will stand forever!

USSF Office of Scientific Integration
@OSIGenBoatright
Records are meant to be broken. Stay
tuned for results of the latest trials of
bionic prosthetics for athletes. —Major
General Richard Boatwright, USSF/OSI

Simon Q @TheExtremeIronMan
@OSIGenBoatright, no fair, man! That's
cheating!

ChirpChat, April 2042

True to the prediction, Shepard was back in less than two
and a half hours. Jen was amazed. He'd been averaging

over forty miles per hour—even with the steep uphill climb of the Kohala Mountain Road—while cycling, and then almost fifty miles per hour on the speed run. The ultramarathon pace had to be over twenty miles per hour. It made her wonder what his swim time was. Either the run or cycling pace would be miraculous for a normal person, but six and a half hours to cover two hundred miles on foot and bike was still impossible even for the most elite of athletes. Perhaps, someday, an unaugmented human might manage to break one record—but certainly not both in the same day.

Jen had learned that Shepard was anything but a normal human. She'd called her editor, despite it being the middle of the night in Richmond, and he'd sent her everything that had been made public in the aftermath of the incident last year. He told her that if she could get the rest of the story, he'd get The Powers That Be to greenlight the interview.

She'd decided that it would be best to be honest, since the reports made him out to be a man who considered honor to be the most important character trait. She was sitting in her same spot when the SUV pulled up in advance of Shepard's return. This time the man—her editor identified him as Doctor Nikhil Pillarisetty—pulled out a small black bag and white coat before coming over to sit next to her.

He smiled, but didn't say a word before Shepard came running up. Much to her own surprise, she remained silent herself, and didn't try to pump the man for information.

"Are you following me?" Shepard asked her, not even panting.

"Yes, Colonel. I noticed your private competition and would like to talk with you about it."

"I guess that would mean you're a reporter. I don't talk to reporters."

"Colonel Shepard, it's true that I'm an investigative reporter, but that's not what I want to talk about. I am intrigued about why you were out here running your own ExtremeIron triathlon."

Before Shepard could answer or Jen could make another comment, Pillarisetty interrupted. He'd put on his white coat and was holding a blood pressure cuff and stethoscope. "Okay buddy, give me your arm. Let's see how you're doing here."

Pillarisetty put the cuff on Shepard's right bicep, pumped it up, held the stethoscope to the inside of the elbow below the cuff, and looked at his watch. After a minute he pulled the stethoscope away, deflated the cuff and nodded in satisfaction. "Okay, shirt off, let's have a listen." He put the stethoscope against Shepard's chest— Jen noted several fine scars, at the left shoulder and down the midline. The doctor paused a moment, then moved around to the back. "Heart sounds good." He repeated the process by placing a palm-sized electronic device against chest and back. "LVAD's within spec, too. Okay, put your shirt back on, I don't need to see your pasty-pale skin."

Jen stifled a laugh. Shepard was anything *but* pale, even if he wasn't as dark as herself or Pillarisetty.

"Here, put this on." Nik handed Shepard a small sensor and instructed him to place it on the index finger of the right hand. Once again, he nodded. "This looks good, Shep. I wouldn't think that you had been exercising at all."

"You could've gotten all of that from the embedded sensors. For that matter, my wristcomm logged it all as well. You don't have to go all Dr. Welby on me, Nik." He stole a glance toward Jen. "Besides, we have an audience."

"It's okay, I called Marty and the home office while you were doing your Superman impression. The chase cars got her ident and called into OSI. General Boatright said it's been long enough; Ms. Butler has a decent reputation and it's okay for you to talk to her. Just remember, low profile."

"Colonel Shepard, does that mean an interview?" Jen asked tentatively.

"I'll think about it. What I seriously need right now is a shower and to change. Then, I'm probably going to clean out a buffet somewhere. That or just order three or four entrees for supper." Shepard paused for a moment. "Tell you what, there's a little place down the road—about three quarters of a mile—just past the seawall. It's called Big Island Alehouse; although the locals might still call it 'Humpy's'." It's a nice little bar with good pub food. Give me . . . oh, ninety minutes, and I'll meet you there. We'll talk but I gotta warn you, it's not going to be private. Nik's my friend, but I suspect he's got instructions to watch me like a mother hen."

"Mind your manners, Shep."

"Yes, Mother. Anyway, it's not just a formality. He *will* be there too."

"Yeah, someone's got to charm the wait staff and reassure them that he's not *just* a mindless eating machine!" Pillarisetty said.

"That's okay by me. I am not trying to do a hit piece. I think there's much more to your story than anyone realizes. Wouldn't you like the world to know who the real Glenn Shepard is?"

"Lady? I'm not sure I know, myself." Shepard grabbed the rest of his gear, nodded to Pillarisetty, and crossed the street to the SUV.

"Oh, I can tell you stories, ma'am," Pillarisetty replied with a laugh.

"Do *not* let him get started!" Shepard called back without turning around. "If you want to know my story, well . . . I can tell you a few things, but to be honest with you, I don't have a whole lot of trust to spare. Earn that, and then we'll see."

"See you in three hours, Ms. Butler! Better bring your wallet, just in case he sticks you with the bill!" Pillarisetty laughed.

"Wait, he said ninety minutes!"

"Yes, he did." Pillarisetty called back over his shoulder. "But I'm going to force him to slow down and maybe even take a nap. If that changes, I'll comm you."

"Um, how do you have my comm code?"

Pillarisetty turned, winked at her, then turned back and followed his friend.

Big Island Alehouse was a nice little shorefront place and like the earlier restaurant, had an indoor bar on the lower level and open-air dining on the upper level. It also offered a great selection of beers, including several local brews. Several people she'd consulted also recommended the pub's food, particularly the kalua pork nachos and the fish and chips. The latter was often made with "catch of the day" and the fries were golden brown and crispy-hot.

Jennifer decided she would go with an order of the nachos and a Fire Rock Pale Ale while waiting for Shepard to show up.

She was somewhat surprised to see that instead of coming up the main stairway from the dining room the two came across a walkway that spanned two neighboring buildings. She cocked an eyebrow, and Glenn replied, "Laverne's has an elevator. Better that than stairs." His companion was walking with paired canes rather than the crutches she'd seen earlier.

There's more than one story here, she thought to herself. *Best not get ahead of myself, though.*

Jen stood and held out her hand as the two approached her table. "Colonel Shepard, I'm very pleased to meet you. I'm Jennifer Butler. I suspect you already know that I write for the *Richmond Times*, but I assure you that I am not tailing you, nor am I here on an assignment. Actually, I'm supposed to be on vacation. My editor told me to get out of town and lay low."

Shepard's expression was neutral, as was his handshake. Doctor Pillarisetty, on the other hand, had a friendly face and enthusiastic greeting. He set one of the canes aside to grasp and pump her hand—such a contrast to his reserved companion.

Shepard motioned for her to sit, and then surprised her by moving to get her chair. The three spoke of inconsequential things—the weather, the menu, Kona vs. Big Island beer, kalua pork vs. kalbi ribs—until orders were placed. Not surprisingly, Shepard ordered appetizers and two entrées, commenting to the server that he might be ordering more.

Soon the drinks and nachos were delivered, so Jen decided to dive right in. "Colonel Shepard—or do you prefer Doctor Shepard?"

"Actually, I'm retired. No longer a colonel, and not presently licensed to practice. Just call me Shepard, or Glenn."

"And I'm Nik—just a k, no c—or Vin, or Vindaloo, 'The Swarthy Menace,' or just Doc, since the flyboy here is bad at the social niceties."

"Vindaloo?" Jen was a bit confused by Nik's comments.

"It started as a joke and kinda stuck," Glenn responded in a deadpan manner. "Nik's pretty irreverent."

"No, I'm the comic relief," Nik corrected.

"Ah. Okay. Well, Glenn, I will get right to it. I'm not on assignment, I'm not recording this, I'm just trying to satisfy my curiosity. I saw you come out of the water and get on your bike. A while back, I did a profile on a lawyer who was a triathlete, so I recognized the ExtremeIron course. Then I realized where I'd seen you before—the rescue a year ago. I looked you up, and couldn't find out much about you. *That's* what piqued my interest. It seems that no one ever told your story. I promise not to do a hit piece. I really don't do that kind of thing."

"I rather think you do. Considering that the reason you're here is the piece you did on the corruption in Councilman Garner's office," Glenn said with a hint of challenge in his voice.

"I usually write profiles—at least for Richmond. They started me off with Sunday supplements, then science pieces. Then I got assignments to cover the releases of biographies of Admirals, Generals, business leaders and the like. I stay away from celebrities; they don't need my help to blow their own horns. That's what I was trying to do with Garner, but some things didn't add up. I didn't look for trouble, but it sure found me—or him, to be exact."

"It couldn't have happened to a nicer guy," growled Nik. "I've met a few of the . . . victims . . . of his type of 'community engagement.' I used to do *pro bono* work for an inner-city free clinic." He cocked his head toward Glenn. "I'm Shep's head shrinker now. I'm not sure which is worse."

"He's my rehabilitation therapist," Glenn corrected with a smile. "And turned out to be my best friend, much to the surprise of both of us. Since I wanted to test myself, I thought it might be a good idea to have a doc to check me over to certify that I was in good health . . ."

". . . And of sound mind, which is rather dubious. If you ask me."

"Well, that describes both of us, now doesn't it, Nik?" Glenn laughed.

Jen laughed with them. It was clear that there was a strong bond between them. Nik cared for Glenn, and Glenn trusted Nik. This was not the usual doctor-patient relationship. Perhaps it was because they were both medical professionals, perhaps it was a shared experience in injury and rehabilitation. Since Nik was the one who'd said that someone had vouched for her, she figured she should ask her questions of both of them and see which one responded.

"The news article on you was from a year ago. What was that about?" Jennifer asked.

"I had just finished rehab and wanted to visit my aunt and uncle. Nik and I decided to drive from Texas to Virginia and got caught in a tornado. When the storm passed, I saw a car rolled over, almost upside-down; a mother and two children were trapped. I'm a doctor, I couldn't leave them there even if I'm not certified to practice in North Carolina. I would do whatever it took to get them out, and that's what I did."

"Whatever it takes him. That's how he got into this mess," Nik added.

"Yes, that is, in fact, how I got into it. How much have you learned about what happened to me?"

"Frankly, nothing. The official Space Force statements didn't say anything. A deeper dive only revealed that you were part of a new rehabilitation program for injured vets. Nothing else. I mean it's pretty obvious from seeing you in a swimsuit that you've had extensive surgery, the evidence suggests prosthetic limbs, but that's really all I know. There was nothing else to find."

There was silence for a long time. Glenn looked conflicted. He raised his left hand to his ear, touched it briefly, then put his hand on the top of his head and brushed it back and forth a few times. Catching himself in what appeared to be a nervous habit, he looked over at Nik. His friend smiled back and nodded.

"It started on the Moon." Glenn sighed as he put his hand back down on the table. Jen noted that up to this point, he'd handled his drink and food with his right hand. "Three years ago, I was up there as medical officer in charge of monitoring tests of the Dragonfly vehicle—the ultralight aircraft designed for use on Mars. It won't actually 'fly' on the Moon, though, and the reaction control thrusters are tricky and not all that stable. The Dragonfly flipped over and trapped the pilot. The hypergolic propellants burned—even in vacuum. I pulled the pilot out, but got burned. It wasn't too bad—a little bit of plastic surgery and replacement of my left arm and I would have been as good as new, certified for flight and able to go to Mars as planned. Unfortunately, an explosion blew me into a nearby rock outcropping and shattered my legs."

"Oh! Oh my." Jen stared at him wide-eyed.

"So, they stuck him in the paint and body shop and rebuilt both legs, an arm, an eye and an ear with advanced bionics," Nik said.

"OPSEC, Nik."

"It's really not classified, just obscure. If she knows where to look, it's all there. Besides which, General Boatright said it's okay. Deep background and all that, although he would like to speak with Ms. Butler as well. An interview, not a threat."

"As a matter of fact, he called me about an hour before I met the two of you. He said he is ready to start getting you in front of the public again, so I can interview you and even write a biography if I wished. I still have to talk with the Public Affairs Office before publication, but it seems they would like to play up how you are an inspiration to injured vets who want to return to duty and normal life. They want to use you as an example."

"As a figurehead more likely," Glenn snarled. "They've been a little slow at that return to duty part. In fact, after the event in North Carolina, I was told it wasn't going to happen for at least a year or two—if ever."

"Well, maybe I can do something to help with that. Tell me about yourself—you're an astronaut. You were part of the Return to the Moon mission in 2029, and were on the crew for the Mars colony-building missions. Why? What motivates you to go through all of this?" Jen waved her arm vaguely at Glenn. "What makes this worthwhile to you?"

CHAPTER 14:
Loss and Love

❄️

Simon Q @TheExtremeIronMan
Twenty-five percent faster than the best
human record with DARPA's new
prosthetics? Where can I get some?
USSF Office of Scientific Integration
@OSIGenBoatright
@TheExtremeIronMan, I thought you said
that was cheating?
Simon Q @TheExtremeIronMan
@OSIGenBoatright, gotta get out in front
of the curve, man.

ChirpChat, April 2042

*Chip Hairston hadn't intended to spend the first day at
his new school in the principal's office. It wasn't his fault,
really, it's just that when the teacher got to the end of the
roll and called his name, he didn't answer. Ms. Stuyvesant
looked at the sheet of paper. Hairston was the last name*

on the roll, it had just been added this morning. There were twenty-nine names and only one of the thirty desks was vacant; the only person not to answer roll call had been the dark-haired sixth-grader in front of her.

She called his name again, "Chip Hairston." She looked over the top of her glasses with her most intimidating look and addressed the boy. "Chip? Is that your name?"

"No, ma'am," was all the answer she received.

By now she was feeling uneasy about the boy who had just transferred in from out of state. "Well then, what *is* your name?" she asked, with just a hint of sarcasm.

"Glenn Armstrong Shepard, ma'am," the boy answered. Again, he fell silent and just stared toward the front of the classroom.

"Well, if your name is not Chip Hairston, you do not belong in my classroom. Why are you here?"

"I was told to come to this classroom." He sat perfectly still. There was no malice on his face, just a faint... determination.

"Do you have a class schedule?" Perhaps there was a mix-up and he was supposed to be in Mister Frangelico's class.

"Yes, ma'am." The boy reached into his backpack and pulled out a much-folded piece of paper. He handed it to the teacher and she unfolded it to read his classroom assignments.

"The name on this class schedule is Chip Hairston. Did you take this from him?"

"No, ma'am."

"Did he switch schedules with you?"

"No, ma'am."

"Well then..." She started tapping her foot. The students who had been in Ms. Stuyvesant's class for the prior two months of the fall term knew that this was the sign of imminent trouble. There was a faint sound of whispers and giggling.

Someone was going to the Principal's Office!

"Well then, how do you explain having Mister Hairston's schedule?"

"That's my schedule. That's just not my name."

Sure enough, Chip Hairston ended up in the principal's office. He was sitting on one of the student-sized hard plastic chairs outside the office of Doctor George Kali, Vice Principal, while his mother, Rosemarie Hairston, tried to explain young Chip's... eccentricity. Chip could hear pieces of the conversation, mostly because his mother's voice kept rising in volume. He wasn't interested in her part of the argument, though. His future depended on what the vice principal had to say. Unfortunately, Doctor Kali didn't seem the sort to raise his voice.

A little while later, Chip's stepfather, Vernell Hairston, came in. Despite continual urging to call him "Dad," Chip had never been comfortable with the idea. Mister and Missus Hairston were showing Doctor Kali a bunch of papers, but the vice principal just kept shaking his head. Finally, he stood and walked to the door, opening it and summoning Chip into the office.

"Young man, what is your name?" Doctor Kali seemed nice enough. He asked in a nice tone of voice, after all.

"My name is Glenn Shepard, sir."

"Yes. Yes, it is." He pressed a button on his deskcomm and spoke after it clicked. "Mrs. Riley, please come and *take Master Shepard back to Ms. Stuyvesant's room. Glenn Shepard is the new student she was expecting, not Master Hairston."*

As the lady from the outer office entered to collect Glenn, the Vice Principal turned his attention back to Glenn's mother and step-father.

"I'm sorry, Mrs. Hairston, absent adoption papers or a court-approved name change signed by a judge, you cannot register him by any other name than what is recorded on his birth certificate. Moreover, you have falsified documents . . ." That was all Glenn could hear before Mrs. Riley closed the office door behind them.

"See? Shep was a troublemaker even at a young age."

"No, I wasn't. I didn't start it," Glenn retorted. "I wasn't really angry over the attempted name change. It just made me sad, because it was her last attempt to suppress the memory of my father. Aunt Sally was the one who told me the most about him . . . that he'd died a hero.

"I don't remember them arguing, but apparently Mom hated Dad's job as a test pilot. That, too, was something I only learned later. Dad had been at the Pentagon on September 11, 2001. I was seven when I first heard about it. Dad was lucky, but Mom often claimed that one day his luck would run out. According to Aunt Sally, there was at least one time when Mom had packed the car and threatened to move back to Illinois and live with Grandma. I vaguely remember packing, but that's all.

"It was at the funeral that I heard about Dad being a hero. He'd walked into the bank at exactly the same time as several men who were about to rob it. One of the robbers seemed very nervous and upset, and started fiddling with something on his belt. It was a grenade, and Dad figured out that it was armed. He leapt up and tackled the man, driving him to the floor behind a desk. He shielded the explosion with his body—and that of the robber. The minister said Dad saved everyone else in the bank that day."

"I'm so sorry," Jen said. The meal was over and the remnants cleared away. They'd had another round of beers, and the server kept refilling their water glasses. Better yet, the crowd was light; they'd been encouraged to stay. Even though Jen wasn't that hungry, she ordered a coconut macadamia pie to share in order to reward the server. There would be a big tip, too; Jen already planned to pay for the meal, and had taken the opportunity to talk to the manager about it.

She and Nik ate a few bites of dessert, but it was quite clear that Glenn was busy replacing calories burned by exertion. She was surprised though, he hadn't ravenously wolfed down the food, like some athletes she'd interviewed over the years. He stayed a gentleman throughout the meal.

"A few weeks after the funeral, Mom started taking down all of Dad's stuff and packing it away. She'd called me her 'little chipmunk' when I was younger, and from that point on, she never called me anything but 'Chip.' She also started calling herself 'Rosemarie Seeley.' I was too young to realize that she'd gone back to using her maiden name. When she married Vernell Hairston, she tried to put every bit of her past behind her, even if it meant changing my name.

"I was born exactly thirty years after the historic landing of Apollo 11 on the Moon. Glenn was my Grampa Shepard's name—so Dad insisted on Armstrong to commemorate the date. Mom said she wouldn't have agreed to the names, but she was still groggy from childbirth.

"Aunt Sally and Uncle Hoop still lived in the house where she and Dad grew up. I visited often and stayed in Dad's old room with his aircraft and spacecraft models and posters. In that house, astronauts were heroes.

"Not to Mom. To her, astronauts were victims—Apollo 1, Challenger, Columbia. She especially hated the last week of January, when all those events had taken place. Then Dad died that same week, and Mom considered it an omen; her family was not meant for space. Mom swore she'd never allow me to follow the same path, and lose me the same way.

"Unfortunately, she'd already lost, she just didn't know it yet."

Jen was moved by Glenn's story. The loss of a father was bad enough, but to have his mother try to erase all memory of him? It wasn't something that she could understand.

She listened closely as Glenn quickly listed off moves and new schools as Rosemarie tried new jobs, new homes, and eventually remarried. Fortunately, she never tried to repeat the mistake of forcing him to change his name. Glenn was a good student, athlete, and a natural leader. He studied martial arts, and wanted to run track for his high school. He told his aunt and uncle that he wanted to go to a service academy, but didn't think he could get the required permission from his mother. He thought of approaching his stepfather, but they'd never been close. As time went on, Glenn and Vernell started to argue . . .

. . . until the day Glenn came home to find his mother crying at the kitchen table. There was a folded paper in front of her, and he could see the letterhead of a local doctor's office. Even as his mother had tried to erase the painful memories, Glenn knew that she still loved him with all of her heart. Unfortunately, ovarian cancer had been growing for way too many years, and was detected much too late to treat. Rosemarie Seeley (neé Shepard) Hairston died of cancer three weeks later, and Glenn never got to run track for his school.

The last anchor in his life was gone . . . first his father, now his mother. All within the same week of the year.

That damnable last week of January.

Glenn was alone with Vernell and neither of them knew quite how to handle it. They grew distant and started arguing more frequently. Glenn's grades slipped and he became sullen and withdrawn. Aunt Sally and Uncle Hoop came to the rescue, and took him in. The warmth of their household gradually brought Glenn out of depression, and Sally's stern eye on his schoolwork helped bring his grades back up. Vernell and Glenn exchanged bland greetings at Christmas, but both of them moved on.

Glenn dug back into his studies, but with a new emphasis—pre-medicine. His grades were high enough for college, and *early admission* to college at that. One month after his seventeenth birthday, Glenn started college as a pre-med major at the University of Virginia on a Space Force ROTC scholarship.

CHAPTER 15:
Profile of Courage

❖

Richmond Times Features @JenButler
Glenn Armstrong Shepard is the type of
hero who quite literally runs toward danger
to help others. See how he has turned
personal tragedy into advantage, and uses
it to help others. Our new multipart feature
starts today, stream it now.

ChirpChat, May 2042

"It doesn't make sense to me," Glenn told her. "All this
fuss of whether I'm more machine than human. I'm a
doctor and a military officer—at least, I was. Every fiber
of my being told me I *had* to rescue that woman and her
children. I mean *how much more human could I be?* But
all the pundits talked about was how much it cost to build
the prosthetics. Not once did they talk about what it all
felt like; what it meant to me."

"Right, so then, explain your prosthetics to me," Jen

replied. "How do they work? How do they feel? What does it mean to be you? I saw you in action and I have to admit that it was incredible, almost superhuman."

"Not quite, I still have a purely biological body. According to the tests they've run me through, I've gained about twenty-five percent over an unaugmented person."

"I'm pretty sure you were going faster than that."

"Cycling, yes, I'm about fifty percent faster, but that's done mostly with the bionics in my legs. I tried to see if the extra red-blood cell capacity of living above nine thousand feet of elevation would give me even more of a boost, but it's mostly in cardiovascular endurance, which doesn't really interact with my bionics other than keeping my heart and respiration rates down."

"How was your swim time? I didn't see you start, just the finish,"

Glenn made a face. "I made lousy time, about half as fast as the record."

"What?" Jen was surprised by the admission. "Why?"

"He hasn't been swimming for a year," Nik said, and elbowed his friend in the ribs. "He thought it should just come naturally, instead of having to pay the price in training like he did with everything else."

"'No pain, no gain'?"

"Something like that," Glenn said, morosely. "I had plenty of that in rehab. I admit it was stupid to think I could just swim a record without practice. I didn't even think about the fact that I don't float naturally, now."

"Oh." Jen thought about it for a moment. "So, how much heavier are the prosthetics?"

"Not much, but it's enough to change my overall density. Artificial limbs don't have any fat contributing to buoyancy. The weight's not bad on land. About thirty years ago, a DARPA program started work on 'wearable' prosthetics, so they make them the same weight as flesh and blood."

"Okay then, what hurts?"

Glenn and Nik exchanged a look and Jen worried that she may have ventured into forbidden territory.

"Oh. Should I not ask that question?"

"No, it's okay," Glenn answered. He looked again at Nik, who nodded in return. "Frankly, Ms. Butler, everything hurts."

"Not surprising, considering the workout today."

"No, not that. Everything hurts, all the time. There are times I regret doing this, but it was my idea. I have to see it through."

"I'm so sorry."

"No, don't be sorry about it. I'm a volunteer, and frankly, knowing what I know now, I'd still do it. But every step, every 'revision' surgery, takes a toll."

"How many surgeries have you had?"

"Counting the original amputations?" Glenn looked at Nik. "Ten?" Receiving a nod, he continued, "Ten."

"Wow! That many, what were they?"

"Amputate the legs, amputate the arm, implant the artificial thigh bones, implant a shoulder socket. Then there's the implants of eye and ear, skin grafts, repair of the eye and ear, replace the bionic controller in my hip...I think that's it."

"You forgot the LVAD," Nik said.

"Oh yeah, the LVAD. How could I forget the deal-breaker for the Space Force?"

"I got most of that, but what's an LVAD, and why is it a deal-breaker?"

"Left Ventricular Assist Device. It's a pump."

"Wait, isn't that an artificial heart?"

"Not really, and not really 'left ventricular' in my case, it's attached in-parallel with my heart and helps redistribute fluid—lymph and blood—to assist with heat dissipation. Most of the medical field and public know them as LVADs, so I'm stuck with the name. Still, it's a deal-breaker; Space Force was coming around on the subject of prosthetics, but anything to do with the heart . . ."

"Damned short-sighted," Nik grumped. "He's stronger than any astronaut, and able to endure way more,"

"But at the cost of pain?" Jen asked.

Both men nodded.

"Got it, but you still haven't told me where it hurts."

"Well, my hips are constantly straining, because of the imbalance in strength between the bionics and my natural bone and muscle. The small of my back and my ribs hurt because no matter how I try, I can *feel* the weight difference on my left side. My right arm tries to do the same as the left, and it can't. The left arm isn't as coordinated as the right, so I unconsciously put even more strain on my right side. The eye and ear inputs can often have me at the edge of a headache, every single one of the scars *itches*, and even after three years we're still adjusting the sensitivity of the artificial tactile sensors in the bionics."

"How are you still upright, given what you did today?"

Glenn jerked a thumb in Nik's direction. "I have my own doc."

It was late, and the wait staff were clearly hovering, waiting to clean tables.

"Okay, one last, strange question. It's—okay, it's weird, but please understand, I'm a woman, and I notice these things . . . Shepard, you don't smell different. I can tell you were exercising and have showered since then. You're not wearing cologne that I can tell. You smell . . . normal."

The two men sat in shock for a moment, then Nik started to laugh. Glenn looked indignant. "What did you expect me to smell like? Machine oil and ozone? Hot electronics?"

"Well, no, but half of your body is artificial . . ."

". . . and half of me is natural. I assure you, my adrenal glands and sweat glands work just fine. The bionics *don't* emit any odors."

"Hormonally, he's just fine. Fully functional in every way."

"Shut up, Nik," Glenn said, but there was no anger in his voice or expression, just exasperation. Instead of responding to Jen, he signaled the server for the check, and then protested when he learned that she had pre-paid it.

He went over to the bar to speak with the manager, and there was some exchange going on. She'd have to check her account to see if he'd had her charges reversed and paid the bill himself.

The trio moved to an area with benches outside the

front of the restaurant. It was time to go their separate ways—but Jen felt that she didn't want the evening to end. She wanted to tell this story, but it wasn't *just* the story— she wanted to know more.

"I have to go back up to PTC in the morning. I was *supposed* to be on leave, but my next assignment came through today and MarsX wants me to collect my stuff and pack up. I'm still not due in D.C. for another four weeks, but PTC has a battalion coming in for an exercise and *they* need the space."

"I thought you were going to Maui?" Nik asked.

"Yeah, I need to work on my tan." Glenn said it with a straight face, but there was a twinkle in his eye as he did so.

Inside jokes, Jen thought. *These two have been through a lot together.*

"I would really like to follow up with some specifics for the article. Can we talk later?"

"My good lady, you can ask me anything!" Pillarisetty winked at her.

"I will take you up on that, Doctor—and please, call me Jennifer. I can't imagine the tales Shepard's headshrinker can tell."

"And you, Ms. Butler? Are you heading directly back to Richmond to write your exposé?"

Jen looked at Shepard. There didn't seem to be any malice in his comments. In fact, there was that same twinkle in his eyes...

Wait, one of those eyes is artificial—how can it twinkle? But she liked the twinkle.

"No, Mr. Shepard, I will likely just dictate and edit on my tablet from the hotel room. Besides, I really do

need to follow up—" She thought about it for a moment.
"—with each of you, I think. I will be here for at least
another week up at the Waikoloa resort. I'll give you both
my card. Please call me."

"Glad to!" Pillarisetty stood up and placed his canes to
one side. He looked at his wristcomm. "Well, Shep, it's
already tomorrow, so if you're going up the mountain
while it's still morning, we'd better get going." He stepped
over to Jen to shake hands, and surprised her when he
took hers in both of his hands. "A pleasure, Ms. Butler.
I'll call you tomorrow to set up a time."

As he stepped away, Shepard also rose and took her
hand. She was even more surprised when he held it for a
few moments before letting go. He smiled at her . . . and
she smiled, too. "Later this week or next, Jennifer?"

She gulped. "Why, yes, Colonel—I mean Mister—
Shepard."

"Please, call me Shep."

It was going to take a few weeks for Jen to write her
article. She needed to get more perspective on Shepard,
as well as try to fill in several gaps in the public record
regarding his accident. She started with Nik. Glenn—
Shep—would be up at PTC for the next couple of days,
and Nik needed to head back to Texas, but he had an
evening flight, and plenty of time for a long lunch.

After getting some background on Nik—former boxer,
injured his back in an automobile accident, studied
medicine with an eye toward emergency medicine, but
gravitated to psychiatry after working with injured kids—
the conversation turned to his friendship with Shepard.

"He doesn't make friends easily. Too many losses," Nik told her. "Before me, his last really close friend had been a doc on Asimov Station."

"'...*had been*...' Oh! You mean..."

"Yeah, *that* one. The one who died when some rich, old S.O.B. locked the escape pod hatch with only himself in it. Anyway, he and I are a lot alike. We're not letting our injuries stop us from what we want to do. He *was* my patient, but *now* he's my friend."

"How about girlfriends? Any romantic involvement?"

Nik gave her a concerned look. "He's...delicate. From what I know of him, I'd say he had one great love, and that ended badly. Even worse, she took his place on the Mars mission. He's convinced it was her plan all along."

"The accident, too?"

"No, not like that. More that she was looking for any opening. He says that her going to Mars is just to spite him for events in their past."

"Is that what you think? Did she do it to spite him?"

"She's not my patient, so I really can't say—and couldn't say even if she *was* my patient. But I don't think that's a factor. It scarred him, though, and recent events haven't helped."

"The accident."

"More like the aftermath. He's tried a few dates, and they ended...well, not so much that they ended badly, just...they were the wrong women."

"I'm afraid I don't understand."

Nik turned looked straight at her, and it was somewhat disturbing to see such a stern look in his otherwise friendly face. "Let me put it this way. Glenn Shepard does not need a mother, an angel, a guardian, or a fangirl. He needs a friend. If anything else develops, fine. Otherwise, it's best to leave it at that."

"Oh, okay. Message received loud and clear. You don't have to worry, I'm writing a profile, not looking for a conquest."

He gave her that look again. "Uh huh. Listen to me, Jennifer. Shep is fragile. Promise me you won't break him, with your story or otherwise."

"I promise, Nik."

"Good, now let me tell you the story about Shep and the HR lady . . ."

Shep was more reserved, less spontaneous. She supposed it was unsurprising that he would be clinically detached when he discussed his injuries and bionic components. He seldom talked about the eye and ear— they were mostly invisible to the casual observer—and he was still hurt by the negative press from more than a year ago.

She interviewed him twice over comm, but then asked to meet him for more "off-the-record" conversation.

He told her that he was well aware that there was no such thing as truly "off-the-record." Nevertheless, he spoke a bit about his life, experiences, and the accident. He was right, the journalist in her was always listening— but not for tricks and traps, rather, she listened for hints of who Glenn Shepard was as a person. It was more than just the story; these sessions truly shaped what she would write.

She returned to the subject of how he had dealt with

the pain of the long recovery. He was silent for a long time. This was one of those times when the recorder was off, so she waited patiently. His face fell. He was usually so expressive—from his pleasant smile during small talk to a more serious face when recounting details of the tornado. He grimaced, and the lower eyelid of his right eye twitched.

"Badly, I suppose," he said finally. "I was a whiny brat for a while, but Aunt Sally came in one day when I was throwing a temper tantrum. She brought me up short. Marty—that's Doctor Spruce—and Nik also helped me understand that what I was going through was no more, nor less, than any other injured vet in that hospital. Moreover, I was going to be able to walk and function normally, not all of those soldiers would get the same chance. I *had* to be an example and pave the way to improve the quality of life for amputees."

Their next meeting was over dinner, then drinks on the beach watching the waves. During those meetings, she caught him a few times looking at her with a strange expression. *Is it attraction? Curiosity? Uncertainty?* she asked herself. For that matter, she was not entirely sure she knew her own feelings.

Shepard had instituted a *quid pro quo* as the interviews continued. He would answer her questions, but then had questions for her . . . and some were silly, "Would you choose mint chocolate chip or rocky road ice cream?" "Is white chocolate really chocolate?" or "Biscuits or corn muffins?" Other questions were more serious, about her own background and experiences.

He's probing for the same type of character background I am, she thought. *He just doesn't know how to phrase the questions.* So, she told him of growing up south of Atlanta, of moving out at eighteen to enter a journalism program, of her internship at the *Dallas Morning News* after graduation, how her skin color had influenced what stories the editors would allow her to write in the early days. She described the down-and-dirty world of investigative journalism, and how the nasty business had cost her several relationships—including an almost-marriage where police took the groom from the church, minutes before the ceremony.

"I became disillusioned with always looking for the worst in people, so I quit the paper and moved from Dallas to Richmond. Leo—my publisher, these days—was an old college classmate. I now get to write about unsung heroes and ordinary people accomplishing extraordinary tasks. Commissioner Garner? That was an accident. He did good things, but he was using money and applying it in ways his constituents wouldn't approve."

All trace of sun was gone from the sky; the hotel staff were lighting tiki torches along the paths. Shep walked her out to her car, then took her hand and held it way longer than a simple handshake.

She didn't know why she did it. It wasn't like her to be so impulsive, but after pulling out so much of his inner self, he'd cracked her own carefully maintained shell. She pulled his arm, reached up and wrapped her arms around him, and lifted up on her toes to give him a quick peck on the cheek.

His arms fluttered. She'd caught him off guard.

Good.

She let go quickly. There was no sense in making it any

more awkward. Shepard was heading to the neighboring island of Maui in the morning. She was mostly done with her writing and would probably only need a couple more details to finish off the article. They would probably do that over comm—and she *knew* that it simply wouldn't feel the same.

Face it, girl. You've fallen—hard, she thought to herself. Glenn Armstrong Shepard was a man who thought of others nearly to the point of ignoring his own needs. More than that, he was a hero—even if he was uncomfortable with the label and denied his own heroism. *That* was the story she needed to tell, and she was honored that he—and the general—had decided to trust her with it. But it was more than that. She'd discovered the man inside and decided that she wanted more.

The Times contacted the Kailua-Kona and Honolulu news outlets, and they'd been proud to run the story as a wire-service feature on the front page, since it featured local sights and businesses. Jen had been sure to mention the places where she, Pillarisetty and Shepard had met, even to the point of praising the local food and drink specialties. She knew that it was these "local color" details that made a story *real* to the readers, and established the sense of trust that was so important to getting both a wide readership, and access to the subjects of her interviews.

She'd asked the *Big Island News* to run a promotion flexi copy of the issue. While most readers used comms or tablets to get their "newspapers," some still liked the anachronistic feel of a hardcopy in their hands. Programmable polymer "paper" was a far cry from newsprint, but physical news copy was still available in major markets. This one had to be flown over from Honolulu, but Jen waited patiently at the airport for the delivery, before boarding her own flight to the neighboring island of Maui.

Shepard was finishing out his leave at one of the resorts in Ka'anapali, just north of the old whaling village of Lahaina. A commercial flight would have taken her to the main airport at Kahului, but that would have left her dependent on a rental or expensive autocab ride to Lahaina. While less than twenty-five miles distance, the combination of heavy traffic, narrow roads, and the relaxed attitude of *Island Time* meant a long, expensive commute to the resort area on the western lobe of the dumbbell-shaped island. Her charter took her instead to the Kapalua-West Maui Airport, only five miles from Lahaina, and even closer to the Ka'anapali resorts. Despite the proximity to Shepard's hotel, she had commed him to meet her at the banyan tree in the center of Lahaina, the only surviving landmark of the tragic 2023 fire. A short autocab ride delivered her to the iconic plaza, home of the oldest living tree in Hawaii. She grabbed a shave ice from a vendor at the near permanent arts-and-crafts market under the limbs of the tree which covered over two acres, and walked down toward one of the corners of the plaza adjacent to a plaque marking the pre-2023 location of the old courthouse for Maui County. There was a low rock wall, and she sat, ate her shave ice—still getting syrup on her hand—and waited.

Shepard rode up on a rented bicycle. Given both the short distance from the resort, and the tourist crowds, it made sense—especially since she knew he could keep pace with the vehicular traffic. He noticed her, then took note of the rock wall and her shave ice, and grinned.

She held up a water bottle, glistening with condensation. "That looks like hard work. I've got an extra bottle of water here. It's cold, do you want one?"

His grin got even wider, and Jen felt that funny feeling in her stomach again.

"Why, thank you, ma'am, don't mind if I do." This time he accepted the offered water, got off of the bike and leaned it against the wall.

As he sat down, Jen pulled the flexi copy of the *Big Island News* out of her bag. "The article."

He accepted it with a slight nod. Their fingers touched as he took the flexi and it felt almost as if a spark jumped between them. "Thank you for this. I've read it, but Momma will want a copy to keep. She's probably bought out all the flexi in Lexington by now to give to her friends. She never thinks to get her own."

"So . . . you like it?"

"Yes, Ms. Butler, I do. General Boatright called to tell me he likes it, too, and the Top Brass is quite pleased. I imagine your publisher and editor have gotten a few calls from Very Important People. More importantly, Momma wants to know when I'm bringing you home to meet her."

Jen blushed. "Is that . . . Is that in our future?"

"Well, I'm going to be in Greenbelt, Maryland, you're based in Richmond, Virginia. That's only an hour on the National Capital hyperloop and Lexington's only two, two-and-a-half hours by car from either one."

"Oh," she said. Then the implications hit her. "Oh!"

"Yeah. Oh. C'mon, let me turn this bike in and get us a pair of electrics. I promise not to override the motor, that way you can keep up."

"Where are we going?"

"Hula Grill—it's a nice restaurant up at Whaler's Village, near the resorts. You can get a table practically on the beach and watch the sunset."

"That's quite a few hours off."

"I know. In the meantime, let me show you some of the sights of West Maui."

CHAPTER 16:
Tropical Heat

DARPA @YesDARPA
> Announcing the 2042 Anthony Tether
> Conference. Join us next month as we
> showcase state-of-the-art prosthetic
> development in tribute to former DARPA
> Director (2001-2009), Dr. Anthony Tether.

USSF Office of Scientific Integration
@OSIGenBoatright
> OSI is proud to announce that Colonel
> Glenn Shepard will be participating in the
> 2042 Tether Conference. Our program on
> lifestyle and occupational prosthetics is
> out of this world!
>
> ChirpChat, June 2042

Instead of bikes, they opted for a scooter, and Jen rode
behind Shep as he took them north to the surfing areas of
Napili and Honolua bays, the beaches of Kapalua and

Punalau, and the dramatic sight of the Nakalele Blowhole, where ocean waves drove a spray of water dozens of feet in the air through a gap in the lava rock lining the shore. She'd converted the arm strap of her purse into shoulder straps, and wore it as a backpack while she placed her arms around him and leaned into his back for the ride.

After an afternoon of sightseeing, followed by macadamia nut-crusted Mahi-Mahi, and an unobstructed view of the nearby island of Lanai, Shep announced that if they wanted to try to catch the famous "green-flash" of tropical sunset, they'd need to relocate to the balcony of his room a bit farther up the coast. His building had oceanfront rooms facing due west, looking between Lanai and Molokai. Moreover, it was on a slight cliff, so they'd gain the benefit of catching the light from the sun bending over the horizon.

As they sat, watching, Shep reached his right hand over and took Jen's hand. She held their linked hands up in the fading light, and looked at them and then at him. She then reached over, grabbed his left hand, and held both of his up to compare. "You *have* tanned! Your skin is darker! How did you manage to match the color?"

"Spray tan," he said, and laughed.

"Seriously?"

"Serious—" He broke off as she poked him with the umbrella from her Mai-Tai. "Okay, it's a new development. When they re-skinned me after North Carolina, there was a crystal suspension in the mix, one that can be polarized with an acoustic signal, sort of like the privacy glass used in offices, or the rapid photosensors that keep bright flashes from overloading my bionic eye.

I scan my tanned natural skin with my wristcomm, and it sends a signal to adjust the SymSkyn pigment. There's only one problem—I can *hear* the damned signal, and it gives me headaches. I have to hope I get the tint matched the first time or I get a migraine from the ultrasonics."

"I noticed you wincing in the shopping center."

"Uh huh. The jewelry shop had an old security system, and it *screeched*."

"Yikes. I wouldn't have thought of that."

"I can filter most of it out, as long as I'm expecting it. The problem is that it doesn't have to be close for me to hear it. I can still hear the drums from the luau."

"Well, it *is* just around Black Rock Point."

"Not that one, the Huaka'i, up at the Diamond Resort."

"That's . . . what? A mile away?"

"One and a half."

"Well, drums *do* carry long distances, especially over water."

"True, but I can differentiate the different types of drums and hear the announcer as well. I occasionally catch bits of conversation from the boats offshore. Clear enough to know who's talking, and who's making love."

The conversation made her shiver despite the warm night. She decided to change the topic. "And your eye? What do you see besides the sunset?"

He held up a finger, then pointed toward the setting sun. "Wait for it . . ."

Jen turned to watch as the last sliver of sun slipped below the horizon. There was the faintest hint of green to the upper edge of the red disk, then a faint line of green flashed upward as the last of the red disappeared.

"What did I see? I saw the spectrum analysis of the sunset change. I was able to detect which photons were coming straight at us, and which were bent by the atmosphere. I could tell that the flash was coming because of the change in the refracted light. I can look up and see stars a bit before the sky is dark enough, and I can make out individual objects over on Lanai and Molokai."

"That's . . . simply amazing." Jen marveled at the superhuman capability of the man next to her, in stark contrast to the very warm, very real hand she held. She turned toward Shep, reached out her right hand to touch the left side of his face and turn his head in her direction. She held him for a moment, the feel of smooth skin and fine hairs under her touch. "And what do you see now?"

"I see—" But he never got to finish the sentence as Jen leaned over and kissed him.

When they broke for air, Shep pulled back slightly. "Um, I should warn you . . ."

Jen placed a forefinger over his lips. "Shh. I know. No agenda; just me and you."

"In that case . . ." Shep pulled out of her embrace, stood up, then leaned her over to pick her up in his arms. He was extremely careful with the left arm, as if afraid he'd break her. He just used it to support her weight and wrapped his right arm around her as he whispered in her ear, "We'll be more comfortable inside."

A few hours later, they sat on the balcony again, looking up at the stars. Shep was dressed in shorts, Jen wore only a long T-shirt as she sat in his lap. His left hand rested on her hip, underneath the shirt, and he stroked his fingers idly against her skin. He was practicing his fine motor movements, but she could tell they weren't easy. He'd done well enough, though.

With few light sources to their west, and the building blocking any light from the resort, the sky was filled with points of light. She asked, and he supplied all of the names—both real and fictional. They'd discovered a shared love of old science fiction adventures, and the talk quickly turned to Barsoom and Trantor, the Ringworld and galactic empires.

They sat silently for long intervals as well, with Jen leaning her head on Shep's left shoulder. She couldn't feel the transition from biological to bionic. She knew it was there, but tonight, it simply didn't matter; he caressed her equally well with right hand and left.

After a long silence, Shep spoke, "You flatter me, Ms. Butler."

"Oh? And just what did I do to deserve the last name basis again?" Jen arched an eyebrow. An ordinary man would not be able to see it in the dark, but she now knew from experience that Shep would.

He laughed. "Toothbrush, change of underwear, a sleep shirt."

It was time to tease him back. Jen pulled back a bit and looked him in the eye. She affected her best South Georgia accent from her younger days and drawled, "Why sir, you malign my intentions! It is merely an old reporter's habit. Always expect the flight to be canceled or the client to postpone until the next day!"

"So, you *haven't* been chasing me since the day I ran my extreme triathlon?" He moved his hand off of her hip—his fingertips reaching for points a bit higher up.

Jen mock slapped his hand. "Well, I may have chased, but I never imagined just what it was I've caught!" It felt good to press herself against his chest and feel the deep, rumbling sensation of his laugh in response. He'd gone from taciturn and distrusting to this warm, gentle man over the weeks since they'd met.

"Oh, I am well and truly caught, milady. Hook, line and sinker."

The response to the article was excellent. There were still a few xenophobes and conspiracy theorists who feared the mix of man and machine, but on the whole the comments and reactions were positive. Her publisher called the next morning, while Jen and Shep lingered over coffee and fresh pineapple on the balcony.

"Jennifer! My dear, the response to your article is fantastic! It's been picked up by the wire services and has already been reprinted a dozen times—and that was just up until noon today!" Leo Garcia always seemed to speak in exclamation points. Jen imagined him signaling the punctuation with his hands as he talked on the comm.

"So, I guess you liked it."

"Like it? I love it!" Leo said. "In fact, I got a call this morning from your General Boatright! I had to resist the urge to call you immediately because I knew it was two A.M. and you'd be asleep, but I have to tell you the good news! Space Force and MarsX love the article, it makes them look good having such a genuine hero, and they want a couple of follow-ups!"

Jen smiled to herself at the memory of just what she had been doing at two A.M. "What kind of follow-up?"

"Well, for one, the general thinks you should work with Shepard on his biography—do it as an '... autobiography as told to ...' book like you did with that chess master a couple years back!"

Jen had ghostwritten four autobiographies, including the chess guy, and they'd been well received.

"Uh huh, I can see doing that. I'll need some travel time to finish out the interviews and talk to his friends and family members."

"All doable, Jennifer, I've got my top people on it already."

She paused a moment. A subconscious thought was trying to get her attention. "Wait, you said a 'couple of follow-ups'?"

"Oh, yes! MarsX wants you to do a piece on their astronaut training program. They can embed you with the next training class."

Jen thought about Shep's report of his year at the high elevations on Hawaii. While it was appealing to think of writing—and experiencing—something that was such a huge part of Shep's life, she was less than thrilled with the idea of a long separation just when they were starting to explore a relationship. "Um, okay. Let's talk more about that one before I commit. It's a physical challenge as well as a time commitment. If I'm going to be in the training class, I should ensure I fulfill all of the physical demands."

"No problem! We're thinking you should do the bio first, and maybe give us a feature on Boatright and the surgeon—what's his name, Spruce? Yeah, Martin Spruce. Do those first, then we'll see about the MarsX class. They don't start for another six months."

"Oh. Okay. That sounds reasonable."

"Good. You've got another week. Spend it interviewing your bionic astronaut, and then get back here to the office. You don't need to lay low any more. I've talked with legal, and they've talked with Garner. They pointed out that you now have some very powerful friends with the ability to drop things on him from very high altitudes! You don't need to worry about him or his cronies from here on out. Enjoy the rest of your tropical vacation, then get back here and get to work."

Jen disconnected from the call, and looked over at Shep, who was looking back at her with one eyebrow raised. The fact that it was his left eyebrow made her giggle. "Is that a bionic eyebrow?"

"Nope, just the work of an excellent plastic surgeon."

"Well, I have another week, and it seems Leo wants me to ghostwrite your autobiography. Can you stand my presence for a bit longer?"

"That depends, are you going to commute from Kona or join me over here?"

"I have to go collect my things and check out of the hotel."

"There's a flight at noon from Kapalua. I'll go with you."

"Trying to make sure I come back?"

"Do I need to?" Shep gave her a look with wide eyes and an innocent expression, then laughed. "No, I have to drive up to Pohakuloa and supervise the packing of something that needs to be shipped back to the clinic. We can also go up to the telescopes on top of Mauna Kea. Since you're going to write more, let me get you a tour of HI-SLOPE."

"Oooh, that sounds good. More than just a trip over and back. Better pack a bag, Shep."

"And book myself a room, too."

Jen stood up, grabbed the cushion off her chair and hit Shepard with it. "Silly man."

He reached out and pulled her down onto his lap.

She dropped the pillow and wrapped her arms around him as he kissed her.

The "something" at PTC was an exoskeleton similar to ones Jen had seen developed for soldiers and civilians in jobs that required heavy lifting. Shep had told her that there were several differences. He strapped on the exo and proceeded down the runway at the nearby Bradshaw Army Airfield. Despite having spent almost a month at sea level and not reacclimating himself to the elevation, he'd accelerated to almost forty miles per hour, then backed off to around thirty miles per hour for more than four laps around the thirty-seven-hundred-foot-long runway. Barely even breathing heavily as he finished the 5K run, Shep dismounted from the exo, then stood next to it as he moved his arms and legs and demonstrated the ability to control the exo's movements even without being strapped inside. He walked the electromechanical skeleton over to their rented car and lifted one end off the ground.

"The same signals I use to operate my bionics can be used to command the exoskeleton."

"But . . . you moved its right arm, too," Jen protested.

"Yeah, well, there are pickups on those nerves for balance and coordination. It also lets me do magic tricks."

"Hmm, maybe it's just as well I didn't put this in the article." Jen made a scary face, then laughed at Shep's reaction. She wasn't quite sure when they'd progressed to the point that *she* could tease him about his bionics, but Nik had told her that when *he* started making jokes, it was a very good sign.

Thanks to Shep's connections, they'd been able to visit the telescope complex at the summit of Mauna Kea after dark, and even observe some of the images collected through the thirty-meter telescope—the largest optical telescope in the world, and the highest elevation of any extra-large telescope. No longer just looking for planets around distant stars, the telescope was now engaged in getting all the information they could to determine if those planets could support life.

Dr. Johannsen, the astronomer operating the system that evening, was describing the current image. "That's Trappist-2, a star about thirty-nine light years away. At least one world is in the zone where water is a liquid."

"The Goldilocks zone?" Jen had read the term in some of her favorite science and science fiction books.

"Exactly. Here's additional evidence we could find life there . . ." He shifted the display to a spectroscopic graph, and pointed out a line indicating absorption of red and blue light, but not green. "That's close enough to chlorophyll absorption to suggest plant life. Here's another chart. Those two peaks are carbon dioxide and methane, in an atmosphere of mostly oxygen and nitrogen."

"Liquid water, breathable atmosphere, plant life, and methane . . . cow flatulence?"

The astronomer laughed, and Jen could see Shep behind him trying to keep a straight face. "Close enough. It's a sign of respiration and digestion, so there's likely life there. I've heard that they want to call the planet Cistercia, after the Trappist monks of the Cistercian Order."

"Hmm, I like the sound of that. A world out there that just might hold life." She turned to Shep. "The analysis, did your eye give you all of that, too?"

"Maybe if I was looking at the image directly. Off a screen? No. Although, Professor Johannsen, I have to say you have very good monitors. I did get a hint of chlorophyll absorption out of it."

"Hmm, maybe you *should* look at some of the raw imagery sometime."

"I'll mention it to NASA. They're going to have me analyzing lots of data from satellite sensors and space telescopes. They might be interested."

Shep and Jen thanked the professor for the tour and headed back down the dormant volcano to Waikoloa. It had been a long, busy day and was after midnight when they finally got to the hotel. They didn't need to leave in a hurry, but the clock was definitely ticking down to time for them to get back to the "real world," as Jen had begun to think of it. She felt like she could spend forever in this beautiful, complex tropical paradise with Shep. Unfortunately, they both had jobs to get back to.

Until then, they had six more days, and she was determined that they would spend those days together.

CHAPTER 17:
Game, Set . . .

George J @spacefan
> He really just ripped off the door and
> turned over the car on his own?

WSJS+ Local and National NewsStream
@yournewsnowNC
> @spacefan, let's not forget the brave
> residents of Mount Airy who assisted in
> the rescue.

George J @spacefan
> @yournewsnowNC, sure, they helped,
> but HE RIPPED THE DOOR OFF THE
> CAR WITH HIS BARE HANDS!
>   ChirpChat, September 2042

Jen stepped off the train platform feeling nervous. The
odd sensation in the pit of her stomach had increased over
the ride up to Maryland. She and Shepard had been
looking forward to this weekend, so why did it also fill her

with this sense of unease? After all, she'd talked with Sally Pritchard over the comm when she interviewed her for her for both the article and the biography. Today they would meet face to face for the first time.

She'd returned to Richmond three months ago. The interlude in Hawaii had been wonderful, but the *Times* wanted her back in the office, even if she was working on astronaut features and the Shepard biography. Shep had been assigned as a civilian medical consultant to MarsX and NASA, which entailed frequent trips between D.C., Houston, and Tucson. He was officially based at NASA's Goddard Space Center in Greenbelt, Maryland, where he had real-time access to telemetry from the Moon, Mars, and *Percheron*—the ship which carried personnel from Earth to Mars and back. She rode the hyperloop from Richmond to the Baltimore-Washington International Airport on those rare weekends he was in town. From there it was thirty minutes by surface rail to Greenbelt. She hadn't thought too hard during the ride regarding their plans for the weekend, but as she walked out of the station into the housing development, her thoughts kept returning to the upcoming meeting.

Sally was "the other woman" in Shep's heart—or maybe that was the other way around—*Jen* was the other woman. After all, he called her "Momma."

This was a long holiday weekend—at least for Shep— not so much for her, since the newspaper only took off Monday for Labor Day. However, NASA gave Shep Friday off as well, so she coerced Leo into letting her take the day in the guise of working on the biography.

Shep's townhouse was within walking distance from the

Greenbelt rail station. She let herself in with the key he'd given her soon after he'd rented the place from a friend. That person had only lived here for a few years, and rented it out to NASA staff who were assigned to Goddard for intervals too long for a hotel, and not long enough for purchase or rental. It was fully furnished, which was fortunate, since Shep didn't have much of his own.

She left her rolling suitcase on the lower floor. They'd be headed out to the garage on this level soon. She went up the steps to the next floor. The kitchen and living room were neat and clean . . . but Shep wasn't there. There was a faint buzzing sound coming from upstairs.

Jen walked up to the bedroom floor and found him in the bathroom, cordless clippers in hand as he clipped his hair back to its customary half-inch buzz cut. "You know, if you let somebody help you with that, she might be able to even out the back and catch those stray hairs from around your ears." She'd teased him about his habit of cutting his own hair and offered to do it several times. This was the first time she'd actually caught him in the act.

She reached over, took the clippers from his hand, and touched him on the back to get him to lean over. He was taller than she was, and she needed to get the back of his neck. It took a couple minutes to clean up the edges. When she was done, she laid her hand flat on his bare back and told him to stand up and look in the mirror.

He smiled. As far as Jen was concerned, it lit up the room and chased away her earlier unease. "Thanks, love," he said.

In the bedroom, he grabbed a polo shirt and put it on.

"Okay hon, I'm ready, let's go." He carried a small duffel, since he only needed a few incidentals for the weekend. Most of his possessions and clothes were still stored at Aunt Sally's.

They walked back down to the first floor and out to the garage. He owned a classic Mustang convertible—bright red in its day. It was well kept, and sixty years of care and rebuilding had kept it close to showroom appearance. She tossed her suitcase in the back seat, and Shepard followed it with his duffel. He put the top down and they pulled out into the warm summer day.

Jen had a hat as well as a scarf to tie it down, but there was just something anachronistic about riding in the convertible. She generally didn't need sunscreen, but since she could still burn, and the white interior reflected back onto her shoulders and face, she'd applied a little as a precaution.

One of the nicer benefits of her article had been that Virginia allowed Shepard to renew his driver's license without the handicap endorsement, and *with* the manual drive endorsement for the classic car. The model dated back almost eighty years, although this particular car was about twenty years younger. No one dared call it "antique" to Shep's face. The engine had been changed out to accommodate new fuels and electronic systems, but it was a completely manual car. There was no self-driving or automation. Shep relished the act of driving—it was a link to the freedom he'd felt as a pilot and astronaut. He hadn't yet been able to renew his pilot certification, so "flying" down the interstate with the top down was the closest thing. For now.

The small city of Lexington in central Virginia was the home of one of the oldest private universities in America—Washington and Lee University. The town was actually due west from Richmond, but since one goal of this weekend was the road trip with Shep, it would be a more roundabout trip than if she gone there directly.

The area of town near the university and neighboring Virginia Military Institute hadn't changed much in the nearly three hundred years since founding of the Augusta Academy, which would eventually become WLU. Stately buildings of WLU and VMI led to the intersection of Washington and Jefferson streets, which were lined with classical small town buildings, housing shops and offices. Those in turn gave way to a small business district, and then to suburbs serving the colleges and the larger cities of Roanoke and Charlottesville, each less than an hour commute via auto-drive.

Shep's Aunt Sally lived just outside Lexington in a small development where houses didn't crowd up so much against their neighbors. It was a classic farmhouse with wrap-around porch and bedrooms peeking out through dormer windows on the upper floor. Jen thought it looked like it could have come straight out of the early half of the twentieth century. She was not far off. Shep told her that the house had been rebuilt several times, including modernization in the 1990s and renovation in the early 2000s.

Sally was standing at the door as they drove up. She was a slight woman of five-and-a-half feet in height. Her blonde hair had faded with age, never truly becoming gray, never quite turning white—it had simply become lighter as time progressed. She had pale skin with fine lines around the mouth and the palest blue eyes Jen had ever seen. The contrast with Shep's black hair and hazel eyes was striking, and Jen supposed he must have gotten those looks from his mother. Shep's aunt had a bright smile and glistening eyes to welcome home the nephew she loved and raised. She held her arms wide and Shep rushed up to hug her.

"Hi, Momma. I'm home."

Jen held out her hand, but Sally shook her head and embraced her as well.

"I am so glad to meet you, Jen. Glennie hasn't talked about anyone, or anything, else in weeks! Welcome. Welcome home."

The Shepard-Pritchard home showed signs of having been modified for the time when Uncle Hoop had been wheelchair-bound. There were ramps instead of steps and low door handles that could be accessed from a seated position. Jen had wondered if Shep had also had to use them in that configuration while he was recuperating, but he'd told her that this was only his second visit home since the accident.

The inside of the house was cozy. It was not absolutely neat, but it was clean. Jen hadn't been sure exactly what to expect; modern entertainments still clung to stereotypes of last-century décor or hordes of cats, but the house looked welcoming and comfortable.

They moved to the living room, where the mantle over the fireplace caught her eye. On it were three wooden cases—two were triangular and contained folded flags and medals. On the right was Roland Shepard's, a U.S. flag with two stars—a bronze star for 9/11, and a silver star awarded posthumously for bravery. In the center was Hugh Pritchard's United Kingdom flag, along with a silver star and purple heart. The square case on the left had no flag, for it was Shep's. It contained a purple heart, two silver stars, a bronze star, a civilian bravery medal awarded by the State Police of North Carolina, and a Coast Guard Gold Lifesaving medal.

Shep received a call on his wristcomm and stepped away to take it, so Sally took Jen on a tour of the rest of the house. The kitchen was open and filled with low counters and cabinets for Hoop. The garage held a white Mustang convertible, twin to the one Shep was driving. Sally explained that this one had been Roland's, and it had been the reason Hoop had bought the red one. Shep had insisted that she keep her brother's car, while he took the one his uncle had used to teach him to drive.

The bedrooms were upstairs: a master bedroom, guest room, and Shep's room—much as he'd left it when he went to medical school. There were a few medals, trophies, and certificates from school years—both for Roland and for Shep. There was a framed print of the famous "Earthrise" picture from the Apollo 8 mission, another of an astronaut standing on the Moon, and a picture of stars and galaxies as seen by the Hubble and James Webb space telescopes. On the back of the closet was a poster of a 1970's model with long wavy, blonde hair, posing in a one-piece swimsuit. Sally explained that it had originally been her brother's, and Shep had never removed it.

"Momma, I can't believe you saved all of this," Shep said from the doorway, his call completed.

"Of course, honey. These are your memories. I kept them for you." She pointed to a couple of framed news articles—the first was about Shep performing the first appendectomy in space as part of the 2029 Moon mission. The second article was Jen's.

Jen blushed when she realized that Sally was watching her as she stared at the articles.

"You did a good job, honey. I'm proud of my Glennie, and I'm proud of you for seeing the young man I know and I love."

Jen didn't know what to say. It was flattering and embarrassing at the same time. "Thank you, I guess. I just write what I see."

Sally took her hand and squeezed it. "As I said, you *see* what I *know*." Sparing her further embarrassment, she turned to Shep. "All done? Your phone call? I hope it was good news."

"It is. It turns out I have business in Richmond on Tuesday morning."

"Oh?"

He looked a bit sheepish. "Yeah, I have to go see the medical licensing board. I'm getting my license back!"

"Oh, good." Sally clapped her hands. "About time. That sounds like reason to celebrate. There's pot roast in the oven and champagne chilling. I knew this would be a day to celebrate."

Dinner conversation turned to stories of Hawaii and tales of Shep's time at the high-elevation training sites. "Have they decided what they're going to do with you next?" Sally asked.

"They're still talking about whether or not I can be certified for space travel. They won't even send me to low orbit, let alone the Moon or Mars. I've put in a request for the human spaceflight lab at Johnson Space Center—either that or Space Force's lab in Tucson. Part of what they have me doing at Goddard is reading satellite sensor data on radiation, gravity, magnetic flux, and all of the other conditions and comparing it against the tests performed on my bionics. I think they're hoping it will discourage me, but as far as I'm concerned, there's nothing up there that can make any difference with how I function. In fact, my bionics were specifically designed so that I could go back into space. There are distinct advantages to having a person who cannot be as severely injured in space by mechanical, radiation, gravity, or oxygen levels. All of these things I can do it better."

"I'm sure you can, honey. I believe in you."

"I'm glad somebody does, I guess." He grinned at Jen. "Well okay, two of you. I'm just not sure everybody else does, especially Mission Medical—and you know who is on Mission Medical."

"Yvette? You still blame her, don't you, honey."

"Of course, I do. She blocked me at every turn and then took the position that I wanted. The Mars mission was mine. She didn't want it. She'd left the Force—told me that was my dream, not hers. ROTC was just a scholarship program. But I knew she wanted to go to space, and she always managed to take what I had my eye on. What was she doing on the Moon in the first place? Why was she even there? What gave her the right to make decisions for me?"

Shep was angry, but it was clear from Sally's face that she'd heard this before and tried to talk him down from it on repeated occasions. Jen stayed quiet; this wasn't really her argument.

"Look at it from her perspective," Sally suggested softly. "Her father lingered for a long time with Alzheimer's Disease. He required constant care. Her mother's stroke put her in a wheelchair and she couldn't even feed herself. All Yvette could see was that you were going to be crippled—losing your legs, likely losing an arm. Someone would have to care for you and she just didn't think it right to make a decision that would cause you to be in pain and to require care for the rest of your life."

"It wasn't her decision to make," he growled, "I told her they could fit me for bionics. I wouldn't have been confined to a wheelchair even with standard prosthetics, and I certainly am not now. She wanted me out of the way so she could take the Mars mission. She didn't have the vision to see what I can do. She still doesn't. General Boatright showed me the letter where she told Command—in her official capacity with Mission Medical—that there was no way any medical officer would put a cripple back into space. She's been sitting on Mars for two years and has no idea what I'm capable of, yet she's still telling others what I can and can't do."

"Is it really her you're mad at?" Jen almost whispered it. She half wanted him not to hear, but she knew better. She was less certain about whether the intent of her question would be understood. She wasn't sure this was entirely about Yvette. She'd seen that, deep down, he still had a lot of insecurity. That insecurity occasionally came out as anger at the world for not believing in him.

Shep sighed and the tension released. "No, not entirely. Command doesn't have to listen to her. She doesn't know what I'm capable of. For that matter, you two, Marty, and Nik are the only ones on my side. The general? I sometimes think he only half believes it, although those chirps of his lately have been pretty supportive. I guess some people will have doubts until I rub their noses in it."

He looked a bit ashamed at his own outburst and hung his head. They continued eating in silence for a few moments before Sally spoke up.

"Jennifer, sweetie, your article really does help. A number of my friends read it and told me how proud they are to have known Glennie when he was growing up. They said I must be proud—and I am. Of both of you. What you've done—what you're doing—is very important. Write your book and tell the world what he can do. This is how we convince them of the strength of character he has."

She turned to Shep. "You, young man, you're mad at the world. I thought I taught you better than that. It's just the same as you were after your mother died. I thought you had gotten over that, too, but here you are again. No one died this time. You lived and you get to go on living and you get to make a difference. You *have* made a difference. We will deal with that—all of it. You concentrate on getting back to space."

CHAPTER 18:
. . . Match

❄

Richmond Times Features @LeoGarcia
Streaming live tonight, our own Jennifer
Butler talks with astronaut, doctor,
survivor, and hero Glenn Armstrong
Shepard. Download his new biography,
on sale wherever you buy eBooks.
O'Dour @TheOakTree
I'm not a Martian, I just want to work
there. MarsX needs regular people who
want to work there, too.

ChirpChat, November 2042

The biography was a success. Her editor suggested the title, *Forged in Fire: The Glenn Armstrong Shepard Story*. Shep thought it was cheesy, and made it sound like it was about a blacksmith. Jen liked it, and the publisher greenlit the printing of a hardback edition. Nik told him that at least it wasn't titled *Spare Parts* or *Batteries Not Included*.

Shep was still working for MarsX, on loan to NASA. The release of the book had finally prompted Space Force to upgrade him from medical inactive reserve, to ready reserve. Thus, all three agencies had to agree to the book tour schedule—as well as Jen's publisher, but eventually they all agreed, and the two set off on a multi-city tour for a month.

The tour was good, but grueling. Fifteen cities in thirty days—it amazed Shep that there were still so many bookstores in an age of ubiquitous digital media, but he was booked for one or two book signings per city. There were also interviews for local news media, as well as 'netcasts and network features whenever they hit a major city.

Jen wasn't ready to go back to writing Sunday features. Oh, she'd been writing steadily since Hawaii—small interviews that didn't require deep background, profiles of local celebrities, even an article on the research being jointly sponsored by DARPA and General Boatright's new Office of Scientific Integration. One of her local profiles looked like it might uncover another scandal—but nothing as big as the Garner mess.

Her issue was the amount of time spent on the Shepard interview and biography. So much of it had been researched and written on her "off" time that she'd essentially been working double hours for the past few months. Her last free weekend had been the Labor Day trip to Aunt Sally's two months ago, and that had been a different sort of stress.

She was in a position to take weekends off to do something other than promotion or signings, but Shep was now in Houston almost full time. She needed a break, but the publisher and MarsX were pushing for her to start the astronaut training features. Jen's career was at a high mark, and she needed to capitalize on it—but her heart was in Texas, and she needed to figure out what that meant to her, first.

"Leo, I need to take a leave of absence."

"And hello to you, too, famous author! How's your day, Leo? How's your partner, Leo? You're looking mighty good, there, Leo. Did you lose weight, Leo? Sorry to barge in unannounced, Leo." The publisher looked up from his screen with a half-amused, half-exasperated expression.

"Sorry, Leo. I guess I'm a bit preoccupied." She stopped for a moment and took a good look at Leo Garcia. He was in his early sixties, with receding blond hair, a broad face, and the roundness of a person who spent more time sitting than walking. The thing is, though, he did seem to have lost weight.

"You *have* been losing weight. You look good, Leo, what's the secret?"

"Dana's been making me walk more. We're up to two miles every evening, and I'm trying to get another couple miles during the day." Leo's partner, Dana, was a runner, and had been after him to get more active for as long as Jen had known them.

"Good for you. Now about that leave."

Leo sighed. "I guess two sentences are better than none. Didn't you just have *two* leaves of absence, Jen? I seem to recall a month in Hawaii and a book tour ..."

"Both of those were work, and you know it. I wasn't

even in Kona for a week before I started in on Shepard...
I mean on his story."

"Interesting little slip, there, Jennie. This wouldn't have
anything to do with the Bionic Man being in Houston,
would it?"

"Yes, that has everything to do with it. I *need* to see if
this is going to work. I *want* to give it more time."

"Yeah, well, MarsX and Space Force think you should
start in on the training article right away. The new class is
about to start next month in Tucson, and that's a pretty
hard deadline."

"I know, and I've been thinking about that. MarsX,
Space Force, NASA, they all start their astronaut classes
with physical exams in Houston, then MarsX goes to
Tucson, Space Force to Wright Patterson Aerospace Base,
and NASA..."

"...stays in Houston. I see. Got it. You figure if you
start with the NASA class..."

"...and make some overnights to sit in on classes in
Arizona and Ohio..."

"...it will handle the joint training aspects. Okay, let
me talk with General Boatright and the editorial board.
Go. Be with Shepard. You'll be on unpaid leave until we
make a decision, but you've only got a month until NASA
and MarsX start their new classes. You'll have to be back
on the payroll by then." Leo paused for emphasis.
"Provided you stick with this job."

Jen rushed over and hugged the pudgy publisher.

He blushed and muttered, "Dana will be jealous. Now
go."

※ ※ ※

Jen was torn—close up her apartment in Richmond and move to Houston, or just ask a friend to watch it and get an extended-stay room near Johnson Space Center? Shep was no help, he was staying in visitor quarters associated with Joint Reserve Base Ellington five miles from NASA. That wasn't an option for her, plus it didn't give them any opportunity to be together.

In the end she decided on a short-term rental for business executives who needed lodging only for one to two months. After all, when she started the astronaut training feature, she'd be housed with the other candidates. If things worked out with Shep . . . well, they'd make other arrangements.

Houston was close enough for Nik to visit, or for Shep to go back to San Antonio to visit folks at SAMMC or the rehab hospital. One weekend three weeks after Jen arrived, they'd done exactly that. The docs had encouraged the visit, saying that it was good for their patients to see one of their own number walking around unassisted.

The effect on Shep was mixed. It was good for the patients, but it brought home to him that he *still* wasn't back to "normal"—at least in terms of doing the job he wanted to do. It was as if a shadow had come over Shep's mood—until late that afternoon when he received a comm that he needed to take in private.

When he returned from the call, his mood was much lighter, but he wouldn't tell her about it. Instead, he insisted that they go to dinner—all of them, Shep and Jen, Marty and his wife, Nik, and the nurse that he had *finally* started dating.

Dinner had a much brighter mood than earlier in the day. Nik and Shep teased Marty about being married to his work, and that his wife must be the "other woman." Much to their surprise, Marty's wife, Aaliyah, joined in, telling of how she sometimes had to ambush him and lock him in his office in order to force him to allow the residents and junior doctors to take a meal break. Nik's friend, Sheila, then told the tale of how she'd finally had to ask Nik on a date, because if she'd waited on Nik, he'd still be dithering.

Jen waited to see if Shep would counter with one of his own stories, when he broke into a big grin and blurted out . . .

"I'm going to the Moon."

. . . and her heart broke.

"No, I can't let you do that."

"Damn it, it's not for you to decide, Shepard."

"Yes, it is. It's for me to decide not to get in your way."

She'd put on a good face for the rest of dinner, but the moment they'd left the restaurant, the argument started.

"You are not in my way if I decide you're not. I don't care if you're going to the Moon. They need journalists there, too. That's what O'Dour was saying this morning. He's encouraging NASA and MarsX to start looking at historians, artists, journalists, others."

"That's easy for him to say, he's a billionaire with lots of space-based business. That doesn't mean they have to listen to him."

"So, you're pushing me away, instead."

"No. I'm saying that you have your career and your life.

I'm headed away for who knows how long, and I don't want to hold you back."

"You aren't holding me back! I'm perfectly willing to wait for you or follow you. I'm going to be embedded in astronaut training, anyway. If they'll have me as a real candidate, I can come join you!"

"It's risky, and it'll jeopardize your job."

"To hell with the job, I'm thinking of *us*."

"And I'm thinking of *you*. I'm not worth it."

"Yes, you are. I love you. You are so worth it to me. Just try to get that through your thick synthetic skull."

They were back in Houston, sitting in Shep's car outside Jen's rental. It wasn't his classic sports car, but rather one provided by NASA for his use. It was a convertible, and an unseasonably warm night, so they'd left the top down for the drive back from San Antonio. It had slowed the argument by keeping them from shouting over the wind noise, but now they needed to keep their voices down to not attract attention.

"My skull is real bone. My arm and legs are synthetic."

"You know what I mean. Now stop arguing and look at me." She reached out and put her hand under his chin and rotated his head to get his full attention. "Glenn Shepard. Marry me."

Shep's mouth dropped open, and there was just enough incidental light for her see his expression. He closed his mouth, and his expression softened.

"No."

Now it was Jen's turn to be shocked.

"What? Why?"

"I told you, I don't want to hold you back."

"You're not doing that. *I* asked *you*."

"I love you for that, I truly do. But, I'm not...it wouldn't be fair to you."

"Why? I love you."

"I'm scarred, Jen. Frankly, I'm scared, too. What if I can't survive the Moon? What if the bionics fail? What if...heaven forbid, my mother was right, and we're not meant for space?"

"I don't care, and no matter what you say, you aren't cursed. You spent ten years in space before your accident."

"So, maybe that's all I get. I can't live with the idea you'd be waiting for me and I never come back."

"Women—and men—have been waiting for loved ones for as long as there has been love...and men...and women. So, I'm going to ask one more time. Marry me."

"No. Not...yet."

"Well then, I'm coming out into space for you—like it or not." But as soon the words were spoken, she saw his face fall, and the darkness in his expression came back. In that moment, she knew it had been exactly the wrong thing to say.

PART 3
THE RETURN

CHAPTER 19:
Exploring Beautiful Places

❂

Richmond Times Features @JenButler
Join me for a look inside astronaut
training for NASA and MarsX. The growing
habitats and space stations need . . . well,
everyone! Tonight, I'll show you what it's
like during the first month of physical
training and medical screening. *Stream it
now @RTFchannel11016.*

Mars Exploration Consortium
@TheRealMarsX
@JenButler, thanks for a wonderful
feature! We can't wait to see the next
installment.

ChirpChat, January 2043

The Moonbase assignment was important, but terribly
frustrating as well. Glenn was officially employed by
NASA and working on behalf of MarsX. The problem was

that Moonbase was Space Force territory, and several of the crew seemed to resent his presence. USSF seemed to be ignoring him—after all, according to them, he wasn't fit for space, so he wasn't really there. Even within the can-do MarsX corporate culture there was political maneuvering by the consortium backers. The chief of the medical section belonged to one of those consortium cliques, and while he trusted Glenn, he was reluctant to put much faith in Glenn's feelings about some discrepancies in the Mars Three crew medical results.

On the other hand, NASA was hedging their bets by giving him access to the data. It bothered him that the space agency seemed to be two different organizations. One part—the best part—truly wanted to be in space. The other part—the bureaucratic one—only seemed to care about keeping their jobs. "Play it safe, take the easy road. Don't raise your head. Don't attract attention and you get to keep your job when the next political administration takes office." Of course, that raised the question of *which part* was responsible for hiring him. Then again, he suspected that General Boatright had a hand in it. NASA's bipolar nature might not be responsible at all.

The job was to review medical telemetry and develop a plan for treating the Mars Three crew when they returned later in the year. They'd been on-site for two years and the replacement crew was due to arrive at Mars on the brand-new *Percheron* Earth-Mars transfer ship in three more months. After another three months handing over their jobs to their replacements, *Percheron* would begin the six-month return journey, reacclimating the crew to Earth gravity and atmosphere.

Even there, competing fiefdoms and overlapping areas of authority muddied the waters. MarsX crews were trained to NASA standards, and were *supposed* to follow all of the medical guidelines learned over eighty-plus years of spaceflight. *Percheron* was commissioned by NASA for Mars transfer as well as supplying planned asteroid mining and exploration missions. In turn, the United States Space Force *operated* the ship and all U.S.-majority space infrastructure—such as Moonbase and Heinlein Station—in order to avoid a repeat of the Asimov Station disaster.

Glenn's gut was telling him that either the Mars Three crew had ignored the rules, or the precautions to maintain crew health for two and a half years on Mars were wrong. There was evidence of bone and muscle loss that simply should not have occurred given the zero-point-three-seven-gee gravity of Mars. Crews in weightlessness, or in one-sixth gee on the Moon, needed to exercise to maintain muscle and bone strength. It had been thought that Mars gravity should be sufficient to at least partially prevent deterioration. Therefore, the daily exercise requirement had been reduced to just one hour per day, as compared to the two-hour-a-day requirement that had been standard for decades.

If there was continued loss, then either the guidelines were wrong—a NASA issue, or the crew was not doing even that one hour of daily exercise—a MarsX problem. Either way, it also suggested that this problem had not been detected and addressed by the Mars Three medical officer, Dr. Yvette Barbier.

That was the real problem. It would be easy for Glenn

to blame it all on Yvette. She should be monitoring crew health. She should have noticed the deterioration, and should have enforced—or even increased—the exercise requirement. To be fair, though, this was the first long-duration mission to Mars, four times longer than Mars Two, and twelve times longer than Mars One.

The whole situation was fraught with unknowns. In fact, that was the ultimate reason he'd been assigned to Moonbase. *Someone* needed to come up with a plan. Even if General Boatright couldn't get him restored to independent flight status, at least he'd managed to convince all of the parties that Glenn's brain still worked properly. So, Glenn sent his reports to both General Boatright and to Mission Medical Command. MMC then sent them to NASA and MarsX Mission Control in Houston and Tucson. From there, it seemed as if the reports simply disappeared into a black hole.

He talked with Nik almost daily. It was good to get some of the frustration out. Nik didn't know the nuances of the crew medical issues, but his background made him an excellent sounding board for Glenn's thoughts. For that matter, he could listen and help Glenn identify aspects of the data he'd missed. They also brought Marty in from time to time. The three of them could deal with the medical data, but were stymied when there was no response whatsoever from the Earth-based commands.

When frustrations were high, Glenn liked to go out onto the surface of the Moon. Some segments of the Moonbase community weren't concerned with his accident and rehab. As far as the rank-and-file workers and technicians were concerned, he was still accredited as a Moon-rated astronaut. Some of them had even been here when he was Moonbase CMO. If Glenn wanted to don his spacesuit and go out onto the lunar surface, who were they to stop him? For that matter, if he wanted to check out a moon buggy that was none of their business either—and if he had a special purpose for that buggy, well, Moonbase Command didn't need to know.

"Hey, Glenn, headed out again?"

"Sure thing, Guenter."

"Buggy number three is ready for you, and you only. Still working on the special modifications?"

"Just a few more tests, I think."

"I have to admit, it's elegant code."

"Yes, DARPA did good. They just were slow to realize it could be used for something other than my exo."

"As I said, elegant. The control interfaces look pretty good. I've been thinking of using some of it to update the existing drive-by-wire controls. They aren't causing issues with the overall control system, and might even help in the long run, so I don't have a problem with it. Think DARPA will mind?"

Glenn laughed. "Unlikely. As you said, it's just drive-by-wire with an ultra-short decision loop. Thanks, Guenter. I'll take it from here." He waved and climbed into the moon buggy.

When Glenn had gone back to the "paint and body shop" after the tornado rescue, he'd received an update to the processor that mediated signals from his nervous system to the bionics. One bonus was software to allow him to extend that control to other computer-driven devices, and a set of chips that had come packaged in a case with the OSI logo on the cover. He'd started by installing one of the chips in his tablet and comm and playing with the resulting brain-to-computer interface to get a feel for how it operated. There was also a letter in the case from General Boatright instructing him to "test the interface under various field conditions." Included was a list of names of specialists he should work with in the course of his tests.

Sergeant Guenter Wendt's name had been on the list, and he was in charge of Moonbase's surface vehicles. Moon buggies had a remote-control link to allow them to be teleoperated and returned to Moonbase in case something happened to the human operators. Buggy Three had been sidelined waiting for an unstated maintenance procedure, but Guenter assured him it was perfectly functional, just "out of date." He had no problem inserting one of the chips in the buggy's computer and keeping the vehicle out of general service so that the experiments wouldn't affect anyone else. Glenn suspected the "upgrade" the buggy was waiting on *was* the OSI chip, but Guenter only smiled when asked.

Glenn stepped into the buggy, closed the hatch, and powered it up. Even as the cabin pressure came up, the world of the vehicle and garage came alive around him. He could now utilize his bionic eye and ear as a "heads-up" display, and enter commands to the computers by *thinking* about the muscle movements behind touch and gestures. The system displays and sounds felt as if he was seeing and hearing them naturally, and he could *feel* the buggy much the way he felt his arms and legs. All he had to do was think of moving forward, and the buggy started out the open garage doors, and onto the Moon's surface. Throttle, direction, turns—it didn't matter. The buggy responded flawlessly. It was even equipped with small reaction-control jets allowing it to "hop" to clear terrain obstacles. He thought about jumping with his legs, and the hopper controls obeyed. The first time he tried it, it hadn't worked, but there was a learning system built into the interface. His bionic interface computer was able to learn his commands and teach them to whatever system he commanded. It also allowed him to experiment and get more out of his bionic interface than anyone had even imagined.

There was a freedom to being out on the Moon surface like this, just Glenn, the buggy, the vacuum. One of the Apollo astronauts had called it "magnificent desolation," but to Glenn, there was no desolation to the Moon's surface. It had beauty. It had grandeur. The sharp-edged shadows, and white and black contrasts revealed all of the features in exquisite detail. It wasn't all colorless, either. When he looked up, there was the Earth with all its blues, whites, greens, and browns, hanging over the horizon.

Apollo 15 astronaut Dave Scott had said, "There's something to be said for the exploring of beautiful places. It's good for the spirit!" For a short time, Glenn could forget about regret, disappointment, and the frustration of dealing with bureaucrats back on Earth.

It was indeed good for his spirit to be out here.

An advantage of his bionic ear was the direct interface to secure comms. He reported back to the laboratory whenever he ran his moon buggy experiments, and didn't want anyone eavesdropping.

"Okay, Ian, are you there?"

"Yup, just waiting."

"Just sitting there all the time waiting for me to call?"

"Nope, Guenter gave me the heads-up that you took Buggy Three out for a spin."

"Spies. I'm surrounded by spies."

"You *do* know that the original OSI worked within the intelligence agencies."

"Sure, sixty years ago—and it was Justice Department, not intel. Enough of that. Do you want the results?"

"Sure thing, fire away, Shep."

"Right. Here you go. I have a zero-point-zero-two-microsecond delay between commands to the steering apparatus and executing of the command. There's a zero-point-zero-one-microsecond delay between a jump command and activation of the thrusters. The heads-up display is working just fine although I'm still not getting the interior temperature and partial pressure of oh-two."

"Thanks, Glenn, your signals are looking good. We do have a new update for you. I'll squirt it to your tablet as a secured file. When you open it, it will automatically download and update your processor, and that will automatically update the interface chips."

"Um, do you ever worry about my processor being hacked?"

"Do you ever worry about solving million-bit encryption? That doesn't even take into account the quantum entanglement required to even talk to your processor. At this point, your tablet interface thinks it's part of your body. Digital viruses are cleared by your brain the same way biological viruses are handled by your immune system. For that matter, there's a few quantum links in that direction as well."

"Ouch, thinking like that makes my brain hurt."

"That's just quantum physics, don't try to understand it. Anyway, I think we can either get rid of those lags, or at least get them down to the nanosecond level. Let me talk to the guys in the lab and figure out what we can do about adding features to the heads-up display. Overall, the data you're sending us looks great." There was a pause on the comm, and sounds of clicking that were the audible reminder of the encrypted comm. "Last question. Any muscle twitches whenever you give the commands?"

"No, not really. I did at first, but it became fairly easy to direct the commands. I can readily switch back and forth—like if I want to press on the rudder pedal as opposed to simply commanding it. I haven't had any trouble."

"That's good. It's working the way it's supposed to. I'll send you that update and get to work on the display. Has anybody up there figured out what's you're doing yet?"

"Guenter, of course."

"Of course, but besides him?"

"Nope. I'm only using one buggy so it's not showing up anywhere else."

"That's good, then. Okay, I'll get back to Guenter on the upgrades he wants, and I've already sent the file to your comm. Have fun experimenting."

CHAPTER 20:
Visions . . .

Mars Exploration Consortium
  @TheRealMarsX
  Mars Three crew inflated the guest
  quarters module today. It is the fifth
  permanent structure, making the facility
  the largest—and first permanent
  installation, on Mars. With the arrival of
  the replacement crew in two months, the
  facility and mission have been renamed
  'Marsbase One.'
O'Dour @TheOakTree
  @TheRealMarsX, has anyone found my
  car . . . keys?
                              ChirpChat, February 2043

"What the hell?" Glenn called Marty as soon as he finished reading the latest communication from MarsX Mission Medical Command. "'Marsbase One crew is in good health and good spirits as they prepare to welcome their replacements. More than two years on Mars does not seem to have adversely affected the health of any of the crew. Chief medical officer Yvette Barbier foresees no problems for the upcoming six-month return trip to Earth.'"

"And?" Marty prompted.

"She—or MMC—is leaving out a lot. Green—Steve, not Melissa—was suffering from scurvy until I pointed it out to them last month. Amit is showing signs of unacceptable bone loss. Taketani has a rash that won't respond to topical steroids. It's probably fungal. What in the world—or out of it—is going on up there? I think they're going to need to be quarantined both here and on Earth. They are all showing odd titers for immunoglobins. IgG and IgM are low, and IgE is elevated. It's amazing they're not having hives, urticaria and asthma—I worry about exposure even to the replacement crew."

"Shep, it's the first time that any astronaut crew has been totally away for Earth this long. Six months out, more than two years on the surface. By the time they get home, it will be over three years. Moonbase and Heinlein Station are still working on thirteen-month maximum shifts. Do you really expect there to be no medical complications? Look, I know you're just blowing off steam, but you've got to be careful. Don't give anyone reason to question your professionalism."

Despite being operated by Space Force, Moonbase had a sizeable civilian contingent as well. Normally, it was a close-knit community—very often, the astronauts and specialists trained together, or knew each other professionally.

So why does it feel as if I'm being shunned? Glenn asked himself.

The dining hall was run by a contract service, much as had military base dining facilities since the turn of the twentieth century. There was a mix of freshly cooked food, prepackaged food that simply needed reheating, and what would be considered "vending machine" food on Earth—mainly snacks and beverages. Residents held their wristcomms up to a reader, then selected food items or placed an order at the service window. There were sufficient tables and seating for groups of two to eight people at a time—but there didn't seem to be any vacancies today. He'd approached one table of scientists from the bio and chem labs to see if he could squeeze in, but they'd quickly closed the gap as he approached.

In another corner were four people seated at a table for six. He'd noticed several glances his way, followed by whispers, and hard looks. Despite what might have been gossip at his expense, he'd walked over to join them, only to have everyone get up and depart before he reached the table. Guenter was seated alone at a table for two, and waved when he'd entered the dining hall, but he'd been called away. He shrugged—an odd-looking gesture in one-tenth gee—and gave a small wave of regret as he exited.

Yeah, I'm being shunned.

"It's a hell of a thing, Nik. I trained with these folks. Some of us have been friends for years."

"It's different, now, Shep. Even if you weren't the lone dissenter in MMC, you're the Other to them."

It was an ongoing topic from early therapy sessions. Humans naturally feared or distrusted anything that was too obviously different than their experience. Animators and model makers had discovered what was called the *Uncanny Valley*—clearly cartoonish characters were accepted, and as the illustration became more realistic, people reacted to it accordingly. However, there was a point at which the imitation of a human became close to, but not quite realistic. A "valley" appeared in the curve of steadily increasing attraction because the simulation was uncanny, inhuman, or unrealistic.

Nik warned that Shep's bionics could trigger an Uncanny Valley reaction in some, although they'd both thought that the positive publicity he'd received courtesy of Jen had mostly eliminated negative reactions. It was possible they were wrong. It was also possible this was the rejection of someone perceived as an outsider who was criticizing too much.

"I know, Nik, but this is new. It wasn't like this when I first got here."

"Then they're reacting to you. How's your attitude?"

"A quarter million miles, give or take a thousand."

"*Attitude,* not altitude. Damn flyboy jokes."

"Same thing. I'm a quarter million miles from friends and family."

"Uh huh, and how is she?"

"How would I know? She's at HI-SLOPE undergoing isolation phase."

"So, did you talk to her *before* the phase started?"

"No."

"Have you heard from her?"

"Yeah, she commed me at Thanksgiving, Christmas, and New Year's."

"And did you answer the phone?"

"I texted her back."

"You *idiot*! You *texted* her back? Dammit, Shep, what's wrong with you?"

"I . . . I'm . . . it's too soon. I was an idiot, but I can't take it back."

"So, call her, text her—send her flowers and a Valentine's Day card! It's only two days away."

"I can't. She's in strict isolation with her training group for another month."

"Send a card. Not an email, not a text, a real-life physical Valentine's Day card. Even deep space missions have communication from home. I bet you could even get your buddy Professor Johannsen to deliver it."

"Um, but I still need to get a card and figure out what to say."

"You won't have to say anything. Sending the card will *be* the message."

"Still, quarter million miles, remember? How am I going to find a card on a paperless base . . . in space . . . and get it to Mauna Kea?"

"Good grief, Shep, you're hopeless. You go on the internet, search Valentine's Day cards, pick the one you like, they'll print it in Waimea, or more likely in Kona or Hilo, and they'll stick it on a drone and deliver it."

"Eleven thousand feet up the side of Mauna Kea?"

"Okay, so they put it in a pizza delivery autocar. It'll just cost a bit more. Do it, Shep."

"I—I'll think about it."

"Hopeless idiot. I'm not entirely sure what she sees in you, and it's for sure you're better off with her than without her, you jerk. *FIX this!* I have spoken."

"Yes, Nik," Glenn replied sheepishly.

Living in space caused many problems. Aside from vacuum and radiation, the biggest issue was gravity. The initial space stations were in free-fall—zero gee. They now all had rotating living quarters to simulate gravity, but that didn't change the fact that the Moon—at one-sixth gee— and Mars—at just over one-third gee—simply were not the conditions under which humans had evolved.

Normally, gravity pulled blood and other fluids to the legs and extremities. Not so in low gravity, and pressure issues in the brain, eyes, and around the heart led to neurological and cardiovascular problems. It was also difficult to maintain bone and muscle strength without devoting a significant amount of each waking cycle to exercise. Moonbase personnel had a rigorous physical program and regular medical checkups. The first two Mars missions weren't long enough to test extended duration exposure to zero point three seven gees. The data Glenn saw suggested either that the Mars Three— sorry, *Marsbase One*—crew had slacked off on their exercise, or that Mars gravity was still not sufficient to maintain Earth-like physical health.

That wasn't what really worried Shepard, though. He was concerned that three years' isolation would adversely affect the immune health of the crew. History was filled with stories of visitors from distant lands infecting indigenous populations with diseases they'd never previously encountered. Science fiction writers and futurists had predicted that distant star colonies could experience immunological drift, especially if one colony developed resistance and became carriers of pathogens that other colonies had not experienced in years, decades, or even centuries. The data that he was tasked with analyzing suggested that there had been immunological drift in the Mars personnel in under three years. Partially because they had remained in closed, sterile environments the whole time.

The components of the immune system primarily responsible for antibody production—IgG and IgM— appeared to be reduced, while the immunoglobin mediating allergic response—IgE—was elevated. More importantly, there was also reduction in B and T type white blood cells. Immunodeficiencies heightened the risk of opportunistic infections in which normally benign pathogens could become life-threatening.

Something needed to be done if it was true. He didn't shy away from pulling Rick Morykwas out of the Dragonfly wreckage. He didn't back down from rescuing that mother and children from their overturned car. For that matter, he didn't back down from returning to Moonbase, even though he was not entirely trusted up here.

It didn't matter whether or not his own health was on the line—the health and safety of others was more important. He'd taken an oath to heal the sick and treat the injured. He'd also taken an oath to serve his country and fellow man. He'd renewed one, and still felt himself bound to the other even if Command didn't agree. Glenn held himself accountable to both of those oaths.

Glenn Shepard never backed down from a challenge, and it was doubly important that he not back down from this one. There was a job to do, and he was the person to do it.

CHAPTER 21:
. . . and Portents

Gavin T @TaketaniDoc

Marsbase Two crew is on the ground at
Marsbase! This is a historic moment as
we prepare to hand over Marsbase.
Previous missions were transients; but
Marsbase crew are *residents*!
—Gavin Taketani, Ph.D., Marsbase One
Commander

USSF Office of Scientific Integration
@OSIGenBoatright

US Space Force announces a new
division organized within OSI named
'Moon, Mars and Beyond.' MoMaB will
provide infrastructure support for
Moonbase, Heinlein Station and now
Marsbase. We are here to assist civilian
exploration and colonization missions by
NASA, MarsX, and allied international

space programs. The high frontier has a
new home at Space Force OSI!
                            ChirpChat, May 2043

"Somewhat as a voice in the wilderness, I would like to pass on a few thoughts..."

That wasn't the exact wording Glenn used in his most recent report to MarsX Mission Medical Command, but he'd paraphrased it. That phrase was a legend within the NASA community; in 1961, engineer John Houbolt jumped chain of command and wrote the phrase in a letter to NASA associate administrator Robert Seamans detailing a plan to deliver astronauts to the Moon via a controversial method. The concept, lunar orbit rendezvous, became the actual method used by the Apollo program. If Houbolt's letter had not got the attention it deserved, the Apollo program likely would not have achieved success. The man—and phrase—were a legend, and Glenn wondered whether or not he would have to do something similar in order to call attention to his concerns.

Thus, it came as a surprise when he received a call from NASA medical division regarding the readings from *Percheron*. "Hey Glenn, I want you to take a look at something. We're starting to see an increased incidence of headaches, blurriness of vision, and dizziness among the *Percheron* crew."

"Juan, thanks for sending this. I've been concentrating mostly on the Marsbase crew—and that's been doubled for the past month. I haven't really looked at *Percheron*, but I'll go over this and get back with you. Who's been affected?"

"It's the female crew for the most part. Captain LeBlanc is the one who's first complained, but several others as well—navigator Katou, hydroponics engineer Takeda."

"All female?"

"So far. Bialik, the ship's medic, reported a few other crewmembers affected showing the headaches, but mostly it's the women. It's got us scratching our heads down here. Doc Shelhamer suggested we look for something hormonal, thinking that if it was air quality, it should be affecting everybody equally."

"That's true, but there's always some differential sensitivity. I've got a model here that I can run it through and see what I come up with."

"A model? What kind of model?"

"It's actually a metabolic model that was designed to monitor my health up here in the Moonbase environment. Since my blood volume and oxygen needs have been so severely altered, the guys back at the bionic shop put together a model to try to figure out my oxygen requirements in a spacesuit. It's a really good closed environment model, so I'll see if I can tweak some of the genetic and hormonal factors. That should give us a model of oh-two and cee-oh-two flux in *Percheron* among the crewmembers. It might be just as simple as turning up the oxygen and checking the carbon dioxide scrubbers. You know how much trouble that was for Apollo and Mir."

"That was actually the first thing we thought of. Takeda has been running diagnostics of the air system every six hours since the reports started coming in. Also, it's not all bottled air, the hydroponic plant provides about half of the breathable air, scrubs it, and supplements the food. In fact, carbon dioxide imbalances would affect the algae tanks right away. Since there's been no change, we're not entirely sure where this could be coming from."

"Well, it *is* a new ship. This is the maiden voyage and you built it to be used for multiple trips back and forth. Six months out, three months at Mars, six months back, then wait for a year in Earth orbit. You know what they say about complex systems; 'the more they fancy up the plumbing, the easier it is to gum up the works.'"

"Don't go quoting Scotty on me, Glenn. I'm the one who's been monitoring this the whole time while you've been sitting on your ass up there."

"'Smile when you say that, pardner . . .' There's not a whole lot of sitting being done up here, yet no one seems to be paying any attention to the reports I'm sending."

"Oh, I can assure you that they are paying attention, Glenn. This is . . . well . . . It's not that they're ignoring you, but I'm not entirely sure they're ready to face what you're trying to tell them. Either all of the models are wrong, or the crew has been slacking off on their conditioning. I've seen the telemetry, and it certainly doesn't look like anybody slacking off."

"Which leads to a question of whether the data is being falsified."

"Hey!"

"Easy, Juan, I'm not saying it is. It's just the next thing on a long list of possibilities to check."

"Yeah, well, nobody's going to be ready to accept that, either. Just keep the thought to yourself right now and keep your eyes open for further development. You're doing good work and some of us are paying attention. You need to know that."

"Yeah, I do, thanks. As I've said before, I feel like I'm shouting into the wind."

"Oh, gee, thanks, I had almost managed to forget about that one."

"What, my last report?"

"Yes, that one. It caused a bit of a stir among the NASA liaison team. A few execs were not entirely amused. Of course, that's because they are well aware of what happened the last time someone used the phrase in a report and made certain *other* individuals look like fools."

"That was not my intent, Juan. I hope they understand that. It's just that I think whatever's wrong with the data could mean serious consequences—at the very least, extended rehabilitation when they get back to Earth."

"Right, and at least one of our advisors suggested maybe they don't come back to Earth and just stay on Moonbase."

"I can't believe they're serious. Some of these people have family. We have no right to keep them separated for the rest of their lives."

"No, no, that's not it at all. The conversation was simply that there's no need to bring them down to Earth—*yet*. We could keep them on Moonbase or send them up to O'Neill or Clarke. Given *Percheron's* ring plus the multiple gravity decks, at O'Neill we can put them at one-third gravity, then move them up to one-half, then three-quarters and finally, full gravity to allow them to gradually reacclimate before we bring them back down to Earth."

"That could take years, Juan. Are they seriously talking about years?"

"Yes . . . possibly. Look, I know it's not ideal, but we'll figure it out. Just . . . keep sending me copies of your analyses. I'm on your side and there's a few more here that think the same way. If you can figure out this headache thing that might help to raise your status."

"Raise my status. That's a laugh. I had status once. Look at me now."

"Quit your bitching, Glenn. You know that the half-life of bureaucratic memory is the election cycle; it's only been one cycle since you got injured."

"That's not much consolation. No one seems to remember anything anymore."

"Not just there. Here, too. Run this data through your model. For that matter, run the Marsbase data through your model as well. I'm hoping you find something that the rest of us are missing. Work the problem, Glenn."

"Got it. Juan, I'm on this. Shepard out."

Percheron had eight crew who operated the ship throughout the entire round-trip from Earth to Mars and back. Lieutenant Colonel Gee LeBlanc, *Percheron's* captain; Second Lieutenant Mila Katou, navigator and third officer; Master Sergeant Marta Bialik, medic; and Technical Sergeant Hana Takeda, hydrology technician—all of the females—showed the first symptoms of headache and nausea. Technical Sergeant Jonas Christensen, drive-systems technician, was the first male to report neurological symptoms, progressing to nausea and vertigo. Major Maxim Dvorak, the first officer and pilot, was next, but never seemed to progress much past a headache, while Technical Sergeant Eric Philips, engineering, reported headaches and insomnia, and Captain Angus Scott, the chief engineer, hadn't reported anything other than mild headache. On the other hand, a note from the captain said that Scott had been quite irritable and argumentative.

All of *Percheron's* permanent crew were affected to various degrees, with the females much more severe than the men. Glenn looked closer into the oxygen and carbon-dioxide levels on *Percheron*. Unlike early space vessels and orbital stations, the craft was pressurized to an atmosphere close to Earth normal, although it was similar to airliners, with internal air pressure equivalent to a seven-thousand-foot elevation on Earth. It was only about twenty percent less than sea level pressure and oxygen. That meant it wouldn't be necessary to fine-tune it to anything different from normal atmospheric composition. Still, that didn't mean they couldn't be tweaked a little. Both the scrubbers and hydroponic air system were handling the balance. The only adjustment Glenn really had to recommend was a slight increase in partial pressure of oxygen. NASA and Space Force recommended the same thing, and a few weeks of the new mix seemed to have alleviated most of the headaches.

With that problem solved, NASA and MarsX turned their attention to the next phase. It was approaching the three-month mark; Marsbase had been turned over to its new residents, and *Percheron's* passengers were on their way up to board the transport for the return trip. After more than three years away from Earth, they were ready to come home.

※ ※ ※

Percheron no sooner started the engines to break Mars orbit when new medical problems started to crop up. This time it was the Mars personnel showing signs of headache, insomnia, and irritability. That argued for an infectious agent, and all of the medical advice sent from Earth assumed bacterial or viral contamination and/or infection.

MMC thought that it was norovirus, a stomach infection responsible for most of the symptoms of "stomach flu" or a "stomach bug." Strangely, the females once again showed symptoms first. Rachel Amit, habitat engineer, Maia D'Cruz, geologist, and Melissa Green, dietician and botanist, were affected. Within a week, severe headaches were reported by the men: Gavin Taketani, mission commander, Steven Green, construction engineer and brother to Melissa Green, Victor Grigorescu, hydrologist, and Surya Mishra, who managed Marsbase's remotely operated vehicles.

Surprisingly, Yvette Barbier seemed to be the only one who wasn't affected. Since *Percheron* only had a medic, and not a doctor, she took over as senior medical officer and started treating the illness, assuming as before that it was some form of mild viral infection. Most of the crew responded to treatments, but there were lingering issues.

Neither MMC nor Yvette were saying anything yet, but Glenn began to doubt that they were dealing with a virus.

He continued to monitor crew health, and sent a message to Juan—*If not viral . . . could it be food poisoning?* NASA and Yvette seemed to have come to the same conclusion, since the next report stated that affected crew were started on medications to treat both possibilities, i.e., viral and bacterial contamination of the foods.

Again, the treatments worked for a short time, then new symptoms emerged. Many crew—particular those directly involved in the operation of *Percheron* (and thus those who had been on the ship the longest) reported much more severe headaches, and started to show signs of anxiety, agitation, nervousness. None of the symptoms were totally consistent with a foodborne illness. On the other hand, there was still a possibility of fungal growth or "ergot alkaloids" in spoiled food. The problem with both diagnosis and treatment was the increasing neurological symptoms which affected crew performance.

One of things that baffled the medical team was how the *Percheron* crew seemed to be suffering worse than the civilians who'd been picked up from Marsbase. As Glenn examined the data, his first thought was that there was a contaminant in the ship's environmental systems. The *Percheron* crew could have been exposed to it for the six-month outward voyage and the three months in orbit at Mars. The Marsbase One crew would have only started their exposure in the last few weeks. A major limitation in his analysis was that the Marsbase Two team were not reporting anything unusual. He tried to contact several former colleagues at NASA and Space Force to request additional laboratory tests.

So far, none of his requests had been answered.

Glenn was in his small office outside the Moonbase sickbay when his wristcomm pinged at the same time the incoming message indicator lit up on the display of his desk computer. The header of the message confused him. *Was this supposed to be for him?* It wasn't addressed to him, but rather to the Moonbase medical officer. *Does she know I'm here?*

To: *Moonbase CMO*
From: *Marsbase One CMO*
Subject: *Crew illness.*

I'm attaching new blood and serum tests from Percheron *and Marsbase crew. The suspected stomach virus is not responding to conventional antivirals or antibacterials, nor to isolation of affected individuals. Symptoms now include anxiety, irritability, depression, and at least one instance of hallucination. It appears first—and worst—in females, but then males show similar symptoms, just not as severe. I am now examining the possibility that the issue could be chemical or hormonal in nature, but I'm just not seeing it in patient vitals. I've drawn blood and analyzed it for blood gases, electrolytes, trace elements, lipid profile. The reports are attached.*

I am not ruling out human-transmissible factors, and have directed crew to self-isolate as much as possible.

Please advise if you see anything I've missed.
Y. *Barbier*

After reading the message, Glenn looked at the header again—it was directed to the chief medical officer of Moonbase, but also contained a specific routing to him. The timestamps on basic text and this version didn't match, though, so he wondered if this was a copy or forwarded to him as an afterthought. On the other hand, she probably didn't even know he was here, despite his assignment being part of MarsX MMC's official roster. It might be another example of being out of the decision loop, or avoiding a reaction to putting his name on the broader distribution.

She wasn't specifically asking for his help, but *someone* was.

Reading between the lines suggested that she was out of her depth. On the other hand, this could be precisely the opening he needed. He opened the attachments and started looking at the data. It was all the data he would've asked the SF medic to collect on his behalf. That Yvette had done so and sent it to Moonbase and Earth, meant that she was at least thinking along some of the same lines. He needed to look at this very carefully to figure out what other tests or information they needed.

There simply was nothing in the blood tests—or any of the vitals—to explain the crew reactions. There were other tests and Glenn turned his attention to those results. Iron levels looked fine, electrolytes, the same. Some of the neurotransmitters were high, especially norepinephrine—often mistakenly called "adrenaline." Dopamine levels were slightly reduced. That could explain the headaches, insomnia, and general irritability. On the other hand, headaches, and insomnia increased feelings of stress and that could elevate norepinephrine. So . . . cause? . . . or effect?

The neurotransmitter changes suggested a more systemic action. Glenn had a nagging suspicion he should recognize this, but it was just too indicative of an environmental contaminant. It had to be something in either the food, the water, or the air. Symptoms like these had been at the root of "sick building syndrome" back when office buildings and residences began to use totally sealed heating and air-conditioning systems. Recirculating the same air concentrated contaminants, and something as simple as a puddle of water in the bottom of an air shaft could make the entire population of a building sick. Allergies and chemical sensitivities were among the *milder* effects, as strange as that seemed, with Legionnaires' Disease being one of the more severe examples.

The problem was that food and water supplies *should* have remained sealed since *Percheron* left Earth orbit. The food came from Earth, while the water was produced in orbit from asteroid ice using vacuum distillation. The bottled air had been produced by electrolysis from that same ice, then conditioned in the massive greenhouse and garden that served Moonbase. It was the purest air they could produce, without any of the potential pollutants or airborne contaminants of Earth's atmosphere.

Given that *Percheron*'s own hydroponics suite seemed to be functioning normally, it had to be food or water, but he couldn't figure out how. On the other hand, on Earth they would simply re-sterilize everything. Heat, pressure, and steam were often used to kill bacteria, degrade viral nucleic acids, and kill any remaining spores. There were also chemicals that would do the same—ethylene oxide, hydrogen peroxide vapor, nitrogen oxide or supercritical carbon dioxide. Chemical means were not an option, though. The sealed air system was too delicate to use any means that would upset the delicate balance of oxygen, nitrogen, carbon dioxide and water vapor.

It also meant that high pressure steam similar to a hospital autoclave was also not ideal. On the other hand, the Earth-bound food industry increasingly used hard radiation for sterilization of food. It didn't leave any residue and didn't change the taste of the food.

There was plenty of radiation in space.

To: MarsX Mission Medical Command
From: medical consultant
Re: Potential food contamination

Has anyone considered vacuum and irradiation to sterilize the food? They can't use vacuum on the water supply, but should be able to put it into radiation transparent vessels. It can all be put into a cargo hold, open the hatch to expose it to vacuum, and rotate the ship to expose the hold to full sunlight.

I'm not saying this is the only answer—and maybe not even the best answer—but it would certainly provide a way to eliminate food contamination.

The fact that this is showing up in the Percheron *crew and in the women* first *certainly suggests that it's something with a long exposure period. On that basis alone, I don't see this being a contaminant brought back from Mars, but rather, inherent to the* Percheron *supplies.*

—Shepard

CHAPTER 22:
Radical Solutions

Gavin T @TaketaniDoc
Farewell Mars!
Richmond Times Features @JenButler
Whoo, six months isolation on top of a
volcano is no joke, but sometimes a
sense of humor is necessary. Tonight's
live-stream looks at crew psychology—
and outtakes from our less serious
moments. Inside Astronaut Training—
Streaming live at 1900 EST on
@RTFchannel11016.
ChirpChat, August 2043

Either Glenn wasn't the only one to think about sterilizing
the food supply, or someone at MMC was finally listening.
A couple days after he sent his recommendation, Jeff
Ling, the Moonbase chief medical officer, came to see
him. The man was ten years younger than Glenn, and had

been a resident on temporary duty to Moonbase when Glenn had been CMO. While he didn't always share the concerns over lapses in Marsbase crew health maintenance, he had sought out Glenn's analysis of the Marsbase One and *Percheron* crew issues.

"Shep, the head of human spaceflight at Johnson thinks it's food contamination and that they should sterilize the stores. He's been talking to the Tucson Boys and Girls Club and says they are thinking along the same lines. That's as close as you're going to get to an acknowledgement that you're right."

"Good. So, who tells her, and when?"

"It needs to come from Space Force, since Doc Barbier is acting *Percheron* medical officer, which puts her under my authority as CMO Third Space Wing. I'll send the comm this afternoon, but put everybody's name on it. However, I wanted to talk with you, first. I want to put your name at the head of the list and to hell with what anyone else thinks. You have more experience than the rest of us and I wanted to see if you've thought of anything else to add. After all, I haven't forgotten everything I learned from you—the most important fact being that nothing is *ever* final."

Glenn put his fingertips together and affected an old man's voice. "Good, good, my young padawan. You have learned well." They both laughed, then the medical officer left to send his communication.

Finally, someone *was listening.*

The technique was as easy as Glenn had said; put the food and water into the cargo hold and open the door to expose it to hard vacuum and solar radiation. The not-so-easy part was that food would have to be removed from the sealed vacuum and radiation-proof packaging for the treatment, then crew would have to repackage the food to store it for a few more months. It would have to be done by vac-suited crewmembers, since repressurizing the hold before sealing the food would defeat the purpose of the sterilization process. Sterilizing the water was more difficult. Exposure to vacuum would boil the water, leaving only a cloud of ice crystals floating in vacuum. The low boiling point wouldn't do anything to kill bacteria or viruses, so the water would be pumped into radiation transparent containers, large water bladders similar to giant water balloons. Those would be placed in the cargo hold, then exposed to the ionizing radiation by direct exposure to sunlight.

That was the plan. It just didn't work out that way. Glenn watched and listened with a sense of growing horror to the recordings transmitted back to Earth from *Percheron*.

"Captain! Captain, what you doing?"

Approximately two months' worth of food and water had been placed into the cargo hold in preparation for the vacuum and radiation sterilization.

"Captain, please! Please don't do this."

The transmission originated on the bridge of *Percheron*. Captain LeBlanc had been complaining of strange dreams and had been showing signs of anxiety and nervousness. *Percheron*'s medic had asked Dr. Barbier to prescribe some antianxiety medications in hopes of calming the captain down, but she'd begun acting erratically and saying things that did not make sense.

"They want it. They want it all, but they can't have it. I'm not going to let them have it."

"Captain who are you talking about? There's nobody else here."

"They want it, they do. They told me in my sleep. They came and told me they wanted our food, our people, everything. I can't let them have it."

"Captain, please stay away from those controls. Security! Security to the bridge!"

Security on *Percheron* was two Space Force soldiers who doubled up in other jobs—Master Sergeant Bialik, the medic, and Technical Sergeant Philips, the assistant to the ship's engineer. The bridge hatch opened to reveal the two soldiers who immediately moved to separate First Officer Dvorak and Captain LeBlanc. The latter had one arm out and was reaching for a small blinking button on the ship status panel. That button should have been covered by a safety latch, but a jagged piece of plastic, with a few drops of blood hovering in the free-fall environment of the bridge stood testament to the ongoing struggle between the two officers.

LeBlanc was raving. Her words did not make sense—something about aliens wanting their food and water, and planning to kidnap the crew. While Master Sergeant Bialik stood back with Major Dvorak, Tech Sergeant Philips kept the captain away from the console ... until she kneed him in the groin, causing him to double over and release his grip. Dvorak and Bialik were too far away as LeBlanc reached out and pressed the flashing button.

Percheron shuddered.

Depressurization alarms throughout the ship could be heard over the various comm feeds. The view shook slightly as airtight bulkheads closed. Red lights appeared at many places on the status console as a recorded alert sounded.

"Depressurization, cargo bay one. Depressurization event, cargo bay one. Alert. Alert. Alert."

The food! The water!

If the cargo bay was depressurized without gradually pumping out the atmosphere, it was possible that the food and water was damaged or even blown out into space. The two soldiers subdued the captain, although she continued to struggle. Major Dvorak moved to the console to assess the damage.

"Bridge to engineering. Chief engineer Scott, please tell me the cargo was secured."

"Bridge, this is Lieutenant Katou. Scotty's not here—he was in the cargo hold. We were trying to secure the load and he shoved me toward the hatch as the bay doors blew out."

"Katou! Can you see in there? What's the status?"

Another voice came over the comm. "Oh! Oh, my God! It's all blown out!"

"Calm down. Who is this?"

"It's Doctor Barbier; I'm in the observation galley. I saw it happen. The cargo bay doors just blew outward. Engineer Scott pushed Lieutenant Katou toward the hatch, but Scotty was in there without a suit! He's gone. The food is gone—the water is gone—oh my God, what are we going to do?"

※※※

The conference call was one of the largest in the history of spaceflight. In addition to the Houston and Tucson mission control centers, medical officers in Dayton, Huntsville, and Moonbase were joined by Dvorak, Barbier, and Bialik. The communications delay between Earth and Moon was only about one-and-a-half seconds, but *Percheron* was still in close enough proximity to Mars to cause a nearly twenty-minute one-way comm lag.

Captain LeBlanc continued to rave about aliens trying to steal crew provisions. Yvette had run a brain scan which confirmed that the captain was experiencing elevated activity in the visual and auditory processing centers of her brain. Her neurotransmitter levels were also elevated—likely the source of the anxiety and insomnia before the incident. She was hallucinating, but as far as LeBlanc was concerned, her brain was telling her that there was actually something there, real, or not.

It was only the start of *Percheron*'s crew problems, though. With the loss of the chief engineer and medical disability of Captain LeBlanc, the ship was short-staffed. Major Dvorak and Lieutenant Katou could fill in, but no one knew the ship like Scotty. Dvorak also had to act as ship's captain and mission commander, unless he wanted to yield to returning Marsbase One commander, Gavin Taketani. They could draft the Marsbase engineers, too, but Amit's specialty was habitats, while Steve Green specialized in construction. No, they were better off with Katou and Philips—at least they were familiar with the ship's fission-fusion drive system.

To make matters worse, more crew members were reporting irritability and mood swings. Once again, it was worse in women than in men—at least the female *Percheron* crew showed symptoms earlier, and with greater severity, but now all showed the effects of a disturbance in the human body's delicate endocrine balance. Ground-based medical teams were still saying that the problem had to be in the food, while the space-based medical teams cautioned that even sterilization might not be enough if the issue was chemical and not biological.

On top of that, there was the issue of two months' worth of lost supplies.

"We send them food. That's what we do. We send them more food and water—something where *we* do the quality control. Something that we know is good."

"Jason, that is just nuts! We can't do that. How are we going to send a ship, hit a moving target, and get it there before things get even worse?"

"We strap on every single booster we can get our hands on. We can use an unoccupied drone. We did it with cargo ships to get the basic components to Mars. We sent out drones, and they were there waiting when the astronauts arrived."

"But we have to hit a moving target! *Percheron* is on its return already. Their trajectory changed again when the cargo hatch was blown."

While the rest of the team argued, Glenn sat silently and thought about the problem. They needed to get resupply to *Percheron*; it would need to go on a fast drone. That meant putting every booster they could manage on it and accelerating to a high rate of speed so that it wouldn't take six months to reach the ship.

Of course, no matter how they did it, it wouldn't necessarily take six months for a cargo drone to get to *Percheron*—they could meet it halfway in two to three months. The current argument was in favor of simply supplying enough food and water to get home. Glenn knew that the problem was not simply about having the supplies to get home. The crew was sick; in two months they could be dead or dying. Only *Percheron* crew were seriously affected so far, but the Marsbase crew would be next.

"So, we strap on every booster we've got. If we can do a six gee or even a ten gee for an hour, it would be enough to get that drone moving at a high rate of speed. We can get it there in a week or two instead of months!"

"Jason, did I mention that you're nuts?"

Six gees, ten gees—Glenn thought about it. There was another problem that no one had yet mentioned. Even if the drone only took a week to reach *Percheron*, would the crew be coherent enough to complete the remote docking procedures and bring the drone on board? The deterioration of the captain had been much too fast. Even more important—someone had to unload the medical supplies and treat the crew once the cargo drone arrived.

Glenn started tapping on his comm tablet to send a secure message to Marty.

> To: *Martin Spruce*
> From: *Shepard*
> Subject: *Gee Tolerance*
>   *Marty, what's my maximum tolerance?*
>   *—Shep*

※ ※ ※

About a minute later Glenn got a response.

Maximum G tolerance likely around six gees.
Shep, what are you thinking?
—M

Glenn turned off his microphone. He'd already turned off his video link. There was no need to waste Orbit to Earth bandwidth for the dozens of people on the call. With the audio turned down, he commed Marty.

"What the hell are you planning to do, Shep?"

"And a jolly good afternoon to you, too, Marty!" Glenn replied in a cheerful voice.

"Don't give me that. General Boatright made me listen in on this cluster—" He broke off before completing the phrase.

"Well then, you know we need to get supplies out to *Percheron* fast. These guys are talking about strapping on every booster they can get their hands on and boosting at six or ten gees for an hour to gain enough velocity to make the trip in a week. They want to send an unmanned pod, but I'm afraid that unmanned is just going to add to the disaster. There needs to be somebody on board. There needs to be someone who can tolerate high gee-load."

"You're a fool, Shep."

"No, Doc, this has to be done. I'm the one to do it, we both know that."

"No, not that kind of fool. It's that old saying about how fools rush in where angels fear to tread. You're a fool, Shep, but you're right, you're the fool we need. I'll have the lab team work on it, and I'll figure out how to broach the subject with General Boatright. By the way, we've got a new suit for you for extravehicular activity. Boats wanted me to send it up next month, but I think you're going to need it right away. If there's a way to do this, we'll figure it out, but we can't let anybody else know."

"Sure, but you're talking about checking it out with General Boatright. How is that not letting anybody know?"

"We can trust him. We have all along. You'd be surprised, Shep."

"Okay. Well, I trust *you* and if you think that's the best way to do it."

"Definitely the best way to go, Shep. The general knows your capabilities as well as we do. He's your advocate; he's been fighting to get you back into space. He authorized the new EVA suit, and as I said, he wanted me to send it to you soon. I'll have it put on the next shuttle."

"That sounds like a plan. I guess I need to get myself on the crew that's packing supplies."

"I suspect the general can help with that as well. After all, you're the most experienced medical officer in orbit right now."

"Yeah, I've heard that somewhere recently. Okay, I need to get back to this whine-fest. Keep me posted, Marty."

"Yeah, well, before you do that. Have you talked to Jen?"

"Geez, you're as bad as Nik."

"Yes, I am. We care about you, and we like Jen. She was good for you."

"Look, I sent her a card, but as soon as she got out of the isolation phase, this whole situation blew up."

"That's—a partial excuse, but I'm not letting you off the hook. You need to call her."

"Why? What do you know that I don't?"

"It's not that, it's just—you're about to do something stupid. Before you do that, you need to settle things."

"Yes, Mother."

"Don't make me call your Aunt Sally."

"Ugh. You fight dirty."

"I mean it, Shep. *Do it.*"

"Yes, Marty. I will. Now, I really do need to get back to this conference call."

Glenn listened as the arguments went back and forth. The plan was now to send freshly packed food from Earth. There was discussion of sending water, but it was shouted down by others complaining about the cost in ground-to-orbit lift just to get water to space when there were other sources. That led to discussions of how to ensure they sent pure (or at least, clean) water and air. Eventually they settled on water from asteroid ice. The growing space stations at the L2, L4, and L5 Lagrange points were mostly supplied by capturing near-Earth asteroids with high ice content. Additional supplies of air would be produced from asteroids that were heated to release water and nitrogen. The water would be distilled and electrolyzed, and the nitrogen and oxygen combined into breathable air.

Everything that could be, would be packaged on Earth, boosted to orbit, combined with additional supplies in orbit, packed into a cargo pod, then sent on its way. It would take every booster they could spare—and a few they couldn't—to send the cargo drone on its way. The argument then turned to how to ensure that the pod would be able to rendezvous with *Percheron*. It would be moving at an extremely high velocity in the opposite direction, and would need to turn and decelerate to match trajectory with the Mars ship. That meant more fuel, more thrusters . . . and more weight.

Space Force was confident that they would be able to do everything by remote control. They would preprogram course correction and matching to get the cargo drone alongside *Percheron*. From there, the Space Force crew of *Percheron* would be perfectly capable of snagging the pod and bringing it to dock with the ship and unload the supplies. The MarsX personnel were not quite convinced but it really wasn't up to them. *Percheron* belonged to NASA and Space Force. They were the ones who built it, operated it, and crewed it. MarsX was just along for the ride.

The NASA teams were mostly silent. They knew how hard it was to do rendezvous in low orbit, high orbit, even lunar orbit, but they'd managed it at the Moon and Mars. On the other hand, those events had the benefit of alert and confident crews.

"Has anybody considered the fact that the *Percheron* crew may be too sick, or even disabled by the time the cargo pod gets there?"

Glenn was surprised somebody else was thinking on the same lines. He looked back at the conference indicators to see who spoke. *Ah, it was Ling.*

The Space Force and NASA experts dismissed the concerns. If need be, they could handle rendezvous and docking by remote—even with up to forty minutes' round-trip transmission lag. Glenn thought they were overconfident. Again, Ling expressed Glenn's unvoiced concerns.

"But with the time lag, wouldn't it be more prudent to send someone with the cargo pod?" Ling's question was met by laughs.

"No human can survive the acceleration," NASA administrator Chuck Gallant said. "If we make it safe enough for an astronaut, the supplies won't get there in time."

"I can think of someone who could do it. Shepard could."

"The clockwork astronaut?" Gallant scoffed. "Hell no, we're not putting a cripple with an artificial heart on a high-speed rocket."

"That's not very inclusive of you, Chuck," a new voice said.

"Who said that?"

There were chuckles and muttering, but with most participants having turned off their video feeds, there was no way to know who had spoken. After a few more heated words, the conference broke up. They had a plan to pack a cargo pod with clean food, water, and air, plus a bunch of fuel. They would strap on as many boosters as they could manage, and send the pod like a bat out of hell to rescue *Percheron*. What was *not* in the plan was a final determination of how to manage rendezvous if the crew was incapacitated.

Deep in his heart, Glenn knew that the basic concept would work, but it needed something more.

It needed him.

CHAPTER 23:
Putting It Together

Scott K @Kman549

International Space Expo '43. This year's theme 'Tomorrow the Stars' was on full display with the latest equipment for mining and construction. The Space Force display of new suit designs was absolutely amazing! I'll be posting pictures in the thread below.

USSF Office of Scientific Integration
@OSIGenBoatright

@Kman549, thanks for the kind words, Scott. OSI is all about pushing the boundaries of what's possible!

ChirpChat, September 2043

The new spacesuit had a lot in common with Glenn's old exoskeleton. Ian wanted to call it the Fireball XL Five, but apparently General Boatright had vetoed that name.

For now, they were simply calling it the hard suit. At first glance, Glenn liked it; it was less confining, and in a way, much less restricting than a spacesuit. This suit was similar to deep water diving suits, with hard coverings and articulation joints at wrists and elbows, shoulders, knees, and hips. However, servo motors controlled those joints to assist with movement to provide both greater protection and greater mobility to an astronaut. Glenn's own experience with the fire on the Dragonfly trainer was one reason that was used to justify the new suit.

Superhuman strength wasn't necessarily needed on the Moon or orbital. Reduced gravity meant that less muscle was needed to lift and move objects. On the other hand, every object still had its same mass—and therefore inertia—that it would have on Earth. Once an object was moving, it required a greater amount of force and control to stop it. Thus, this new spacesuit design was all about exerting the type of force needed in low gravity and low atmosphere environments while maximizing astronaut protection. Computer-controlled servos compensated for mass and inertia, while longer life support and the ability to integrate propulsion made it practically a personalized spaceship. The design had been developed for orbital construction crews.

A non-augmented human would operate the hard suit much the same way they operated an exoskeleton; pressure sensitive pads around the ankles, knees, hips, shoulders, elbows, and wrists translated movements to servomotors. Glenn's was originally operated the same way, allowing him to move about while learning to adapt to his bionics before they had been turned up to full power. Much like his later exo, though, Glenn's embedded bionic processor could directly interface with the hard suit to operate it by thought alone.

Glenn packed the suit into his special moonbuggy and took it out of Mare Imbrium into Mare Serenitatis where he knew he wouldn't be observed. His next test would kick up quite a bit of dust, so he needed to be out of line-of-sight from Moonbase. While the chief medical officer and Guenter knew what he was doing, it wouldn't be a good idea to have casual observers watching. The hard suit was in the cargo compartment, so he needed to pressurize the compartment to just below the pressure of the cab, climb into the suit, seal it, then seal off the cockpit area of the buggy. That kept the dust out, and the base monitors would continue to show normal pressure while he pumped down the cargo compartment and opened the hatch.

The cargo compartment had a distinctive smell. Apollo astronauts had described it as "spent gunpowder." To Glenn, it smelled of ashes leftover from a charcoal fire. As a doctor and scientist, Glenn knew that lunar regolith actually had no smell, since any aromatic chemicals had long boiled off in the vacuum, but that the highly charged ions reacted with moisture in the human nose. That didn't make it any less distinctive, and the smell brought back memories of Fourth of July cookouts and fireworks.

Every time Glenn stepped out onto the lunar surface, he marveled at the beauty. He looked up at the Earth hanging almost directly overhead, and noted the odd sensation of moving *inside* the suit and not having the exterior move unless he commanded it to do so. He'd done several tests in the garage before this point, but this was his first experiment in full vacuum on the lunar surface.

He checked his commlink back to the Moon buggy, then sent a ping to Guenter to make sure the technician knew he was out of the buggy. Next was a secure comm link to the bionics laboratory on Earth.

"Okay Ian, I'm ready to let 'er rip."

"Roger, Glenn. Take it easy at first, just start off walking. Good . . . starting to get some readings. Internals are steady, externals are . . . whoa, that was a sharp temperature jump. You in full sun?"

"Confirmed, Ian. I stepped out of the shade of the buggy into direct sun."

"Okay, Glenn. External temp is stable at one-oh-three Celsius, internal temp is one-niner degrees cee—are you sure that's not a bit cool for you? You can kick it up a bit."

"Sweat doesn't evaporate as well in a suit, even the extra breathing room in here won't help if I get dripping wet from exertion. Better to be a bit cool now than risk moisture penetration into suit systems."

"Understood, Glenn. Okay, all systems reporting green. Go ahead and take it out for a run."

"I'm going to try for twenty-five kph, around fifteen miles per hour. I can maintain that on my own pretty easily on Earth. In this suit on the Moon should be a breeze."

"A breeze in the vacuum. Very funny, Shep," Ian replied. "Okay, according to readings you're operating strictly on the force feedback servos. Those are operating just fine, but I'm going to send a lockout code to shut them off. Think about interfacing directly with your bionic control computer."

"Wait one, I don't want you sending the code while I'm in mid-leap and I lock up and go tumbling. Okay, I'm stopped now. Send it." Several green lights in Glenn's heads-up display turned amber, and a red light turned green.

"Sent. Now, it's just like your exo. Take a step."

"Okay . . . that felt a bit like swimming in molasses for a moment, but it passed. Speeding up . . . That's better. I'm moving along in an easy lope with about ten meters per bounce."

"Copy. I've got the same on this end. System integration is nominal, lags are down in the picosecond range. No problems. All right, you can give it a little bit of gas, if you want."

Glenn grunted to himself as he realized that he was still continuing to move his legs and arms in time with the motions of the suit. In truth, he could pull his legs up in a tuck and let the suit do all of the work—either that, or let the suit move the limbs passively. For now, he decided to stay in the same position, wearing the suit like any other garment, but he stopped exerting force with his muscles, and the external speed started to climb. "All right, all okay. Five-zero kph and bounding along. I stopped thinking about my legs and just told the suit to move and it got a lot easier."

"Excellent, Glenn. See if you can take it up to seventy-five."

"Seven-five acknowledged and kicking up some dust. Are you reading the camera on the Moon buggy?"

"I am but you're actually out of the picture. One of the L1 satellites has you in view, but I'll pan the buggy camera a little bit . . . Oh, ho, ho! Nice rooster tail there, Speedy! You're kicking up more than just a little bit of dust. I'm also reading one hundred kilometers per hour."

"I thought I'd push it a bit more. One hundred kay, running on the surface of the Moon. Not bad. Not half bad at all." he paused a moment, then resumed. "One request, though."

"Oh, what's that?"

"Can you give me maneuvering jets? The bounds are getting a bit long. Moving this fast in low gee makes me risk losing contact with the surface. I think I'm going to need some extra boost to stay grounded."

"Hmm, not a bad idea. I know that there was talk of an orbital version of the suit. Let me talk it over with the dev team. So, tabling that for now, how are you feeling, Shep?"

"Okay, felt a bit of a twinge for a moment back down around seventy-five. Kind of like a pulled chest muscle, but it passed quickly."

"Hmm, I'm not seeing anything here. Biotelemetry doesn't show anything, but then I don't get the full bio readout. Are you being monitored back at Moonbase?"

"The CMO gets a readout. It was a condition of my being up here in the first place. He won't tell anybody, though. The general swore him to secrecy."

"I suggest you check in with him . . . that is, if he doesn't call you before you get back. Still, time to slow it back down."

"Agreed, I'm starting to feel a cramp or something,

probably an intercostal muscle in the chest, but I'm coming back down through fifty kays, headed for twenty-five. I'm also starting to circle back; it's going to take a while."

"That's fine. Keep it down to twenty-five and I'll keep the force-feedback servos offline for now. How are you feeling?"

"The cramp is easing up; it now just feels like a muscle twitch. Probably just time for a visit with the massage terrorist. I think it will be okay, so let's call this one a good test."

"Looks good, here, Glenn. I can stay on the line for bit, but will clear off the comm frequency and just keep your telemetry up. Call me if you need me."

"Roger, Ian. The buggy's in sight and I'm slowing down to a walk. The test is done and all is well. Glenn out."

When Glenn got back inside the buggy and out of the exo, he still felt a slight twinge in his chest. Something wasn't quite right, but it didn't seem serious. He would see if he could get some time with the Moonbase resident massage therapist—a position he'd created when he was Moonbase CMO after witnessing firsthand the need for someone with those skills. One of the issues with working in reduced gravity was an increased frequency of muscle strains and sprains. It was easy to forget that decreased gravity and weight did not change mass. Large, heavy objects—or ones moving one hundred kilometers per hour—still required exertion to start and stop movement. This twinge had all the hallmarks of a pulled muscle, so he'd consult her . . . later. For now, it was time to get back to his quarters, take a nice hot shower, and check on correspondence regarding the *Percheron*.

"Dr. Shepard, I'm so sorry, but I've been looking at the medical telemetry from your surface excursion. I'm not happy with your heart function and circulation." Jeff Ling had stopped by Glenn's quarters later that evening.

Glenn had just gotten off a very awkward comm with Jen. He'd followed Marty's advice and reached out to her. Deep down, he knew he'd hurt her and needed to try to repair the damage done to their relationship. She seemed receptive to the call, but cool. He was unsure if it would be possible to regain the old warmth and feeling, but he was coming to realize that he needed to try, so he'd talked for most of the call, trying to fill her in on what he'd been doing. He couldn't say everything via unsecured comm, particularly given what he was planning, but that was probably for the best.

Unfortunately, he had a feeling that what the CMO would say next was going to sideline all of his plans.

"What kind of a problem, Jeff?"

"You need to get back under full gravity, or even higher. It's not a problem now, but I can see you losing muscle tone. With your reduced blood volume and shorter circulation system, you need Earth normal, or even higher gravity for short periods. I'm recommending you head up to O'Neill station and take advantage of their one-gee and one-point-two-gee habitat wheels." O'Neill station was at Earth's fifth Lagrange point—the same orbit as the Moon, but following in the orbit by sixty degrees. That's where they were assembling the cargo pod.

Glenn fought to suppress a grin. "So, what you're telling me is that I need to spend some time in a higher gee environment for my cardiac health. Is that right?"

"Yes, that's pretty much it, Shep. I'm also going to prescribe some specific exercises. I think you need to do more cardio, plus something to improve your core muscle strengths. Crunches are good, but planks are better. You can do those in the one-gee areas, but I think you should do at least an hour of exercise each day in the one-point-two-gee ring. Oh, and don't spend any more time in the point-eight-gee wheel than you need to. I'll be monitoring to see if this improves your readings."

Ling seemed to have a bit of a facial twitch. *Wait, did he just wink?* Glenn thought, then continued aloud. "Well Jeff, I know some of the docs have doubts about how well I can perform in space. God knows I've been fighting Space Force on it for the past four years. If you think I need to do it, I'll go."

"Yes, Shep, I think it will be a great value to go out to O'Neill and build up some cardiovascular stamina."

Oh, this was not suspicious at all. Ling was sending him to the exact same place where the cargo pod was being assembled.

This had General Boatright written all over it.

The emergency cargo pod was being assembled at L5 Lagrange point so that it wouldn't have to interact with Earth or Moon gravity. The L4 and L5 points, also known as the leading and trailing "trojans," already had a velocity advantage over anything originating in a close Earth orbit, since they shared the same orbit and velocity as the Moon. A "slingshot" trajectory around the Earth for additional gravity assist was out of the question, because the craft would have to dive too deep into Earth's atmosphere to get sufficient acceleration, so the trailing Lagrange point gave the optimum trade-off of access and launch position.

If someone wanted to send Glenn to O'Neill—where he'd be in a position to work with loading the cargo pod—that was fine with him. If the doctor wanted him to spend a couple hours a day on cardiovascular conditioning in higher gravity than the Moon . . . well, that was fine, too.

It was a setup.

Of course, it was a setup, but it was exactly the setup he wanted.

CHAPTER 24:
Don't Call It Piracy

Mars Exploration Consortium
@TheRealMarsX

At MarsX, we're all about improving access to deep space resources. High-speed cargo transit to Mars vicinity has been in the works for some time, and the recent successful Marsbase missions indicate it is time for a trial. Earth to Mars in one month is becoming a reality.

USSF Office of Scientific Integration
@OSIGenBoatright

To clarify, the upcoming cargo ship to Mars will be unmanned. OSI MoMaB is proud to support and coordinate the test of novel high-acceleration means to deliver essential supplies to Mars and Beyond!

ChirpChat, September 2043

☀☀☀

Glenn, like all astronauts, had very little personal gear to pack. The proliferation of private cargo ventures and reusable launch vehicles had made it easier to travel off Earth, but space and weight were still at a premium. Ships and stations provided uniforms, bedding, and sundries, so he only had one suit of formal civilian clothes, a few flowery print shirts from Hawaii, and his old Space Force dress uniform. The latter had been re-tailored after his rehabilitation since it needed to accommodate his bionics. Mainly, his personal effects consisted of an electronic book reader, a digital picture frame, two hardbound books of classic science fiction and an autographed copy of Homer Hickam's *Don't Blow Yourself Up*. He'd met the rocketry pioneer and science historian when he was twenty-two, at a space science conference in Tucson, Arizona. He'd bought the book for Hoop, but his uncle had insisted that Glenn read it, too.

During his recovery from the accident, Hoop had brought it to him in the hospital, tapped the cover and asked "What have you learned?"

"I need to do a better job of not blowing myself up, I guess," was Glenn's response.

The digital display frame was for pictures of important events and people. There was one of Aunt Sally and Uncle Hoop from back when he was young and they were raising him. Nik had caught a picture of him yanking the door off the wrecked car in North Carolina, with the local sheriff looking on in awe. There was also a picture of Jennifer in Maui, and of the two of them with Aunt Sally. Finally, he had a collage of pictures from the rehab hospital. Various patients showed off their advanced prosthetic and bionic limbs, with interspersed shots of Marty, Nik, and Jakob.

There wasn't much to put in the shipping module, since most of his possessions were with Aunt Sally. *Home* was Hoop and Sally's house in Lexington; this was just a place to work. He liked Moonbase and its people, but he wouldn't mind leaving.

He had a job to do and that job was on O'Neill Station.

"Hi, Jen. How is the on-the-job research going?" After having monopolized the last call talking about his own concerns, Glenn figured he needed to let her talk this time.

"It's not too bad. I just got back from Maui working up in the Haleakala crater training area."

"Really? Seen any green flashes lately?"

"Ha, ha, very funny. Not exactly easy to do when you're inside a crater at twelve thousand feet of elevation. On the other hand, sunrises are spectacular. They let us go up to the summit the other day. It's fantastic to watch the sun come up from there."

"Did you turn to the west to see the shadow of the mountain?"

"I did. That triangular shadow is wonderful...but cold."

"Cold? Really? Don't they have you in spacesuits up there? I was always too warm in the simulation exercises."

"We wear them in the crater. For one thing, with the silicates in the dust, it's best not to breathe too much. With some of the heavy work we also need the extra oxygen. On the one hand, exertion warms me up, on the other hand, getting sweaty ends up giving me chills. On average, it's colder than my preference since we need to stay at a temperature that doesn't result in perspiration."

"True, it's a consideration up here, too. The fans in the suits and venting of pressurized air can chill you pretty quickly."

"I can't really complain, though, this is fascinating. It's interesting, a good place to train, good people, and I'm learning new stuff every day."

"Your text said something about continuing training after this cycle. What happened to going through the first two stages, writing the feature, then going home to write your book?"

"Well, my editor wants me home. I've been recording one feature a month and he's been releasing them on a regular basis, but he wants me to get the book finished so that he can put me on other projects. Leo, my publisher, changed all of that. He negotiated a contract change so that I don't work for the news outlet anymore, I now work for the communications company which owns it, but on loan to the public affairs offices of NASA and MarsX. I sort of work for them now. As long as I keep serializing the monthly features, there's an editor in the PAO assembling them and sending them back to me for editing and approval. We've almost got enough for the first book."

"'First book'? Really? That implies multiple books and a continuing series. What exactly do they have in mind?"

"I'm not entirely sure, but Leo mentioned that my work caught the attention of that general of yours."

"Huh. Boatright's at it again. He's becoming a bit of a

puppet master. He's been pretty supportive, but I never really know what he's planning."

"Leo said something about reporting off-Earth. That would be nice, but I can't help but think that we need to resolve matters between us."

"I . . . I know. I'm sorry. I panicked. Then I was too embarrassed to admit I was wrong."

"Damn right, you were. I went off to training thinking that it was pointless because you wouldn't be there when I was done. You hurt me, Glenn."

Ouch, he thought. *She called me Glenn, not Shep.*

"Oh." It was all he could think of to say. He'd already said he was sorry, but it seemed so inadequate.

"Anyway, it seems to me that you're about to head off and do something stupid and heroic again, and I really want to get this settled. I do still love you, even if you broke my heart."

"I love you too, but what I said back then stands, I'm . . . well, I can't say, but yeah, it's probably stupid, and I don't want that to splash back on you. I couldn't stand it if it held you back."

"You're still a fool, Glenn Shepard. Do what you have to do, then come back to me and settle this."

Before he could say a word in response, Jen cut the connection.

"So, did you talk with her?"

"Yeah, I did, Nik. We've been on comm a couple of times, and a few texts in between."

"And?"

"I don't want to talk about it."

"You're a fool Shep."

"Almost her exact words."

"Almost?"

"Ok, her exact words, except she called me 'Glenn.'"

"Ouch. Sheila's stayed in touch with her. She's hurting. It's like being abandoned at the altar all over again."

"Oh, I never thought of that."

"Of course not. It's because you're a fool. Enough of that. How are things going for you at O'Neill? Keeping up the heavy gee conditioning?"

"I'm exercising. Still, that's not the only thing I'm doing. This isn't just a rehab assignment. Most of the time I'm working on the packing list for the cargo ship and participating in the planning meetings with respect to medical supplies. They keep arguing over the weight of the food and water vs. fuel consumption. Now they're talking about sending extra fuel because telemetry says *Percheron* made excess maneuvers. That might be more erratic behavior, so I'm pushing for additional medical supplies. General Boatright got me assigned to figuring out what could be causing the medical and behavioral issues so that we have the appropriate meds in the shipment."

"Like what?"

"Well, we can't rule out toxicity, so we'll need chelators, maybe even dialysis supplies if it's not overtly viral or bacterial. The latest report says LeBlanc is suffering from liver failure. It could be parasitic from something growing in the hydroponic sections, so, we need herbicides and fungicides—both industrial and medical, and at that, ointments, powders, oral meds and injectables. The outbound flight took honeybees for the greenhouse dome, so we need insecticides . . . not to mention counteragents and antitoxins for all of that."

"They have flowers and insects?"

"Mars base does, but *Percheron* only has dwarf fruit trees. Those provide good sources of vitamins, and they taste good. Still, they had to be pollinated, and they used the outbound honeybees for that."

"You think flies or mosquitoes might have gotten in with the honeybees?"

"We can't rule it out. Someone needs to go there and look. We can't count on the crew being able to do it. They've had what, a month now? Still no resolution." Glenn sighed. "Then again, you already know my views on that."

"Yes, I know that you think you have to go because you don't trust Yvette to make the right decisions. You feel you're the only one who can withstand the gee forces of the launch and arrive with a clear head."

"I don't know if it's a matter of trust, but the medical reports are getting worse. It's not bad enough that the captain became delusional, but some of the other reports suggest increases in depression and OCD-like behaviors. The amazing thing is that Yvette hasn't appeared affected until now, but these latest reports? She's seeing things that aren't there."

"So, you're the psychiatrist, now?"

"Do you think it likely that only a single individual on that ship could remain unaffected?"

"No, but this sounds like you think she falsified earlier reports."

"Not that so much as she's not aware of her own impairment—but this latest report? Dvorak and Taketani conspiring to remove her? Confining them to their quarters? I don't know Dvorak, but I trained with Gavin Taketani. He's a mediator, not confrontational if he can help it. If he *is* plotting against her, he would have to have a damned good reason. As it is, she ordered all of the crew to isolate in their quarters and has effectively taken command in the captain's absence."

"So, Dvorak—he's the XO, right? He didn't challenge her?"

"We don't know if he did or not, other than this odd report of conspiracy. She's invoked medical authority, and been rational until just recently. She relieved the captain of command and has been giving orders. She's in the command hierarchy—at least as far as MarsX is concerned, although I'm not sure why Space Force is going along with it."

"Perhaps because she's the person best able to solve this."

"But what if she's not? Able, that is. She reported doing a medical exam on Engineer Scott! Scott was blown out into space when Captain LeBlanc blew the cargo hold."

"It could be a simple name error. A mistake due to stress and overwork."

"No, it's not. She's impaired, and she can't see it. Everyone else is in awe of her handling of the problem to date, and they don't see that she's now in as bad a shape as everyone else."

"There it is. You don't trust her."

"Yeah, that's fair. The reports of crew health from Mars

didn't make sense. She should have been on top of things, and she wasn't."

"If there was even a problem in the first place."

"Sure. *If.* But there *were* docs in NASA and MarsX who agreed that something was wrong. They were just reluctant to pin it on their golden girl."

"And that galls you, doesn't it?"

"Wait—when did this turn into a psychotherapy session?"

"Hello? Psychiatrist here! You have to know that my brain is always analyzing."

"Okay, okay. The truth is, I think the situation is too volatile. If she's unaffected, then my whole role is to get the cargo pod docked with *Percheron.* But I don't think that's the case. It's not just a feeling, I've been analyzing the medical telemetry. Her heart rate and endocrine levels are way up. Her norepinephrine levels are also off. She's impaired, and there needs to be an unimpaired doc on-site."

"Provided you survive the trip. How are the chest twinges?" Nik asked.

"Nothing to worry about; it was just a muscle cramp. One of the fittings in the suit was too tight across my chest. It crimped a medical lead and gave me a bruise. That's all it was."

"But the Moonbase CMO wrote that report . . ."

"That's right, he did. He needed a reason to send me to O'Neill. The truth of the matter is that I *do* need to prepare for a lot of gees. Being able to train in full gee and the one-point-two-gee section of the habitat wheel is a hell of a lot better than starting from the one-sixth gee of Moonbase. Plus, I'm here, with access to the cargo ship."

"I know you said that it was just an excuse. But are you sure? What if there really is something to the medical readouts?"

"Look, I know you, Marty, Jen, even the general worry about me, but it's okay. Want to know the truth? I'm worried, too. This is risky—both to health and career."

"Uh huh. It's also a good reason not to run back into a burning crash site."

"It's not burning. This is different."

"Not, it's not, but it's what happened to us in North Carolina. You can't stand by and watch when someone needs help. That's why we're all worried for you."

"Look, I'm just doing my job."

"You're doing *more* than your job. Hey, we understand—I understand. Deep in her heart, Jen understands, too."

"I know, Nik. I know all the reasons why I shouldn't do this—and you know all the reasons why I think I should. Give everyone my best, and if you or Sheila talks to Jen, help explain it to her, please?"

"Nope, you're going to have to come back here and do that yourself, buddy. I won't tell you to be careful, but you still need to try to stay safe."

After Glenn signed off the comm, he sat and thought for a few moments.

That conversation didn't sound ominous at all, now, did it?

To send a cargo drone to rendezvous with *Percheron* in the shortest time possible, NASA, Space Force and MarsX had pulled every solid and liquid fuel booster in the system in orbit. They even pulled the brand-new Helicity2 hybrid electric-plasma-fusion drive planned for the next-generation Mars-transfer ships *Augeron* and *Clydesdale*. The cargo drone would have a propulsion section ten times larger than the actual cargo pod, allowing for excess weight (and volume) capacity in the cargo pod. It would be filled with an expandable foam to keep the contents from shifting under thrust. Glenn had spent some time with the engineers designing that ballast section, and knew they were concerned about filling and expanding the foam from the outside, and not getting a complete penetration of the ballast throughout the open spaces.

Glenn had a plan for that.

George Mellies was an orbital construction engineer. His was also one of the names on the list from General Boatright. Glenn's new orbital-work exoskeleton was practically a wearable spacecraft, and George had also been part of *that* design team. Ian had finally come up with a name—or at least an acronym—for it. Mobility In Limiting Environment Suit—or MILES. George passed along several messages from the dev team as well as from General Boatright. The MILES was capable of more than a week's life support, power, and mobility, with external connections for additional power and supplies as well as waste venting.

Once again, Boatright seemed to be way ahead of him.

Glenn suggested to George that the ballast foam could be sprayed from the inside, embedding his suit in foam— and incidentally inside the cargo pod before its high-speed trip across the Solar System. George's team was already ahead of him, and packed the pod with tanks and dispensers not only for the quick-hardening foam, but for a catalyst to dissolve it when Glenn needed to get out of the pod.

They still needed to figure out the best position for Glenn within the cargo space. He needed to have his back to a bulkhead and be lying on his back in the MILES suit for the best acceleration tolerance. He also needed waste disposal, heat dissipation and supplemental power connections. The pod was a standard design with compartments for cargo as well as a small cockpit—even though it would not be needed for this flight, and would be filled with the ballast foam. Therefore, George and Glenn decided to pack the MILES suit and a personal stock of food, air, and water in the cockpit before the foam was dispensed. As a bonus, he could use the space and supplies to allow himself to remain isolated from the *Percheron* crew if necessary. Finally, there was the matter of connecting the interface module to interface his bionic control computer to the ship's controls.

"Well, this baby is ready to fly across the sky like a bat out of hell," George said to the multi-site conference call as they finished the last of the preparations.

"Hmm, '*Bat*' would be a good name for the craft," Glenn mused. He was on the call to discuss the latest in medical reports from *Percheron*. As far as he could tell, no one outside OSI had any inkling of his plans, but he still needed to be cautious.

"Absolutely not," said a Space Force general. "This is the first use of a Helicity Two drive; according to the propulsion team, there's never been a ship named *Helicity*

One, so that's what they are proposing. MarsX wants *Ares Q*, and NASA suggested *Schiaparelli*." There were nods all around the video conference as each name was mentioned. The general continued. "Unfortunately for all of you, Space Force nomenclature applies to all non-crewed flights, so this flight is designated C-21-MX."

The NASA flight director in charge of the meeting grimaced, but held his peace. "Since that's settled, let's hear the medical report."

Nearly everyone on *Percheron* was reporting one or more neurological symptoms such as anxiety, insomnia, stress reactions, irritability, and anger. Arguments and fights were common. Most concerning were reports of auditory and visual hallucinations, leading to claims that the ship was haunted—with ghostly figures of family members, construction workers, and astronauts roaming the passages. The engineer said there were strange individuals in red shirts in the engine room. The first officer claimed a nineteenth-century sailor was on the bridge calculating position with sextant. Yvette mentioned that Bialik was hearing injured soldiers crying in pain. She prescribed sleeping pills and anxiety medication to everyone, but that didn't seem to be helping. The best thing they could do was to simply keep their distance from each other . . . on a spacecraft with four months remaining to get to Earth. The situation was bad, and it was getting worse. Once again, the female crew were exhibiting more symptoms than males.

Glenn stressed that finding; it had to mean something. He'd even suggested that hormonal agents be included in the cargo in case they needed to balance testosterone and estrogen, or supplements such as progesterone. MMC had overruled him; after all, the women were on ovulation blockers, and Yvette didn't even need those. Still, Glenn had direct access to the cargo, and he'd seen to the composition of medical supplies himself.

He also made sure to have pharmaceuticals, medical devices, and other supplies to perform diagnostics. *Percheron* had essential medical scanning and imaging, but some tests required lab work, and he did not know how much would still be available on the ship. This was really where Glenn's concerns about the crew function came to the fore—diagnosing the illness and treating it would require concentration, focused attention, and scholarly inquiry. Yvette truly did not lack the ability, no matter how he groused in his private moments. What concerned him was that the unknown disorder seemed to be affecting the very abilities needed to respond to this emergency. They were not only *not* going to be able to treat themselves, they likely wouldn't even be able to capture and dock the cargo ship.

Glenn knew that he had to go. He, of all people, could withstand the high gee-forces, thanks to his bionics. His shortened circulatory system meant less fluid to pool under acceleration, and less stress on his heart. Bionic limb strength would enable him to move in high gee if necessary, and he could even wirelessly interface with the *Bat*'s and even *Percheron*'s controls.

The C-21-MX *would* be crewed, and it *would* have a name.

He wouldn't need to move out of his protective cocoon until arrival unless there was an emergency. If there was, he could supplement the remote controls with his own local controls. The MILES suit would provide air, water, food, heating, and cooling. It would cushion him from the gee-forces as much as possible, and his additional gravity training and core conditioning would help. He was the best situated, trained, and equipped doctor to solve this problem.

It was time for him to go.

CHAPTER 25:
Weighty Matters

✦

United States Space Force @USSFActual
Launch of the unmanned C-21-MX is
scheduled for Midnight, GMT on the 25th.
Tammie D. @SMagnolia
@USSFActual, will we be able to see it?
USSF Office of Scientific Integration
@OSIGenBoatright
@SMagnolia, yes, Tammie, the east coast
of the United States should be able to see
the initial boost between 8:00 and 8:10
PM. C-21-MX will be launching from
O'Neill station, and should be visible
without magnification about thirty degrees
above the western horizon. After the initial
boost, viewers with at least 25x
magnification should also be able to see
the Helicity2 plume from one to three
hours after sunset. OSI MoMaB is excited
to support this unique test.
ChirpChat, September 2043

※※※

Official mission clock called for launch of the *Bat* within twenty-four hours; the best launch window was within twelve hours. *Bat*—still officially the C-21-MX—was undergoing tests for remote control of engines, navigation, and docking. This was a "plugs out" test in NASA vernacular, meaning that all physical links had been disconnected, and only internal systems were active. It was the perfect time for Glenn to enter the cargo pod and become situated in the unused cockpit area. George and his team had argued to spray the ballast foam after the test—supposedly via a remote link—then repeat the plugs out test to ensure that none of the systems were affected. While the foam was setting, Glenn would test his own command and control links while the link to Mission Control was inactive.

Once he made his way to the cargo pod, he waited for the signal from George to release the foam. It was time to record a few messages.

"My dearest Jennifer. By the time you get this. *Bat* will have launched and I will be committed to my plan. This is something I have to do. Although you may not agree with my reasons, you should know that I *must try*. I will do this, but then I'm coming back. I'm coming back for you, my dearest love, please believe that—*I* do. That's my answer to the question you asked, as well. I will, and I do. Yours, forever and always, Shep."

The next message was both more difficult, and more likely to cause a reaction. He could make the promise to Jen because he knew his actions were likely to end his career, and he'd be grounded the rest of his life. It was worth giving up a dream of space to be able to share the rest of his life with her. He had lived the reality of space travel, and was doing exactly what he was trained for—in truth, what he was *made* for. If the consequence was never coming back into space, it would be okay.

"To NASA and MarsX Mission Control. Right about now you should realize that your weight calculations on the C-21-MX are off. However, thrust and guidance have been adjusted to the new values. This cargo ship is not unmanned, and so I have christened it the *Bat*. I hope that history records this not as an act of piracy, but as a mission of mercy. The crew health on *Percheron* is critical, and I do not think they will be able to rendezvous and dock with *Bat*, and then diagnose and treat themselves—at least, not without the assistance of someone who has not been affected. Automated systems are all fine and good, but we already know that crew members behaving erratically have altered *Percheron*'s course and status. The more-than-twenty-minute communications lag will make remote-controlled docking extremely difficult.

"I have argued for a manned mission, and made the case that my unique condition will make this survivable. Someone has to treat the *Percheron* crew. As of launch time, the medic is in a coma and the Marsbase medical officer is . . . not functioning at one hundred percent; there may not be competent medical care by the time *Bat* arrives. I know there have been doubts about my suitability for space missions, but I can handle this. My uniquely remodeled physiology—including my LVAD— will enable me to withstand the high gravity boost to get to *Percheron*. The automated systems will remain online, but do not attempt to bring me back or I will override it.

"I will reopen communications with Mission Control after the acceleration phase is complete. I will also record and send status messages to keep Mission Medical in the loop. I have to do this, not to prove my own capabilities, but more importantly, to save lives.

"May God and history forgive me, even if you do not. This must be done.

"Shepard, out."

The recordings would be sent after the initial burn of the strap-on boosters. The engineers had calculated that a six-gee burn for ten minutes, followed by two gees for ten hours, would boost the cargo ship to a speed of over two million kilometers an hour. At that speed, *Bat* could make the trip to Mars itself in five days. Of course, there was acceleration and deceleration time, plus maneuvering to catch up with *Percheron* on its ballistic course back to Earth, but the plan was for a total of twenty-two hours of acceleration and deceleration and one hundred twenty-two hours of coasting. This should be a six-day trip if all went well. If it didn't . . . well, the computer in the MILES suit had been updated with multiple course and trajectory programs, as well as a backup link between his bionic control interface and *Bat's* engine and navigational controls.

Glenn knew that General Boatright had been at work behind the scenes. He'd pushed to get Glenn assigned to the Moon, provided the MILES suit, and given him the team to pull this off by arranging the contacts behind much of this endeavor. In fact, the general had been involved since his accident and authorized the release of classified material used for his bionic rehabilitation. There was more to this than met the eye, and while the back-channel plotting bothered Glenn, it encouraged him even more. He had a powerful patron, and he had a team supporting him.

Enough woolgathering, it was time to brace himself for acceleration.

There were numerous bumps and shocks as *Bat* was disconnected from the support framework used during construction. Glenn connected his control interface to *Bat*'s computers. He would have anywhere from ten to thirty minutes before Mission Control detected his intrusion; fortunately, there were only ten minutes left in the launch countdown. It felt as if he was reaching out his arm to the navigation controls, and his legs and feet to the engine controls. His bionic eye now showed a view of space, and the heads-up display became ship's status. He could see stars, but more than that, he could see the solar wind and all of the electromagnetic flux that surrounded the vessel. He could hear the communications between the tugs and the local controller at O'Neill. His legs conveyed the vibrations of the fuel pumps and a subtle background hum as the Helicity2 drive began to warm up. He could feel the drive controls with his feet, and he knew that all he needed to do was to think about where he wanted to go, and the controls would follow.

In the corner of his vision, a countdown clock was getting closer and closer to zero. Another overlay showed course calculations, constantly updated with trajectory and timing based on immediate launch. His feed also showed updated information from *Percheron*—it seemed that it was continuing to stray off course, whether from leaks, or accidental thruster firing, or deliberate action. If the latter, it pointed to more deterioration of the crew's mental state. Time was of the essence, and the new trajectory calculations suggested that the programmed launch time might be too late.

A message popped up in his vision, flashing to get his attention:

Launch now—Boatright.

The countdown still had five minutes, but he could sense additional data being loaded into *Bat* via his secure comm. Glenn had to trust that it was the updated course. He had to act now. He thought about pressing a switch, and the interface interpreted it as taking control of *Bat*.

He flexed his legs and *jumped*.

Glenn didn't actually move, he was secured in the acceleration cushions of the MILES suit, embedded in foam in the nose of the cargo pod. However, the intent to move his legs was interpreted as activating the boosters. He *felt* the thrusters with his legs, and the maneuvering systems as his hands. *Bat's* sensors and instruments were his eye and ear. Acceleration pushed him into the cushions, and he thought of turning a dial in order to increase his oxygen flow to help with the stress and strain of increasing gee forces.

Glenn had taken control of *Bat* and was on his way.

The comm systems were filled with expressions of concern that *Bat* had malfunctioned. Mission Control was talking about aberrant signals, NASA worried about the trajectory implications, and MarsX was concerned that the early launch would jeopardize the entire mission. A new voice came over the comm, and all of the other chatter was cut off.

"Ladies and gentlemen, this is Major General Richard Boatwright of Space Force, Office of Scientific Integration. As you know, we are the support and liaison element of this mission. We have dedicated considerable effort, including computing resources, to continue to analyze the dynamic rendezvous parameters. No offense to our colleagues at NASA, but we feel we have the best and most recent launch and trajectory information for the C-21-MX. Deep Space Tracking indicates that recent changes to *Percheron* trajectory render the NASA trajectory too late and too inefficient. *Percheron's* continued course deviation would require too much maneuvering at rendezvous unless we moved up the launch and altered trajectory to compensate.

"Do not be concerned; the *Bat*—excuse me, the C-21-MX—is perfectly under control. I'm sending one of my officers, Lieutenant Colonel Richardson, over with the updates and to act as liaison. Don't worry, we'll take it from here."

The chatter resumed, now with added recriminations from Space Force's First Space Wing, which operated the Earth Traffic Deconfliction Zone, which was supposed to have control over any and all craft operating in near-Earth space. NASA voices countered that the cargo ship had launched from O'Neill, which was *not* "near-Earth" and hence under their jurisdiction. Space Force countered that Moon-Lagrange space was the responsibility of the Second Space Wing, and thus they should *still* have authority. The weakest argument came from MarsX, who protested that the ship was headed to meet their personnel, thus control should have been theirs.

General Boatright came back on the channel, cutting off all other voices and sternly reprimanded them that this situation was *precisely* why his office had taken control. Moreover, he had the explicit permission of the United States president and the chief executives of England, France, Germany, Brazil, and Japan—the voting partners of the Mars and Outer System Exploration Consortium, the combined national space programs backing MarsX. Space Force personnel continued to protest until the Chief of Space Operations sent word that—as Boatright had informed them—this was precisely the reason why OSI MoMaB had been placed in charge, and that authority for mission came under the aegis of the USSF *Third* Space Wing—all space operations traversing the space inside the asteroid belt—and *not* the First or Second Space Wings. He then commanded the USSF personnel to shut up and follow orders or be dismissed from the Force.

Glenn listened for a time, but as the acceleration continued and gee-forces increased, he had less concentration to spend on the comm. Boatright still had not revealed the stowaway on *Bat*, but that was sure to come later, after Glenn's pre-recorded message was received.

Call it privateering if one must; he would face those consequences in time. For now, though, it hurt. Crunches and core exercises had been part of his routine ever since the scolding he'd received from his physical trainer. Now those muscle contractions were essential to maintain blood flow and stay conscious. Just because he didn't have legs for blood to pool didn't mean it wouldn't settle somewhere else—like his abdomen. Then again, that's what the LVAD was for. By design, his torso and head were flat with respect to the direction of acceleration, but even minor differences in elevation were magnified by the gee force. He just needed to keep crunching his abdominal muscles to keep blood flowing to the heart and LVAD, and from there to his brain.

Pilots endured six gees all the time . . . but for only seconds each instance. He needed to stay alert and conscious for ten minutes. Not impossible, but difficult and a big strain on his heart, lungs, and muscles. He just had to concentrate.

CHAPTER 26:
Express Delivery

USSF Office of Scientific Integration
@OSIGenBoatright

> The Moon, Mars and Beyond division of
> OSI, announces that the C-21-MX cargo
> vessel, christened the *Bat*, will
> rendezvous with *Percheron* mid-flight on
> its return to Earth. Moreover, *Bat* is
> indeed a manned vessel, as a proof-of-
> concept demonstration of emergency
> resupply and rescue capabilities as
> humanity expands beyond Earth orbit.
> Colonel Glenn Shepard, our first bionically
> augmented astronaut, is aboard *Bat* and
> will return to Earth with *Percheron* and the
> Marsbase One crew in four months.
> > ChirpChat, September 2043

As acceleration continued to build, Glenn was pressed
deeper into the cushioned lining of his MILES suit. He

could start to feel some of the harder components of the
suit underneath the cushions. Those could cause
significant bruising, and he wondered if he needed to try
to adjust his position. While he could slightly move his
legs and left arm, moving his torso was impossible under
acceleration. It felt as if all his internal organs were being
pulled through his spine, but the support and position
meant that the pressure was still tolerable. The vision
grayed out in his right eye but his left eye continued to
feed information to his brain. Not only the remote feeds
and information that interfaced through his bionic system,
but also visual information from the inside of his suit. He
could still hear comm chatter, but it faded in importance
and seemed to be coming from a long distance away.

There was a brief lessening of thrust, and then several
sharp jolts as the solid fuel boosters burned out and the
liquid-fueled boosters throttled up to full thrust. The gee-
force indicator continued to climb through two gees. An
intense low-frequency vibration signaled that plasma
fusion from the Helicity2 drive had started up. The
combined force of rockets and fusion drive would top out
at six point five gees before the liquid-fueled engines cut
out. The fusion drive would continue to thrust at two gees
for another ten hours.

Fighter pilots experienced six gees and more in dives
and dogfights; and roller coaster enthusiasts could
experience as much as eight to nine gees, but those
accelerations only lasted for one or two seconds. Glenn
had experienced six gees in a centrifuge at Joint Aerospace
Base Wright-Patterson in Ohio, but without bionics,
LVAD, or high-gee training, he'd only managed thirty

seconds before losing consciousness. The accelerometer indicated six point two six gees. Amazingly, Glenn was still conscious, but it *hurt*. Fortunately, the readout monitoring his LVAD stayed in the green, and the core conditioning exercises seemed to have helped, but his abdominal muscles would be awfully sore.

With a sudden sensation of relief, the acceleration cut off. The moment acceleration eased, he sent a command to loosen restraints so that he could move his arms and legs. He rocked his head left and right, and rotated his neck without fear of serious injury. He was functional and awake, having survived the worst of the acceleration. The two-gee constant acceleration of the Helicity2 drive still held him tight against the acceleration padding. Double his body weight for ten hours would wear him down, but it was tolerable since he really didn't need to move around. It was difficult to move, but not impossible; the stress was worth it for the resulting velocity.

The Helicity2 combined a low-thrust ion drive which fed a higher-thrust plasma drive, which in turn incorporated a fusion "afterburner" to propel him to speeds one hundred times faster than even the New Horizons probe, which had achieved a speed of fifty thousand kilometers per hour—after *months* of constant acceleration. For him, it would only be ten hours and ten minutes of acceleration, then he would drift for nearly five days, then decelerate for a day. Fortunately, *deceleration* would only be at one gee of thrust. Then he would find out exactly what was wrong with the crew aboard *Percheron*.

☀☀☀

Glenn slept when he could. He continued to monitor communication from Mission Control, particularly once his presence on *Bat* was revealed. Fortunately, the general had told everyone that Glenn would be staying quiescent to save air and resources. There wasn't much extra room inside the MILES, but he was able to pull his arms and legs out of the suit's appendages to work out the cramps and strains. He could also eat, drink and deal with waste elimination. For the rest of it, he slept . . . and dreamed.

Surprisingly, these were not the PTSD nightmares he still experienced on occasion. If they were, he would have had to sedate himself to avoid thrashing about and injuring himself in the confines of the MILES suit. After all, Nik wasn't there to apply his "squirt-gun therapy." On the other hand, Nik had supplied him with music and voice recordings to assist with meditation and to keep him in a relaxed state.

Much to Glenn's amazement, it worked. Most of his onboard dreams were not anxiety inducing at all, rather, there was a surreal feeling to them. In one, he was flying through space, unencumbered by ship or suit. He spread his arms to reveal great, golden wings and flew from the Earth to Mars. In another, he felt himself riding one of the massive rockets of the Apollo program, or the historic moments of his namesakes John Glenn, Neil Armstrong, and Alan Shepard. He dreamed that he was flying over Mars looking down on the Valles Marinaris and coming to rest at the summit of Olympus Mons. He looked out over plains of red with dust storms that billowed in the air, but with pressure so low, they barely fluttered pieces of paper.

He awoke with tears in his eyes after he dreamed of

hearing a symphony from the stars. In it, heavy molecules born in the heart of a supernova accelerated to near light speed, then traveled for eons before encountering an object and dying in a shower of radiation. Every component of the dream—from dramatic stellar explosion to the sensation of light on his skin—was transformed into music, and it was glorious.

Not all of the dreams were so pleasant, but for those, he was much more of an onlooker—the *Apollo One* fire, *Challenger* explosion, *Columbia* breakup, and the Asimov Station disaster. He dreamed that he was an investigator trying to solve the problems and awoke feeling that a solution had been at his fingertips right up until the moment he emerged from the dream state. He supposed the meditation helped to reduce any risk of nightmare, since what he did *not* see in those dreams was the Dragonfly or himself.

He slept deeply for much of the first two days, restoring his body from the stress of acceleration. Once he felt rested, he read transcripts of communications between *Percheron* and Earth, logged his medical data for Marty, recorded his thoughts for Nik, and slept lightly, with more frequent dreams. He saw his mother, and the father he barely knew. He dreamed of his aunt and uncle who showed him the love that his life had been missing. He had dream-conversations with Rosemarie, his mother, about the love she tried to express, and couldn't, about her cancer, and her fears that he would grow up to be just like his father. He tried to reassure her that he was not— but deep in his heart, he knew it to be a lie. He was exactly the same type of person as his father.

He relived arguments with Marty, Nik, the other patients in the rehabilitation unit. There were both good and bad memories, but they didn't seem to bother him. It was more like reliving an incident, coming to terms with it, and then moving on. He recalled several incidents with Yvette, the passion of arguing, and the heat of lovemaking. He saw other friends and lovers, but every time he tried to concentrate on a face, each and every one of them transformed into Jen. Despite the memory of his mother's cancer, the estrangement from his step-father, and the memory of his own pain, he could feel Jen's love, and that filled him with peace.

Glenn awoke from a therapy he never knew he needed. Nik probably had something to do with it, after all, he'd provided the soundtrack, but Glenn realized he didn't mind. He was refreshed and focused. An alert showed in his vision informing him that he'd awakened in time for the deceleration maneuver and burn. *Bat* rotated automatically without incident. The Helicity2 drive started back up with a slight hitch, but that smoothed out once the magnetic containment strengthened and the plasma began to fuse, slowing the headlong rush toward Mars.

After five days of floating, the sensation of gravity was a bit of a shock, but at one gee, it felt as normal as lying down on Earth. He tightened his core muscles and resumed the breathing exercises he'd used during acceleration. This time it would last for a full day but at the end he would be matching course with *Percheron*.

It took twenty-one hours to bring *Bat* to rest with respect to its original course, then another four hours to accelerate back toward Earth, at an angle to their original course. *Bat* had come on a straight trajectory, but *Percheron* was not aimed at Earth, but rather, the point where Earth would be in another four months. Thus, it was necessary to speed up to catch *Percheron*, then slow slightly so as to not overshoot. As the clock ticked down, *Bat's* instruments started to scan for the other ship. There didn't appear to be anything out there, suggesting that *Percheron* had deviated from its course yet again.

It was time to open up the comm link to Earth and see if he could get updated tracking information from them. He sent a standard inquiry ping to notify Mission Control that he was online.

After fifteen minutes he heard, "Space Force Office of Scientific Integration. Lieutenant Colonel Richardson, speaking." The voice on comm sounded familiar, but he didn't know of an LTC Richardson in NASA, MarsX, or Space Force Mission Control. On the other hand, OSI was General Boatright's division, so it seemed they'd been waiting for his comm.

"This is Glenn Shepard in *Bat*, requesting updated trajectory and course corrections for *Percheron*."

Again, the fifteen-minute wait.

"Acknowledged, Colonel Shepard. This is Andrew Richardson from MoMaB section, and I'm your liaison. You are right on time. The general has updated information for you and has been expecting your call. Stand by."

As I figured, thought Glenn. *He seems to have taken over this mission. Here I thought I risked going rogue, pirating this cargo ship, and flying off on a mission Space Force wouldn't allow, but General Boatright has been in the middle of it all along.* Still, he was unsure of the reception he would receive—cool distance or warm welcome.

It was less than two additional minutes before Boatright came online. There were no pleasantries, but also nothing about his actions—just business. The general started in with a list of contingencies and instructions to get *Bat* moving immediately to match *Percheron's* new course. Once again Mission Control had recorded erratic firing of thrusters, and once even the main engines, as if someone on board was fighting to gain or regain control of the ship. The course correction was slight, but he'd need another ten minutes of two-gee acceleration, a couple hours to coast, and several minutes of deceleration to come up alongside *Percheron*.

Then Boatright surprised him.

"How are you doing, Shep?"

He called me Shep? Glenn didn't expect that.

"I'm sore, sir. I came through the acceleration okay, and five days of rest helped the recovery, but I'm looking forward to getting out of *Bat* and moving around."

"I'm sure you are, but don't be too eager to get out of your MILES. We still don't know what's causing the crew sickness on *Percheron*, so you'll have to stay isolated for a while yet."

"Yes, sir; agreed, sir."

"It's gotten worse, Shep. They lost Captain LeBlanc—multiple organ failure."

"So, who's in charge?"

"It *should* be Major Dvorak, the executive officer, but it seems as if Doctor Barbier is in command."

"What? How did that happen?"

"Her reports state that all *Percheron* crew are in unstable health. As senior medical authority, she's best qualified."

"Everyone went along with it? Even Gavin? He's still her boss in MarsX."

"Yes, but she's got rank, too. After all, the Force put her back in as Selected Reserve before she went to Mars. She went to active status when Bialik got sick. She's a Major, and they're going back to her commissioning for term of service. She's senior to Dvorak."

"Oh, joy."

"There's a bright spot. You're back in the Space Force, too—Selected Reserve, IMA—with your old rank, Colonel, full bird. The CSO called Resources Command directly."

"I'm an Individual Mobilization Augmentee? Thank you, sir."

"Don't thank me. You're under a microscope and on the clock, but I have confidence in you. Your Ms. Butler and I are working the public angle to get you all the support we can. Now, get to work Shep, and good luck."

"Again, thank you, sir. I will."

Boatright put Richardson back on the comm to wait for Glenn's acknowledgement and to transmit the course changes. They were also being uploaded to *Bat's* navigational system, but Glenn would provide immediate fine corrections as needed without the comm delay Earth-based remote control. Even with the additional thrust, it was necessary to slowly approach the ship to avoid drive exhaust damage, so he had a few more hours of waiting.

So, he waited.

After the latest cycle of acceleration, coast, and deceleration, *Percheron* was still not evident on instruments. He was about to call Richardson again when he expanded his tracking search to a broad spectrum of electromagnetic radiation . . .

. . . and there it was.

CHAPTER 27:
A Walk in the Dark

※

USSF Media Office @JBSpaceNews

Bat has rendezvoused with *Percheron*. MarsX logistics, NASA trajectory planning, and our own onboard Space Force pilot have succeeded in bringing two spacecraft together in the depths of space. Not since NASA's own 'Dr. Rendezvous,' Edwin 'Buzz' Aldrin, wrote his dissertation on *Line-of-Sight Guidance Techniques for Manned Orbital Rendezvous*, has there been such a feat of physics, mathematics, and human ingenuity.

ChirpChat, October 2043

Percheron showed up in infrared, but was not visible to the eye or on comm. Its tracking beacon was silent and it was completely dark.

There should have been running lights. It seemed silly that a ship built to spend six months in the dark, not encountering any other crewed or uncrewed vehicles, would need external lights, but NASA and Space Force had long insisted all space vessels needed to have both visible light and radio beacons in order to be detected against the background of space. At the very least, blinking lights in bright colors would be obvious against the backdrop of unblinking stars.

Nevertheless, *Percheron* was dark. He wasn't surprised that there was no indication of drive or thruster activity; after all, except for incidental course corrections, the ship should be coasting for four more months. The alarming fact was that the running lights were turned off and the automatic beacon that *couldn't* be turned off . . . was not functioning. What Glenn *should* be seeing was a brightly lit ring of rectangular modules rotating around a long, thin main hull with lights fore, aft and at the docking bays. The ship's beacon should be announcing its presence and warning him off of any potential collision.

The thing is, not only were there no lights, but the habitat ring didn't appear to be rotating. Astronauts traveling to Mars needed to maintain conditions equivalent to the Martian gravity of approximately one-third gee. On return to Earth, they needed to gradually build back up to one gee. Therefore, the personnel quarters on *Percheron* were in a rotating ring similar to wheeled space stations such as Clarke and O'Neill. There were also zero-gee (or low-gee during thrust) sections in the main hull—bridge, and some labs forward of the ring—and hydroponics, shuttle docking, cargo bays, fuel tankage and engines aft of the ring. Those sections might very well be lightly staffed at any given time during the journey, but the habitat ring would always be occupied. It should have been rotating and well-lit.

The upload from Earth included recognition and acknowledgement codes for *Percheron*. The programs were automatic. As soon as *Bat* arrived, the handshake should have been exchanged between the two ships. Soon after, the larger ship should have initiated procedures to allow docking. Earth-based Mission Control could take over, but the round-trip messaging time was fifteen minutes. Remotely operated docking would be an extremely slow and error-prone process.

No one had anticipated that *Percheron* would not respond to hails, and that even the automated handshake would be ineffective.

Well, Glenn and General Boatright had.

That was why Glenn was here.

As soon as Glenn reported that *Percheron* was not responding, he received a new upload from Richardson. It contained two parts, one to load into *Bat*'s computer for docking and navigational control, the second was for remote control of *Percheron*'s maneuvering thrusters. The latter program was almost sure to be a necessity, but it needed to be uploaded from the bridge of the larger ship.

Percheron was slowly spinning along its long axis. It wasn't enough to create any semblance of gravity in the habitat ring, so he was uncertain why it was occurring. It might have been a "barbecue roll" commonly used by NASA in the past to dissipate radiative energy received from the Sun and prevent one side of the ship from overheating. Unfortunately, even if it had been initiated as a fail-safe, the ship was now in precession, making docking even more complicated.

Precession was spin plus additional rotation not perfectly in alignment with the spin axis. Instead of smoothly spinning, the two ends of the spin axis moved in slow circles, much the same as a toy top just starting to slow down. If that precession became extreme, the ship would wobble and become unstable.

When the Gemini space program first began to experiment with docking two spacecraft, they had to learn to deal with wobbles and rotation in more than one axis— like precession. Neil Armstrong and Dave Scott docked their Gemini 8 capsule with an Agena Target Vehicle on March 16, 1966, but soon had to abort their mission and separate the two vehicles because a maneuvering thruster stuck in the on condition, putting the docked spacecraft into a dangerous precession. Once separated, however, the tumble was fast enough to risk collision or the astronauts blacking out from excessive gee force.

Percheron's precession was nowhere near that severe, but it did create dangerous conditions for docking. One contingency was to attach the two ships by a tether and "reel in" the cargo module. Unfortunately, as long as one ship was rotating with respect to the other, the tether would wrap around one, bringing the two together at an uncontrolled speed. Moreover, that speed would increase as the distance between the two dropped, causing a crash and damage to one or both ships.

Bat was small compared to *Percheron*, so it would

certainly be the one whipped along like a ball on the end of a string. Another possible solution would be to use *Bat's* drive to *pull* the roll out of *Percheron*, or even to separate *Bat's* cargo pod from the drive section, tether all three components together and somehow use counterbalancing weights to control the spin.

The chances of any of those solutions going out of control were simply too high to risk. Glenn would need to cross over to *Percheron* and take control.

The engineers had planned for this as well. The ballast foam dissolved with a catalyst and a high-frequency vibration pulse. Fortunately, the suit and vacuum in the ballast compartment kept him from hearing the ultrasonic burst as headache-inducing sound. With internal bulkheads separating the cockpit from vacuum-sensitive cargo, all he had to do was dissolve the foam, open the hatch, and step out. The MILES suit's propulsion system could take him on multiple trips between *Bat* and *Percheron*.

He would head for the open cargo bay with its blown hatch where he would eventually dock *Bat's* cargo pod, sealing it in place of the missing outer cover. There were personnel hatches and smaller cargo entrances, but none of those could handle the girth of the MILES suit.

Glenn had been on extravehicular activity many times before, but he'd rarely made solo spacewalks. He'd practiced all of the necessary maneuvers—under supervision—at O'Neill Station, but now he would have to do it on his own, more than two hundred million kilometers from Earth. If he knew the status of the personnel inside the ship, he might have been able to arrange a spotter. He could use a tether between ships for security, but it had to be detached before he entered the cargo bay, lest it become fouled on the rotating *Percheron*.

This was his challenge. He needed to do it himself, without a net, without a safety rope...and without hesitation.

Just get out there and do it, he told himself.

The cargo bay had an airlock on the inside, though more to serve as a precaution against accidental decompression of the bay than for working access into the ship. For one thing, it was smaller than his MILES suit; he would have to exit the suit and be exposed to vacuum for a brief time. There were three entry points large enough to accommodate the MILES: the two shuttle docking ports—one of which was unoccupied, since its shuttle was still at Mars; and the secondary cargo bay. Unfortunately, entering any of those places presumed personnel on the inside of *Percheron* operating controls associated with docking or cargo transfer.

Given that there was still no response to his comms, the best option was still the cargo bay. It was just a walk in the dark, plus a walk in the vacuum.

Fortunately, Glenn and his "handlers" had prepared a backup plan for loss of pressure during a long flight from Earth. Inside the MILES suit he wore a skintight garment with what were euphemistically referred to as "hygiene attachments." It was similar to a pilot's gee-suit, which maintained positive pressure throughout acceleration to assist in fluid balance and to prevent blood pooling. It would be sufficient to maintain his body's internal pressure against vacuum for a short period of time. He only needed about a minute outside of the MILES to enter the airlock. With the skinsuit maintaining internal pressure, he just needed a helmet and air supply. He attached a mating collar to his suit, then sealed a tight-fitting helmet to the collar. The helmet attached to a small portable air supply, replicating his comms, his heads-up displays, and providing access to a small stock of water and nutrients. It was effectively a second space suit that he wore within the MILES. It would not protect him from full exposure to open space—for one thing, it had no insulation, and he would get cold very quickly—but it would be enough to make the transfer.

Theoretically.

Glenn maneuvered the MILES across the gap between *Bat* and *Percheron*. As much as he wanted to stop and admire the view of unfiltered stars, he figured there would be plenty of time for that once he completed his job. He had to accelerate slightly to catch up with the cargo bay as the ship rotation caused it to disappear around the curvature of the hull.

He hit the interior wall of the cargo bay with a jolt. There were no warning lights in his heads-up display, so he likely hadn't damaged anything on the MILES. It was a plain bulkhead, so it was unlikely that he damaged anything on *Percheron*, either.

Oh well. Any landing you can walk away from, he thought to himself, *and I definitely plan to walk away from this one.*

He switched on the magnetic soles of the MILES, and commanded the suit to walk toward the airlock door. He needed to get as close as possible, yet still leave maneuvering space. He set his miniaturized spacecraft to stand by, and prepared to open the hatch in the belly of the suit, but not before making one last check to ensure that the control panel next to the airlock was functional. It showed one red and one green light, indicating that it was powered and registering air on the inside and vacuum on the outside.

With that confirmed, there was one more thing he needed to do. His bionic eye and ear were tied into a comm system, with electronics under the skin of his left ear. Not only could he receive comm signals silently through the bionics, they could also record and transmit what he saw and learned. He programmed the MILES to pick up and relay those recordings back to Earth. Colonel Richardson had provided a comm address to send the data. He would very likely be called upon to justify his decisions and actions. This was his backup and permanent record—not to mention his defense or prosecution if it was ever needed.

He was ready. He opened the suit, stepped out, and immediately felt his skin temperature dropping. Vacuum was an insulator; without a source or sink for temperature, he shouldn't have felt a thing. It must be sublimation of moisture caught in the weave of his skinsuit.

Glenn stepped over to the airlock and examined the control panel. He pressed the button to begin the cycle, removing the air from the inside, and releasing the outer door—but the indicators did not change. They still showed pressure on the other side of the door. The automated system appeared to be off-line. He activated the control again, and this time a new indicator showed a malfunction in the automated controls. Fortunately, there was a manual override behind the panel. Unfortunately, that meant heading back to the MILES and opening an external storage compartment to retrieve a pouch of tools.

Once he had the tools, he decided he'd better keep them with him. After all, if one system malfunctioned, others would also. He reached into the pouch to get a screwdriver, and almost dropped it due to numbness of his fingers. He transferred it to his left hand and used it to pry off the panel, revealing a crank handle and latch. He put the screwdriver back in the pouch, unfolded the handle and began to operate the hand pump. There was resistance, and he had difficulty keeping his footing—the MILES had magnetic soles, but the skinsuit was designed for interior use, and only had Velcro. He settled for bracing his feet on the motionless MILES, and using the augmented strength of his left arm to rotate the crank. He felt himself begin to sweat, which presented its own hazard, from moisture freezing on the surface of the skinsuit,

He needed to hurry.

The crank encountered more resistance, and he stopped to check the indicators. The interior of the airlock was now in vacuum, with only a simple latch to release the door. Once inside, he secured the door, opened the inside panel, and repeated the process to repressurize the chamber. This time it went faster, since he didn't have to operate a pump; after the first partial turn, the valve opened and air rushed in. His ears popped; the interior of *Percheron* was at a higher pressure than he had maintained in the MILES. With pressure equalized once again, the inner door simply latched in place.

He opened the door and stepped onto *Percheron*.

During the outbound trip, Glenn had studied ship schematics and medical reports and thought about what he would do on arrival. Obviously the first thing to do was to get the cargo pod mated with the larger vessel to enable transfer of food, water, and medicines. That had been obvious, but what to do once inside? Yvette had ordered all personnel to self-isolate. Should he also remain completely isolated? If whatever was affecting the crew was airborne or in the food and water, he needed to prevent any chance of it affecting him. Frankly, none of those *could* affect him if he chose to remain sealed up in the MILES, eating and drinking only from stocks he had brought from Earth.

On the other hand, he needed a place to eat, sleep and clean up. He'd been in the MILES for a week with no bathing and no change of clothes. The hygiene connections worked flawlessly, but once in atmosphere, he would need to get out of the skinsuit and put on some real clothing. He also needed a bunk with more space than the inside of the MILES. The second Mars ground-to-orbit shuttle was still attached to the outside of *Percheron* or he could repressurize the cockpit of the *Bat* and rig a hammock once some of the cargo was offloaded. Either option would let him stay away from the crew for large portions of the day with an air supply that was filtered in case he had to reduce exposure to outside contaminants.

The skinsuit alone wouldn't provide complete protection though, since it allowed limited diffusions of sweat and exchange of air molecules. He would still be exposed to anything in *Percheron*'s air. Which meant that since he would be exposed via his skin, he could open his helmet for brief moments as long as he turned up the oxygen feed to minimize exposure.

And that was a big mistake.

Glenn was pretty sure he stank after a week in *Bat*, but the first whiff of *Percheron* air suggested that no one was going to notice. He could smell waste overflow, organic rot, and possibly spoiled food, plus many unwashed bodies. It was a good thing he'd brought his own air. He closed the helmet, checked his oxygen supply, and even turned it up a bit to clear away the smell.

He had four hours of air before he would need to replenish. Hopefully that would be enough time to take care of his next task.

CHAPTER 28:
Old Flame

Yvonne A. @AlphaTeam21

Has anyone noticed that the *Percheron* website hasn't updated? My husband and I wanted to see if his telescope would show us the rendezvous. After all, we should have been able to see that funny new drive on *Bat*, but we couldn't see anything where the website said the ships would be.

Mars Exploration Consortium @TheRealMarsX

@AlphaTeam21, a server failure has resulted in a delay updating our websites. Please see our website for the latest news and exciting opportunities in MarsX!

George J @spacefan

@TheRealMarsX, what the heck? That doesn't make sense. Did you and @USSFActual trade chirp writers?

ChirpChat, October 2043

✳✳✳

There was no one in the corridor outside the cargo bay.

He hadn't really expected a greeting, but the rendezvous comm signals from *Bat* and Mission Control should have been noticed by somebody. He'd also banged around quite a bit during his landing in the cargo bay. While sound wasn't transmitted through vacuum, it certainly carried through solid bulkheads.

Still, there was no one investigating either comms or sounds. Not a good sign.

He knew that a direct route to the bridge, and the maneuvering controls, would not take him anywhere near the personnel quarters, since he would be in the main hull and not the habitat ring. Since no one met him at the cargo bay, it was unlikely that he would encounter anyone if he went straight to the bridge with no diversions.

There was no gravity, so he didn't walk to the bridge— it was more like a swimming motion. Each passageway had rungs up two sides. Under thrust, they would be ladders; in zero gee, they were handholds for starting and stopping. The central core of *Percheron* was designed not to rotate, so it was almost always in zero gee. Even now, the slow roll of the ship was not sufficient for any noticeable artificial gravity. This close to the axis of rotation, the only force affecting a moving person was air resistance or collision with another object. The handholds or rungs were designed so that an astronaut simply grabbed one and pushed off to start, or held on to stop. Glenn had plenty of zero-gee training and had learned to simply slap a rung with palm of the hand or sole of the foot, and to only touch one to stop or change direction.

As he started down the corridor, he caught himself in the learned habit of using both hands. He needed to limit himself strictly to his biological hand and arm. The risk of propelling himself too fast and having a catastrophic collision was too great for him to risk using his bionic arm.

On the other hand, Glenn thought to himself with a chuckle, *I should keep that arm in front of me to provide steering, like Superman!*

He was amazed that so many of the doorways he passed were open or ajar. Space Force policy—not to mention Yvette's isolation order—should have every hatch closed and locked. Civilian vessels would at least have hatches and doorways closed in case of loss of atmospheric pressure. He still opened the helmet periodically to sample the air. The smell would reveal much about each compartment and its status. The food storage compartment had a faint smell of rotting food, while the zero-gee galley next to it had a slightly burnt smell coming from within. This was strange, since zero-gee food preparation *should* have been in totally sealed containers and dispensers. The aeroponics garden, on the other hand, gave off pleasant smells of plants, water, and fresh air. It was the first indication that some systems might be functioning normally. Through one of the hatches, he heard a voice male muttering to himself. Glenn thought about stopping to investigate, but he needed to get *Percheron* stabilized and *Bat* docked, first.

He reached the bridge. At least *this* entry hatch was closed. There was a small window, and he looked through it. As he'd expected, there was no one inside.

He opened the hatch, entered, and sealed it behind

him. He also locked it with a physical bar to prevent any interruption until he had completed stabilizing of the ship. He lifted the faceplate of his helmet again—he would need the heads-up display in a few moments, but he wanted to look around and take a sniff. The smell was not as bad as in the corridor, suggesting that no one had been in here lately. On the other hand, it also suggested that *Percheron's* erratic roll could be due to malfunction rather than malfeasance.

The general atmosphere of neglect extended to the bridge as well. Several safety covers were missing— notably, the one that Captain LeBlanc forcibly removed in order to blow the cargo bay hatch. Many status indicators were amber and quite a few others were red; the low number of systems reading green appalled him. He could only hope that the maneuvering systems were sufficiently functional for next task.

Time to get to work. Glenn realized he'd thought that to himself way too many times, lately, but it was true. He reached into an outside pocket on his skinsuit and pulled out a small circuit board. On the back wall of the bridge was a cabinet, behind which were communications relays for remote operation from Earth, Mars, or one of the shuttles. Those links provided a failsafe in an emergency in case no one was onboard, or if those individuals were incapacitated.

At least, that was the plan. Somehow, that link had been turned off. Mission Control had attempted to take control, or even transfer control to *Bat* once Glenn arrived. The chip in his hand would not just restore the remote communications link, it contained the codes he'd been given by OSI to allow direct access through the wireless interface which operated his bionics.

He opened the panel, and checked the relays. As expected, the fourth one down on the left was missing. It floated in the bottom of the compartment . . . broken in two. Glenn inserted his chip, watched until it lit internally with an orange, then blue glow, accompanied by activation of his heads-up display.

Despite the fact that Glenn could now take direct command of *Percheron*'s maneuvering system, it still took nearly two hours of increasingly fine control of the thrusters for him to null out the irregular motion of the ship. Counterintuitively, he first had to increase the roll to eliminate the precession, then he had to cancel the roll. It was a complicated three-dimensional problem, and he had to take it slowly to prevent the wobble from getting worse.

Stopping the roll presented a further problem—should he restart the habitat ring rotation? If so, he would need to counter that force to ensure that he didn't simply have ship's core and ring rotating in opposite directions. That result would reduce the artificial gravity generated in the ring by rotation, and wouldn't solve his issues with docking *Bat*. In the end, he decided to leave the ring as he found it, and address that problem later, after *Bat* was docked.

By the time he was done, indicators showed that the reaction gas for the maneuvering thrusters was quite low—he'd had to burn fuel for some of the maneuvers. The gas could be replenished, as long as they had fuel for the main drive. He wondered if *Percheron* had wobbled because the reaction gas was too low to null it out, or if reaction gas was low from the events that caused the wobble. He activated the systems that would replenish the reactants before shutting down and locking out bridge controls so that no one else on the ship could activate it. That act compounded his piracy, but at he at least restored the Earthside remote controls.

He also found and activated the telemetry link to Earth. He sent a message to his own comm system on *Bat* for relay to Earth informing them that the automated attitude control and remote systems were back online.

It was done, but it had been way too much time since he'd checked his oxygen supply. From a starting point of four hours, he now only had an hour left. Still, plenty of time, and he always had the option of simply switching to ship's air, but he wanted to put that off as long as possible. It meant not cutting the time any closer than he was right now. He unsealed the bridge hatch, then secured it behind him. He considered locking it, but figured that the bridge control lockout, and new sealant on the comm locker, would prevent problems for now. He headed back down the passageway toward the cargo bay—and for the first time, encountered one of the crew.

Yvette was waiting for him just outside the cargo bay airlock.

She wasn't just standing outside the airlock, but was blocking it, her pose defiant. She'd grabbed a rung on one side of the airlock, and stuck a foot through a rung on the opposite side of the doorway. She wasn't in a skinsuit, but in a dirty singlet with short arms and legs—the sort of garment one wore underneath clothing that offered more protection and concealment. Her normally tidy hair fanned out around her head in all directions. She was dirty; her face and arms showed smudges, her fingernails had black grime under them. There was a sheen of sweat to her face, her eyes were red-rimmed and sunken, cheeks hollow . . . and she looked angry.

"I knew someone was here. I saw someone moving on my monitors and followed you, but you locked me out of the bridge. Who are you? What are you doing here?" It didn't seem as if she recognized him. Of course, he had his helmet closed, breathing only the air from his internal supply, which had now dropped below one hour remaining.

"Yvette, it's me. Glenn Shepard." He hoped it would be enough to identify himself. He activated a control with his chin to turn on a light inside his helmet. The light made it more difficult to see out, and impossible to use his heads-up displays, but it was there to allow a companion to see the face of an injured partner.

"You lie. Glenn Shepard's dead. Who are you and what do you want? Did you cause this?"

"I'm not dead Yvette, you sent me to Earth for reconstructive surgery."

"No, that's a lie. He's dead. I saw him die."

"You didn't see me die, Yvette, you saved my life."

"No, he died. I killed him. I cut off his legs and killed him."

"I don't want to fight you, but I need to get through that hatch."

"I can't let you do that. You're just going to let the aliens get us. They got the captain and they poisoned us. You just want to let them in."

Conversation and reason were not going to work if she was delirious. It gave him no consolation to realize he'd been right; in fact, it broke his heart. He'd told Space Force that a human was needed on *Bat* just in case the crew was incapacitated. Yvette was the medical officer—the one who *must* be healthy and sane in order to treat the rest of the crew. If she was delirious, it was a big problem. He needed to get past her, though, and he might very well injure her in the process. As a doctor, he'd taken an oath to first do no harm. Still, if he couldn't reason with her, he would have to physically remove her from her position blocking the hatch.

He was bigger and stronger, but in zero gee, that didn't count for much. Yvette was manic, and under the circumstances, that outweighed—literally—any advantage he might have.

"Please, I need to get through the hatch. I have supplies. I have food. I have water and medicine. I've come to help you."

"No, you're one of them. I can't let you do that."

"Yvette, please it's me, Glenn. Honest, I'm here to help you. I don't want to hurt you—but I Must. Get. Through. That. Hatch!"

She wasn't giving up. He could see the skin on the back of her hand turn white as she clenched down even harder on the rung. She tried to reach her other arm to a rung on the other side, and couldn't reach far enough. Instead, she reached back and grabbed the same rung with both hands and tried to do the same with her opposite foot to firm up her position across the hatch.

That was the opening Glenn needed. She'd had to turn

her back slightly toward him. He reached out and grabbed the rung she failed to grasp. He pulled himself close and then reached across her shoulders and around in front of her neck. She wasn't wearing a skinsuit, and there was no collar ring for a helmet. There was nothing to block him from trying a breath hold—but he would need to do it with his right arm—the natural one, not the bionic.

"Please, don't make me do this Yvette. I don't want to do this. I don't want to hurt you, but you must get out of my way."

She tried to bite him. Yvette growled and grunted, squirmed, and tried to get away from the hold. Glenn had to use the same arm for the breath hold as he'd used to grab the rung earlier. He was now depending on her to anchor him as he tightened his arm around her throat. This was the tricky part. To avoid injuring her, he needed to get the crook of his elbow directly in front of her throat so that his bicep and lower arm pressed against her carotid arteries. He'd learned martial arts for the exercise, but this was the first time he had to do it for real. He'd dreaded the thought that someday he might have to use it on a patient; he never dreamed he would have to use it on his former fiancée.

Yvette continued to struggle. She reached one arm up and grabbed at his. This loosened her grip and he kicked with his feet to pull her away from her handhold. They began to drift down the corridor now that neither of them was holding onto the rungs. She reached up and started to claw at his face, but his faceplate was closed.

She was so close that the interior light reflected, and was affecting his ability to see. He turned it off with the chin switch, and the motion rocked his head back. Yvette took that opportunity to try to twist in his grip, and they started to tumble. His head hit the bulkhead wall, and then her head hit his. His helmet took the impact, but an indicator turned from green to amber in his status display. The neck seal had been compromised. That would be a problem when he stepped out into the vacuum of the cargo bay, but he still had to get past Yvette.

Fortunately, Yvette's struggling stopped, and she slumped in his arms. He checked her eyes—unconscious, not dead.

They were still drifting down the corridor. He swam toward the wall, much the same way as a lifeguard—he was *not* going to let Yvette go, just yet. He grabbed a rung and brought them up to the wall. He placed one of her arms through a rung, and then pushed that hand into a pocket of her singlet. That should at least keep her from drifting off until she woke up. He moved back to the airlock and entered it, closing and locking the hatch behind him. He'd restored the automated controls while on the bridge, it was one of many systems that appeared to have been simply turned off. As the chamber pumped down, he turned up his oxygen feed. He could hear air hissing, and his ears popped. The neck seal was definitely damaged, but he could still make it. As long as he could get back into the MILES, he would be back in a pressurized environment, but with limited oxygen. He opened the airlock outer door and quickly stepped over to the MILES. He climbed in and closed the belly hatch.

Twenty minutes of air.

He looked out through the open cargo bay and couldn't

see *Bat*. Of course, he'd made quite a few maneuvers to stabilize *Percheron*, so there'd been no guarantee that the cargo ship would be in close proximity. He triggered a comm signal to flash *Bat's* exterior lights. He saw them blinking quite a distance away—maybe two or three kilometers.

He fired his maneuvering jets at full thrust. He didn't have time to waste. He also braked hard, and soon hit *Bat* feet first with a jolt. The magnetic soles held, and he walked back to his access hatch. Once inside, he inflated a pressurized emergency bubble, opened his MILES suit, and drank in the blessed, clean air. Even with the confined space and his own body odor, it smelled sweet compared to *Percheron*.

He checked the gauges on the MILES and his portable life support pack.

Two minutes remaining. That was too close for comfort, but there was no time to dwell on it. He had to get *Bat* docked with *Percheron*. After that, he could figure out how to rescue a ship full of people who had gone crazy.

CHAPTER 29:
Out of Hell, and into . . . Hell

USSF Media Office @JBSpaceNews

The data from Colonel Shepard's flight on *Bat* will be essential to understanding how to improve gee tolerance in all of our astronauts. When we combine that with the new drive systems that allowed *Bat* to rendezvous with *Percheron* in just over six days, we will soon be able to extend humanity's reach to the asteroids and other planets.

ChirpChat, October 2043

The first order of business was to change out the air supply for both the MILES and the portable pack he used with the skinsuit. Next was to see what had happened to the seal on his helmet when he hit the bulkhead. The *Bat's* cockpit was independently sealed from the cargo spaces, so he could pressurize it and get out of the MILES.

Being out of the MILES also gave him the opportunity to check his skinsuit and helmet. He could see that the flexible seal which mated with the neck ring had gotten pinched between ring and helmet. The gasket was cut two-thirds of the way through. He would patch it with sealant goo for now, a standard repair for anything short of large gaping holes. The goo was thick and flexible, and maintained those properties in both air and vacuum, making it suitable for patching to pressure suits and spacecraft hulls. It would suffice until he could dig into *Percheron's* stores for a replacement neck ring. Hopefully, once he got the cargo pod mated to *Percheron*, he wouldn't have to transit through any low-pressure zones.

It was also a good time to take a rest break to eat, and drink. He pulled out a drinking bulb containing powdered flavoring solution. All he needed to do was to add water from a dispenser, such as the ones in the MILES and in his compartment on the *Bat*. The military called the resulting drink "bug juice," but astronauts called it "tang" even though it wasn't the original trademarked orange drink made popular by the Apollo program. He also decided to splurge on a freeze-dried meal since he'd eaten ration bars for the past six days. The prepackaged, self-heating meal was quite a bit better than the survival rations he'd trained on, but he couldn't use the heater on the *Bat*. The heater pack generated hydrogen gas; *Percheron* would have a compartment in the galley with a recapture system for volatile gases, but there was nothing like that in the limited confines of the survival bubble.

Ah well, cold spaghetti with meat sauce is still better than flavored paste, he thought. *Plus, I have hot sauce, and that helps everything.*

He contemplated taking a nap before returning to *Percheron*. His last excursion had taken six hours and he was still a bit tired from the high acceleration of the outboard journey. Things were bad in the *Percheron* but would they be that much worse if he took a nap?

Logic said no, but Glenn's conscience said yes. He tried to suit back up, and found himself fumbling with catches and fasteners.

Sleep it is!

Six hours, another meal, a wipe-down with a moist towelette later, he suited back up, pumped down the compartment, and prepared to dock the *Bat* with the cargo bay. The process went better than his first spacewalk. He attached a tether and remote-controlled winch to the latch point in the center of the docking attachment on the cargo pod. He then fired his maneuvering jets and traveled over to *Percheron*, dragging the tether to a latch point on the opposite side of the cargo bay from the open hatch. Next, he went back to *Bat*, released the attachments between cargo and drive sections, and connected a reciprocal tether between cargo pod and the massive drive. The two opposing systems would serve to dampen any sudden moves, and allow him to control the velocity of the cargo pod so that it didn't crash in the *Percheron*. Finally, Glenn positioned himself just inside the entrance to the cargo bay and started the system to slowly winch the cargo pod between the *Bat* and *Percheron*'s cargo bay.

It took almost an hour to close the two-point-five-kilometer distance between *Bat* and *Percheron*. When the pod was ten meters out, he slowed winch speed; at two meters, he stopped it entirely. The pod was larger than the bay, so it needed to be precisely aligned to attach to the external hull of *Percheron* and seal off the open cargo bay. In its current position, the docking mechanism was just off-center and slightly askew from the cargo bay opening. The final positioning would have to be done with his own muscle power; fortunately, he had a bionic assist.

He climbed up the tether and onto the hull of *Percheron* so that he could use rungs set into the side of the cargo pod to rotate it to align it with the cargo bay opening. He ran additional tethers from the pod through rings set at multiple points around the inside rim of the bay opening. That way he could do the final adjustment from a single location inside the bay.

He climbed back into the bay, braced himself, and made light tugs on the tethers to gently move the pod into contact with the opening. One side was still moving too fast, and he reached his left hand into the rapidly closing gap. A flesh-and-blood hand would have been crushed, but he was able to exert enough force with just his fingers to prevent a collision that would have damaged the seal between cargo pod and bay. It took nearly an hour to finally line it all up and complete the attachments.

Finally, it was done and the seal appeared to be good enough to repressurize the cargo bay. Glenn had thought that the hardest part of his mission was over when he endured the high acceleration of the trip to *Percheron*. He now knew otherwise—he'd worked harder today than he had in quite some time. Frankly, he would be exhausted if he had a full flesh and blood body. His bionic legs and arm had made the difference both in strength and endurance. All of this would go into a report to Space Force, NASA, and MarsX. They needed to get bionically enhanced individuals out into space—he'd just proven that there were some jobs that needed abilities beyond the capabilities of a non-enhanced human.

Having that happen would be reward enough. Still, the job wasn't anywhere near over.

Much as it pained him to admit it, he knew that before he went back into *Percheron*, he was going to have to find a way to make the ship's crew aware of his presence. They were likely still locked in their quarters, since none of the reports said that she'd rescinded the isolation orders. The strange encounter with Yvette—supposedly the "most rational" of the crew—meant he couldn't predict their response to his sudden presence on the ship.

The relay he'd repaired on *Percheron*'s bridge gave him a local control interface only. While present on the bridge, he could operate *Percheron*'s maneuvering thrusters and engines much the same way as he had those on the *Bat*. Once he left the bridge, the distance was too far for the control linkage. On the other hand, the repeater in the MILES gave him access to internal communications.

"This is Glenn Shepard in the cargo ship *Bat*, C-21-MX, hailing *Percheron*. *Percheron*, do you read?" He'd attempted communication when he'd first arrived, but it hadn't been answered. This time Glenn was sending his message through all of the internal comm channels. He repeated the message a few more times and then added, "*Percheron*, this is Shepard. I've brought food, water, fuel, and medical supplies. My ship is docked to your cargo bay. I'm going to be coming inside soon, but I need to stay in my isolation suit for now. Don't be afraid; I've come to help."

There was no response for several minutes and then Yvette's weak voice came over the comm. "Glenn Shepard? What are you doing here?"

Well, *that* certainly did not sound like the Yvette he'd encountered in the hallway. Maybe she was a little more rational now. Glenn checked his intercom link and discovered that she was talking from the ship's medical bay. He switched his own comm from general broadcast to her intercom station. "Yvette? Yes, it's me Glenn. I brought a cargo ship with supplies and medicine to help you."

"I didn't mean for someone to come out here! I just wanted advice." Yvette's voice turned hard. Glenn supposed it meant she wasn't entirely out of her mood swings, but he could work with that.

"Space Force sent me out here. A crew member was required for final course corrections and docking. You also need a doctor unaffected by whatever has happened on your ship." That wasn't strictly true, since Space Force didn't send him, although it could be argued that General Boatright had done exactly that. The latter statement about needing an unaffected doctor was certainly true. "I'll be coming in through Cargo Bay One. Make sure people are aware that I'm coming. We should probably get them together and check everybody out."

"No! You can't come in that way. The bay door was blown and it's open to vacuum." Yvette's voice was back to normal. Showing concern and awareness of current conditions was good.

"That's not a problem. I've docked the cargo module to the outside of Bay One. It's sealed tight, and we can restore atmosphere to the bay to make it easier to transfer the cargo." While that was true, Glenn was still not sure about mixing atmospheres between *Bat* and *Percheron*. For now, he'd repressurize with argon—he'd brought sufficient for this purpose and for isolating and cleaning compartments in *Percheron* if needed. As long as he had pressure, he wouldn't need the MILES, just his skinsuit.

"Oh, okay. Let me get the captain, and we will meet you at the airlock for Cargo Bay One."

"Captain LeBlanc?" Glenn wondered to himself who she was referring to. General Boatright had told him that Captain LeBlanc died from liver failure while he was en route. The first officer, Major Dvorak, should have stepped in to fill the captain's duties, but Yvette had pulled rank.

"No, Major Dvorak. Commander LeBlanc didn't make it."

"Oh, I'm sorry to hear that. Okay, fifteen minutes?"

"Sure, that will do."

Glenn had not gotten out of his skinsuit, so there was little to do in preparation but grab his helmet, depressurize the cockpit, and go. He still needed to pressurize the cargo bay with argon gas, so that he could pass easily between *Bat* and *Percheron* without having to get into the MILES.

He considered other supplies. Did he need self-defense? Tools? Medicines?

He settled for a large flashlight that could be used as a club, and a small backpack with medical supplies—essentially an overgrown first aid kit. He would also take the portable life support pack and maintain isolation from the crew.

He opened a valve on one of the argon tanks and watched the indicators. He would match pressure between *Bat*, the bay and *Percheron*. That would help maintain isolation and hopefully keep the ship's air out of *Bat*. For that matter, unlike the previous time, he didn't intend to open his helmet at all since he would be around people who might be carriers for the unknown disease.

It was still cold inside the bay. Even though the atmosphere was not breathable, it was preferable to vacuum since it would hold sufficient heat that his sweat didn't freeze. The automated airlock controls were back online, so he could have simply opened the doors, since there was equal pressure on both sides, but it was safer to continue to use the standard cycle.

The indicators turned green, telling him it was safe to open the inner door into the ship.

CHAPTER 30:
Greetings and Suspicions

❂

Mat L. @MyWife'sCarIsASpaceShip
    WHAT THE HELL? I haven't heard from
    my wife in a week and now my comms
    are bouncing back as undeliverable?
    What is happening on *Percheron*?
United States Space Force @USSFActual
    @MyWife'sCarIsASpaceship, we are not
    permitted to release that information on a
    public channel. Please contact the USSF
    Resource Command for more information.
                          ChirpChat, October 2043

This time there was a greeting party waiting for him.
Yvette was joined by Dvorak, and a man in a stained USSF
jumpsuit. The nametape said Philips, which meant he was
the engineering technician who would have had to take
over engineer Scott's duties. All three looked worn and
haggard. Yvette looked a bit better than the previous time

he'd seen her, except for the bruise on her head. Apparently, she'd taken some time to check her appearance, but the other two were tired and there was something of a wild look to their eyes. Whatever was affecting the crew was starting to take a terrible toll.

"Hello sirs, ma'am, I'm Colonel Glenn Shepard, and I've brought supplies to assist." Glenn hoped staying slightly formal would be of use in setting them at ease, and soften what he had to say next. "Please excuse me if I don't take off my helmet. For now, I need to maintain isolation until we can get a handle on just what it is that has been happening here. I know that you've been suffering and that you really don't know what's going on. Earth is too far away to help, but that's why I'm here."

"Thank you, Colonel Shepard," Dvorak replied. "We appreciate you coming out here. Frankly, we didn't know that your ship had arrived or we would've tried to help you with the docking maneuvers. I'm glad to see that NASA was able to handle the remote controls, although frankly I'm surprised that they sent a passenger."

Dvorak's manner was somewhat wary. He kept glancing at Yvette, and it was clear that he really didn't know much about Glenn, his bionics, or how he came to be there. That also meant Yvette hadn't said anything about encountering him outside the cargo bay airlock...or she didn't remember.

"That must've been a long, lonely journey by yourself. How long have you been in transit? It must've been months," Philips said.

"We have an updated drive. It was scheduled to be installed in *Augeron*, but we put it in service early and added some extra boost. It was a bit of a crunch under heavy acceleration, but we were able to shorten the transit time." Glenn didn't want to go into the details; after Yvette's—and Captain LeBlanc's—alien delusions, he didn't want to trigger paranoia or anxiety that would make them uncooperative. On the other hand, lying wouldn't help, either. Best to keep explanations simple until he'd had more time to assess the crew.

"Ah, I've read about a new drive system in one of my journals. At least, the last one I was able to get."

Yvette gave Philips a sharp look, but he seemed oblivious.

"It's the Helicity drive, right? Constant thrust and no need for a rotating habitat ring? That must be nice, we've had issues with our ring this trip."

Yvette continued to glare at Philips, but she didn't say anything.

Glenn was a bit surprised when Philips mentioned the habitat ring. It was on his list of concerns, but neither immediate, nor within his expertise. What he needed to do was to find out what was wrong with the crew and get them treated. Then, they could get back to doing the jobs that they were trained for.

"Helicity2, actually. I don't know if it's possible to transfer the drive section from the C-21-MX cargo ship I came in, but perhaps we can see about putting that drive to some additional use. First, though, let's look after your crew health."

"It's bad, Colonel," Dvorak said, and Philips nodded, then noticed Yvette's expression. They both adopted neutral expressions and didn't elaborate.

"We lost the captain to liver failure and medic Bialik is suffering from pancreatic disorder of some sort—her blood sugar is erratic and uncontrollable. Several others of the crew are starting to show signs of organ failure. None of us is sleeping well," Yvette told him.

"No one has heard from the chief engineer, either. He won't answer my calls, and I've looked for him all over the place!" Philips said. He stole a glance at Yvette and muttered, "Of course, I don't get out much, now."

Oh, this is bad, Glenn thought. *There is some strange dynamic going on with these three. Yvette's reports said she recommended a self-isolation protocol, but they seem to be actively* afraid *of her. Could she have locked them in their quarters? Philips thinks the chief engineer is just missing, yet everyone should have heard the open comm as he was pulled into the Black when LeBlanc blew the cargo hatch. What is going on here?*

"I'd like to start by reviewing the physical exams on all of the crew. Yvette, please show me your readings and interpretations of the problem. If we have to rerun any tests, I've brought additional test kits and reagents, plus a few instruments to supplement what you have here." Glenn knew he had to handle this carefully. When they were residents, they argued over patients and treatments. Toward the end of that time, she had accused him of trying to take over and undermine her position as chief resident. He *could* just step in and take control now, but it would cause problems later. He wanted to put that step off as long as possible.

"Well, I've done everything that I can do; there's nothing else to be done about the situation. I appreciate the additional medical supplies but I really don't see what you can do that I haven't!" Yvette bristled.

"Oh, I'm not here to take over," Glenn said, thinking guiltily that he'd just resolved not to lie—and doing it anyway. "Someone needed to pilot the cargo ship and now that I'm here, Mission Medical asked me to send them the most up to date information. There seems to have been some trouble with the comms."

"That's just 'New Ship Syndrome,'" Philips said, this time without looking at Yvette. "This is really our shakedown cruise. There should have been much more troubleshooting done before we left Earth. We have warped bulkheads, sticking hatches, and the air and water are terrible. I suppose you can't smell it in your suit, but it's getting worse. Systems simply are not working right on this ship, so it doesn't surprise me if comms are down, too."

The whole exchange was making Glenn uneasy. The stories didn't add up, and their behavior was strange. Someone had deliberately damaged the comm—he'd seen that evidence himself. These were astronauts experienced in deep space operations—he *knew* the selection process. If the first officer, acting engineer and medical officer were as impaired as this conversation suggested, they'd be lucky to last the four months left to get them home.

Was there an alternative that would get them home sooner? Could he somehow rig the Helicity2 engine from the *Bat* to the *Percheron* and accelerate the ship to a faster rendezvous? They didn't have the solid fuel boosters or the liquid fuel rockets which had accelerated the *Bat* to the high speeds he'd experienced on the outbound trip, but he wasn't sure that would have been sufficient for a ship as large as *Percheron*, nor did he have the time to engineer the assembly so that it wouldn't fall apart.

Stop that. You're a doctor, not a ship's engineer, he told himself. *Concentrate on examining the crew and finding out why they were sick.*

He was likely to have to conduct the medical tests himself at some point. That would certainly play into Yvette's insecurities, and thus yet another problem he'd have to solve.

"One problem at a time." Glenn said it out loud, but it was a reminder to himself as well. First the crew health; he needed to solve that before taking on anything else.

"Well, Colonel, I'm sure you have things to do, and I need to get back to my ponies," Dvorak said.

Ponies? thought Glenn. *More strange behavior; on the other hand, it wouldn't do to challenge the comment at this time.* "Oh, I understand sir. I will let you get back to your business. Engineer Philips, I'm sure you've got to get back to your engine room as well."

"*Weel, them wee bairns're purrin' like kittens. They tend theysel's these days, but dinna ye be pushin' 'em. Ye wouldnae want them ta fly apar' now, would ye?*" The engineer's accent came as a surprise, and he gave Philips a sharp look. The missing chief engineer was Scottish— was this a joke? Imitation? Delusion? He'd have to look into what recorded entertainments the crew were watching. This could be a personality change or just copying a certain science fiction stereotype. It was still disturbing, though, when combined with all of the other odd behaviors he was seeing.

"Yvette, if we can go take a look at those records? I do need to bring myself up to speed to make my report. After that, I can let you get about your business as well."

Yvette didn't say anything, just released her grip from the handhold and made a "follow me" gesture as she started to drift down the corridor toward the med bay.

CHAPTER 31:
Incubator

✦

Matt L. @MyWife'sCarIsASpaceShip
Something's wrong on *Percheron.*
George J @spacefan
@MyWife'sCarIsASpaceShip, you really
think they'd actually tell us?
USSF Media Office @JBSpaceNews
@MyWife'sCarIsASpaceShip,
@spacefan, Lieutenant General Richard
Boatright, director of the USSF Office of
Scientific Integration, and the Moon, Mars
and Beyond Division, will be making a
public announcement regarding the SFSS
Ares Percheron this evening at nineteen
hundred hours, Eastern Time.
ChirpChat, October 2043

Glenn had been this way before, but instead of
proceeding all the way to the bridge, Yvette stopped at a

point where two hatches were placed directly opposite each other along the corridor. One hatch was open, in defiance of ship's standard safety procedures, although the other was closed.

On the other side of the hatch was a perpendicular corridor that arched up (and down) out of sight. It extended completely around the central corridor and served as the fixed hub for the rotating habitat wheel. Most corridors within the ship had at least one wall covered in hatches for access to pipes, wiring, and essential life-support components; however, this space was largely empty except for racks of vac-suits and emergency loss-of-pressure gear. On the other side of the outer wall would be a similar circular ring that rotated around the core of the ship. The transition between fixed and rotating segments was at high risk of depressurization, so there needed to be a pressure suit for every crewmember and passenger on each side of the connection. All of the hatches—fixed side, rotating side, and transition—needed to be kept sealed and secured at all times, too, so the fact that Yvette had nonchalantly drifted right through an open hatch disturbed Glenn even more.

He checked the pressure readings in his heads-up display. The pressurization system, at least, seemed to be functioning normally, so he wasn't too worried about following Yvette as she moved to one of the hatches to the rotating section—but not before he closed and secured the hatch through which they'd entered.

The outer hatches were about five meters wide, unlike many of the other hatches that were just wide enough to allow one or two people to pass. Yvette undogged the hatch, revealing a shallow room with another wide hatch not quite opposite the first.

This then, was the actual transition from stationary to rotating sections. The hatches had to be wide since they would only be aligned for seconds at a time while the habitat ring was rotating. The transition room was deep enough to allow several people—or pieces of equipment—to enter before transitioning through the opposed hatches into the outer hub and one of the spokes that led down (under spin) into the ring.

Once again, they encountered a hatch that had been carelessly left open, and Glenn marveled that the whole ship had not suffered from depressurization rather than just cargo bay one. After passing through the open hatch, Glenn again secured it behind them. *Preventable accidents were not going to happen on his watch!*

Rungs led down the sides of the spoke corridor, as well as a track for securing and lowering equipment. If the ring were rotating, they'd need to climb down as centrifugal gravity increased, but without the rotation, they could simply drift along the hundred-meter-long corridor to the ring. A retractable ladder extended from the end of the spoke to the ring "floor." It was designed to be retracted when the ring was not rotating—not only would it not be needed, it would be an obstacle blocking free passage down the corridor. He was unsurprised to see that like so many of the safety features on the ship, the ladder had not been stowed for zero gee, but extended halfway into the ring corridor—neither fully retracted nor extended. On the other hand, for once, every door and hatch seemed to be closed.

Several items of trash drifted in the ring corridor; more debris had accumulated near the air vents. The smell was worse here. Even though his helmet was still sealed, the damaged neck ring allowed in some of the stench of burnt food, unwashed bodies, and bodily wastes. Glenn was tempted to turn up his oxygen supply, but the problem with that was that he still only had eight hours of air despite bringing extra for this trip. There were additional canisters in the cargo bay, but he needed to turn his attention to the crew now.

Even before looking at the crew records, though, he should determine whether or not he could get by with just biosafety filters. Glenn pulled an instrument off his belt and examined a screen on its upper surface. The sampler included multiple chemical and biological sensors. It utilized a hybrid organic and electronic chip that mimicked many functions of liver tissue. Just as the human liver detoxified the blood and metabolized almost anything a person consumed, the device detected toxins, metabolites, contaminants, and reported on how those items could be filtered, detoxified, or eliminated from air, water, or food.

He was not surprised to see that the instrument reported high levels of organic contaminants. The fecal bacterium, *Escherichia coli*, was prominent; that indicated failure of hygiene—either the ship's systems or the crew's behavior. Of course, the smell earlier had suggested he'd get that result. Carbon dioxide was elevated, but not dangerous. That was expected in the residential areas. Likewise, the presence of complex esters and aldehydes—body odor—as well as caramelized proteins and carbohydrates—cooked food. What was surprising was high levels of putrescene and cadaverine. Spoiled meat was the most likely explanation, but it did make Glenn wonder what had been done with the captain's body.

Okay, best to stay sealed up.

He followed Yvette down the curving corridor until she turned into the only open doorway. The first room of the medical bay was tiny, with a single chair bolted to the deck in front of computer consoles and a diagnostic display which was showing medical readings from a patient. Through another door was a larger room with two diagnostic beds, one of which was occupied by the Space Force medic, Master Sergeant Bialik.

Reports had mentioned signs of a pancreatic disorder and difficulty maintaining Bialik's blood sugar within safe levels. Her case might be a good place to start, but Glenn first needed to access the medical records and interface some of his own instruments with those of the med bay. He started into the larger room, but Yvette blocked his way with a belligerent expression on her face.

"You said you wanted to look at the records to bring yourself up to speed. I have treatment of the crew in hand. I don't need you butting in." She pointed to chair in front of a computer console. "Use that."

Glenn moved over to the chair, used the rung underneath it to lower himself, and then secured the "seatbelt" which would hold him in place in zero gee. He could have used the wireless communication capability provided by his bionics, but chose to use the keyboard and touch pad. He tapped in the credentials issued when he'd been assigned to the Mars Three crew many years ago, and was surprised that it still worked. He stole a glance at Yvette; she had a sour look on her face, which probably meant that she took the active login as just another indication that he was here to force her out of her job.

He didn't have time to deal with it now, so he simply called up crew medical records from a point at least a month back, and started reading. There wasn't much more in the records than what he already knew. Two major illnesses that he knew about were prominent— Captain LeBlanc's liver failure, and Master Sergeant Bialik's apparent pancreatic failure. Two new entries, though, pointed to a disturbing pattern. Hydroponics engineer Takeda was showing signs of kidney failure, while third officer Katou was showing the first signs of liver failure, just like the captain.

Every female crewmember who had accompanied *Percheron* from Earth to Mars and back was exhibiting some form of organ failure. The men were all sick, too, although none were as severe as the women. The crew picked up from Marsbase were now reporting all of the original symptoms reported by the ship's crew. Most of that only dated back about a month, suggesting that either the Mars explorers had caught the disease from the ship's crew, or that the causative agent had been on the ship for some time. The crew had longer exposure, but it was still here to affect the Marsbase personnel . . . and eventually Glenn.

The clock was ticking.

Yvette watched him the entire time he reviewed medical records. He made a few mental notes that he would discuss with MMC later but he was hesitant to enter anything into the computer. Some of the blood work looked remarkably like heavy metal poisoning, and that should respond well to treatment—but would that be enough?

Yvette's delusion that he was after her job was still hanging between them. The problem was—it wasn't entirely delusion. He needed to figure out if he was going to continue to try to work with Yvette or just pull rank and relieve her.

She took *this job from me. It's mine by right, not hers,* he thought to himself, and was almost immediately ashamed of it. That was actually why he *shouldn't* just relieve her. He wanted to talk with General Boatright or Colonel Richardson about it first, but he suspected he knew what they would say—he should have locked her up after the attack, and not let personal feelings cloud his judgement. He had rank, seniority, and authority. He needed to do what was best for his patients, and not worry about his—or her—feelings.

Still, he wanted to work *with* her, if he could. She'd been here, he hadn't.

He wasn't able to insert an interface chip for remote operation. Yvette simply watched him too closely. He wouldn't be downloading the records for later review—at least, not this time—and would have to settle for visual inspection and downloading the long way—telemetry from *Percheron* to Earth and then back to *Bat*. The communication lag was down to fifteen minutes each way, but the number of relays from computer to computer meant he wouldn't receive all of the records for several hours.

☀ ☀ ☀

"Have you put Takeda on dialysis? That could also help with Bialik's blood glucose levels. For that matter, even Katou could benefit."

"Of course, I considered dialysis," Yvette snapped. "We don't have the facilities for it. You're just like everyone else—demanding that I do procedures requiring resources I simply do not have!"

Her response surprised Glenn. While not having the resources might have been true on Mars, the diagnostic beds on *Percheron* were the best medical science could design. They were equipped with internal components for dialysis, imaging, ultrasound, anesthesia, bone setting, neuromuscular monitoring, and even surgical support. The only thing Yvette should have had to do to implement dialysis would have been insert a catheter into a central vein and connect it to the biobed. The bed would do the rest— running blood through osmotic filters and sending the filtered blood back to the body. Even if she could do nothing about the cause of organ failure, she could treat the effects.

"I don't understand . . ." Glenn said. "You should have all the supplies in your stocks. Even if you don't, I brought replacement filters, solutions, and supplies. You've *seen* the designs of these beds. They were going to be installed at Marsbase on the next cycle!"

"You have undermined me every step. You would not let me make my own decisions, said bad things about me to Command, and told them I was incapable of doing the job. You wanted them to wait for you, instead of letting me do the job I trained for."

"Well, yes, it's true I wanted to go to Mars; I trained for it for years, too. But I never did those other things."

"Yes, you did. Now you're here to take over and finish the job."

Glenn said nothing. The problem was that her statement could very well end up to be true. Everything he was seeing indicated that he needed to dismiss her and take over. The records for the past week showed fewer and fewer entries, as if Yvette had stopped reporting on any but her sickest patients. If he said "No," now, and then had to relieve her of duties, she wouldn't believe him.

He should simply insert one of his control chips into the med bay computer, and go back to *Bat*. He felt a throbbing pain begin to grow in his temples. He checked his air mix, and saw that the carbon dioxide levels were high; that explained his growing headache. That prompted him to check *Percheron's* air as well. Carbon dioxide levels were even higher than he noted before; still not dangerous, but it could explain Yvette's belligerence.

"We're not going to solve anything by arguing. There are other things to do. I need to get back to *Bat* and start unloading food and water. I assure you; I did not come here just to replace you. I'm here to help, so perhaps the best thing for me to do right now is to go away."

The statement earned a scowl from Yvette, but she did at least offer to guide him. When Glenn declined, her scowl deepened.

Great, that just confirmed to her that I'm just going to push her aside, Glenn thought. *The problem is, the longer this drags out, the more likely I'll need to do exactly that.*

CHAPTER 32:
Shepard's Flock

USSF Office of Scientific Integration
@OSIGenBoatright

Mission Control has received several
reports of illness on *Percheron*. The *Bat*
experimental cargo ship, piloted by
Colonel Glenn Shepard, has delivered
essential medical supplies to the ship to
assist in diagnosis and treatment. At this
time, we do not know the full nature of the
illness. We cannot comment on who is
affected, nor the severity of effects until
we receive the results of Colonel
Shepard's analysis.

Richmond Times Features @JenButler

My readers may recall that in addition to
his other qualifications, Colonel Shepard
is a USSF flight surgeon who has served
on Earth and the Moon, and trained with

the Mars Three crew. I have full faith and
confidence in Colonel Shepard's ability to
figure out what is wrong and bring our
people home safely.

ChirpChat, October 2043

The next order of business was to ensure that he had a place to sleep where he could isolate from the rest of the crew. While going back to *Bat* was an option, it wouldn't be very comfortable since he would have to either rearrange the tiny cockpit or sleep in the MILES. On the other hand, *Percheron's* remaining ground-to-orbit shuttle had bunks for the pilots as well as a hygiene closet and small galley.

The shuttle was everything the specs said it would be. It was attached at two points to the bigger ship. An airlock transfer hatch connected to the pilot and passenger compartment, while a cargo hatch mated directly to *Percheron's* Cargo Bay Three. The latter was a three-way connector which allowed access to Bay Three, the shuttle's cargo hold, or the outside of both ships to facilitate transfers in air or vacuum. The personnel airlock meant that the shuttle's habitable compartments always stayed pressurized.

The shuttle rode on the outside of *Percheron*. It would have been unwieldy in atmosphere, but the Earth to Mars transfer ship was never meant to operate anywhere except interplanetary space. The shuttle, on the other hand, had a smooth, aerodynamic shape similar to an arrowhead. It had large fuel tanks, heat-distributing coating, and engines that could operate in vacuum or the thin atmosphere of Mars. In normal operation, it could make the round-trip from *Percheron* to the Mars surface, and back—twice—in one fueling. It could also land on Earth, but would require a booster stage to return to orbit.

The shuttles were intended to be a workhorse for Mars or the new asteroid bases that NASA and Space Force planned to start establishing in the next five years. They would pick up two additional shuttles prior to returning to Mars, leave both, and bring home the one that had stayed behind on the previous trip.

That all presupposed that *Percheron* returned to Earth, let alone Mars.

So far, during this trip, the shuttle had been unused. It meant that air, food, and water stored on the shuttle had not been accessed or mixed with anything on *Percheron*. Since the shuttle had been assembled on Earth and flown up to the final ship's assembly at O'Neill Station, there was an extremely low risk that it had experienced the same contamination. Glenn could always discard it all and replace with supplies he'd brought with him on *Bat*, just to be safe.

The risk was low enough that Glenn decided to chance it. The crew compartment was smaller than a cabin on *Percheron*, but larger than *Bat*'s cockpit. Most important, it gave him a space where he could get out of his skinsuit and use the hygiene facilities away from the crew.

This would do.

Having addressed the question of where he would rest and sleep, Glenn sent a message off to Mission Medical to officially request updated crew medical records. To avoid the question of why he couldn't just get them from

Yvette now that he was onboard *Percheron*, he cited the internal comm issues he'd encountered on arrival. The fact that he'd *fixed* the comm didn't need to be mentioned, but if queried, he could also claim he was testing whether the automatic backup of the mission records was reactivated once the comm was restored. That, of course, raised an issue of whether the backup *was* working, but he did still have direct access in the med bay.

It would take time for the transmission to get to Earth, work its way through MMC bureaucracy, and get the data sent back. He could deal with the contingencies of whether the data was accurate later. Now it was time to work on transferring food, water, and medicine from *Bat* to *Percheron*.

He still wanted to keep *Bat* isolated, which meant keeping the argon atmosphere in Cargo Bay One. He would use the cargo hatch on the outward facing side of *Bat*, and spacewalk items from there to Bay Two.

This was actually a good opportunity for Glenn to fulfill a secondary objective. He'd been told by George Mellies to make every effort to retain *Bat*'s drive section. At the very least, the Helicity2 Drive would be recycled onto a new spacecraft at Earth. There was even a chance it would be needed to send items back at a faster rate than *Percheron*'s Hohmann orbit. For that reason, Glenn had attached tethers between *Percheron*, the cargo module, and *Bat*'s drive. If he added guide lines from the drive section to Cargo Bay Two, as well as tethers to fore and aft attachment points on *Percheron*, he'd have a network to automate transfer of cargo from *Bat* to Bay Two.

Glenn went back to Bay One, reentered the MILES and returned to *Bat*. From there, he passed through to the other side, exited, and began placing tethers and transfer cables.

NASA preferred to keep extravehicular activity to approximately two hours at a time. Glenn had already exceeded that limit on the two previous EVAs—and he knew that construction crews at O'Neill regularly spent four to six hours in the *Black* at a time. With the previous hours sealed up in his suit, he needed to ensure that he had plenty of air, water, and food for the next step . . . and it was a good thing, too.

Placing the additional tethers and making sure that they were tight without introducing any additional motion to *Bat*'s cargo module or drive section took him another four hours. Upon completion, he had all components secure, plus transfer cables in place to allow him to transfer cargo from *Bat* to *Percheron* by remotely operated cargo drones.

He went back inside by way of the shuttle, so that he could leave the MILES suit in a place where he would not need to pass through either *Bat* or *Percheron* to get to it. He donned a thermal insulating garment, went to Cargo Bay Two, pumped it down, opened the outer door, and began commanding the cargo drones to pull pallets from *Bat*, across the cable network to Bay Two, and stack the food and water containers inside the bay. When he'd transferred about one-fourth of *Bat*'s cargo, he shut down the transfer, sent the drones back to *Bat* and repressurized the bay.

Percheron now had about a month-and-a-half of uncontaminated food and water in Bay Two, plus medicines and hygiene supplies. There was still more on *Bat*; he'd brought enough to provide a twenty-five percent margin for what was required to get back to Earth since they couldn't count on ship's stores being usable. He hoped it was enough.

Next, Glenn needed to start talking to the crew. He found Dvorak's quarters and touched the annunciator pad next to the door. It slid open to reveal the man standing inside with an open book in his hand. He was surprised to see a physical book printed on paper pages—but then again, Glenn also kept a few favored novels in physical form. Officially, books were discouraged in spaceflight due to weight and fire hazard, but a few prized personal possessions were allowed.

"Have you read this?" Dvorak asked Glenn, holding up the book so that the title could be seen clearly—Sun Tzu's *The Art of War*. "It's fascinating. There's a lot of stuff in here about making the first move, getting in the first strike, holding the high ground, and fighting back when cornered. You should read it; you might need it."

Glenn took the book and looked at it, then back at Dvorak. "What are you saying, sir? Do you think there's going to be a fight?"

"I'm just saying that Barbier is going to give you trouble. She's been a thorn in my side the entire trip and she locked us all in our quarters when this whole thing started. She claimed medical authority and she outranks me. Everyone else went along with her. I'm damned glad you're here. I don't trust her, and if you need to lock her up to keep her from doing anything more to injure us, I'll have your back."

What? Dvorak thought Yvette caused *the trouble on Percheron?* This was almost as disturbing as her paranoia. While he would ordinarily be happy to have Major Dvorak's support, he wasn't sure how much to believe. He'd seen Yvette's capacity for anger, but the attack earlier had to be the disease, not her. "Sir, if you thought that Doctor Barbier was responsible, why haven't you said anything?"

"Because she's listening to us—she's listening to all of us. She made us get shots and I know she implanted tracking chips and listening devices in each person. I've seen that display in her medical bay, it tracks everybody on this ship. She knows where we are, everything we say, and is listening in on whatever we're thinking."

It was true that the medical bay had a tracking system, but it was tied to the wristcomms and proximity sensors throughout the ship. It was essential to know the location of all personnel so that they could be found and contacted in an emergency.

Glenn decided not to respond to the latter comment. Let the man think he was taking seriously the implication that Yvette was eavesdropping on them. They spoke a few more minutes about the supplies Glenn had deposited in Bay Two, and Dvorak showed him the collection of "ponies" he'd mentioned earlier—several toy horses with brightly colored bodies, hair, and little marks such as hearts or flowers on the sides. The contrast between the Sun Tzu book and the children's toys was jarring, and Dvorak's manner as he showed off each toy was disturbing. Glenn disengaged as quickly as he dared, thanked Dvorak, and said he needed to go find Tech

Sergeant Philips to inform him that supplies had been transferred.

The engineer didn't answer the door at his quarters, so Glenn left the habitat ring and headed for the aft engineering office. When he couldn't find Philips there, either, he decided to simply use the ship's internal comm to send an alert to everyone aboard regarding the fresh supplies of food and water in Cargo Bay Two.

He could have sent the message directly via his heads-up display, but elected to use the comm panel in Engineering. Something about Dvorak's comment made him think about keeping some of his abilities to himself for now. The personnel display he'd seen in the med bay showed that most of the people onboard were in fixed positions, with hardly any movement about the ship. Using the comm or activating controls would be logged, so if he was going to keep his built-in comm to himself, he needed to be seen using a comm panel.

There was something else nagging at him as well. Dvorak had mentioned Yvette locking him in his quarters, and Philips said he "didn't get out much." The crew—especially the Marsbase personnel—were acting strangely. The first new person aboard in over a month, and no one was interested in seeing who it was? People he'd trained with for the Mars Three mission weren't interested in seeing him?

He expected to have seen nearly *everyone* aboard by now, and yet he'd only seen Yvette, Dvorak, and Philips, plus Bialik on the diagnostic bed. He needed to conduct his own medical examinations of everyone aboard—not to mention a post-mortem on LeBlanc, presuming her body had been appropriately stored for return to her family. The big question was whether he would have Yvette's cooperation or if he would have to do exactly as Major Dvorak said and push her aside.

This was his flock, he was the shepherd, and no one was going to block him from doing his job!

CHAPTER 33:
Ship of Lies

✦

George J @spacefan
  @OSIGenBoatright, you're the only one
  telling us what's going on. So, what's
  going on?
USSF Office of Scientific Integration
  @OSIGenBoatright
  @spacefan, please understand that we
  first have an obligation to the families of
  the *Percheron* and Marsbase crews. We
  are investigating an illness onboard
  Percheron and don't have anything to
  report, yet. The current Marsbase Two
  crew is unaffected. Colonel Shepard will
  get to the bottom of this.
  Please be patient with us and I will
  personally post updates as soon as we
  know more.
  —RB

  ChirpChat, October 2043

  ❊❊❊

377

It was time for another rest break. He'd seen no sign that *Percheron* was maintaining any sort of uniform day-night schedule, and the trip out on *Bat* had certainly messed up his own circadian rhythm. He decided to just work until he was tired, sleep, then resume his investigations. A meal and a zero-gee shower would feel good now that he had actual quarters.

He could also use the heater module in the shuttle's compact kitchen for food preparation. Freeze-dried spaghetti with meat sauce tasted pretty good when properly rehydrated and heated.

In the "morning," he checked his messages and found that the medical records had started to arrive. He had the records for the Space Force crew, and another message indicating that the records for the MarsX personnel were cleared to transmit but not yet queued.

This would do, these eight individuals had been first to show symptoms. He'd seen the records provided via MMC many times before, so he wasn't certain what he was looking for except for timestamps and the editing logs. These records were *supposed* to be untouched, direct from *Percheron's* daily data upload. If there was anything deleted or altered, it would show in the change log. As for information omitted or falsified—well, that was what doing his own medical exams would reveal.

So far, the only discrepancy he could discern was a six-day gap in the telemetry that perfectly coincided with his flight on *Bat*. It was a pretty big coincidence and may have something to do with the broken comm board he'd discovered on the bridge. While he felt it unlikely that the component was damaged by accident, that explanation was still a possibility. However, this new information moved it into the category of sabotage.

Everything he saw, everything he heard, said the situation was bad and getting worse. He couldn't entirely dismiss Dvorak's comments as paranoia—after all, he'd seen Yvette's behavior. He opened up a message window and started a new message addressed only to General Boatright. Despite encryption, every instinct said he was being watched, and he needed to be discreet.

General: Increasingly likely I will need to exercise rank option. Situation aboard in flux.

Glenn sent the message and continued reading and eating.

Thirty minutes later he received a response.

Understand the options. Additional instructions enroute. Leave the details to me. Good luck.

Another message caught his eye. He'd been copied on yet another complaint from MarsX that, as head of the Mars Three mission, Gavin Taketani should have been considered for command of *Percheron* when LeBlanc was removed.

Thinking on the matter, Glenn could understand why not—despite the honorific "commander," Taketani was an administrator, not a military leader. He had a Master's in Business Administration and a Doctorate in Public Policy from Georgetown University—perfect credentials for a project leader, but that didn't make him appropriate for a military command. Despite being a strictly civilian agency, NASA still chose mission leaders from a pool of multidisciplinary scientists and engineers with some military command background. Leadership of *Percheron's* Space Force crew required someone with military credentials and rank, no matter how brief the experience.

Still, it was odd that Taketani had not been part of the greeting party. Yvette had worked with Gavin for more than three years, and he'd certainly been a capable leader. Even without rank, he could provide counsel and advice. His absence was odd—much like everything else since Glenn's arrival.

Glenn accessed the internal comm from the shuttle and tracked down his former boss. "Doctor Taketani, this is Glenn Shepard. I would like to speak with you and find out how you're feeling and how your crew is doing."

There was an immediate reply from Taketani, but it was timecoded for a communication delay. "Doctor Shepard, so good to hear from you! Are the flowers blooming in Tucson? They certainly are here!"

Ouch. That was a signal often used by space agency insiders to suggest that things were not well. Flowers blooming on Earth—in this case, MarsX Mission Control in Tucson—meant that someone was grounded for illness. While few ships had hydroponics or flowers to bloom, the phrase "flowers are blooming" applied to a ship or space station meant sick astronauts.

Well, at least he's aware of the illness onboard, Glenn thought.

"Sir, I'm on *Percheron*. I brought food, water, medicines, and other supplies. I need to speak with you."

This time the reply took longer to arrive, and came in two parts. The first was a text attachment that consisted solely of a line of question marks. The second was audio. "I was not aware. Come to my quarters." This was followed by another text listing his compartment number in the habitat ring.

Glenn palmed the annunciator plate outside the indicated cabin, and Taketani answered. He was wearing a silk robe and held a small pair of scissors in his left hand. The quarters were a complete surprise to Glenn—after the filth and lack of hygiene he'd seen so far, the quarters were neat and clean. Every item in the room appeared to be placed with precision, including the leaves that had clearly just been trimmed from a bonsai tree located on a table in the precise center of the room.

Glenn had gotten used to the background of odors that seeped through his suit. Inside the compartment he noted their absence. Instead, there was a slight flowery fragrance. *Did this mean Taketani is unaffected by whatever is influencing the rest of the crew?* Glenn wondered to himself. *If so, that's important. I need to figure out exactly what's different.*

"Glenn Shepard, you're looking well. I must say that I'm surprised Space Force sent anyone out here. You must have been in transit a long time; how did you know we needed your assistance?" Taketani's tone was friendly, and he continued to fuss with his tiny, precise plants while he spoke.

"To answer the second part of your question first, I was part of the review team working with Mission Medical. As for the trip out here, they sent me out on a very fast ship. There are some new experimental drives and I had to endure some very hard acceleration." Taketani was an administrator, but he'd been CEO of a space habitat construction company before Marsbase. Even without a background in spacecraft engineering or physics, he had a reasonable knowledge of both.

"Ah, new drives and a fast transit, plus a mid-course rendezvous. How exciting! Just exactly how much gee-force did you have to endure, Colonel? I would speculate that you had to experience five or six gees. Did they put you to sleep for it? Or is it something to do with your prosthetics?"

Of course, Taketani would know about that. He always paid attention to personnel details. "Bionics played a major part. Blood can't pool in my legs or left arm. I also have a pump similar to an artificial heart that keeps fluids moving. I stayed awake for all of the acceleration. Let me tell, you, sir, six gees *hurts.*" Glenn started to feel at ease. Here, at least, was one person who appeared to be not just functional, but rational.

"Yes, I asked for a report on you. Some mid-level flunky in Space Force told me it was confidential, but a general came to visit me before we had to make the final decision on medical officer. He showed me diagrams of your bioneural interfaces—I believe he called them 'bionics.' He and others in Space Force wanted to delay the mission until you could join us, but NASA and MarsX said that the launch window was too critical."

"Perhaps it is just as well. Here I am now, able to offer my help. You mentioned that the flowers were blooming."

Taketani looked around furtively, then moved to the door. He thumbed the actuator panel, and it turned from green to red. "Hmm, interesting. She hasn't let us have control of our own locks."

"Sir?"

"I haven't been able to control when my door is locked or unlocked. There was a span of two weeks in which I was completely locked in. Yvette said there was a contagious virus."

"When was this, sir?"

"Right after the incident with Captain LeBlanc. Everyone was confined to quarters for two weeks. She told us it would slow down the spread of whatever was causing our illness."

"She . . . Yvette?"

"Yes, she told everyone that she was the highest-ranking officer, so she was in command."

"And everyone went along with it? Major Dvorak didn't challenge her?"

"She has medical authority and she outranks him, or has seniority, or something like that. He grumbled to me about it. I told him I would back him if he challenged her . . . and we got locked up very soon after. The locks released about a week ago, but I haven't particularly wanted to go out. Less chance of a random encounter with her, or any of her supporters."

"Who's supporting her?"

"The Space Force noncoms, a few of the Marsbase people, the nighttime housekeeping crew."

Wait . . . what?

"Sir? *Housekeeping* crew?"

"Oh sure. They were stowaways. Every ship has them. They used to clean up while we were sleeping, but they stopped doing that during the lockdown. I haven't seen them lately, but then I never let them in here—before or after—I do my own cleaning."

Neat as it was, Glenn started to notice a few disturbing details. Items on the work-desk were not just precisely aligned, but appeared to have been epoxied into place. There was no way Taketani could have used the stylus for his tablet, since it was apparent that both were permanently affixed to the desk surface. Other than the bonsai garden, it appeared that every loose item had been glued into place—or stitched, in the case of the bedding.

Taketani was affected by the strange malady, too. The man's normal neatness and precision had turned into severe obsessive-compulsive disorder. Worse, the delusion of stowaway housekeepers made Glenn start to wonder about the other things he'd just heard. Were they really locked down for two weeks? MarsX, NASA and Space Force had all agreed to Yvette's recommendation for self-isolation to prevent spread of infection, but that certainly hadn't been effective, nor was it as severe as had just been implied.

Did she do it just to prevent someone challenging her for command? Or was that more delusion?

The commander offered tea, and Glenn expected to be offered a drinking bulb, since they were still under weightless conditions. Instead, Taketani reached for an Oriental tea service. As he lifted one of the delicate porcelain cups, the saucer came with it. Glenn discreetly tested a cup nearest to him—yes, the saucers were glued in place. He couldn't see as the tea was poured, but when handed the cup, he found it to be half-filled with a translucent brown substance. It might have been tea, once, but not now. He touched the tip of his smallest finger to the surface of the "liquid," supposedly to check temperature. More epoxy, just tea-colored.

Glenn mimed drinking the tea as Taketani continued to talk.

"It's good, isn't it? It's an oolong variant I grew in the greenhouse on Mars. It's my own special blend!"

Glenn nodded. "Sir, I think it's going to be necessary to redo some of the crew medical exams—for everyone. Major Dvorak has given permission for everyone assigned to *Percheron*, but I'd like yours for the Marsbase One staff. With your permission, I'll review crew records and call each person in for a checkup. I'm worried that the illness affecting so many could put you all in danger when you return to Earth."

Glenn was ashamed of yet another lie—this time to his former superior. He knew it was a bad practice and he'd been determined not to lie to them—after all, this malady was causing people to lie to themselves via delusions and hallucinations. It wasn't a lie, though, not really; there *was* danger on return to Earth, but even more so here and now. Whatever was affecting the crew was immediate and it seemed to be contagious. He had only a limited time to figure out what was happening, otherwise this crew might never return to Earth.

Glenn simply could not allow that to happen. For one thing, he'd promised Jen. He'd also made a promise to this crew when he'd been one of them many years ago. He owed them; he owed them all.

※ ※ ※

As it turned out Glenn didn't have to worry about pulling rank or being the one to announce that he was taking over. His wristcomm announced a high priority incoming message from General Philip Bolger-Cortez, Chief of Space Operations, and Chief of Staff of the United States Space Force. It was a change-of-command order addressed to first officer, Major Maxim Dvorak, Acting Captain, *Percheron*, with copies to Taketani, Yvette, and himself.

Dvorak was directed to hand over command of *Percheron* to Colonel Glenn Armstrong Shepard. It included two addenda. The first was from Doctor Aaron Haskins, director of MarsX, which further instructed Doctor Gavin Taketani to turn over command of his Marsbase personnel to Shepard. The second addendum was from Boatright and MoMaB directing Glenn to assume the Chief Medical Officer role in addition to the captaincy.

So, this is what Boatright meant when he said leave the details to him. Interesting. "Hi, boss. Thanks for the support," he said to no one. It would be added to his sight and sound recordings as part of his personal telemetry. His guardian angel would receive Glenn's thanks later in the day.

The orders established that Glenn was now completely in charge, with authority to do whatever was necessary to get *Percheron* and her crew home safely. Once again it brought home the inescapable fact that he would be held accountable if things went wrong—that was always the unmentioned assumption of command.

Taking command as captain and leaving Yvette as

CMO would have been a two-edged sword. One of the loopholes in ship command was that the chief medical officer had say over whether a captain was medically fit to command. Of course, neither Master Sergeant Bialik— who *should* be the de facto CMO of *Percheron*—nor Yvette, CMO of Marsbase One, had relieved Captain LeBlanc of duty in the immediate aftermath of the incident with the cargo hatch. Naming him CMO as well as captain avoided the possibility she'd be able to relieve him capriciously, even as it removed a valid check on his own actions.

Everything he did would be scrutinized. Nothing new there, that was a given from the start.

Doing the exams would be somewhat awkward with him still in his skinsuit and wearing a helmet. He'd cleaned his skinsuit the best he could—there was a 'fresher compartment on the shuttle specifically designed for skinsuits—but he couldn't do anything with the helmet. He sprayed it with the same chemical used for dry cleaning of uniforms, rinsed it, dried it, then sprayed it with disinfectant, rinsed and dried it again. It got rid of his own body odor, and left him with something a bit more pleasant to smell.

On the other hand, the sense of smell is often a doctor's best diagnostic instrument. He'd probably have to turn up his oxygen and lift the helmet a few times to take a sniff.

This time, as he passed through the central corridor of the ship, he noticed that some of the previously closed hatches and doors were now open, while some of the previously open ones were now closed. The hatch to the zero-gee aeroponics facility was now closed—a good thing, since the compartment had been designed to force ship's air through the plants to freshen and clean it. The hatch to Cargo Bay Two was open, and he saw two persons removing food pallets, presumably to transfer them to galley storage.

However, when they saw him, they retreated back into the cargo bay and put the pallets down. Glenn could see that some of the food and water had been removed, so it was getting distributed. Unfortunately, the behavior of the two he saw—Grigorescu and Mishra from Marsbase— meant that he'd have to follow-up to ensure that the items had actually gone to common storage and were not being hoarded somewhere else.

Every crew member he encountered so far was showing evidence of behavior that would've been screened out by astronaut selection processes. Even latent tendencies toward paranoia, OCD, or hoarding should have been detected in the years-long training.

This time when he entered the med bay, Yvette looked up and smiled brightly. She'd put on fresh makeup and attempted to do something with her hair. "Hi, boss," she said in a friendly open manner. "What can I do to help? We need to start running physicals on the crew, right?"

He must have gotten used to tang of the ship's air— that or his freshly laundered skinsuit was affecting his sense of smell . . .

No, that's Yvette! A faint lilac scent made it into his helmet. *She's wearing perfume!*

As pleasant as her greeting was, it was just as disturbing as the other two personalities. Paranoid delusions, sullen and angry, and now bright and cheerful—none of those were traits he normally associated with her. Driven, meticulous, and circumspect had been her characteristics during residency—unless they were arguing, but that was mainly differences of opinion over treatment. Most of the time, neither of them was wrong, but they'd each had a tendency to stand their ground until forced to yield by higher authority. Of course, that same passion for their work had transformed into other . . . passions, but that was almost twenty years ago.

He supposed that the message from Space Force and MarsX could very well have produced a change in her attitude. Still, it wasn't normal, so that made him suspicious. After all, no one in this crew was acting normally . . .

. . . as she proved with her next move.

Yvette came over and pulled herself right up next to Glenn. She'd bumped him with her hip, which caused him to drift slightly away, but she reached an arm out, grabbed his waist, and pulled him close. She then leaned in and said, "I've missed you, Shep."

It took all of Glenn's willpower not to push her away, but to play along just enough to know whether this was yet another personality change, or if there was actual affection underneath her behavior. "Yes, it's been a long time, many miles and life changes, too."

"I've missed you in so many ways," she whispered. Her other arm came around to grab his shoulder and turn him so that they were facing each other. She briefly kissed his helmet faceplate and reached for the seals of his skinsuit. "You should close that door so that no one interrupts us."

Glenn was stunned.

Paranoid, then angry, now lustful. While their time together had been fiery, that fire usually came when arguments turned into passionate lovemaking. She had never been a seductress—this aspect was simply not her style.

Why did she start now? Glenn thought. He gently pushed her back. She didn't resist, but she didn't let go either. "Yvette, we need to do the crew physicals first."

She blushed and her expression changed slightly—less seductive and a bit confused. "Oh yes, sorry, work before pleasure. Shep always was a dull boy that way." The corner of her mouth quirked up in what he supposed was a smile. It was probably meant to be teasing—under the circumstances, a better outcome than the reaction to rejection that he'd feared.

"Yes, yes, work before play. Hold onto that thought for now, we'll get back to this later." Another lie. He'd been so determined not to lie, but here was another. Whatever this disease was, it caused its victims to lie to themselves, and he wasn't doing any better.

He *had* to do better. No more lies.

CHAPTER 34:
Detective Work

United States Space Force @USSFActual

We are sad to announce that *Percheron* captain, Commander Gee LeBlanc, and her chief engineer, Lieutenant Commander Angus Scott, have lost their lives in the performance of their duties. Captain LeBlanc suffered from a previously undiagnosed liver failure, while Engineer Scott lost his life to vacuum exposure during an extravehicular activity. We previously delayed announcements until the families of the affected crew could be contacted.

George J @spacefan

@OSIGenBoatright, is this true? And what about the widespread sickness that was reported?

USSF Office of Scientific Integration
@OSIGenBoatright

> @spacefan, yes, George, this is
> unfortunate but true. We haven't yet been
> able to confirm if Captain LeBlanc's
> condition is related to the illness
> previously reported. Rest assured that
> Colonel Glenn Shepard is aboard
> *Percheron* as my personal representative.
> He will get to the bottom of it.
>
> ChirpChat, October 2043

Glenn and Yvette agreed on an order of examinations for everyone to be seen in med bay. Her manner was completely professional; he hoped it continued long enough for the exams to be productive.

The most severe were Bialik, Takeda and Katou; they would start with those three. Both Bialik and Takeda were lying on treatment beds in the med bay. Glenn wanted to start with Hana Takeda because she'd collapsed about thirty minutes before he'd arrived, and she looked as if she'd need dialysis as soon as possible. The hydroponics technician was pale, with a yellowish tinge to her skin. She was also delirious—a sign of advanced uremia—because her kidneys could not remove all of the uric acid and other toxic metabolites from the bloodstream. Dialysis was almost always the treatment-of-choice under those conditions, and it pained Glenn that Yvette had not diagnosed and prescribed dialysis before this point.

Yvette and Glenn both looked for the dialysis tubing and cannula that should have been stocked in the med bay. They were unable to find the supplies, so Glenn simply directed her to open the large protective case he'd brought with him from *Bat's* supplies. In it were most of the items he expected to need that day, including dialysis supplies. Hana was already lying on the biobed, so it was a simple matter of unpacking tubing and catheter, inserting the sterile tube through a vein under the collarbone, connecting it to ports behind a panel in the bed itself, then slowly advancing the catheter down to the superior vena cava while watching the progress on a combination ultrasound/infrared/x-ray imaging monitor. Once the tip was at the entrance to the heart, the double-barreled catheter would both draw venous blood to pass through the dialysis machine, and return the filtered blood to be pumped onward by the heart.

Again, Yvette performed efficiently and competently, with no hint she'd ever been opposed to the treatment. What was strange, though, was that not only had she been telling the truth about not having (or at least being able to find) the dialysis supplies, the access panel for the dialysis ports was still factory sealed. In addition, the software menu for programming the dialysis was in a hidden menu and locked with the factory access codes. Fortunately, Glenn's preparations had included learning everything he could about the biobeds. It didn't all add up yet, but in this, Yvette had been telling the truth.

They moved on to Marta Bialik. Her pancreatic failure was causing wild swings in blood sugar due to erratic insulin production. Abnormally high and low blood glucose levels were beginning to cause extreme pain from damage to nerves in her fingers and toes—a symptom usually associated with advanced type 2 diabetes. With two biobeds in the med bay, they could also put Bialik on dialysis. That would at least help control the blood glucose and other toxins to stabilize the medic for now. Yvette prepped her second patient, and started the dialysis, which went considerably easier the second time.

With two crewmembers being treated in the main room of the med bay, they needed facilities for examining the other patients. There was an additional room designed for isolation of a patient with contagious illness. It was a small room with a single chair and an adjustable cot that doubled as patient transport or examination platform. There were fewer *treatment* options, but sufficient *examination* instruments to examine the rest of the *Percheron* crew. It also had an extremely large observation window so that he could keep an eye on Yvette and his two existing patients while he met with the remainder, or he could swap places and keep an eye on *her*.

The only problem was the door lock. It was meant to be operated from the outside to prevent an infectious patient from getting out. Glenn checked his heads-up display for med bay access, and found that as captain, he could disable the door lock remotely and disallow any other access—in fact, he was the first person on the ship to access *any* door lock control subroutine. It was an odd fact, especially given Taketani's comments about being locked in. He would need to look into that, later.

With that worry taken care of, he called Mila Katou to the med bay. Her condition was better than Bialik and Takeda, but just barely. She was weak, had evidence of recent small hemorrhages on chest, back and abdomen;

soreness of, and possible bleeding in, her esophagus; and several red, inflamed patches of skin that were hard to the touch. Glenn checked her eyes, and noted yellowing of the sclera—the whites of her eyes.

Much like the reports on Captain LeBlanc, Katou was showing serious signs of liver failure. There was medication she could be given right now. Dialysis would help with the fluid retention and once they identified the agent causing the damage, removing that cause should help with recovery. If not, he would perform a detailed tissue scan of the liver to see the extent of the damage. If the damaged tissue was less than two-thirds of the organ, he could surgically remove the damage and let the remaining good tissue regenerate itself. Worst case, she'd need a liver transplant.

There was a bioprinter on the Marsbase, but he was uncertain if *Percheron* had been provided with one. Still, he'd need some of Mila's stem cells to seed the printer if it was available.

Yvette must have been thinking along the same lines. "You know, we have stem cells banked for everyone aboard. They are in the deep-cold storage aft of the water tanks. We could probably work up a treatment for her."

That was true, with the right differentiating agents, he could resect her liver and regenerate it from a stem cell culture. It was worth thinking about. It also brought to mind the question of what Yvette had done with the captain's corpse.

"Yvette? I'd like to compare Katou's symptoms with LeBlanc's. Where did you store the body?"

"Gee? I mean, the captain? The same deep-cold unit. It's set at minus eighty degrees Celsius. The Marsbase crew stored seed, ova, sperm, and other long-term reserved biologicals in there on the outbound trip. It had plenty of room for the body. Just the stem cell bank and some emergency biologicals in there now. I debated putting it in the galley freezer, but figured it wasn't cold enough."

"What? With the food?"

"No, we stored the food in Cargo Bay One. It was in vacuum already."

"Weren't you afraid of desiccating it?"

"The food or the body? Don't be silly. Although, now that I think about it, Maxim wanted to store the *captain's* body in Cargo Bay One, and Gavin said we should just pitch her out an airlock and tie her off to the outside, but as you said it's cold and in vacuum, so that wouldn't do."

Yvette continued. Her voice and mannerisms had been light and somewhat playful, but now she turned serious. "That's why I had to take command and have them stay in their rooms. They act like silly little children, always doing whatever pops into their heads."

Now that *wasn't creepy at all.*

Glenn swallowed and cleared his throat. "Okay, when we're done with exams and can move Marta or Hana off of a treatment bed, we need to go get LeBlanc's body so I can do an exam."

"No need, I'll just tell Eric and Jonas to fetch her. They'll do *anything* I ask them to. Such puppy dogs."

Glenn desperately needed to change this conversation, there was a strange look in Yvette's eyes, and he'd seen something like it when she'd attacked him three days ago.

"No problem, let's finish the exams first. The rest of the *Percheron* personnel are next."

Scott, the engineer, had been lost during the depressurization of Cargo Bay One. There would be only the records of his symptoms and Yvette's exam. Without a body, there wasn't much else he could do. The other three males—Dvorak, Philips, and Christenson—were sick with gastrointestinal complications and some neurological symptoms. He'd already seen signs of aberrant behavior in Dvorak and Philips—the first officer had brought one of his ponies to the exam and kept cuddling and stroking it; the engineering technician answered all questions with a Scottish brogue, but declined to say *why* he'd affected the accent. Jonas Christensen was nervous and anxious. His eyes continually darted around the room. They seldom stopped, except when he looked toward Yvette and she was not looking back. Those times, his eyes opened wide and his pupils dilated.

He's afraid, Glenn thought. *No! He's in love!*

Glenn now had some idea why Dvorak and the others hadn't objected to Yvette taking over command. Their neuropsychological symptoms ranged from the sick—way too many; the afraid—and he wasn't entirely sure how many those were; to the adoring. So far, Philips and Christensen fell into the latter category.

The Marsbase personnel showed a similar pattern with female members more severely affected than males. Organ failure had yet to appear in any of them, but they all showed some form of neurological symptoms such as migraines, insomnia, anxiety, and something like attention deficit disorder. Doctor Melissa Green, the Marsbase botanist and dietician, was the worst affected—that is, if Glenn reserved judgement on Yvette—with erratic behavior that bordered on schizophrenic. Her brother, Stephen, the lead construction engineer, was also the most severely affected male. He alternated bouts of insomnia during the ship's "night" with narcolepsy during the waking hours, resulting in extreme fatigue and inability to concentrate on any complex tasks.

Glenn found the two quite intriguing—they were fraternal twins, with as close to the same genetics as he was going to get onboard. He expected any environmental contaminant to affect them equally. The fact that Melissa was so much more severely affected than Steve meant that the apparent sexual dimorphism with respect to susceptibility was real, and not coincidental to different genetics, exposure sites, times, or durations. He needed to be looking for something that was either made worse by estrogen, or counteracted by testosterone.

Surya Mishra and Victor Grigorescu, the two men he'd seen removing food from Cargo Bay Two, were the least affected, although their tests revealed high blood alcohol content. After those two exams were complete, Yvette confided that Dvorak and Taketani suspected the pair had built a still and were making their own booze. Given all of the other problems, neither leader had felt it worthwhile to hunt down the still and halt production. They felt that if the two wanted to drink away their problems . . . well, it was no worse than anyone else's coping mechanism. While Glenn understood the sentiment, it was his job to get everyone home safely . . . and sober. He would need to run additional tests to ensure that the two were not getting any metal toxins from the distillation process.

Habitat engineer Rachel Amit and geologist Maia D'Cruz were the final two Marsbase crew, and the last two females. They reported digestive problems, particularly a phenomenon known as "dumping" where the intestines emptied themselves almost as fast as food could arrive from the stomach. One of the characteristics of the disorder was liver inflammation, as it attempted to keep up with the production of bile salts depleted due to the extremely fast emptying of bowels. Aside from the recurring indications of liver involvement, none of this made sense.

On the one hand, some of the symptoms appeared to be consistent with metal toxicity. On the other, there were symptoms consistent with a gastrointestinal toxin. In either case, it was unclear if the toxin was biological or environmental in source. Neither the exams they'd just conducted, nor Yvette's prior analyses, had shown any sign of virus or bacteria that could be responsible for these symptoms.

He turned his attention to the possibility of metal poisoning from Mishra and Grigorescu's still. He asked Yvette if she had run tests for heavy metal contamination, and she showed him the results. The tests had been run over a month ago, though, and while there were traces, it was nothing specific. On the other hand, both were showing signs of dehydration now—and had been when the tests were run. They were likely drinking more of their moonshine than water, so it would have been easy to miss.

He needed more samples.

Glenn was contemplating whether an Earth virus or bacterium could have mutated either in space or on Mars to cause this malady, when twin notifications announced the end of the first cycle of dialysis for Bialik and Takeda. The system retained the dialysate—the fluid and dissolved substances—removed from the bloodstream of the two crewmembers. It could provide additional clues as to what was affecting the crew.

One wall of the med bay, adjacent to the one with the treatment beds, was completely filled with medical laboratory instrumentation. A small drawer was provided to input solid tissue samples, another for semisolids such as bodily wastes and blood, while two injection ports were dedicated to liquid samples. A small console allowed the doctor to select from standard blood analyses, biopsies, chromatography, spectroscopy, and pretty much every medical test the ship designers could include. After Glenn's experience when he'd had to perform an appendectomy—alone—on a fellow astronaut while orbiting the Moon, his input had been solicited for design of this med bay. Thus, Glenn knew what tests should be possible, and he'd programmed the treatment beds to automatically send dialysate samples to the "lab wall" for a comprehensive panel of tests.

There was still one crew exam left undone, but Glenn was deliberately stalling on that one. As he went to the lab console to inspect the test results, he reflected on the fact that things had been going so well between himself and Yvette throughout the afternoon. He was reluctant to change that dynamic by insisting on including her in the crew exams. He injected the blood samples from Mishra and Grigorescu and queued up a test for heavy metals before he opened the reports on Bialik and Takeda.

The screen first showed colorimetric and microscopic images of Bialik's samples. The first item that struck Glenn was the color of her samples—dialysate was mostly a buffer solution plus blood plasma with the blood cells removed. It should have been straw-colored, but this was a light bluish-green. Certain metals would cause that, but then, so would excess chlorophyll from green, leafy plants in the diet.

The problem was that the dietary supplementation from shipboard aeroponics and hydroponics wouldn't provide enough chlorophyll to turn plasma this particular color.

Microscopy of the Bialik's dialysis was relatively normal, although the presence of broken and ruptured white blood cells was high, which was to be expected from the inflammation and immune system damage that accompanied pancreatic disease.

Takeda's dialysate was similar to Bialik's, with a more distinct greenish tint, but similar cellular debris. Neither patient showed any sign of bacterial or viral contamination, and there were no fragments of parasites or fungus.

Glenn felt that the green color was important and programmed the lab wall to perform the same heavy metal tests on the dialysate that he'd programmed for Mishra and Grigorescu's blood samples. Takeda was awake, now, and looking better, so Glenn dismissed her back to her quarters to rest, with instructions to return in eight hours for another session.

With that done, he couldn't put it off any longer . . .

※ ※ ※

"Yvette time for your checkup."

"Okay. Do you want to do this right here? Or where we did the other exams?" She seemed to be taking it well and Glenn took that as a positive sign.

"Let's do it in the isolation room. We have all of our instruments back there."

"Good. We have more privacy, too."

Oops, Glenn thought to himself.

Yvette practically rushed back to the exam room. They still had no rotational gravity, so she just flung herself across the med bay to the open door of the isolation chamber and disappeared from his view. Glenn took his time, though, pausing to look at Bialik who now appeared to be sleeping comfortably without the signs of obvious pain she'd had earlier—even when unconscious. Her skin color looked better, too.

As he drifted through the open doorway to the isolation room. He felt a hand reach out and grab the neck ring of his ship suit. Once clear of the doorway, the door closed, and he could hear the latch engage. Yvette put her other hand at the back of his neck and struggled with the helmet catch as she lifted the faceplate and gave him the long kiss she'd attempted earlier that day.

He'd gotten through the entire day without even lifting the faceplate, but now she'd opened it and was kissing him. If the disease was infectious through personal contact, he was exposed now.

When she came up for air, she stopped struggling with his helmet, leaving it still attached, but only partially latched. She started removing her clothes.

"No! No, Yvette, you can't do this."

"Oh, but you wanted to examine me, Shep. I thought this would make it so much easier for you."

"In this case, I'm your doctor. I must remain professional, and I know you don't really want to do this. It's not right."

"Oh, but I want to. I want you so badly," Yvette replied in a husky voice. "I've missed you, Shep, and I want you. I know you want me too."

"Yvette, this is not right. Us . . . we . . . that was so long ago, and I'm . . . I'm with someone."

"She's not here now, is she?"

"Well, no, but . . ."

"Then she doesn't matter. I'm engaged too, but he's not here, either. You are. It's been so long, Shep, I *need* you!"

"They *do* matter, Yvette. We made promises." In the heat of the moment, he couldn't take the time to consider whether her supposed fiancé was real or imaginary. He had to take that at face value for now.

She was completely naked and pressed herself against him. He was still in his skinsuit; the tight weave dulled sensations on his skin, but not completely. Moreover, he could feel her body heat radiating through the thin material. It was starting to invoke a physical reaction . . . he needed to stop this.

"Yvette, this isn't right. You're acting irrationally." As soon as the words were out of his mouth. He knew it was a mistake.

"Irrational? You think I'm irrational!" Just that quickly, Yvette's mood changed. Now instead of trying to get him out of his skinsuit, Yvette started scratching and clawing at him. She braced her feet on the table and pushed him forcefully toward the ceiling, causing him to hit the bulkhead hard enough for the back of his head to hit the inside of his helmet.

That hurt, he thought to himself.

He also felt the helmet separate from the neck ring even though the latch was still partially engaged. His own motion made the helmet come loose and start to drift. With a damaged helmet and neck ring, his plan of trying to remaining isolated—at least from the rest of the crew—while solving the mysterious disease was now completely out of the question. The helmet separation also caused his self-contained air supply to cut off. He was breathing ship's air, now. He hoped the causative agent wasn't airborne, or at least that it wouldn't affect him quickly.

That was for later. Right now, he was under attack and needed to stop Yvette before she hurt him.

There was a spray hypodermic of midazolam on the instrument table over by the cot. It was a strong sedative that was good for stopping seizures. It would also work to at least slow down a person intent on violence. Glenn had included it as a precaution in case any of the other crew had been irrational.

The problem of course, was that it was on the opposite side of the room, and Yvette was coming at him, swinging her fists. In zero gee, the motions were causing her whole body to twist and drift off course, but she was still between him and the table. She began to scream at him, that he was "working for them" and here to "take us all away." Her eyes were wild and unfocused.

As soon as Yvette's motions brought her close to Glenn, she tried to hit him on the head, even though that sent her tumbling back in the opposite direction. The next approach, she extended her fingers and attempted to jab at his eyes. His helmet was also drifting about the room—out of reach, of course—so he had no protection other than to put his arm across his eyes and attempt to push her away with the other hand.

The drifting helmet hit the instrument table, and now the hypo, scissors, a biopsy needle and various bits of gauze and tape joined the floating mess. She grabbed at his ears, pulled him close, and tried to bite him. Fortunately, that brought him closer to the drifting implements and he grabbed the spray hypo. Instead of attempting to turn toward Yvette, he hooked his feet below the cot and waited for her to come at him again while he held the hypo low and to his side. When she reached out again to claw at his face, he grabbed the side of her neck with one hand, pressed the autoinjector in the hollow just under her collarbone and triggered the injection.

Unfortunately, no matter how fast acting, the sedative didn't work immediately, and he needed to push her away and try to keep his distance, lest she actually manage to catch his eyes or ears again. They struggled for several more minutes, while Glenn accumulated scratches. Since he was still wearing his skinsuit, his head and neck were the only things she could reach.

Eventually Yvette stopped fighting and her body went limp. She drifted slowly across the exam room, and Glenn took a moment to catch his breath before he pulled himself to the bulkhead, then reached out to grab the sedated woman and strap her down to the cot. It occurred to him that he still had not done her examination. Given his concerns with how she would react, this was the time to do it. As much as it disturbed him to be examining an unconscious, naked woman—he had to do it.

The exam revealed that she was exhibiting early signs of organ failure. More importantly, she was suffering from encephalitis. The fluid-filled membrane protecting the surface of the brain had become inflamed, putting pressure on the frontal and prefrontal cortex—areas associated with personality and the ability to make rational decisions. Of all of the crew, this reaction was unique to Yvette, but it also explained her irrational actions and changes in personality.

It was also a clue.

There was a particular metal toxicity that could account for everything—every symptom from insomnia to encephalitis—including the irrational behavior of Yvette, Taketani's OCD, and LeBlanc's hallucinations.

He just needed to check the blood and dialysate tests for copper. If he was right, the detective work was over. He needed to find the source and start the crew on chelation treatments. It would stop the deterioration, and reverse the symptoms . . . if he was in time.

He *had* to be. Failure was not an option.

CHAPTER 35:
Under Pressure

❖

Richmond Times Features @JenButler
    Tonight's stream features Mission Medical
    Command, the consolidated team of
    physicians, surgeons, and specialists
    serving NASA and MarsX. We'll also dive
    into the training of USSF flight surgeons.
    Join us in an exploration of the fascinating
    work these highly-trained doctors bring to
    our space missions. *Stream it now
    @RTFchannel11016.*
                    ChirpChat, October 2043

Glenn felt confident as he headed into the main room to
check the toxin analysis results. Something nagged at him
as he closed and latched the door to the isolation room. It
was something about the little room and security, but he
couldn't place it.

First, he needed to check on his patients.

When he'd dismissed Takeda to her quarters, Katou had taken her place and was currently asleep, dialysis finished for now. He checked her condition and set the treatment bed to keep her sedated for the next eight hours so that she could rest. Glenn decided to keep her catheter connected to the treatment bed to facilitate administering the sedative.

Bialik moved slightly and her eyes shifted back and forth beneath the closed eyelids. The readout on the treatment bed indicated that the medic was currently in normal REM sleep, and not showing signs of pain or discomfort. She still needed rest, and the treatment program was due to re-dose her with a sedative in ten minutes. Pancreatic failure didn't typically require dialysis except in severe cases. He might have to surgically implant a dialysis port later, but for now he could disconnect her from the treatment bed. He programmed an immediate dose of sedative instead of waiting, then removed the tubing and capped the catheter for the time being.

He was satisfied that dialysis had been the right call. It would have removed copper from their bloodstreams, if that was indeed the culprit. At the very least, he'd taken steps to keep the deterioration from getting worse. Copper could still linger in cells and lymph fluids, but that could be handled with chelation treatment. Still, these results were one more indication that he was on the right track.

Now to confirm it.

He sat at the console for the lab wall—or rather, pulled himself to the seat and pressed his knees under the console to keep from drifting away. He reached into his belt pouch and pulled out one of his remote chips. The interface behind the analyzer panel was tied into the whole med bay informatics system. He would finally get the remote access he hadn't been able to do while Yvette was watching.

Once the chip was installed, he pulled up the results in his heads-up display. Each of the tests—Bialik and Takeda's dialysate, Mishra and Grigorescu's blood samples—showed high levels of copper.

Now, where's it coming from?

As he had just seen with Bialik and Takeda, the crew could be treated. If the source was in their food or water, it wouldn't matter, since he'd brought replacements from Earth. If it was some other environmental source, though, he needed to find it and shut it off. The tests indicated that ceruloplasmin levels were very high, as well as unbound copper—elemental copper, copper sulfate, copper nitrate, copper arsenate, copper chromate and other salts—this was important for Mishra and Grigorescu's diagnosis, since ceruloplasmin was the body's carrier of copper for normal metabolic functions, as well as ridding the body of excess. Copper sulfate was a soluble component of fungicides and bactericides. He found some metal salts in the results, too, implying that the source was associated with corroded metal, but it wasn't enough to point to the illicit still. Copper sulfate and copper salts were common in many of the agents used to keep fungal growth down in the warm, moist, closed atmosphere of a spaceship. There was still a chance that there was a solid source for the contaminant, but the mostly likely way each crewmember would have been exposed would be the water supply.

There was a water dispenser in the small room with desk and console through which one entered the med bay from the main corridor. Glenn grabbed a syringe and went to the office to get a sample of drinking water. He opened the dispenser valve for just a moment, and a small globule of water formed on the mouth of the tube. He used the syringe to suck up the water, then returned to the analysis wall, injected the sample, then waited for a result.

Copper sulfate.

Time to go looking for copper in the water tanks.

Glenn started out of the med bay, and was hit by the smell of the atmosphere of the rest of the ship. While conducting the exams, he'd increased filtration and airflow in the enclosed medical facility. With his helmet off—and now that he understood the causative agent, he could leave it off—he was hit with the bad smell of the ship's general air supply.

It reminded him both that he had left his helmet in the isolation room where Yvette had knocked it off during their fight, and that he no longer needed his own air supply. He would need it if he planned to enter any of the huge water storage tanks, though; they wouldn't have airflow except through the open inspection hatches. Descending into a tank would require him to bring his own air along.

Yvette was still unconscious from the sedative. As he retrieved his helmet, Glenn realized he had another problem—he was about to leave the med bay, having locked the ship's medical officer in a room, strapped to a cot. Acting captain or not—*superior officer* or not—this was not the sort of action that could go undocumented. Before starting his scavenger hunt, he needed to record a report to Earth.

He wouldn't have trouble with the diagnosis, metal toxicities had been briefly discussed during the pre-*Bat* medical discussions. They had only been dismissed because the teams had been fixated on bacteria or viral causes. He now had definitive tests that showed copper levels were abnormally high. He'd attach those to the report and send it along for information, but make it clear that he had the treatment plan in hand.

As for treating the crew, he planned to use the decades-old standard treatments of penicillamine and dimercaprol. Both were chelating agents to remove excess heavy metals from the body, although they had different routes of administration. Penicillamine could be taken in pill or liquid form by mouth; dimercaprol, also called "British Anti-lewisite," would have to be administered by injection into muscle, so he'd have to call each of the crew back in for shots. There was also a newer treatment with alpha-lipoic acid—an antioxidant with good effect at chelating unbound copper from tissues. It was a common dietary supplement, and he'd brought sufficient stock in *Bat* to treat the crew.

No, the part of his report that would create problems would be the diagnosis of paranoia in First Officer Dvorak, debilitating OCD in Marsbase commander Taketani, and paranoid delusions with schizophrenia-like symptoms in Medical Officer Barbier. Command teams distributed authority precisely so that ultimate authority was not held by any one person. While it was true that a ship's captain was in full command, questionable decisions could be countermanded when first officer and medical officer agreed. Glenn Shepard had been effectively made captain of *Percheron and* commander of the returning Marsbase crew, but the command triad was broken. He had declared both of his potential seconds-in-command— as well as the medical officer—unfit for duty.

He was truly alone, so he'd better be right.

Once more, Glenn transited out of the habitat ring to the ship's core. For the first time since he'd started the medical exams, he realized how much time had passed. He and Yvette had done twelve exams on the ambulatory crew members, as well as two more on Bialik and Takeda. That was fourteen exams—most about thirty minutes, but several had run much longer. They'd also set up three dialysis treatments and the blood, urine, and dialysate analyses. Altogether, he could account for nine hours just on the medical procedures alone. However, that didn't include the fight with Yvette, her exam, securing her, getting Bialik disconnected, and reading the analyses. It had been twelve hours since he'd entered the med bay, and he was feeling the strain. He should go to the bridge and make the report, then back to his shuttle to eat and rest.

The problem was Yvette—she was unconscious in the med bay, and he needed to make his report and inspect the water tank before she woke up.

All he really needed was a ration bar, some tang, and an extra oxygen canister. He'd need the air if he went inside the water tanks—which he admitted to himself was increasingly likely—but it shouldn't require too much more than a single recharge. After all, he'd been breathing ship air for some time now. There were spare air packs scattered throughout the ship, and they were compatible with his suit. It was more important to get reports and messages sent to Earth now that he had an answer, or at least the first part of one.

He didn't even have to go to the bridge to use the comm. The belt pouch of his skinsuit had a ration bar and couple of drink bulbs, and he'd grab an oxygen canister on the way. He dictated a report for Mission Control as he made his way back toward the cargo section. The interface chip in the med bay workstation gave him full access to the medical records and instrument displays on his heads-up display. That same system allowed him to store data and individual views, so he simply attached those files to messages sent directly from his interface to *Percheron*'s bridge comm console, and from there to Earth.

The eye prosthetic not only wrote visual information to an electrode interfaced to the still-intact retina of his left eye, but read information in the visual association areas of his brain. Their purpose was to help focus and refine visual input depending on where he was looking in his visual field, and on which items he focused his attention. It also functioned as a virtual "keyboard" interface in which all he had to do was focus on letters and numbers superimposed over his vision. Using the interface, Glenn's search for files to attach to the report had also revealed time-indexed "snapshots" of his day.

Each was an audio and video clip of varying length, which occurred both at regular intervals, and at events throughout the day when he'd been most stressed. He knew his bionics spied on him; after all, he'd activated the "bodycam" recording function when he boarded *Percheron*. This particular system had done him a great favor, though. He was able to find records of the fights with Yvette, Dvorak's paranoia, and Taketani's delusional OCD. He attached those records as an addendum to his original report and sent those to Earth as well.

Current communications lag was fifteen-and-a-half minutes each way, just over thirty-one minutes for a round-trip message, assuming that Earth answered as soon as they received his report. However, it would take time for the report to go from the comm station to the flight director, through MMC, and up to the director level at NASA, MarsX and Space Force. It would be hours before he could expect a response. There was no point in waiting, so he also recorded messages to Dvorak and Taketani to briefly describe his findings. He ended each message with the information that medical officer Barbier had attacked him and he had secured her in the med bay. She should be okay for the hour or two it would take him to complete his next investigation, but he wanted others to know where she was in case it took him longer than anticipated.

Glenn found himself standing in front of the inspection hatch for Internal Water Storage Three. Normally at this stage of the voyage, *Percheron* would still be drawing water from the second of the four large internal tanks.

IWS One was meant to service the *Percheron* and outbound Marsbase crew during the journey from Earth to Mars. With reduced numbers aboard during the stay at Mars as the Marsbase crews switched off down on the planet, IWS Two would suffice for the entire stay at Mars and well into the return journey. The crew would use approximately half of IWS Three for the rest of the trip back to Earth, leaving IWS Four completely in reserve. However, a malfunction in the IWS Two distribution valves occurred forty-five days into the three-month Mars orbit phase.

The remainder of the water in Tank Two was still there, inaccessible until the ship returned to the dockyard at O'Neill Station. Moreover, the water intended for sterilization by exposure to space radiation had been drawn from IWS Four. Not only was nearly one-fourth of their water supply inaccessible, almost the same amount had been lost when Captain LeBlanc blew the hatch and decompressed Cargo Bay One.

There was additional water storage in external water supply tanks—EWS One through Six—but those tanks were much smaller, and were primarily "gray water" tanks, meant to store wastewater from the hygiene facilities, hydroponics, and cooling systems. It could be filtered and recycled—and was, if needed—but as is, it also served as radiation shielding for *Percheron*'s emergency shelters and core.

Approximately forty-five percent of Tank Three's water remained. It had been in use full use for only three months, and partial use for a month and a-half before that, so this was to be expected. Free water in zero gee was hazardous to humans—it was possible to get trapped in a bubble and not be able to swim one's way out. Glenn needed to move the remaining water out of Tank Two, and he had a choice of sending it to IWS One or Four. Tank One was completely empty, while Tank Four was still fifteen percent full. A control console outside the inspection hatch to Tank Three allowed Glenn to transfer the remaining—presumably copper-contaminated—water to Tank One, preserving the hopefully clean water remaining in Tank Four.

CHAPTER 36:
Crisis

USSF Office of Scientific Integration
@OSIGenBoatright

(1/2) We can now report that the unknown illness affecting *Percheron* has been identified as resulting from an overdose of copper from the treatments intended to reduce fungal and bacterial growth in humid, closed-air spaces. It is not contagious, and has not affected the current Marsbase Two mission. The condition is easily treated, but will take time for individuals to fully recover.

(2/2) Since all *Percheron* and returning Marsbase personnel are affected to varying degrees—including Acting-Captain Dvorak, Marsbase One Director Taketani, and Medical Officer Barbier—USSF today directed Colonel Glenn A. Shepard to assume command of

Percheron and all persons aboard. This
office will provide updates on crew
condition on a weekly basis.
                    ChirpChat, November 2043

The access panel had also given him the option to vent
the entire contents into space, but Glenn really didn't
want to waste any of it. If the source of contamination was
obvious, and could be sealed off, then the water could be
filtered and at least used for hydroponics and hygiene. On
the other hand, once the tank volume dropped below five
percent, it was very difficult to extract the remainder as
long as they were still in zero gee. Even the slightest
engine thrust or roll of the ship would move the water to
the walls of the tank and allow it to be pumped out, but
not when there was no gravity of any sort. Therefore, he
was going to have to waste the final few percent of the
tank's capacity with reduced pressure.

The diagnostics on the access panel tracked pumping
efficiency. Once the water level fell effectively to zero, air
would be pumped out as much as possible. The low
pressure would cause the remaining water to boil, and the
resulting water vapor and residual air would also be
pumped as much as possible. When the pump readout
indicated that no more water or air could be removed
from the tank, Glenn turned off the pumps and opened
the valve to re-equilibrate pressure. There would be water
droplets and humidity, but there should not be any large
globules of water to trap and drown an inspector. It was
still enclosed space, so he would simply put his helmet on
and turn on the oxygen feed.

He looked at the damaged faceplate and neck seal.

Damn, I should have fixed or replaced that on the walk here, he thought to himself. *I've been so busy dealing with everyone else's problems, I haven't looked after myself. Here I am about to walk into a confined space without a working helmet.*

Emergency decompression supplies were located in lockers all over the ship, but the highest concentration was at the hub interface for the rotating habitat ring. He could go back there for a full pressure suit, or check the lockers here. Unfortunately, there were only two in this section, and one was empty except for a plastic bottle filled with a clear liquid. He opened it and sniffed.

Alcohol. High proof, too; from Mishra and Grigorescu's still, no doubt.

The second locker was nearly empty, containing only a pair of magnetic soled boots, another bottle of clear liquid—actually water this time—a packet of ibuprofen, and a tube of sealant goop.

Glenn figured that this was probably a prank, although he wasn't sure who it was intended for. "Take two ibu, drink a bottle of water, and change your socks"—or boots in some circles—had been a joke among military medical personnel for many years. On the other hand, the water and pain reliever would help the headache he'd started to feel, and he could smear extra goop on the damaged neck ring for his helmet. He'd have to increase the airflow because of leakage, but at least he'd be breathing suit air.

To open the inspection hatch, Glenn had to enter a code and supply a biometric authorization. He worried, briefly, but command codes had apparently been uploaded along with the change-of-command orders. With that out of the way, he opened the hatch and entered the tank. It was more than large enough for him to stand upright, and the magnetic soled boots would be useful. He entered the tank, stood with his feet anchored to the hinged side of the hatch, and looked around.

The powerful flashlight that he had carried earlier as a potential weapon, was now put to its original use for illumination. The interior of the tank had a featureless metallic sheen, except for a few droplets of water that had condensed on the cold walls when pressure was restored. He touched a gloved hand to the interior wall. It was smooth, polished steel or aluminum, typical of water storage both on-Earth and off.

One area on the far wall of the tank did not reflect the same uniform sheen.

He released the magnetic locks on his boots to try to float or swim over to the opposite wall, but that was a mistake. He drifted slowly away from the wall, and swimming motions only caused him to tumble. He reactivated the magnetic soles and waited to either bump into another wall of the tank, or for his shoes to come close enough to grab. The magnetic force was adjustable—after all, he needed to be able to lift his feet to walk—so he turned the field strength to maximum and was suddenly jerked toward a wall only a foot away. Unfortunately, both feet were not together, and he landed in an awkward near-split.

That hurt! He turned the magnetic strength back down and shuffled his feet back together. As he slowly and gingerly shuffled to the area of discoloration, he called up the schematic of *Percheron* that he'd stored in his heads-up display buffer when he'd first entered the ship. The compartment on the other side of the discolored bulkhead was a holding tank for bactericide, fungicide, and cleaning agents. It had a valve to pull water from the main tank to mix with powdered chemicals. A fill station in the corridor allowed personnel to obtain the prepared liquid for treating specific problem spots, and a network of special pipes could spray the chemicals in several parts of the ship that required frequent disinfection. As Glenn got closer, he could see a small valve in the middle of the dark patch. That *should* be a one-way valve which took water from the tank for mixing the chemical cleaners. He reached out to touch it, and the valve fell away, revealing corroded metal.

Bingo!

The entire area around the valve was corroding, explaining the discoloration, and suggesting that it stuck open at some point in the past, allowing chemicals to backflow the water tank. The corrosion would have allowed other metals to leach into the water—aluminum, chromium, nickel, and more, which was why the heavy metal toxicity symptoms were not consistent across the crew.

As he was inspecting the area around the leak, he felt and heard vibration as the inspection hatch closed. Before he could get back to the hatch using the particular shuffle of magnetic boots, he heard the locking mechanism engage. A faint hissing noise became louder as his ears popped.

Vacuum purge! The pressure wouldn't drop just to the point where the water boiled, but would go all the way down to hard vacuum. Someone had locked the hatch and trapped him in vacuum with limited air and a skinsuit helmet that wouldn't completely seal.

Glenn's right eardrum began to hurt from dropping pressure. He popped it several times, and kept his mouth open as he struggled with the manual release for the inspection hatch. Suddenly, he heard a screech of stressed metal. The structure of the tank had been compromised by the corrosion, and would collapse inward as pressure decreased.

If the vacuum didn't get him, he would be crushed by the imploding water tank.

The hatch had been designed to lock in place with water pressure inside and air on the outer—corridor side—or vacuum on the inside and air outside. Either way, the mechanism dilated the outer rim of the hatch like an iris, so that its diameter increased, and wedged into the frame to secure it from being blown inward or outward by differential pressure. It was an ingenious design that Glenn felt absolutely no particular need to admire. At least, not under the current circumstances.

Manual operation of the hatch, the inner emergency release, was intended to operate when pressure on both sides of the hatch was equal. The only way to operate it with the pressure rapidly dropping was to physically pry it open and break the seal. It would cause decompression of the immediate corridor, but emergency bulkheads would protect the rest of the ship.

There was nothing in the tank that he could use to pry the hatch and crack the seal...except...

He felt a stabbing pain in his right ear, then felt a pop, and nothing. The only sound now came through the cochlear implant in his left ear. The vacuum had ruptured his eardrum. It was now or never.

He needed a prybar. In its absence, he needed to make one, just as he did back in North Carolina when he'd pried the door off of the overturned car. Nik had dubbed that move the "bionic knife hand." Glenn put the fingers of his left hand together, palm flat, in a blade shape. He gave a mental command that locked the finger and wrist joints together to keep the whole thing rigid, then moved to a position straddling the hatch and turned the magnetic locks on his boots to maximum. He stabbed down with as much bionic force as he could, driving the hand into the edge of the hatch.

One advantage of bionics was the ability to turn off the sensation of pain. There were still many red lights and indicators in his heads-up display and the helmet indicators told him that the fabric of his skinsuit gloves was compromised. It didn't work on the first try; he needed to repeat the motion at three more places around the hatch rim, watching the seal deform a bit more each time. The synthetic skin of his fingers as well as the artificial muscle underneath was shredding, but still remained operable enough that when his fingers penetrated the rim of the hatch on the fourth try, he unlocked the fingers, curled them, and pulled.

Much like the car door in North Carolina, the hatch came flying off—but so did the lower half of his arm.

Damn, he hadn't expected that.

He wanted to stop and gasp for breath, after all, a rush

of air just came in through the busted hatch. Unfortunately, the vacuum purge cycle was still ongoing and alarms began to sound in the corridor announcing decompression and risk of vacuum exposure. As he pulled himself out of the tank using his right arm, he saw Yvette standing next to the access control panel.

Oh crap, that's what I forgot. I'd disabled the lock on the isolation room door.

Yvette looked down at her hands in horror.

Glenn suspected she just realized what she'd done. He swung himself toward the panel and reached for it with his left hand.

His missing left hand.

The movement caused him to twist awkwardly. He grabbed a handhold with his right hand, pulled himself over to the console, and canceled the vacuum purge. The rush of air stopped; both ends of the corridor were already sealed with emergency pressure doors, and he felt a muted sense of the pressure in his right ear along with a stabbing pain in his right eye as normal pressure was restored.

Now, there would be hell to pay in more ways than one. He'd identified both the unknown malady and its source, escaped death, and put the offending tank permanently out of commission. He had a plan to treat the crew and get them home safely to Earth. He even had replacement supplies to make sure they could get there.

He'd escaped death, and it only cost him his left forearm and his remaining natural eardrum. For now.

Yvette was floating in the hallway, staring at him in shock. "What have I done? I didn't know!" she screamed. Then she tried to lunge back toward the control panel.

Glenn deflected her, and she turned on him. Her expression turned to rage, and she beat at him with closed fists. "It's bad water! We have to get rid of it!"

He quickly moved his right arm to block her, and in the process, his right fist collided with her jaw. With a sob and a sigh, she slumped unconscious.

Glenn may have figured out the disease, the source, the treatment, and the way to save his own life, but he had one more . . . critical . . . crisis to solve. Everyone would be treated and brought back to health as much as possible, but he *needed* to stabilize Yvette.

He wasn't sure that he could take another three-and-a-half months of her swinging from lust to rage on a chemical imbalance.

The trip back to the med bay took much longer than usual, with an unconscious Yvette being dragged along by his right hand, and the step-shuffle of magnetic boots. Flying down the corridors in zero gee required at least one free hand, and he was currently short two. Entering the med bay, he found Bialik up and gingerly moving around the room. She looked up in horror as the two entered the treatment room.

"Oh, Colonel Shepard, I'm so sorry! I only saw the change of command after I let Doctor Barbier out of the restraints. She said you attacked her!"

Glenn nodded wearily and maneuvered Yvette over to the open treatment table. Bialik stared at the empty magnetic coupling where his left forearm would have been. "S'okay. You didn't know, but you need to follow my orders, now. She's very sick and mentally altered. She needs dialysis, but give her five migs of midazolam before you start."

"You want me to give her versed? The dialysis will pull that right back out."

"I know. You're going to repeat it once the first pass of dialysis is done," Glenn told the medic. "Repeat every four hours at half the dose while we get her treated. You should prep some haloperidol, too. Just in case."

"Yes, Doctor . . . um, Captain . . . ah . . . Colonel."

Glenn looked closely at the medic. She looked tired, her eyes sunken, skin pale—but not yellow, so the dialysis had removed much of the copper from her system. "Help me with these restraints, then go rest on the isolation room cot. Later, if you're feeling up to it, I'll need your help getting everyone a shot of dimercaprol. You all need penicillamine, too, and prepare for it to smell much, much worse in here. If I can trust you with giving Doctor Barbier her medications, I need to go get some rest."

Bialik nodded. She still looked weak, but was so much better than before. "Yes, Colonel."

When he got back to the shuttle, Glenn checked his comms, but there was still nothing from Earth. He was so tired, and he needed sleep.

Screw them. Who cared what they thought?

He decided to take a nap and check again in a couple hours, but thought better and recorded a message to General Boatright, first. He recapped the events, and ended with a summary of the most recent events and his concern for Yvette. He wanted to end on a more positive note, so he included the fact that Bialik and Takeda had responded well to dialysis.

It was eight hours before he woke, to a whole series of messages from Houston, Tucson, the Moon, and the Third Space Wing headquarters on Heinlein Station. The NASA and MarsX messages were full of second guessing, but the message from his old friend the Moonbase CMO was simply congratulations and wanted him to relay the whole story over a beer. Heinlein confirmed his diagnosis and treatment plan and told him to ignore Houston and Tucson—he was in command, and he'd done what he'd been authorized to do.

The worst was over—*but was it?* He still needed to dialyze the rest of the personnel, get chelation treatments started, get Philips to inspect the spin hub, and restart the habitat ring. He could probably get Steve Green to help with that.

Then there was the matter of treating the psychoses and delusions so many had experienced. Fortunately, he knew a good psychiatrist. The worst was over, the hard work was about to start . . . and he would be doing it one-handed.

After a delicious meal of freeze-dried chili-mac and tang, Glenn received a message consisting of just a package ident and stowage manifest from *Bat*. It wasn't one of the cargo cases he'd offloaded already, so he got into the MILES and went over to the cargo pod. It was a long, narrow cargo case, with a square cross-section; about fifty centimeters on a side and two meters long. It wasn't particularly heavy, which made Glenn quite curious. He took it back to his shuttle and opened it. Inside was a complete replacement arm with a tag stating that it was a present from Marty and Nik. "In case you need to use the 'Bionic Knife Hand' again; it's not fine-tuned, but better than nothing."

Below that was a message in Boatright's hand: "I wouldn't want you to be unarmed."

PART 4
AFTERMATH

CHAPTER 37:
Recovery

Beth L @SpaceNewsNetwork
The *Percheron* crew are healing. Her commander, Colonel Glenn Shepard, reports that all personnel are responding to treatment. Today the ship made several minor corrections to her course to bring them back to the optimum trajectory for return to Earth in just over three months. Several ship's systems are still undergoing maintenance, but they plan to spin up the habitat ring later this week to gradually acclimate the crew to a return to Earth normal gravity.
Godspeed, *Percheron*, our prayers are with you.

ChirpChat, November 2043

"Damn it, Christensen, it *has* to be here."

"Yes, sir. I understand, but are you sure it didn't drift

out through the hatch while you were getting everything repressurized? After all, restoring air pressure in the tank would have created outward air flow."

"Sure, but the corridor was sealed by pressure doors at the time. There was nothing out here. Besides, it's brightly lit out there."

"Which leads me to wonder . . . If you don't mind my asking, how did you see the faulty valve?"

Glenn grinned at Christensen and tapped his head beside his left eye. Rather, he tapped his helmet—one with a functioning neck seal this time. "Bionic eye. I shined my light on the far wall and saw an odd reflectance."

"And that same bionic eye can't see your arm?" Christensen asked plaintively.

"Sorry, I tried, but I'm not picking anything up. That's why we have to search ourselves."

"Okay, sir, but why look for it at all? You have your replacement, what do you want with your old banged-up arm?"

"We'll be back at Earth in a week. I need to be able to turn it into the lab guys for analysis."

"What analysis? It's broken."

"Ah, but that's what they want to analyze. I've received numerous comms over the past four months asking for particulars about how much force I exerted, what are the materials of the hatch and pressure seal, what was I doing when it detached. It's all information they could get from shipbuilding specs and my medical telemetry. I think it's all mainly a reminder that the arm was issued to me, and I have to turn it in at the end of deployment."

"What happens if they decide to discontinue maintenance and updates? Could they take it all back, since it's 'issued'?"

"I suppose. It happened with the guy who got the first bionic arm back in the 2010's. It was part of an experimental project, and when the project ended, there was no funding for him to keep it. The bionic one was taken away and replaced with a purely passive one. But public outcry—particularly among the researchers involved—convinced the government to find a way to pay for maintenance and give his arm back. So, there's always that option. Besides, they can't take everything away. Certain parts are more essential than others."

Glenn felt a twinge in his chest. For just a moment, he could feel and hear his heartbeat. It was the same odd sensation he'd felt on the Moon and passed off as a muscle cramp. It had happened several times per month since the trip on *Bat*. It was just another bit of damage he'd have to wait to have repaired.

"Here sir, if you'd help me turn over the hatch, it seems to be stuck to the wall." Christensen was looking at the pressure hatch Glenn had forcibly removed. The hinges were bent and twisted, and the rim of the hatch was crumpled.

"Aha! So *that's* where you've been hiding!" Glenn said as he reached out to remove the bionic arm from where it was stuck to the underside of the hatch.

"Why's it sticking like that?"

"Magnetic bearing at the elbow. I guess it's still energized."

"Would have been nice to know that an hour ago, sir."

"Sorry, Sergeant. I didn't expect it to still be active after nearly four months."

"Yes, sir. Now, can we get out of here? Knowing what happened to you, this place gives me the creeps."

"Me, too, Jonas. Me, too."

In the first week after the incident in Water Tank Number Three, Glenn asked Philips to set up additional cots in the med bay. Yvette was locked in the isolation room and he needed to use the biobeds for dialysis. There were three patients who needed continued observation. Fortunately, the habitat ring was still motionless, so the cots didn't need to be located on the "floor." Unfortunately, Philips was occupied pulling debris from the rotation mechanism and repairing minor issues so that he *could* get the ring rotating.

Steve Green offered to fill in and assist Philips with other engineering projects—like assembling cots from spare components intended for the shuttles. There was room on the med bay walls away from the monitoring consoles and the lab wall, so quick-dry epoxy and space tape sufficed to provide bedding for mounting four cots on the "ceiling" of the med bay. It was only temporary, since they couldn't have five people concentrated in one small compartment once the habitat ring was spun up.

Bialik started to show improvement after the first dialysis treatment. She'd gotten up on her own after that first session, although she had still been very weak. Glenn started her on a high-protein, low-carbohydrate diet, and insulin to help stabilize her metabolism. She'd lost almost fifteen percent of her body weight between the pancreatitis and zero gee, and Glenn wanted to start supplementing her diet with additional fats—provided her kidneys and liver stayed healthy.

Daily dialysis was beneficial for Takeda, and after a week, she started to show residual kidney function. She would continue with weekly dialysis until they got back to Earth. As with Bialik, Glenn considered her stabilized—not cured. She would need additional treatment, possibly including stem cells or transplant, when they returned to Earth.

Glenn kept Yvette sedated for most of the first week, until he was certain that the both the copper and excess norepinephrine had been flushed from her body. He hadn't needed to repeat the haloperidol, which was a good thing, and had switched her to aripiprazole, a much more appropriate antipsychotic for long-term treatment. It meant that she wasn't sedated full time, so she remained confined to the isolation room, but with increasingly longer durations in which she was allowed out—but only under his supervision, and as long as she didn't leave the med bay.

Katou was not recovering as fast as Glenn had hoped. Her liver toxicity was advanced, and he feared she'd need a transplant before they got back to Earth. A resection of the damaged portion of her liver and transfusion of stem cells with trophic factors into her hepatic artery *might* help regenerate the organ temporarily, but it also might not be enough.

Glenn needed to do an autopsy on Gee LeBlanc to see just how badly damaged the captain's liver had been. If he knew *what* to expect, he might be able to halt or slow down Mila's decline.

He had Christensen retrieve LeBlanc's body from the deep freeze, and slowly warm it back to just below freezing. That would avoid degradation of tissue as it thawed, but would leave the skin and internal tissues stiff and hard to cut. Fortunately, he could do much of the examination with imaging; unfortunately, he would still need to visibly examine the liver.

"Do you want me to scrub in and assist?" This was one of the times when Yvette was calm and lucid, and she'd been helping Bialik store medical supplies from *Bat*.

Glenn weighed the options between having two capable hands—after all, his bionic hand was still only partially tuned—versus Yvette holding a scalpel in those hands. "No, but I want you to observe. See if I miss anything."

Imaging showed no evidence of severe damage to any of the organs other than liver and brain. Necropsy—removal of tissue samples for testing—showed copper accumulation, and a severe imbalance of hormones and neurotransmitters. Patches of skin, esophagus and intestines showed signs of bleeding, but those were small and diffuse—consistent with liver damage. The brain scan did *not* show signs of bleeding—deposits of iron from hemoglobin would show up white—nor any of the dark patches indicative of clots or stroke. There *was* a faint white rim to the surface of the brain which suggested damage from compression. Liver failure often resulted in cerebral edema, which would compress the surface of the brain, and could explain the captain's delusions. On the other hand, it could also have been due to neurotransmitter imbalance.

Glenn was finally left with the task of opening the

corpse to examine the liver. The normally smooth, dark organ was mottled and lumpy.

"Cirrhosis," Yvette said.

"Yes, and it's pretty bad. I wouldn't have expected this. Was the captain drinking?" Glenn asked her.

"Not that I know of. She looked the other way at Philips and Christensen's still, but I wouldn't think she'd be drinking the hooch."

"It's possible she'd had a brush with hepatitis. It's curable if caught quickly, so it might not even be in her records."

The liver was normally divided by a thick band of tissue—the falciform ligament—which divided the liver into two lobes, and attached the organ to the wall of the abdomen. The surface of the smaller lobe was darker and smoother, with a texture similar to a football.

Glenn lifted the liver and looked at the underside. "There's some sparing of the left lateral lobe. A resection might have saved her. There's enough to regenerate."

"True, but you'd have to leave enough of the caudate and quadrate lobes to support the hepatic artery and vein, portal vein, and bile duct." Yvette pointed to the small sections on the underside of the liver above and below a cluster of blood vessels. The tissue was almost black. "She was bleeding here. It wouldn't have been stable."

"I agree. We'd best do some scans of Katou and make sure she's not this bad."

Just then they heard a thumping sound and Bialik shouted, "Colonel, it's Mila. She's seizing."

Glenn turned a bit too quickly and drifted away from the biobed. He kept turning until he was able to right himself with his left hand on the other bed. There was an odd feeling, and he looked down to see that he'd crushed the edge of the bed. Fortunately, it wasn't where any of the instrumentation was located, but it was a reminder that he still didn't have very fine control of his bionic hand.

"It's cerebral edema. I need to..." Yvette stopped. "You need to...no, let me start again. Doctor Shepard, you may need to relieve the pressure. Dexamethasone and mannitol will help, but they won't be fast."

"I'll need to release the pressure with a drain."

"Y-yes." Yvette drew out the word. She was hesitating to say something.

"Spit it out. I've never known you to hold back criticism," Glenn snapped.

She looked as if she'd been slapped. "I know. But if anything, I've learned how wrong I could be, too."

Glenn sighed. "I apologize. That wasn't called for. What were you going to suggest?"

"You need help." She pointed to his left arm. "You need *my* help."

Glenn held up his left hand and wiggled his fingers. The feedback was just a bit off, and they moved out of sequence. He sighed again.

Yvette continued in a quiet, almost plaintive voice. "I was going to suggest that I help you. If you can find it in your heart to trust me...and to forgive me."

The surgery took several hours. Glenn incised the scalp and cut a small burr hole through the skull behind Katou's left ear. The membrane lining the brain immediately bulged out, and Yvette threaded a thin catheter under the membrane to relieve the fluid pressure. Once that was done, she carefully repaired the incision with microscopic sutures, leaving Glenn to pack the hole in the skull with sterile foam, and close the scalp.

By the end of the procedure, Yvette was starting to shake and twitch. As soon as Katou's scalp was closed, she went to the isolation room and locked herself in. Glenn continued to finish the surgery—one handed—and handed off the post-surgical medication and monitoring duties to Bialik.

Glenn looked through the observation glass, and saw Yvette talking to herself and "pacing"—which in zero gee consisted of launching herself from one wall, tumbling and landing feet-first on the opposite wall, then launching herself back to repeat the back-and-forth motion. He grabbed a dose of sedative, and overrode the lock on the door to enter the room.

"Here's something to help you to relax."

"No!" she snapped. More calmly, but through gritted teeth, she added, "No thank you. I need to learn to deal with my demons."

Glenn left the room, and programmed the lock to release in four hours if he didn't do anything. He continued to watch until she slowed down and moved to the cot. She fastened the zero-gee straps and turned her face away from the window to sleep.

The room camera and microphone were always on, but the volume had been turned up when he entered. Over the monitor he could hear her murmur, "I'm sorry. I'm so sorry."

CHAPTER 38:
Anticipation

USSF Media Office @JBSpaceNews
US Space Force is inviting credentialed
media reporters to cover the return of the
Percheron. This historic event marks the
first round-trip of a reusable Earth-to-Mars
interplanetary ship. The mission has
suffered many triumphs and tragedies,
and will be docking with Heinlein Station
in two weeks.
As a reminder, Heinlein Station is an
access-controlled military base. Reporters
requesting travel to Heinlein are directed
to upload their credentials at the link
below.
ChirpChat, March 2044

Communications between *Percheron* and Earth had
gotten easier over the last four months. As the ship closed

the distance, communications time dropped from more than fifteen minutes when *Bat* arrived, to now just under a minute. With the Mars-transfer ship due to dock at Heinlein Station in just a few days, Nik and Glenn had been discussing with General Boatright that Nik needed to be there to meet the crew.

After all, he was the surrogate psychiatrist for *Percheron*—he'd spent more than two months on comms trying to teach Glenn everything he could about how to treat and counsel a crew that had come so close to death. Once the communications delay had dropped to less than five minutes round trip, he'd been able to conduct counseling sessions himself.

Dialysis, chelation, medication, a few minor surgical procedures, and the crew members began to recover. Bialik and Takeda would need continuing treatment, but they were stable. Katou might still need regeneration; once the cerebral edema stabilized, Glenn resected a patch of necrotic tissue from her liver and started stem cell treatment.

The psychology of the crew was not as simple. Each crew member had to deal not only with how the copper poisoning had affected themselves, but how it had affected the crew dynamic and trust.

Yvette was looking at months to years of treatment and therapy. Nik diagnosed her with schizophrenia, which was not just a neurological disorder, but a psychological one as well. It was possible to correct the underlying organic cause; in her case, neurotransmitter imbalances led to altered cognitive abilities and erratic behavior. The problem was that once the pattern of mood swings, intrusive thoughts, and abnormal memories developed, they became a part of her. On top of that, she would have to face legal and ethical challenges to her actions.

Glenn really hoped Nik could be there. He wasn't sure if Jen would be able to make it, and frankly, he needed to see a friendly face. He may have saved the crew—a crew he'd been part of for years in training before his accident sidelined him—but things had been awkward. Yvette had been with them on Mars; she'd been the authority figure they'd followed during a medical crisis. Despite their doubts, and her own behavior, Taketani and Dvorak had still deferred to her. From time to time over the past four months they slipped back to deferring to her and treated Glenn almost as if he'd usurped her position.

Glenn would need medical attention, too. Space Force was adamant that Yvette could not be reinstated as medical officer, and Bialik didn't have the experience to deal with the lingering effects of his hard acceleration, two vacuum exposures, broken eardrum, fights, damaged bionic arm, and the emergency replacement. MMC was also concerned with possible lung scarring from multiple decompressions, and the sporadic heartbeat irregularity reported a year ago on the Moon had returned. Either condition could ground any astronaut, but more so a triple amputee with "experimental" prosthetics and a history of risk-taking.

It would be a shame if Glenn was banned from spaceflight just when he had proven as capable—in fact more so—than a non-augmented human.

A tall man in uniform knocked on the open door of Nik's office and entered immediately. "Doctor Pillarisetty, pack your go-bag," Lieutenant Colonel Richardson told him. Richardson was the person Boatright had put in charge of communications between *Percheron* and the Earthside mission controllers.

"My go-bag. Does this mean they're letting me go up there?"

"The general has made special arrangements. He assures me that you can handle the acceleration. Once you're in free-fall, you'll probably get along as well as anybody else." Richardson looked meaningfully at the wheelchair at the side of Nik's desk, then smiled.

That was a rarity. In all of the time Nik had interacted with the Space Force officer over the past months, he'd never known the man to smile.

"Well in that case, my go-bag is sitting in the corner there. If you would be so kind as to grab that, I'll be with you in just a moment." Nik pushed his chair back from the desk, and pushed the wheelchair beside it out of the way. He reached down and touched the small control box at his waist, and with the faintest whirring sounds, stood up and walked around the desk.

Richardson's face registered shock at Nik's own variation on the exoskeleton originally developed for Glenn.

"Let's go, Colonel. I've been waiting for this my whole life."

Nik was struck by the similarities in appearance between Heinlein Station and *Percheron*. The reception area had several screens showing the approaching ship. One of them showed the view from a work tug standing off from the docking area. It showed both the station and the spaceship—one looking like a scale model of the other.

Percheron was narrower, but almost as long, as Heinlein's core. The ship's habitat ring was considerably smaller, but it was only designed to accommodate twenty to thirty crew for a year-and-a-half at a time. Other distinguishing features were the engines at one end, external fuel tanks, the ground to orbit shuttle docked just in front of the fuel tanks and the bulge of *Bat*, still attached to Cargo Bay One.

The other two Lagrange stations—O'Neill at L5, and Clarke at L4—each consisted of a single set of nested concentric habitat rings on a short, narrow hub. Heinlein—located at the Earth-Moon L2 Lagrange point—had a broad cylindrical core with a habitat ring at one end, like a wider version of the Mars transfer ship. Eventually, Heinlein would have three rotating rings spaced sequentially along its hub, marking a departure from the wheeled designs of O'Neill and Clarke, or the haphazard cylinder and strut designs of the ISS and ill-fated Asimov Station. Of course, O'Neill and Clarke didn't need additional structures attached to their rings, since they had free-floating shipyards nearby, while Heinlein intended to have shuttles and work boats match orbit and rotation to dock directly to the station.

Bat's drive section was now being detached from the tethers which Glenn had placed, and which had dragged the valuable Helicity2 drive back to the Earth-Moon system. Two construction tugs pulled it loose and matched rotation to dock the drive at a construction bay along the station's spindle. Four more tugs were shepherding *Percheron* to dock bow-to-spindle with the station.

The decision had been made to not return *Percheron* to O'Neill or Clarke because those docks were occupied with construction of two more large transfer ships— *Augeron*, intended to supplement *Percheron* on Earth-to-Mars runs, while the latter ship underwent refitting, and *Clydesdale*, which would initiate a triangle route between Earth, Mars, and the Space Force's planned asteroid base at Ceres. Once all three ships were in use, their Helicity3 drives would allow point-to-point travel to anywhere within the inner solar system in less than a month. There was a fourth-generation Helicity drive in development which would take humans to the moons of Jupiter and Saturn in just a few months per round trip. Nik knew that Glenn had plans to ensure that bionic augmented personnel played an integral role in the exploration and colonization of the solar system, but so much of that would hinge on what was about to happen next.

"*SFSS Ares Percheron* arriving, Bay One."

Nik looked around at the party waiting to greet the first individuals to come through the airlock. Colonel Richardson had been at his side for most the trip so far; it was almost as if the OSI officer considered himself as an aide to *Nik* rather than as an officer awaiting the return of personnel. He proved to be quite personable, very concerned about Glenn, and supportive of Shepard and Boatright's plan to include bionically augmented personnel in space. They'd discussed the reception plan:

a restricted group—including themselves—would meet the crew as they disembarked. Medical technicians would take Bialik, Takeda, and Katou directly to sickbay, and media representatives would be waiting in one of the hangars to officially greet the returning astronauts.

Besides Nik, Richardson, and the three medical personnel, he saw Colonel William Webb, commander of Heinlein Station, and Doctor Peter Schlecht, representing MMC. There were also two stern-faced Space Force police officers, suggesting that somebody—possibly Shep—would be taken into custody as soon as they stepped off of *Percheron*. Rumors had been rampant among news services and social media the past week as *Percheron* entered the Earth-Moon system. Las Vegas was even giving odds on whether Shepard would be tried for piracy, or Barbier would be tried for dereliction of duty.

Nik seriously doubted that Shep would face charges. General Boatright had been extremely supportive, taking both the credit and the blame for Shep being on *Bat* without NASA's or MarsX's knowledge. Jen's articles, and her work with improving USSF's media profile, had done wonders to rally public opinion behind both Shep and the OSI. He might have to testify, but few people truly thought he'd be punished for saving fourteen people.

Another favored topic among the gossip media was whether charges would be brought against anyone associated with the design and construction of *Percheron*. While news that Shepard had discovered the cause of crew illness and "cured" it, those reports had not included any official details of how the water supplies had become contaminated with copper. That didn't stop the information from leaking out, after all, the more people who knew a secret, the less likely it would be kept. Space Force investigated the source of the leaked information—after all, they knew it wasn't them—but with both NASA and MarsX personnel in the loop, the chance of keeping information about the faulty fungicide tank secret was virtually nil.

Nik suspected that Boatright knew information leaks would occur, and had likely planted the seeds for some of the rumors himself. Particularly those regarding the consequences of Shep placing himself in danger aboard *Bat*. The past few months, with Jen advising the general on shaping opinion via chirps, and revamping the USSF Media Office, had paid off in the public seeing Shep as the hero of this story. If anyone had plans to blame or punish Shep for his actions, they'd find public opinion firmly on Shep and the general's side.

An alert sounded and a rotating light above the docking airlock turned from red to amber. The *Percheron* and Marsbase crews were coming home.

CHAPTER 39:
The Return

United States Space Force @USSFActual

Percheron, her remaining crew, and the Marsbase One team are home. Civilians will be returning groundside as soon as they are cleared by Mission Medical; USSF personnel are awaiting orders. Welcome home, spacefarers!

Weekly Solar News @NickSteve

Hey viewers, Nick Steverson here with your weekly dose of dirt. What do you think they're going to do to Shepard? Mutiny trial? Desertion? Abuse of authority? Let me know what YOU think is going to happen at Channel WSN21-043.

USSF Office of Scientific Integration
@OSIGenBoatright

@NickSteve, Mister Steverson, we need to get the sick crewmembers into medical care first, then allow the rest to see their families. Colonel Glenn Shepard suffered several injuries in the performance of his duties and will be going into medical treatment and bionic repair as well.

Please keep in mind that *none* of these brave astronauts would be here without some pretty heroic efforts—particularly those of Glenn Shepard.

ChirpChat, March 2044

A green light lit over the airlock. The atmosphere aboard *Percheron* was tense, the crew should have been excited about being home, but mostly they were tense. Glenn waited by the inner hatch, stabilizing Takeda's and Katou's stretchers with a few light touches of his right hand. Bialik floated nearby. She'd refused one, even though she needed it as much as the other two. They had all done so much better since he'd started treatments, and probably could have gone on their own, but it was a precaution against the variable gravity zones they'd experience on their way to the med bay.

Glenn had argued with Marta that even though Heinlein only maintained one-half gee in their rotating ring, she was still weak from the prolonged period without sufficient gravity. They'd only had *Percheron*'s habitat ring rotating again for three months. The Marsbase One crew had been at point three seven gees for more than two years, and everyone had been at zero gee for two months prior to restarting rotation, so Glenn had slowly increased them all to point four gees before they'd had to shut it all back down for orbital maneuvers. Bialik still insisted, so Glenn kept his left hand at her elbow until the USSF medics came for them.

The light turned amber, then green again. Three medics entered, and took charge of the stretchers and Marta, then cycled back through to the station.

While waiting for the airlock light to turn green again, Glenn pulled himself against the corridor wall. He nodded his head, and the Marsbase personnel queued up to exit. They all wore clean Marsbase uniforms—freshly printed onboard at Shepard's insistence. Taketani would go first, followed by Melissa and Steve Green, then Rachel Amit. They'd cycle the airlock again, then Surya Mishra, Victor Grigorescu, and Maia D'Cruz would enter the station.

Yvette . . . would not be leaving the ship with them.

Once the civilians had departed, Major Dvorak called Erik Philips and Jonas Christensen to attention—not an easy maneuver in zero gee, but Space Force had evolved a work-around.

"You've been an excellent crew. We've made history in ways we desired, and some we didn't. To paraphrase Rhysling, 'Out ride the sons and daughters of Terra, upon our thundering drives.' Until the next great leap, it has been my honor to serve with you."

All three would fit in the airlock, so there was no need to maintain any sort of hierarchy or order of precedence. Still, Philips and Christensen floated two flag-draped black tubes into the lock before they entered, followed by Dvorak.

One held the body of Gee LeBlanc. Her husband and family members had planned a private service in her hometown of Rancho Palos Verdes, California. Boatright, on the other hand, insisted she should be buried in Arlington. Many of the family were living in Hawaii, though, and travel to California would have been a hardship; Washington, D.C. was simply too far. They'd compromised on interment at the National Memorial of the Pacific, Hawaii, located in Punchbowl Crater just northwest of downtown Honolulu.

The casket for Lieutenant Commander Scott would be empty, but nevertheless buried in Arlington near the Challenger memorial. He had only one close family member, a sister—Kirstie—who'd moved back to Scotland to work as a teacher. Their parents had passed away five years before, and been buried back in their native land. General Boatright had insisted the engineer should be honored with other American and Space Force astronauts, and the sister concurred. The ceremony would be small—Boatright insisted on that—but Jen and Nik would be there in Glenn's place.

Glenn planned to be last off the ship, for many reasons. One of those was the woman who floated beside him, face appearing to be set in stone. She'd been crying, earlier, but Doctor Green had assisted her in cleaning up and putting on fresh makeup for the arrival and press conference.

The airlock indicator turned green once again, and two Space Force security officers stepped into the chamber and approached Yvette.

"Turn around. Hands behind your back," one of them said. The fact that they were ignoring Glenn meant that they weren't here for him, but he wasn't out of the woods yet.

"You don't have to do that, she . . ." He tried to say, but Yvette shushed him.

"It's okay, Glenn." She rotated her body to present her hands clasped in the small of her back.

The guard who hadn't spoken placed flexicuffs around her wrists, and rotated her back to face the airlock. He hadn't been forceful while putting on the restraint, and his touch seemed gentle as he lined her up to enter the airlock.

Glenn moved to enter, but the first guard motioned for him to stay.

"Not yet, Doctor Shepard."

As the three cycled through the airlock, Glenn thought about what the man had said. *Doctor, not Colonel. Just exactly what does that mean?*

On the next cycle, the same officer returned. His face looked familiar . . .

"Ian? You're not security!"

"Just floating under the lidar, Doc."

"Well, it's good to see you, but why did you come up from Texas? What's going on?"

"I've got to prep you for the cameras. Once everyone else moves to their places in the station, Boaty's gonna let the newsies into the dock for your triumphal return."

"My triumphal, *what*?"

"It's a show, man, directed by an OSI colonel named Richardson and produced by the general. I see you're wearing the replacement arm we sent. Do you have the other one?"

"What? Why? It's in my quarters back on the shuttle. The attachment's trashed, I can't put it back on."

"No problem, I've got one here for you."

Glenn noticed that Ian was carrying a case much like the one used to ship his replacement arm.

"Dare I ask what's in there?"

"It's the arm you damaged in North Carolina." He opened the case. "We're just going to swap out from the elbow down. I've got a sling, and you're to let the wrist and finger damage show."

"Theater."

"You've got it, Doc. Now let's get you ready for the cameras."

The two cycled through the lock. Ian operated the door and was pretending to manage things so that Glenn wouldn't have to use his left hand. Immediately in front of the airlock were three people, two of whom he immediately recognized—Bill Webb and Nik. The third was in a Space Force uniform; his nametape said "Richardson."

"Colonel Shepard, so glad to have you back," Webb told him, as he and Richardson saluted.

Glenn returned the salute stiffly, and awkwardly. The combination of zero gee, damaged left arm and sling made it a bit difficult to keep from flailing around. Ian touched the back of his elbow and helped stabilize him.

Nik floated up and embraced him in a hug. "Buck, up, buddy, here come the thundering hordes," he whispered.

Extremely bright lights came on and a man with slicked-back hair and a thin mustache pushed a camera and microphone in Glenn's face. Webb tried to push the man out of the way, but he'd secured himself to a rung on the corridor wall, while Webb was free floating. The gesture had no effect on the journalist.

"Colonel Shepard! Nicholas Steverson, Weekly Solar News. Colonel Shepard, is it true they're going to make you a scapegoat?"

Glenn recognized the name. Steverson was well known for sensationalism, conspiracy theories, and overall trashy journalism. He was surprised the reporter had managed to penetrate so far through security.

"Colonel Shepard, why did you steal the C-21-MX? What does your family have to say about your actions? You were seen in the company of reporter Jen Butler for a while there—are you two still an item? What does she have to say about you flying off to rescue a former girlfriend?" It all came out in a rush. It seemed as if the man was trying to ensure that his words would be remembered more than Glenn's. The last part, though, likely cancelled out everything that had come before. "Is it true that NASA and MarsX are trying to cover up an attack by Martians?"

Lieutenant Colonel Webb managed to insert himself between Shepard and Steverson. "Hey, we told you not to do that," he growled. "Wait your turn."

Glenn saw Nik turn to Richardson as if to protest, but saw the latter simply turn his head slightly and wink, then turn back to the spectacle with a neutral expression.

Ah, Glenn thought. *This is all part of the show.*

Webb succeeded in pushing Steverson out of the way this time, and SF security cleared a way for him to proceed to the next compartment, where a small podium was set up.

Ian and Webb helped Glenn up to the stand, where he was peppered with questions for fifteen minutes.

The reporters asked about travel on *Bat*, the effects of high-gee acceleration, how he'd discovered the cause of the illness, how he'd known to check the water tanks . . . There were so many details, and frankly Glenn didn't know how much he should reveal, saying only that his bionics helped him endure the flight, that spaceflight was mostly boredom punctuated by brief flurries of activity, that he used all of the medical diagnostics at his disposal, and relied on *Percheron* crew to assist him in his investigations.

He was asked about Captain LeBlanc's death, and he answered solemnly that copper toxicity had affected her liver, and that the damage had been irreversible. To the best of his knowledge, there had been no public release of information regarding the delusions suffered by many of the crew, so he said nothing about the incidents that happened before the toxicity had become severe. In his mind, certain details could just remain covered by doctor-patient confidentiality.

The next question shook him.

"Doctor . . . Colonel Shepard. Why did Lieutenant Commander Scott die?"

Glenn and Boatright had discussed the fact that someone would ask *how* the engineer died, but neither of them had expected to be asked *why*. He looked closely at the woman who'd asked the question. She was short, with reddish hair, and turned up nose. She had a faint Scottish accent, and was using her wristcomm as a recorder.

He knew her instantly. Glenn had studied every patient

record, from medical to family history. This was Kirstie Scott, Angus' sister.

Glenn cleared his throat, looked her in the eye, and began. "Well, Miss Scott. I want to say first, that your brother died a hero. People on *Percheron* were sick, and they didn't know why. They felt—and Mission Medical agreed—that food and water contamination was likely, but at the time, we were looking for viral or bacterial contamination. Vacuum and solar radiation are excellent sterilization methods for food, and Lieutenant Commander Scott was securing a portion of the onboard food supplies in Cargo Bay One for just that purpose when the hatch blew off. Angus died of vacuum exposure."

A murmur went through the crowd of journalists. For most, this was more detail than they'd known.

"Why did the hatch blow, Colonel?" Kirstie continued, in a quiet voice. "Was it a malfunction? An accident? Deliberate?"

The rest of the crowd went silent to wait for the answer.

This is the moment that makes or breaks my career, Glenn thought. *If the Powers That Be want to keep this secret, they won't be happy with me answering her right now.*

But I have *to.*

"It was an accident, Miss Scott. The hatch release was accidently triggered from the bridge."

"By whom, Colonel Shepard?" Tears streamed down Kirstie's cheeks.

"Captain LeBlanc triggered the hatch release. The cargo bays are not airlocks, their outer doors open directly to space. The hatch opened, and Angus was pulled out into space."

"Why? Were you there when it happened?"

"No, ma'am. It was before I was aboard *Percheron*. As for why? We may never know. Captain LeBlanc was very sick, and we can no longer ask her those questions." Glenn blinked away his own tears. "By God, I wish I'd been there sooner."

Kirstie Scott nodded, muttered her thanks, and put away her comm. Webb pushed up to the podium to inform the group that Shepard needed to be seen by the doctors. Richardson floated up to Glenn and directed him to a hatch guarded by USSF security.

The hatch no sooner closed behind them, and Glenn turned on Richardson with fury in his eyes. "Tell me that wasn't part of your grand plan, your little theater for the masses."

Richardson held up his hands. "It wasn't me, and I can assure you it wasn't the general's intent."

"Intent. So, he knew."

"Not . . . entirely. He brought Miss Scott up here to talk with you. She's been tormented by her brother's death, but the plan was for her to meet with you next. In private, not in front of the cameras."

"Yeah, so I imagine I've blown it, now. Whatever clever little story you and Boatright have cooked up is now shredded, and the media now knows Gee went nuts."

"Actually, Matt LeBlanc filed a freedom of information act request and got all of Commander LeBlanc's medical data. He's been talking about it for the past month. All you did was confirm what people already knew."

"I can't imagine Space Force will be too pleased by that, though."

"If you haven't guessed by now, what the other branches of Space Force think, Boatright doesn't care. He's pretty much holding the reins of power, and has been tapped to be the next CSO."

"You still could have stopped her."

"I could have, but you're a *hero*, Colonel, and the whole world just learned that you're an honest one. Don't dismiss the fact that you're the man of the hour."

"Well, half-man. The other half is a lot of machinery."

"*Bionic* man of the hour. Yes, I could have stopped her, but I didn't. Anyone who knows you—and by the way, I read every single report you've filed, watched four months' worth of bionic bodycam footage, I think I can truthfully say *I know you*—know you wouldn't lie. She needed to hear it from you. The *world* needed to hear it from you."

"Hero, yeah. I'm not any such thing. A hero is some poor fool who doesn't know when to quit. Now, can we get out of here so I can get my arm back?"

CHAPTER 40: Homecoming

Weekly Solar News @NickSteve
Bombshell Wednesday! Hey viewers, did
you see that? Yesterday Shepard
admitted that Captain Gee LeBlanc
murdered one of her crew . . .
404 NOT FOUND
Weekly Solar News in Exile @EHNickSteve
I will not be silenced! The *Percheron
Incident* MUST BE INVESTIGATED!
                              ChirpChat, March 2044

Glenn's comm directed him to the visiting officers' quarters. VOQ space was better than barracks, typically consisting of efficiency and studio apartments for transient officers, or personnel from other branches. Other *Percheron* personnel would be transferred to O'Neill and Clarke, and then to Earth, as needed for their medical care and reacclimation to full gravity. Glenn, on the other hand, had received orders placing him on temporary duty at Heinlein.

At least he'd been able to put his working arm back on, and Ian had been there to tune it—still not perfect, but considerably better than on *Percheron*. At least he wouldn't worry about smashing anything while he slept.

A chime at the door announced Richardson and Nik. The OSI lieutenant colonel was friendly, but formal. He greeted Glenn and apologized for the abrupt introductions earlier. Nik rushed into the room and enveloped Glenn in a hug again.

"Wow, buddy, did you miss me?"

"That's from Jen. She made me promise. But yes, to be honest, we thought we were going to lose you. Andrew and I..." Nik cocked a thumb over his shoulder to indicate Richardson. "Were looking at your bionic cam recordings in real-time—or at least, fifteen minutes delayed—when Yvette locked you in the water tank and started the vacuum purge. That was frightening."

"What's going to happen to her?"

"There will be a hearing," Richardson said. "A formality, because she really can't be held responsible for her actions while impaired, but there are irregularities from before. It will be more of an inquest than a trial. She's still one of ours, and the general insists we be fair. People will want answers."

"Speaking of Boatright, I expected to see him front and center in the greeting party. Jen, too, if she's been helping him with PR, I would have thought she'd have a hand in it, too."

"The general intended to be here, and Miss Butler as

well. They were at a ceremony at Peterson SFB the day before yesterday, and were supposed to catch the last shuttle to make it here on time. Unfortunately, there was a weather delay; the Springs received thirteen inches of snow. Normally not an issue, but they were flying commercial to New Mexico and the flight was canceled. Driving was also out of the question. Jennifer will be here tomorrow, and the general will pay a visit later."

"Oh, okay. Ah, where are my manners. Please, sit." The quarters were compact, but there was a small seating area.

Nik moved to sit down, but Richardson declined. "I should give the two of you time to catch up. Doctor Pillarisetty, you may consider this as part of Colonel Shepard's homecoming brief—or not. Your choice." He went out the door and closed it behind him.

The smile finally slipped from Shepard's face. He looked tired and in pain.

"Hey buddy, welcome home. You look like shit," he told his friend.

"Just tired. I've been up for forty hours getting ready for today, then to get ambushed by Scott's sister. That was brutal."

"Yeah, but you handled that in the best way. There had been discussion about how you would handle it—not planned, but just in case someone asked a hard question like that." Nik smiled. "I told them *exactly* how it would go and you proved me right."

"But no one saw fit to warn me?"

"That's on me. Better for you to react naturally, which you did. The public now sees you as a hero who isn't afraid to speak the truth."

"I'm no hero, Nik. I messed up, plenty, including losing another arm, an eardrum, and I've got chest twinges. When Space Force sees fit to give me leave, I'll be headed back to SAMMC, I'm sure."

"Yeah, me too. Speaking of that, you know Jen will be here tomorrow, Marty's sorry, but he wasn't approved for the gees of a conventional launch. If you need him before the Force releases you, he can take a flyer that does the high-altitude launch and a slower transit. He can be here next week if you say the word. Oh, and Jakob says hi. He's got a new set of legs he wants to show you."

"I'm sure I'm going to be there soon enough." Glenn looked at him intently. "Man, Nik. It is so good to see you. The past months have been like a waking nightmare. I'd have given anything to have you squirting me with water anytime I closed my eyes. Hey, I've been remiss. How's Sheila? How are the two of you doing?"

"Not bad, Shep. We're doing fine, she loves the new clinic and is bossing all of the nurses already. Boatwright actually spun us out of SAMMC and into OSI. In addition to clinic work, he's had me doing intake interviews and evaluations. Anyone that comes to work for him needs to have a flexible mind and be able to handle the twisted sense of humor like we showed in rehab."

"Hah! Y'mean like that stupid HR briefing?"

"Good times, my friend. Good times. We still have the recording from the teleconference, you should have seen Boatright laughing at Mizz Click's face."

"I never knew that part of him. We'd met of course. He was high up in the Flight Medical branch, and we've talked and corresponded many times since, but all very formal."

"He's one of us, Shep. Sneaky old bird, too. It was awfully easy for you to stow away on *Bat* with everything you could possibly need, right? That was him."

"I know that now. It was obvious in hindsight. I got assigned to the medical review team, then to the Moon where I could test vacuum exos, then Clarke, where they were putting together the load-out for *Bat*, then having the MILES suit right there."

"Have you been following ChirpChat? He made it clear that OSI was behind you every step of the way."

"Machiavelli?"

"More benign than that. Oh, I sometimes catch glimpses of a very dark place inside him. He's forbidden me from attempting to psychoanalyze him. But he's a very complex person and I still haven't figured him out. The important part, though, is that he's protective of his people. We're the future, and anyone who works for him will need to deal with people like you, me, Jakob, and the like."

"All of them? Even ramrod straight, Colonel Richardson?"

"Even him, Shep. You'd be surprised. He's a decent guy. We talked a lot on the way up, and even before. He came up through JAG, so for legal reasons Boatright inserted him into the communications loop—you know how the Mercury/Gemini/Apollo program had this rule that only astronauts could be 'capsule communicator' and speak to the astronauts on orbit? Well, Andrew was your capcomm. Every one of your communications back to Earth went to him first. He's also the one who arranged a dedicated communication link, and encryption so that I could privately counsel you and the rest of the ship. We talked a lot about your flock—and even about you. He's very concerned that we make sure you're in an okay mental state right now. The general trusts him, and I trust him. With his legal background, he's the one who's *really* in charge here on Heinlein no matter what anyone else may think."

"And what do you think?"

"Me? Not so worried about you. At least not right now. Once they start the court-martial, though . . ."

"Court-martial. Yeah, I knew that had to be coming. Thanks for confirming it," Glenn said, sarcastically.

"Oh, not *yours*, Shep. *Yvette's*."

"Oh."

"Yeah, 'oh.' They'll get to it eventually, but there will be a lot of bluster about flaws in *Percheron*, first. It's going to be a media circus and the agencies are promising investigations and hearings to figure out who to blame. I was served with papers to testify—before you even made it back. The process server cornered me while we were waiting for *Percheron* to dock, so they knew I'd be here. I think they're expecting to order you—your recall to active duty was formalized when you crossed the threshold down in the docking area. They'll likely order Jen as well."

"Order? She's a civilian. You mean summon."

"Uh, yeah. Working for Boatright, you tend to forget who's on which side of the line. The office is very mixed, service and military-civilian, given all of the medical types."

"Huh. Well, Richardson said something about you starting my debrief?"

"Yes. Right now, if you like. I'll start with your medical exam."

"Again? I've been poked and prodded already, Nik."

"Again. I'm your doctor—at least until we decide to bring Marty up. I need a baseline status for my own records. It's part of the debrief, and I need to record it." Nik stood up easily in the half gravity and reached for a small black bag he'd left beside the door. He pulled out several instruments, clipped a recorder to the collar of his shirt, instructed Glenn take his off, then started applying sensors.

In between Nik looking in his right eye, ear, clucking over the damaged eardrum, muttering over his blood pressure and heart rate, Glenn continued to talk.

"Okay, now the big question. They *are* going to let Jen come see me?"

"Let her? It will be impossible to keep her away. If it wasn't for that delay, she'd have been here for arrival." Nik stopped his exam for a moment to stare at Glenn. "You *do* realize you're a day early, right?"

"Mila's just that good a navigator. Besides, Maxim's no slouch as pilot."

"Ah, okay. Well, if you'd arrived here tomorrow as NASA and MarsX planned, Jen would have been able to make it even with the weather delay. It's just that there was something time-critical she needed to deal with."

Glenn got a horrified look on his face. "Oh my God, please tell me she's not pregnant! I'm not sure I could deal with that right now."

"What? It's been seventeen months since you two were together! Unless there's something you're not telling me." Nik peered at him.

"Oops, yeah. Sorry, it's just that I had this dream and it felt so real."

Nik laughed. "Oh, yes, you and your dreams. No, nothing like that. As I said, it's just something to do with a new assignment. It's just that the . . . meeting . . . was on her schedule and couldn't be moved or postponed—then there was the weather and your early arrival. She'll be up here as fast as the shuttle can bring her."

Glenn looked relieved. "Okay, I can live with that. It's been more than four months—hell, it's been over a year. It's just . . ." Glenn looked down and a wistful look came over his face. He looked back up, and there was a faint sheen of tears in his eyes. "I just need to see her face."

"You can get her on comm. She's enroute now. Less than three seconds communication lag, round trip," Nik reassured his friend.

Glenn swallowed and controlled his expression. "No, that's okay. I can wait, but I do need to see her face to face. I want to hold her, hug her, kiss her, and tell her I was a fool to ever let her go. In person. You should know how important that is, Doctor."

"Trying to teach psychiatry to the psychiatrist, Shep?" Nik punched him lightly on his bionic shoulder as he removed the sensors from the biological one.

Glenn gave a brief laugh. "Yeah, I got it. You know it really is good to see you."

"You too, Shep."

CHAPTER 41:
Reunion

※

USSF Office of Scientific Integration
@OSIGenBoatright
> @EHNickSteve, Mister Steverson, we do
> not blame the patient for the virus they
> harbor. Neither do we attach any blame to
> Captain LeBlanc for the toxin which
> caused her altered mental state.
> There will be investigations and
> consequences where necessary—but
> *only* where necessary. It does no good
> to punish those who have passed. Please
> keep that in mind.

Kirstie S. @KScott @EHNickSteve, I don't
> blame her, I just needed the truth.
> @OSIGenBoatright, thank you for the
> candor your people have shown.

**Weekly Solar News, Office of the
Publisher** @WSNpub
We regret any disturbance caused by our
former reporter. Our sincere apologies to
the LeBlanc and Scott families, as well as
their crewmates. It will not happen again.
ChirpChat, April 2044

Glenn did comm Jen after Nik finished with his exam. They'd talked for an hour—stopping only because the shuttle comm relay was about to switch from Earth-orbit satellites to Moon-orbit satellites.

She'd been very apologetic over her delay, but teased him that it was all his fault for doing so well at treating his patients on *Percheron*, they got home early. She'd told him that the ceremony had been connected to her new book *The Write Stuff: An Inside View of Astronaut Training*.

Her manner had been warm and caring, not the coolness of a year ago, nor the concern of the last four months. Glenn knew he loved her, and he was pretty sure she felt the same about him. Perhaps this time he'd manage to do it right.

Nik was interviewing Glenn when both their wrist-comms chimed, announcing that Jen's shuttle was on final docking maneuvers. Nik put away his recorder and they both headed back to the zero-gee hub and docking port.

The psychiatrist seemed particularly happy about something. Glenn tried to find out what, but Nik was evasive. "You'll see" was all he could get out of the man.

The airlock cycled, and several returning USSF

technicians stepped through. There were a few civilians, including a senator who saw Glenn and came over to speak with him.

"Excellent work, young man," said the septuagenarian, former aerospace CEO. "I want to speak with you more about your experiences—nothing formal, just . . . tell me what it's been like."

"Thank you, Senator Greason. I look forward to that, and I'd love to speak with you about your experience with your space companies."

"Good times and bad, young man. Much the same as the stories you are likely to tell. Here's my contact information." He held up his wristcomm, and Glenn did the same. Personal comm codes and addresses scrolled across the screen of Glenn's wristcomm as it created a new contact. "I need to get to a meeting, and I imagine you're not here to greet me. The pilots invited her up to the cockpit. She'll be just a moment."

The senator and his contingent stepped away, revealing Jen standing in the hatch in a midnight blue Space Force uniform.

Glenn's face brightened as he stood to embrace Jen, but after a quick hug, he pushed back, still holding her arms, and looked her up and down. He took in her new uniform and all of the implications. Her insignia said major, and her branch insignia was for the OSI public affairs office.

It thrilled him that Jen would now have a future in space, but at the same time, he was worried that his own future was still in question. Over the past four months he'd experienced incredible gee-forces on *Bat*, solved the sickness on *Percheron*, endured the attacks by Yvette, and led the long process of restoring order and function to bring them all home. Throughout it all, he'd told himself he was willing to endure it all, and face any punishment, because at least he and Jen would be together on Earth.

This new development, however, might put that in jeopardy.

Jen was assigned to the VOQ, just like Glenn and Nik, but whereas Nik's room was down the corridor, Jen's was right next door. There was even a movable bulkhead that would allow the two suites to be combined, in case more room was needed for VIP guests. It was nice to know the option was there, but for now, it would stay in place. He and Jen had a lot to work out.

Nik had returned to his own suite—supposedly to file reports—a few minutes after they'd gotten back to quarters. Glenn appreciated the consideration for his and Jen's privacy, but another part regretted not having a neutral observer.

Before he left though, Nik reached up—it was a bit of a stretch, even in light gravity, Nik's spinal injury left him eight inches shorter—and tapped Glenn on the side of his head adjacent to the bionic eye. "You can turn that off, now. You're home."

Turn it off? Oh! The automatic recording function had been operating for more than four months. It had been necessary to document every action on *Percheron*, but was no longer needed. His bionics could still spy on him, but it would no longer be part of an official record.

"Yeah, thanks for the reminder, Nik," Glenn told him as he closed the door.

The two stood for several moments in awkward silence. Glenn knew how he felt about her, but despite all of the texts and recorded comms sent back and forth over the past four months, he was still uncertain where he stood with Jen. Frankly, the fact that she was now a member of Space Force confused him. They held very different ranks, and any relationship between the two of them would have to have the permission and approval of their commanders.

They stood for several moments. Glenn was, unwilling—no, he was willing, but he found himself unable to make the first move. Then Jen stepped up and wrapped her arms around him.

"I was such a fool," Glenn whispered.

"I know, Shep, but you're *my* fool and that's all that's important."

Jen was in full Guardian uniform, but Shep wore a simple shipboard jumpsuit. Jen slid her hands through the front seam and around to his back. The top fastener popped open, baring his chest, and she lay her cheek against his skin.

"I've missed you, Shep."

"Can it be this easy?"

"Of course, it can. I forgive you. I know what happened, my words and actions reminded you too much of Yvette. I put pressure on you where no pressure was deserved. The question is whether you can forgive me?"

"Yes, of course I do. You're not her. I know that." He

paused for a moment, and Jen pulled back to look at his face. "Oh God, how I know that now."

Jen said nothing. This was his moment. His catharsis.

"The last four months have been difficult. Yvette's schizophrenia led to many awkward moments. It would have been easy to just go along. To humor her, and try to forestall the swings to anger and irrationality, but it wasn't right. I was there, but my heart was here with you."

"And my heart was with you. Now stop talking." Jen pulled his head down and kissed him long and deep.

They were sitting on the sofa in Glenn's quarters. Efficiency apartments were the same the world over, and apparently off world as well. He had a sleeping area, a kitchenette, compact desk, and seating area with one chair and a sofa bed. The sofa bed wasn't much more than a cot with arms at either end and some cushions on the back, but it was still a place where more than one person could sit.

Glenn sat at the leftmost end, clad only in shorts. Jen, in just a t-shirt, sat sideways, with her back against his side, and her shapely legs stretched the length of the sofa. His arm was draped around her as they sat for a long time in silence.

After a while, Jen broke the silence. "You know what this reminds me of?"

"That night in Maui watching the stars? I'm sorry the view simply isn't as nice up here." Glenn looked pointedly at the blank bulkhead across from them.

"Oh, but I know something you don't," Jen said. She reached for her wrist comm lying on top of the pile of clothes near Glenn's feet. "We can set that wall to display anything we want." She touched a control, and giant viewscreen formed on the blank wall. A few more touches and it showed the view from a tropical beach. Not exactly the same, but close enough to Maui.

"I wonder if there will be a green flash?" Glenn mused aloud.

"Only if the recorder they're using is as sensitive as your eyes, Shep." Jen laughed.

When the sun had disappeared completely below the horizon—sadly, with no green flash—Glenn turned toward Jen, reached over with his left arm, and slipped it in underneath her knees. He then moved his right arm down to catch her around the ribs, and lifted.

"Again?" she asked, and giggled.

"Always," he answered.

Jen was on leave for the next two weeks and Glenn's TDY orders were open-ended, but it wasn't all vacation. Several hours of each day were taken with meetings. Space Force public affairs, HR, and legal all wanted statements.

Doctor Schlecht wanted to discuss the medical findings for each person who'd been aboard *Percheron*. He was particularly interested in the mental abnormalities, so Nik sat in on those meetings to provide the psychiatrist point of view as well. Glenn didn't know what he could provide that wasn't in the reports sent to MMC, but Peter seemed to be satisfied. The director told him that it was the personal touch which counted. He thanked Glenn once again, and apologized for all those times his division had doubted him or second guessed his decisions.

Schlecht hadn't been head of MMC five years ago, but he made it clear that the apology went back to Glenn's accident as well. He was a hero, and needed to be recognized as such.

Glenn didn't feel like a hero, but there was a comm message detailing several citations for bravery. Jen told him that there was talk of him receiving a presidential medal and honors from each of the countries that made up the Mars Exploration Consortium.

There was also a considerable amount of time spent in debrief with Lieutenant Colonel Richardson and General Boatright. Most of the time the general was on comm, but toward the end of the two-week period, he'd actually showed up in person. He greeted Glenn warmly—and Jen even more warmly. If Glenn wasn't so happy, he might have been jealous.

It was clear from the start that Space Force would not tolerate any blame attached to the actions of one Colonel Glenn Shepard. Boatright had anticipated his moves every step of the way, and made sure that orders permitting those actions were in place before they even occurred. It made Glenn wonder about free will, and whether he was so predictable.

Boatright just smiled, and said, "It's all just experience, Shep."

One evening, Glenn asked Jen about the general.

"What's his story? What motivates him?"

"He's one of you, Shep. He was injured in Afghanistan, and spent time in rehab. He's got pins, plates and screws holding one ankle together and is in pain a *lot*, although I've never seen him show it."

"And you know all this, why?"

"I'm a reporter, Shep. I find out things."

"Yeah, that's true. Okay, so he knows rehab, I can see that. It's some motivation, but how does he manage to know me so well?"

"He had a son in the Navy. Pilot. Got shot up and barely made it back to the carrier. He managed to get the jet down. It was a bad landing; he got his EWO clear, but was badly burned in the process. A few weeks later, he cracked open his drug pump and hotwired it into giving him an overdose of morphine. Took his own life because he didn't want to live with the pain."

"Oh, damn. That sucks."

"But that's why, Shep. *You* never gave up. You're him, and you're what his son couldn't be. He'll never tell you this, but you mean a hell of a lot to him."

"Crap. That explains so much."

"Doesn't it, though?"

At the end of two weeks. Jen was packing up to head back to Earth while Glenn and Nik replaced the movable panel between suites.

"Okay, Nik, how is this going to play out? What's next?"

"Jeff Ling will be here tomorrow to sign off on your medical clearance. I've recommended you for higher gravity, and he concurs. He just wanted a chance to see you before you shipped out."

"He's a good man, for an Army doc."

"He said much the same about you, fly-boy. Anyway, you go to Clark for a week of intensive physical therapy in the zero-point-seven-five-gee ring, and if you do okay, they'll move you up to one gee for another week. As long as you can handle that—and there's no reason you shouldn't—then you're headed back to Earth."

"Where? San Antonio? Tucson? D.C.?"

"You've been on continuous ops for almost five months. You're due six weeks full leave on doctor's orders. Take it anywhere you want. You're welcome to come to San Antonio and stay with me and Sheila, or hit the VOQ at SAMMC. But at the end of the June, you'll need to be in D.C."

"Hmm, okay. Fair enough."

"You want my advice? Go home. Go to Lexington and see Aunt Sally."

"Yeah, she's been calling on the comm every other day. It will be good to see her, and damned good to be home."

"With Jen in D.C. you can see each other on the weekends. I'll give you a little bit of time to yourself, but I'll come up for a visit, too. I'd love to see Aunt Sally again, and I'll be there for the circus, too."

"The circus?"

"Senate, MarsX, the internationals—they all want to hold hearings. They've been instructed to wrap it all up before the end of June. Then we concentrate on Yvette's court-martial."

"Ah, so that's been scheduled."

"Yup, July eleventh; a bit over two months from now."

"Will she be ready by then? Two-and-a-half months is

not a lot of time to prepare—hell, *six* months since she started treatment isn't much time for this."

"I give that a qualified maybe. On the other hand, I'm going to have most of those two-and-a-half months to work with her. While you head to Clarke, I'm headed back down the well to see my other patient."

"Good luck with that. Help her; I mean that sincerely."

"Yeah, thanks for that, Shep. I'll do my best; she needs our help and our support."

CHAPTER 42:
Tribunal

USSF Office of Scientific Integration
@OSIGenBoatright

(1/2) How did it happen? I think Frank
Borman said it best when asked to speak
about the Apollo One fire: 'failure of
imagination.'
No one imagined the combination of
circumstances which caused the fire on
Apollo One. Likewise, no one imagined
the conditions which resulted in the Apollo
Thirteen crisis, the loss of Asimov Station,
or the possibility that an astronaut would
develop appendicitis while orbiting the
Moon in a Wyvern craft fifteen years ago.
(2/2) It is pointless to seek to pin the
blame on any one person, company, or
agency. While none of them were
responsible, at the same time, all of them
were responsible—even those of you

> sitting in tribunal, second guessing the
> people who were actually there.
> I ask each of you to think upon this and
> reflect on what *you* would have, or could
> have, done differently.
>
> ChirpChat, June 2044

The weeks at Clark were a lot of hard work, but nothing compared to Glenn's original rehabilitation. For that matter, he'd been through exactly this type of rapid acclimation before. During his tenure as CMO of Moonbase, he'd spent fifteen months at one-sixth gee. Heinlein Station wasn't complete, neither were the low-gee rings at Clarke. He went directly from Moon gravity to Earth gravity without benefit of transition to intermediate gee forces.

On the other hand, reacclimation in those days meant an intensive six days doing almost nothing but resistance exercises, cycling, and running on a treadmill. Nights were spent sleeping head-in, feet-out, in a five-meter centrifuge that simulated one gee (and a lot of dizziness).

All in all, he'd prefer the step-up approach available at Clarke.

As he progressed to the full-gee experience, he noticed that the fine motor control on his bionic arm started to deteriorate. He commed Ian to discuss the problem.

"It's just gee-force compensation. Time for a tune-up, Shep. I'll be up there before you're due to return to Earth. I just need to adjust the force-feedback loops."

"You're going to do it before I go to Aunt Sally's, right? I can't be breaking her plates and glasses."

"No worries. I'll send some update codes that will help out now, and be up there by the end of the week.

"Thanks, Ian. I appreciate it."

By the time Glenn finally got down to Earth, most of his injuries had healed, so he had few worries of Aunt Sally scolding him for getting himself hurt. She would still fuss, but that was expected of the woman who had stood in for his mother for so many years.

His eardrum had mostly healed by the time *Percheron* arrived at Heinlein Station. The docs had pronounced minimal airway scarring from vacuum, and there was no lasting mucous membrane damage. He had chest twinges a few times during extremely intense exercise, but it was minor, and he kept that one to himself.

"Glennie!"

Sally came out of the house when she saw the black USSF vehicle pull into the driveway. She'd barely waited for him to get out of the car before enveloping him in a hug.

"Momma."

"Welcome home, Glennie. I'm glad you're okay. I was so worried when I heard you'd gone flying off on your own."

"Not my own, Momma, I had good people helping me."

"Come inside. I have fresh baked cookies."

Aunt Sally made him sit down at the table while she fussed over making a pot of coffee. She and Uncle Hoop would grind fresh beans and make a pot every morning, but that was simply too much for her to drink on her own. Company was always an occasion for coffee in the Pritchard and Shepard households, though, so she was eager to share a pot with Glenn or any visitors who might come calling.

There were, indeed, fresh-baked cookies. Oatmeal raisin, his favorite. Two cookies and a mug of coffee later, Sally gave him a pointed look.

"Jennifer. What's the story? Have you made up with the dear girl?"

"Yes, Momma. I apologized and she apologized, and we forgave each other. She'll come this weekend."

"Good. She came by when you were gone, you know. It was the day before they announced you were out on *Percheron* dealing with the medical problems, and she came by personally to tell me."

"She told me. She was worried about you getting word from the media."

"I had your initial comm message, though. The one you sent when you launched the *whatchamacallit*—the *Bat*."

"I know you did, but Jen told me the general insisted on the personal touch—although, she would have done it anyway."

"He came by, too. Your general."

"He did?" Glenn was shocked.

"Of course, it's not the first time I'd met him. Rick came to see me after your accident. He talked me through your rehabilitation plan. He also came to talk to me and Hoop before the two of us came to see you. We'd crossed paths in the hospital. He's been looking out for you, you know."

"So I've learned. Huh. That's a lot more personal than I expected."

"Rick likes my peanut butter cookies—you know, the ones with the crisscross pattern on top. I made a pot of that Hawaiian coffee you sent me. He's a very pleasant man."

"Rick. Wow, you're on a first-name basis with the general. I never would have imagined it. That's just not an image I associate with him."

"He cares about you. You remind him of himself. He told me way back when, that you'd use your abilities to help people. That's why he supported the bionics and everything. He said that again when you went to *Percheron*. It's what he would have done in your place."

His month's leave was nearly over. Jen had come from D.C. each weekend, and Nik had come calling as well. They were sitting with the inevitable cups of coffee and plate of cookies in the den watching a video feed from the Hague while Sally puttered about in the kitchen.

The video was coverage of a meeting of the MOSEC— the Mars and Outer System Exploration Consortium, the allied space agencies portion of MarsX. Several of the participating agencies argued that the U.S. and Space Force should bear the brunt of the blame for the "*Percheron* Incident."

General Philip Bolger-Cortez, Chief of Space Operations and senior officer of USSF, argued that the construction phase of civilian space operations fell under NASA jurisdiction. Moreover, *Percheron* had been built by contractors. He further argued that *Percheron* had been built by *MOSEC* contractors, to give the multinationals a larger role in the consortium.

Doctor Aaron Haskins, CEO and president of MarsX, cited the safety record of the Mars missions to date. The *Percheron* Incident had nothing to do with MarsX, Tucson Mission Control, or Mission Medical. Indeed, MarsX personnel could not have foreseen the leak and were therefore not culpable. Furthermore, the valve from water tank to the fungicide reservoir was added as an afterthought based on a NASA design modification.

Next to testify was Eugene Kraft, second in command at NASA. He'd come up through the ranks as a flight director, much like the two men he'd been named for. He denied that the NASA design was at fault. Failure was not an option. Their own history had taught them to check everything.

Glenn, Jen, and Nik watched this prologue to the inquiry and wondered when the representatives would actually ask the people who were there and affected by the copper leak. They didn't have long to wait, although Dvorak was the only crew member to appear in front of the committee, as the only officer available. When the Ecuadoran delegate complained about that fact, Dvorak pointed out that Katou was sick, and LeBlanc and Scott were dead—would Madam Delegate prefer to call in a psychic to continue the questioning?

She ignored the barb, and tried to lay the blame on LeBlanc. The French delegate jumped up and accused the Ecuadoran of "victim-shaming." On the contrary, the Ecuadoran delegate argued, if LeBlanc hadn't wasted most of the contents of IWS Reservoir Four, there would have been more than enough water left, and the crew wouldn't have had to drink from the contaminated tank.

"That's not how it works, that's not how any of it works," Glenn said.

"I know, Shep." Jen told him. "I know how the political and media minds work. These folks are there to be seen and heard—to look good for their constituents."

"Yeah, but they've got the logic wrong. The copper caused LeBlanc's hallucinations. Copper-dependent enzymes turn dopamine into norepinephrine. It works just like methamphetamine overdose. She wouldn't have blown the hatch if she weren't already affected. They were already drinking contaminated water when they lost the contents of Tank Four—besides, standard procedure would have been to finish Tank Three first anyway, so all the water in Tank Four still wouldn't have done any good."

Much to Glenn's surprise, Dvorak responded with exactly that point.

"But why don't you go in the tank and inspect it periodically?" asked the Russian delegate.

"Ladies and gentlemen. We don't go inside a water tank in free-fall because we'd drown before we got out," Dvorak told her.

"But you have spacesuits!" protested the Russian delegate.

"Have you ever tried to swim in a spacesuit, ma'am? No? I thought not. I'd be perfectly happy to give you the experience if you'd come down to Houston."

The gallery broke into laughter, and the chairman gaveled the session to a close for the day.

※ ※ ※

The next day, even though no possible blame could be placed on the Mars Three/Marsbase One crew, the tribunal called Gavin Taketani. For this testimony, they had to link in O'Neill Station and endure a three-second round-trip communications lag. Taketani was scheduled for another month of high-gee rehabilitation for heart function before the docs would approve his return to Earth. The questioning was actually quite awkward, with long pauses in the testimony. Glenn told the other two that the pauses were not lightspeed delay, but rather Taketani was very carefully trying to decide who had asked which question—the video link only showed official MOSEC delegates. Non-signatories weren't supposed to ask questions, although that certainly hadn't stopped the Ecuadoran or Russian so far. They were present because they'd contributed contractors, but were supposed to just be observers, not badgering witnesses.

Taketani described events, procedures, and consequences to the best of his knowledge. Officially, he was a passive onlooker for much of the voyage. Unofficially, he kept to himself, and didn't pay much attention to MarsX or *Percheron* personnel once they'd left Mars. He suggested that the board should really talk to his chief medical officer Yvette Barbier. The board agreed, and summoned her, but received a stern warning citing international standards of health information privacy. Barbier was unavailable due to her own ongoing medical care.

"They won't get her," Nik said.

"She's that bad?" Jen asked.

"No, but she's in therapy and needs to be left alone.

The last thing she needs is these clowns making her relive it."

Glenn grunted agreement.

The hearing broke down into turmoil. No one—not the agencies, the governments, nor the corporations—wanted to accept responsibility.

In the words of America's second man in space, Gus Grissom—"it just blew."

CHAPTER 43:
In the Spotlight

❀

USSF Office of Scientific Integration
@OSIGenBoatright
> Congratulations to Doctor Glenn Shepard
> on your awards. They are well deserved.

O'Dour @TheOakTree
> @OSIGenBoatright, I, for one, would like
> to shake his hand. I can't wait to meet
> him.

ChirpChat, July 2044

Glenn didn't return to Washington D.C. until after the blistering-hot four-day Fourth of July weekend. He had one week to prepare for the start of Yvette's court martial; but before that, was due for several meetings with government leaders.

The first would take place at the Pentagon. Glenn had to report to General Boatright for a briefing. He was surprised to see that the E-ring OSI office was full and bustling with activity just one day past a major holiday weekend. It was even more mind-boggling when he saw an organization chart which showed that OSI now comprised a sizeable percentage of the total Space Force!

The meeting with Boatright was brief. He advised that the OSI position with respect to Yvette's actions was that she was competent, but impaired. He wanted no cover-up—only fairness—but they needed the truth. Glenn would likely be called as a witness for the prosecution, and he was to speak as he wished. Nik was listed as a defense witness, but was also likely to be called by the prosecution. Many of their mutual colleagues would be involved, because OSI and Space Force needed to be seen to take the situation seriously—much more seriously than the "*Percheron* Incident" tribunal.

Which made Glenn's command performance with several ranking senators and congressmen all that more important. These weren't to be formal hearings, but informal, relaxed conversations to allow the lawmakers a chance to hear the details from someone who was there. He'd been assigned a team within the OSI public affairs office to assist with those meetings—mostly just scheduling, but a representative would accompany him to each of the meetings. Glenn argued that legal counsel would be better—someone who could tell his "inquisitors" that he was invoking his right to silence.

The general just smiled. A light flashed on the general's comm board indicating a visitor. He acknowledged the alert and instructed his aide to allow the person to enter.

Boatright rose, and stepped out from behind his desk to greet the visitor. Glenn did likewise, wondering who was so important that the general would interrupt their meeting.

It was Jen, looking beautiful in her uniform.

"Welcome, Major. I was just telling Colonel Shepard that he would have a PAO assistant for his meetings. Colonel Shepard? Meet your new aide."

"Uh, sir. Um. I'm not sure how to say this."

"What, you object to Major Butler? I thought you got along quite well. Quite closely, if I recall." There was a teasing twinkle in his eyes.

"Ah, yes, sir. We do. Which is the problem. Um, conduct unbecoming?"

"Nonsense. I've never seen any hint of inappropriate behavior. You *are* going to do right by her, are you not?"

"Yes, sir! I mean no, sir! I mean . . ."

"Relax, Shep. Jen's orders state that she's been assigned to you *specifically* because she's your biographer and knows you better than anyone else. The 'intimately' part is implied, and allowed under the circumstances. You are unique, Jen is unique. No other two servicemembers could do this job, so we make allowances."

"Ah, thank you, sir."

"Jen isn't your handler, so much as advisor. I've assigned Lieutenant Colonel Richardson as your legal counsel, and he's briefed her on what to expect, but we really don't need to worry about that. Speak your mind, tell the truth. If there's any blowback, Jen's there to see and hear it. We can deal with it later if we have to—but right now, the important part is that we are transparent, we are cooperating, and we are truthful. That's the reputation this office needs to have going forward."

Wow. This was certainly a refreshing change.

The first meeting turned out to be nothing to worry over. They were in Senator Greason's office, along with two other senators from the Extraterrestrial Operations Committee. The former space executive set the tone, which was relaxed and collegial. Glenn was mostly asked about his experience on *Bat*, what steps led him to suspect copper toxicity, and how the patients were doing at present. The conversation then turned to questions of which particular roles could be best fulfilled by astronauts with bionic enhancement.

They talked for almost two hours, and while Glenn agreed afterward that it had been a relatively low-stress event, his own anxiety kept him from being overly comfortable. He was also extremely glad Jen was there. Several times, he reached over to hold her hand, then realized they were both in uniform, and pulled his hand back. Greason noticed, winked, and smiled. The others appeared not to notice.

The second meeting was less comfortable, but still not adversarial. The House meeting was held in one of the congressional hearing rooms, with Glenn and Jen seated at a table in front of a curved bench, behind which sat five representatives from the health and space committees. The questions ranged from details about the medical facilities aboard *Percheron*, to how it felt to ride the first Helicity2 drive. A surprising twist was a question about which state and district had produced the supplies carried on *Bat*.

Glenn couldn't answer, but Jen seemed to have that information readily available on her tablet. Glenn was impressed, and so were the congresspersons. Since they were seated behind a table, Glenn could take her hand—and did.

The most problematic meeting was the one that should have been no problem at all. They were invited to a reception at the New Zealand embassy. New Zealand was a member of MOSEC and Mila Katou had family there. While the country couldn't claim the Space Force officer directly, they were proud of her nonetheless. Mila would be at the reception, briefly, and the event had been set up with the ostensible reason of thanking Glenn for her rescue and life-saving surgery. He was instructed to wear civilian clothes so that he could legally wear the awards presented to him by the French and Japanese governments the previous day. It meant being fitted for a tuxedo just that morning—his previous one was more than five years old, and wasn't sized for his bionic limbs. Jen wore an absolutely stunning emerald green dress, and his breath caught every time he looked at her.

About halfway through the evening, Katou bid her goodbyes. She was still somewhat weak, but her new bioprinted liver was functioning just fine. She just needed to rest. An aide brought a wheelchair, but she waved him off, requesting that Glenn and Jen walk her to her car. She leaned heavily on Glenn's arm, particularly when out of sight of the crowd. When they reached the front door, she looked up a Glenn; he was a good ten inches taller, and she motioned for him to lean down. Mila wrapped her arms around his neck, held him for a moment, then gave him a peck on his cheek.

"Thank you," she said, with tears in her eyes. "I wouldn't be here without you." She said her goodbyes to Jen, the two hugged, then she got into her car to return home.

Glenn stood looking up at the sky for a moment, holding Jen by his side. There were a surprising number of stars visible, but then, D.C. had been working to reduce incident artificial light for the past twenty years. A U.S. vice president had once remarked that it was a shame that the Naval Observatory—which was just across the street from the embassy—couldn't be used to view the night sky because of the city's light pollution.

The two stood, arm in arm, for several minutes looking at those stars while Glenn processed his feelings about what Mila had said.

Two men came out the front door of the embassy, arguing. Glenn and Jen were off to one side, and the men showed no sign of being aware of their presence.

"Senator, we absolutely *must* increase our presence in space. All question of resources aside, we can't have our eggs in only one basket. Diseases travel too far, too fast, and the effects of natural disasters are felt around the world for years after the fact. We need to spread out, colonize planets, moons, asteroids—even go to other stars."

"Hell, no. We need to stay right where we are and work on solving the problems we have."

"We can do that. Every major advance in space brings us a corresponding advance in science and engineering.

The aeroponics facility on O'Neill showed us how to better grow crops in Africa. The hydroponics fields on the Moon are used to *purify* air and water for God's sake!"

"You and all your billionaire buddies need to stop wasting money in space. Stop wasting my constituents' money, too. You, your MarsX club, and Space Force—and their damned mechanical puppet-man while they're at it!"

Glenn now recognized one of the men as O'Dour, the tech genius and billionaire who'd started three space industries and was a partner in MarsX. The other—the Senator—he was less sure of.

Senator Walters from Minnesota, came a silent message over his heads-up display. Jen was tapping at her wristcomm. *Go ahead. Get up there—J.*

Glenn stepped into the slightly brighter area in front of the door. "And just what do you think Mister O'Dour does, Senator Walters? Fly up to four hundred miles, open the hatch and start throwing bricks of gold out the door? Is that how he wastes money in space?"

Walters turned red, but O'Dour just grinned.

"Every single dollar, every yen, pound, euro— whatever—spent on space is spent right here on Earth. Right in your state, even." Data began to scroll in his vision. That was Jen giving him numbers, dollars, places, and names. "Seven NASA astronauts were born in Minnesota. Those are just the ones who flew before private space industry got involved. The University of Minnesota is currently running five research studies funded by NASA, three funded by DARPA, and two more funded by Space Force. The tubing and catheters I used on *Percheron* for dialysis were manufactured by 3M—you might know them as *Minnesota* Mining and Manufacturing. Every dollar spent *on space* is actually spent *on Earth* and represents a job, a wage, a salary... and tax dollars for you to spend, Senator."

Walters was blustering, and turned to leave, but O'Dour grabbed his elbow and turned him back around. "Not yet, Monty. I don't believe the young man is finished. You do recognize him, no? Our 'mechanical puppet-man' of the hour?"

Walters' eyes went wide, and his face paled. "I'm sorry. I didn't recognize you, Colonel."

"That's okay, Senator, you're a busy man, with your constituents' best interests at heart. I should let you go." Glenn smiled.

The senator shook his arm loose from O'Dour's grasp, turned and hurried away, calling for his driver on his wristcomm.

O'Dour stepped up and grabbed Glenn's hand. "Well, done, Shep. May I call you Shep? I'm O'Dour. I'm very pleased to meet you."

Glenn was stunned as he shook the man's hand. The text cleared from his heads-up display, leaving only:

My Hero—J.

CHAPTER 44:
Court Martial

USSF Office of Scientific Integration
  @OSIGenBoatright
  (1/3) People ask me if I think the
  Percheron Incident could have been
  prevented—as if somehow there was a
  failure of our own personnel. The people
  on *Percheron* did their best and never
  failed to do their best—even at risk to
  their own lives. Colonel Glenn Shepard
  risked his life on the *Bat* to go to
  Percheron to treat his fellow Guardians
  and colleagues. Doctor Yvette Barbier
  withstood the influence of the toxin much
  longer than anyone else could possibly
  have done due to a courageous decision
  she had made 20 years previously.
  (2/3) Engineer Scott refused a full
  pressure suit because he needed the

dexterity of his fingers and the ability to
maneuver around the cargo he was
securing in Cargo Bay One. That decision
cost him his life. Captain LeBlanc fought
as long as she could. She led her crew in
the finest tradition before she succumbed
to a disorder that none of us could predict.
Even back on Earth, our Mission Medical
docs used every resource at their
disposal to solve the malady afflicting our
crew.
(3/3) These people are heroes, not
villains. Could this tragedy have been
prevented? We don't know now, and we
may never know the answer. Could we
have addressed it in any other way? No.
Our people acted professionally and did
their best. We can ask no more.
                                          ChirpChat, July 2044

Glenn spent the rest of the weekend dreading the
consequences of his outburst, but none came. Jen assured
him that everything he said—and to whom he had said
it—was well within the boundaries that General Boatright
had set for her and the Public Affairs Office. In fact, they
were surprised that it had taken so long to come across
someone like Senator Walters.

He tried to put that all aside, but still had the nagging
sense of being manipulated into something. He thought
he knew what—Yvette's court martial was due to start, and
he would be called as a witness against her. He had mixed

feelings. On the one hand, he'd harbored resentment for so long that she had outmaneuvered him for so many positions of honor and responsibility. He had doubted her capabilities, and even had to come to the rescue to fix a situation he was certain she'd screwed up. But the four months he'd spent with the *Percheron* and Marsbase crew had shown him a totally different side of Yvette, as seen by the people she cared for.

That was, in fact, the problem. Yvette cared—perhaps too much. There had been a lessening of the exercise requirement because the construction schedule for Marsbase itself had been overly optimistic; it was falling behind, and the people were overextending themselves to meet deadlines. Yvette had stepped in and changed the daily requirements and timetables to provide more rest breaks. One of the changes had been a reduction in mandatory exercise time from sixty to thirty minutes, given the high exertion levels of the rest of the day.

Melissa Green had developed scurvy—not because of any nutritional failing, but because the increased work required increased calories—carbohydrates—which in turn elevated her blood glucose levels. She wasn't diabetic, but her kidneys worked harder, and hence were more active in eliminating Vitamin C, so she suffered a deficiency. Taketani had a rash that was hard to treat because he had a skin sensitivity to the powder they used to prevent chafing in their suits. He could have used talcum powder, but they had none—talc was a respiratory irritant and banned in closed ecosystems because of the possibility of asbestos contamination. Yvette had the geologist, Maia D'Cruz, searching for naturally occurring

talc in the Martian soil to try to manufacture a substitute
for Taketani.

The crew respected and looked up to her, and when
the unknown malady started to affect them, Yvette was
seemingly the only one unaffected. Her excuses about not
having the supplies she needed were quite true. Glenn
had plenty of time to go completely through the ship in
four months. There were too many things missing that
should have been stocked. He found inventory tags and
stickers with blanks for the dates of entries for when the
compartment had been stocked.

She hadn't lied, and she also hadn't confined anyone.
Glenn followed up on the log which showed he was the
first person to activate the command subsystem for door
locks. He was indeed the only one to have used it, when
he disabled the lock in the med bay. On the other hand,
several compartment locks in the habitat ring started
sticking around the same time as the spin had been shut
down.

Yvette was well-liked—even loved—by her crewmates.
She'd been calm and cool and dealt with the sickness to
the best of her ability—until she, too, succumbed. She'd
even been there to help with Katou's surgery, then
confined *herself* when she felt her own self-control
slipping.

No, Glenn no longer harbored a grudge, if for no more
reason than seeing her grief and guilt firsthand. Yvette had
always been driven, and extremely passionate in pursuing
her goals, but there was neither malice nor incompetence
in her actions.

Glenn couldn't blame her—not and be honest with

himself. Considering that his charge from General Boatright was to be honest, he suspected that it would not make him very popular with the court.

He was mistaken.

"Please state your name for the court."

"Yvette Elaine Barbier."

"And your rank, branch, and current duty status."

"Major, United States Space Force, Medical Branch, Active Duty."

"Objection! *Major* Barbier is currently assigned to selected reserve."

"Overruled. The actions we are here to review are the medical duties she performed as an individual mobilization augmentee. We will review her actions as actively deployed."

"Major, what was your role on Marsbase?"

"I was the chief medical officer, in my role as medical liaison to the Mars Exploration Consortium."

"And how did you come to obtain that position?"

"I was selected as a replacement for the medical officer who had been injured and unable to deploy on the Mars Three mission."

"And was that injured officer also a space force officer?"

"Yes, it was Colonel Glenn Shepard, and his injury was quite well documented."

"Were you not instrumental in the decision to exclude Colonel Shepard from the Mars Three mission?"

"I didn't exclude him. I merely supported the decision to offer him a medical retirement."

"But isn't it true that you opposed the rehabilitation plan which would have allowed him to resume his duties? To fulfill the role of medical officer?"

"Objection! My client has already stated that she supported a decision—it is a matter of record that the decision was ultimately made by Command, and not my client."

"Prosecutor Ramirez?"

"It speaks to motive, Your Honor."

"Very well. The objection is overruled."

"Major Barbier, did you object to the rehabilitation plan which would have returned Colonel Shepard to active status and allowed him to rejoin the Mars Three mission?"

"He wanted me to cut off his legs!" Yvette sobbed. "He wanted them cut off so that he could have prosthetics fitted, but there was only a five percent chance of success with each procedure. He could not have lived a normal life with all of the reconstructive surgery they had to do. I couldn't stand to see him in pain and crippled for the rest of his life."

"But if you hadn't amputated his legs, he would have lost them anyway. In fact, he likely would have lost more bone, more tissue, and more function. He would have been crippled anyway."

The proceedings were taking place in an Air Force courtroom on Joint Base Anacostia-Bolling—JBAB— across the Potomac River from Reagan National Airport. Glenn was seated in the gallery, awaiting the call to testify. The questioning made Glenn highly uncomfortable. He was in uniform, but Jen was not, so she sat next to him, and squeezed his hand as the questioning rehashed his accident.

With Yvette on the stand, her attorney, a JAG major named Thomas, and Nik Pillarisetty were seated at the defendant's table. Nik glanced over at Glenn a few times, a look of concern on his face.

Glenn squeezed Jen's hand, took a deep breath, and tuned back in to the questioning.

"Colonel Shepard did not have a DNR—a Do Not Resuscitate order on file, did he?"

"That is correct."

"So, he effectively asked to be resuscitated and treated as needed in the event of serious injury. Is that correct?"

"Yes."

"Therefore, you needed to follow his instructions with respect to saving his life."

"Yes, I guess so."

"Is it not true, that in refusing him the care he requested, you were refusing to do your duty as a doctor? Is that correct?"

"Objection. This has no relevance to the events on Marsbase or *Percheron*."

"Your Honor, I believe it speaks quite strongly to motivations that led Major Barbier to be on Marsbase and in *Percheron* in the first place."

"I'll allow it. Mister Ramirez, let's wrap this up. The objection is overruled, but you need to get to your point."

"Very well. Major Barbier, is it true that despite your medical advice, Colonel Shepard received his bionic rehabilitation and was on his way to recovering sufficient to rejoin the Mars Three expedition?"

"Yes, he was recovering, but I don't think he could have rejoined the Mars Three mission."

"Just answer the question. Did Colonel Shepard recover despite your own medical prognostication?"

"Yes, he did."

"And you objected to that fact."

"No, that's simply not true."

"Objection."

"Sustained. I'm going to go with the defense on this one. Mister Ramirez, make your point and move on."

"Very well, Your Honor. Doctor Barbier, did you specifically prevent Colonel Shepard from joining the Mars Three mission?"

"No, I wouldn't have done that."

"But you didn't think he should be there."

"He hadn't recovered enough to fulfill the duties."

"So, you made sure that you took his place instead."

"Objection!"

"No further questions right now, Your Honor, but I will be recalling the defendant at a later time."

The next morning, the prosecution called Doctor Peter Schlecht and questioned him intensely about the Mars Three crew health reports. The director of MarsX Mission Medical Command insisted that the results were within normal range of variability. Glenn, of course, knew why they had deviated, but it wasn't his time to testify. He wondered exactly what role his testimony would play in the proceedings.

The next topic regarded Yvette's selection for the CMO position, and whether she had deliberately sabotaged Glenn's chance to recover and join the mission, instead of leaving the vacancy she'd filled.

The prosecutor argued that there had been two possible launch dates, six months apart, but MarsX chose the earlier launch window, rather than waiting—and allowing Glenn to join the mission. For the first time in the proceedings, there was information that Glenn hadn't known ahead of time.

"The decision was made to replace Colonel Shepard approximately six weeks before mission launch. In the opinion of this medical board, would Colonel Shepard have been considered fit for duty for the alternate launch window six months later?"

"The medical board determined that it would take Colonel Shepard at least six more months of rehabilitation, and retraining for the mission."

"So, he would have been ready for the later launch."

"We couldn't know for sure, but the later launch had other problems."

"Why is that? Mars is Mars, it would still be there six months later."

"Mars Three was actually three missions—and launches. In Phase One, cargo modules were sent with food, fuel, and air supplies. Phase Two sent the construction materials and infrastructure for the base. Third phase was personnel to construct and work in the base. The first two phases had already launched—in fact, the Phase One ships had already arrived. Those items would have to sit there for another six months before they could be unpacked and inspected. If the crew launched immediately, got to Mars, and found any of the pre-positioned supplies to be lost, broken or faulty, replacements could be launched immediately."

"But couldn't they simply do that six months later?"

"No, the timing of optimum transit to Mars would have required a longer transit time. That would add four more months before the supplies arrived. We didn't have the Helicity2 drive, or the strap-on launch boosters we used to send *Bat* in six days. We launched in the first window—and had the backup plan of resupply in six months. If we launched later and needed the emergency resupply, those would have taken nearly a year to get to Mars. The crew might as well have come back. Mission failure. We simply couldn't wait."

Glenn hadn't known about the timing of the two launch windows. At the time, he'd been too busy feeling sorry for himself.

Ramirez called Jeff Ling, who testified over video link from the Moon. Again, the prosecutor called Yvette's qualifications into question, but Ling professed nothing but respect for her qualifications.

Ramirez then asked why—if everyone was satisfied with Yvette's performance—it was necessary to have Glenn on the team reviewing her findings and decisions.

"Mister Prosecutor, it is obvious that you have never worked in the medical field."

"I fail to see the relevance. Answer the question. If you and Mission Medical had every confidence in Major

Barbier, why did you need Colonel Shepard to review the medical data?"

"As I was about to tell you—in medicine, we seldom take only one view of a medical problem—that's called siloing and it costs lives. Daily rounds are not just for teaching, but to verbalize and discuss a case, the test results, and the diagnosis. Surgical cases are always preceded by a conference involving all of the doctors associated with a case, including the personal physician, specialists such as neurologists, the surgeons, the rehabilitation team. In this case, we needed to bring in the space physiology specialists. Colonel Shepard wasn't the only doctor looking at the data."

"Just the most critical."

"Perhaps. He had a vested interest. He trained with these people. They were friends and colleagues. He, and we, wanted the best for them."

"Objection. Relevance."

"Sustained, Mister Ramirez. I think you've taken this line of questioning far enough."

The second day of the court martial came to a close with Glenn feeling that the testimony had been mostly in Yvette's favor. So far, the only real negatives had been about her motivation and methodology of getting assigned to Mars Three. On the subject of her competency, the prosecution had gotten nowhere.

The problem was—they still hadn't gotten to events on *Percheron*.

CHAPTER 45:
Redemption

Glenn Shepard @BionicMan
> People have called me a hero. That's not
> me. A hero is a person who's in the wrong
> place at the right time. I was always in the
> right place at the wrong time. I did only
> what needed to be done. I am a doctor,
> and I treat patients. Sometimes those
> patients need to be helped to safety
> before I can treat them. It's simple, I just
> do my job.

Butler Media @JenButler
> @BionicMan, that's why you're a hero,
> dearest.

ChirpChat, July 2044

"Thomas hasn't had to do much in cross-examination. The questions he does ask are pretty damaging to the prosecution, but Ramirez seems to be hurting his case all on his own. Still, I can't help thinking that Ramirez still has another shoe to drop. It has to be something they think will trump everything else and convict her," Glenn confided to Jen.

"I would imagine he thinks that your testimony will settle it," she told him.

"I'm not so sure. Ramirez and Thomas both summoned me. I'm not sure if I'm witness for the prosecution or the defense."

"You're the witness for the truth."

"And if one or the other doesn't like what I have to say?"

"That's on them. Just do what's right."

Prosecutor Ramirez started delving into events on *Percheron*. Dvorak was questioned at length as to why he would relinquish command to someone who was basically a reservist, when he was a line officer and second in command of *Percheron*.

"But she outranks me. We're both majors, but she has seniority."

"Major Barbier was not in your chain of command."

"We had orders placing her in our chain of command. She was an Individual Mobilization Augmentee from the Selected Reserve. That meant she was assigned to active duty with the *Percheron* and outranked me. She was our chief medical officer, and the captain was unfit for duty. We were facing an illness that was possibly infectious, and it was for certain that I didn't understand any of it. I offered her command by seniority, but she actually didn't want it. She *did* tell me what to tell the crew. As long I was satisfied with her legitimacy—which I was—the crew would follow."

"But she locked you in your quarters."

"We were in quarantine. She told us all to self-isolate because we didn't know if we'd brought a virus from Earth, or something alien from Mars. We stocked up on rations, went to our quarters, and stayed there. It was all voluntary."

"So, you abandoned your duties to just sit in your quarters."

"*Percheron* was in coast phase. There was nothing critical coming up for two months except routine maintenance. Philips did most of that anyway, and Yvette said it was better to just have one person running around than all of us. Besides, many routine tasks could be performed over individual comms."

"You just listened to her, followed her orders with no question, no critical reasoning. There was no questioning why she was in charge?"

"Major Barbier outranked me. She outranked all of us, and she was our doctor. We know her; we trust her. She's our *doctor*."

Glenn mused over the fact that he certainly couldn't fault Yvette for taking on effective command while *also* being the chief medical officer. After all, that's exactly what he'd done, although he'd eventually shifted more of the ship's command duties to Dvorak as he'd recovered.

The difference was that he'd been ordered to assume both roles. Yvette had done so on her own initiative.

Ramirez questioned Gavin Taketani next.

"Doctor Taketani, you were the seniormost official

present on *Percheron*. You were Mars mission commander. Why didn't you take command when Captain LeBlanc was declared unfit for duty?"

"Excuse me, Mister Ramirez. I am an administrator, not a ship commander. I am neither Space Force officer, nor qualified to command and direct Space Force personnel."

"But Major Barbier worked for you. She was a Space Force officer under your command on Marsbase."

"Yes, but that was on Mars. We were in a MarsX facility that was as much civilian as it was military. On *Percheron* we were on a Space Force ship on which the chain of command was the ultimate authority. I had no rank to order those people around. I had no experience in the operation of a spaceship."

"But Yvette Barbier is a doctor, not a ship captain."

"She was the ranking Space Force officer. She had the authority and seniority to direct Major Dvorak and the others to perform their duties as necessary. We were in good hands. We trusted her."

"And when she locked everybody up?"

"We weren't locked in our quarters. We went there of our own volition. We knew there was a serious possibility that we were facing an infectious disease. We learned later that it was not infectious, and when we did, we came out of our quarters and did our jobs."

Ramirez shook his head in frustration. The prosecution simply was not going the way he expected. Thomas stepped up to cross-examine the witness.

"Doctor Taketani. You are telling us that you and the rest of the Marsbase personnel obeyed the instructions you were given by lawful authority. You trusted her. She was your medical officer, and when people were getting sick, you trusted her instructions to keep you safe. Is that right."

"Yes, that is true. She had our confidence. She had *my* confidence."

"And when Colonel Shepard arrived and took over for Major Barbier, did you extend to him that same confidence?"

"Of course, I've known Glenn Shepard for many years. He trained with us. He was one of us."

"And when he overruled Major Barbier—you were okay with that?"

"Well, everybody on board had been affected one way or another. We hadn't seen much of an effect on Doctor Barbier until she broke down. Colonel Shepard outranked her. He was the senior doctor aboard. He also hadn't been affected like the rest of us."

"One more question. You talk now about how you were all affected. Were you aware of those effects at the time?"

"No. I felt normal, but Yvette told us that we were all acting a little bit strange. We had the headaches and the restlessness, plus lots of us had insomnia. I know there were a few arguments, but we just chalked that up to lack of sleep. It was only when people started falling seriously ill—and when the captain did . . . what she did. We knew something was seriously wrong."

"And Yvette Barbier was your doctor. She would know, right?"

"Exactly. We trusted her just as we trusted Colonel Shepard."

"No further questions, Your Honor."

✳ ✳ ✳

"Colonel Shepard. When you arrived on *Percheron*, the first thing Major Barbier did was to attack you, is that correct?"

"No, that's not what happened."

"Colonel, you are under oath, and we do have the bodycam video of the entire time you were on Percheron. Would you like to try that again?"

"Yvette Barbier did not recognize me. She thought I was an intruder. She fought me to protect her ship."

"Ah, ah, ah, Colonel. You don't know her motivation!"

"Actually, I do. I was her doctor and counselor for much of the trip home. I have medical diagnoses that prove she was in an altered mental state. She did not know what she was doing."

"Did she know what she was doing when she tried to seduce you? That seems such a far cry from attack."

"Copper poisoning causes too much dopamine to be made into norepinephrine. Adrenaline, if you will. A person with excess adrenaline does many things that seem crazy. Moreover, excess norepinephrine causes problems with dopamine-serotonin balance. Virtually every neuropsychological health issue we know has its roots in neurotransmitter imbalance."

"I don't need a chemistry lesson, Colonel. Yvette Barbier attacked you twice, mental disorder or not. She disobeyed orders, usurped the chain of command, attacked a superior officer, did she not?"

"No."

"No? Colonel, I remind you that you are still under oath."

"Yvette Barbier was suffering from schizophrenia.

The name translates to '*of divided mind.*' We often say that a person is 'not in their right mind,' but in this case, it was quite literally true. She conducted herself as a professional—officer and doctor—for as long as she could. Her conscious mind then quite literally watched herself do things she would never do. Yvette will spend a lot of time in therapy, and believe me, she knows what happened. She will live with it for the rest of her life."

Ramirez threw up his hands in disgust. "No further questions, Your Honor."

Thomas stepped in front of the stand. "One question, Colonel. What do you think we should decide regarding Major Barbier?"

"I can't bring myself to blame her. I admit to having held a grudge—wrongly, I might add—and I noticed discrepancies in the medical records from Mars, but I spoke to—hell, I treated—every one of her crewmates. She even assisted me with surgery when I needed her the most. She did nothing wrong. She was as much a victim of copper toxicity as the others."

"Thank you, Colonel."

Court was dismissed for the day. Yvette's commanding officer would have the opportunity to speak in front of the ten-officer trial board the next day. Of course, just like Glenn, Yvette's CO was General Boatright.

Glenn figured he knew what the general would say.

"Mister Thomas, will General Boatright be speaking this morning?"

It was an odd question, since Boatright was sitting right next to Glenn in the gallery.

"No, Your Honor, he communicated to me that everything which needed to be said, has been said."

A whispered, "By you, Shep," came from Glenn's side.

"Very well, the prosecution and defense may present closing arguments."

Ramirez was stern in recounting the charges against Yvette, but the actual content of his summary was weak. Thomas was much more forceful and convincing. It took only an hour for the panel to return a verdict exonerating Yvette.

"Excellent work," said Boatright. "OSI is getting off on the right footing. Well done, everyone. Shep, Jen, I'll see you in the office."

The general went forward to speak with Yvette, and congratulate Major Thomas. Glenn couldn't hear what had been said, but there were tears in her eyes. Nik looked triumphant, though. So that was probably a good thing.

What surprised him was that Yvette came over, shook Jen's hand, and then started a tearful apology. She turned to Glenn, and looked unsure of what to do.

Glenn opened his arms, and she fell into him, sobbing. "I'm so sorry. Thank you, you are so much kinder, so much more *alive* than I ever thought you'd be. I'm sure you've heard this a lot, but you're a hero to me as well."

Glenn looked down in embarrassment.

Jen came over, and put her arms around the two of them. "Yes, he is. He just doesn't know how to admit it. C'mon, let's get out of here."

Yvette disengaged from the two of them. "I'd like to treat the two of you to dinner, but . . ." She looked over a Nik, who simply nodded. "I think I need to sit with my doctor for a while."

"No problem. We'll take you up on it later," Jen told her. "C'mon, hero, let's get out of this place. Too many bad memories."

"Too hot, too . . . I feel like I'm burning . . ."

Glenn collapsed.

CHAPTER 46:
The Beach and the Stars

※

Beth L @SpaceNewsNetwork
Astronaut, doctor, hero. Colonel Glenn
Shepard was rushed to the hospital today
after he collapsed while exiting the
courtroom complex at Joint Base
Anacostia-Bolling. Shepard had been
attending the court martial of Yvette
Barbier, chief medical officer of Mars
Three / Marsbase One.
Shepard's testimony was essential to
acquitting Barbier of malfeasance charges
stemming from her actions during the
Percheron Incident.
Our hearts and prayers are with Colonel
Shepard and his loved ones tonight.
ChirpChat, July 2044

They'd rushed Glenn to Walter Reed National Military
Medical Center to determine why he'd collapsed outside

the courtroom at JBAB. His internal temperature had been elevated, and he was found to be slightly dehydrated, so the docs gave him intravenous fluids, ice packs, and made him stay in the hospital overnight. They ruled it heat exhaustion, even though he'd been in an air-conditioned building when it happened. He was eventually released with orders to see his doctors at SAMMC for further testing.

Glenn couldn't help but feel that this was a terrible setback—he'd be back in rehab in San Antonio, and Jen was in D.C.

Fortunately, Marty and his team found the problem less than a day after Glenn entered the facility. His bionic limbs were mostly powered locally, using a combination of internal—battery—and external—beamed power—sources. They were also basically wireless, at least they had no wires connecting inside the body. That was not the case for his bionic eye and ear, they had to be wired into the comm system built into the fleshy part of his left ear, and to the quantum processor of the bionic integration controller implanted in his left hip. Once again, the wiring was kept to a minimum, and well shielded to prevent short-circuits and other hazards.

The same could not be said for his LVAD. While its usage was non-standard—boosting lymph circulation to prevent heat buildup—it was a commercially available medical device, and one of the power leads had been crimped and lost some of its insulation.

As a result, Glenn had experienced occasional jolts of electricity where the wires passed right under the intercostal muscles of his chest. Marty thought that the short-circuits probably dated back to the year after implant, when he'd been in Hawaii. It explained the occasional twinges on the Moon, and on *Percheron*.

Sometime before or during Yvette's court martial, the wire had broken, and the LVAD stopped functioning. His collapse had been from overheating, not heat exhaustion or a heart attack.

Glenn was able to return to D.C. the next week, but that was short-lived. There was talk of new assignments on Earth, the Moon, Heinlein, or even the upcoming asteroid missions, but he secretly hoped for Mars.

For now, though, he was back in San Antonio, this time working on protocols for service member rehabilitation with bionics. He was writing the book on how augmented humans would serve in the Space Force to do jobs that a normal human could not. The general had also declared that he needed a PAO assistant, so Jen was there too.

They'd rented a small house in the northeast corner of San Antonio. It was an old neighborhood, with lots of retirees—mostly from the Army and Air Force, but it had its share of Navy, Marines, and Coasties. They turned out to be a great resource, too. Glenn was a regular at meetings in the old golf club and recreation center where the retirees talked about their days in service. Glenn's office was at Fort Sam Houston, adjacent to SAMMC. He had ready access to the on-base rehab unit, and Nik and Marty's specialty clinic was just across town.

Jen's office was out at the old Randolph AFB, about the same distance north that Glenn commuted south. It was an ideal arrangement. The general had made it clear that it wasn't fraternization when the commanding officers gave permission. Since that was Boatright for both of them, they had no worries about settling into a domestic arrangement.

Jen came home early. It had been a short day, coming off a week of sixteen-to-twenty-hour days where she'd had to spend half of the time at Randolph, and the other half in Shep's office at Fort Sam. She'd been grocery shopping for a special occasion. She wasn't sure he would want to celebrate, but she wanted to be prepared. It had been two years since the launch of the *Bat*. Writing his biography meant that Jen was intimately familiar with what constituted important dates in his life. It might be a strange event to commemorate it, but she wanted to remember it.

On this day, two years ago, Shep had admitted that he wanted to spend the rest of his life with her.

Nik and Sheila would be coming to dinner. They'd invited Marty and his wife, but the surgeon had to go to Los Angeles to prep a patient for transfer to SAMMC. This one would receive some of the same advanced bionics as Shep.

She looked around at her surroundings. The owner said the house had been in the family for eighty years, but updated several times. There were a few outdated pieces of furniture—and even more in a detached garage out back—supplemented with her own things. Glenn simply didn't have much except for his room at Aunt Sally's apartment. She'd finally exited the lease on her Richmond apartment. It was no longer her home, and she knew that her future held a lot of moving, temporary lodging, and likely prolonged separation.

Let's see—we'll hide Nik and Sheila over there, and they'll jump out... No, too risky. We'll wait out front... No. Nik and Sheila should be sitting on the couch when I open the door. She was in the kitchen when she heard the front door to the apartment. *Oh no, he's early. Nik isn't here yet!*

Shep was in the entrance with a big grin on his face. This was more than just the date on the calendar. He had big news and couldn't wait to share it.

"Hey, love, I've got something to tell you!" He reached out and grabbed her around the waist with his right arm.

"Cool your jets, flyboy. I've got to get dinner out and company's coming."

"Wait, what? Company? What are we having?"

"Well, I was thinking of something Hawaiian, kalbi ribs, some kalua pork, maybe some poké—but I couldn't get the poké. I did manage to find a Golden Wave ale for you, though."

Shep looked dumbstruck. "Really?"

"No, not really. But I have mahi-mahi for the grill, and I wasn't kidding about the beer."

As the implications sunk in, his grin became bigger. "Ah! So that must mean the company is Nik and Sheila! In that case, the news can wait until dinner. Need some help in there?"

"Nope, the mahi is fresh, but the rest is prepack. Nik and Sheila will be here any minute. Go see to our guests."

The small dinner party was a success. Shep did indeed appreciate her timing for the celebration. The fact that Nik was there as well, reinforced the positive nature of the experience. Sheila was intelligent and witty, although quite shy. She sat very close to Nik, holding his arm as if having finally caught him, she had no intention of letting him go.

It was time for Shep's big news.

Nik and Sheila brought a bottle of sparkling white wine, and Shep raised his glass in toast. "To the ladies who make our lives worth living!"

"Hear, hear," Nik said. Sheila blushed, and Jen said nothing.

"Okay, so here it is. Marsbase is expanding. Starting with Marsbase Four, they'll rotate crews more often, but only part of the crew at a time. They'll send out twenty, bring back ten. Next, they'll send thirty and bring back fifteen. Over a five-year period, they want to grow Marsbase into one hundred people—real colonists—and put in an orbital habitat. This one will be called Burroughs Station."

"Sounds good, so what's got you so excited?"

"They want me for Mission Lead—not CMO—but Director of Marsbase. I'll also temporarily command the contingent that will be constructing the Space Force orbital facility—Burroughs Station!"

"Whoa, command! Who let you out of the cage, flyboy?" Nik held out his hand to shake Shep's. "Congratulations, buddy."

Shep and Nik were all grins. Sheila was smiling, and Jen forced a pleased expression, too, but inside, her heart sank.

He's going away again.

Shep was still speaking. "It's going to be hard, though. After the mistakes made with Marsbase One, we've got to handle information flow a lot better than has been done in the past. With a larger civilian population, we also need to manage internal information delivery. That's why I'm getting a dedicated communications and media section." He paused, and cocked an eyebrow at her.

Her wristcomm pinged, despite the fact she'd set it to Do Not Disturb for the evening. She checked the screen and her eyes widened.

"That's why Major Butler has been assigned to assist me. Honey, we're going to Mars."

"Hold on, Shep, aren't you forgetting something?" Nik looked at Glenn and waggled his eyebrows.

"Oh, yeah, thanks, buddy." Shep got up from his chair, set it aside, and got down on one knee. He pulled a small black box out of his pocket, opened it, and held it out to Jen.

Her heart melted. Before he could even say a word, she gave him her answer.

"Yes."

It was a small affair held near the town of Lahaina on Maui. Glenn had argued for Kailua-Kona, on the Big Island where they'd first met, but Jen successfully argued that their best memories were from Maui. There were a few guests, Marty and Aaliyah Spruce, Jen's publisher Leo and Dana, Mila Katou, Gavin Taketani, and Jeff Ling, newly returned from the Moon. Several of the regular HI-SLOPE and Pohakuloa staff from the high elevations of the island who'd worked closely with Glenn or Jen during training had come over on an interisland flyer. Colonel Richardson was there, directing an honor guard of Space Force officers waiting to form the ceremonial arch.

Nik was the best man, and Sheila was maid of honor. Aunt Sally was present as mother of the groom, but Jen had no family to attend. She'd considered asking Leo, but then she received an offer from an unexpected source.

Glenn looked nervous, and yet utterly fierce in his midnight-blue dress uniform with all of his medals. He was outdone only by the two figures coming down the aisle. Jen was simply stunning in a cream-colored dress that perfectly accented her dark skin. She gave General Boatright a quick peck on the cheek, and then a big hug, as he handed her off at the front of the chapel. Boatright smiled broadly at Glenn and then winked. Everything was obviously proceeding exactly as the general had planned.

The chapel faced the ocean, and the ceremony had been timed to end at sunset. So much of it was a blur—Glenn knew he'd recited vows, said "I do," and kissed the bride. That was about all he could remember—that and the fact that his breath caught every time he looked at Jen.

He'd turned off the heads-up display in his left eye for the duration of the ceremony. Jen had teased him that he was *not* allowed to read his vows off a teleprompter. He could memorize them—or not—like anyone else. The display activated though, with an alert just at the end of the ceremony.

Glenn squeezed Jen's hand and cocked his head to call her attention to the sun just disappearing from view. For just a second, the western horizon flashed brilliant green.

EPILOGUE

❦

"Hey, thanks for coming, Shep. I'm sure the patients will appreciate the visit and I know that Jakob and Victoria are really eager to see you." Nik greeted Glenn and Jen as they entered the new rehabilitation hospital. "And by the way, the staff told me to convey their congratulations to you two again. Of course, now you've got Sheila thinking about getting married. I'm not quite sure I'm ready for that leap. So, should I thank you, or be angry with you?"

Glenn laughed. "I think in the long run you'll probably thank us. I know Jen and Sheila have been talking a lot."

"Yes, she said something about making an honest man out of you, Nik," Jen said.

Nik made a face, but then laughed. "I suppose it could be worse, although it'll probably be better to wait until after my surgery."

"Yes, I heard about that. You're due to get a spinal stimulator, right?"

"Uh huh. It's supposed to halt the degeneration and restore lower limb strength. It's been so long since my original injury, that I really hadn't hoped to be free of crutches and wheelchair. The exoskeleton is okay, but it will be nice to be able to walk without the extra support. This is all thanks to you, you know, Glenn. This hospital wouldn't exist without you."

"I don't know about that. On paper, they may credit me, but it was really Marty Spruce's work that led to this. I'm really surprised that they didn't name it for him."

"Well, the original plan was to call it the 'Spruce Center for Neurorehabilitation,' but he just wouldn't go for it."

"At least they didn't call it the 'Shepard Center . . .'" Jen said.

"Or worse, 'Shepard's Flock,'" Glenn replied with a grimace. "I will say that 'The Jack Steele Center for Bionics' does have a nice ring to it."

Nik took his two friends on a tour through the new rehab facility. It was larger than the one where Glenn had met Nik, while he learned to use his new bionic capabilities. The site was located at a decommissioned Air Force base in southeast San Antonio, Texas, not far from the San Antonio Military Medical Center.

The hospital was quite large, and most of the patient facilities were on a single floor. There were the usual patient rooms, configured as studio and efficiency apartments rather than hospital rooms. They allowed the patients to have a measure of privacy and feel more like they were in a residence than a rehabilitation center. There were clinical offices, exam rooms, physical therapy facilities, several therapy pools, and gymnasiums with different equipment to support lower versus upper limb (or combination) rehabilitation. The few upper-level rooms included physician and administrative offices as well as support services.

Nik also showed them classrooms, meeting rooms, and social interaction areas spread through the entire campus. In fact, that's exactly how he described it to his guests. This was the campus of the "university of knuckle down and heal yourself." It didn't have the stigma of a hospital or physical therapy center, but rather a place where someone could live and learn and heal.

"Hey Shep, great to see you again!" Jakob had been one of Glenn's fellow patients during rehabilitation. In fact, it was Jakob that he'd been racing the day Marty Spruce chastised Glenn for inappropriate use of his exoskeleton. It was only Nik's presence racing—and beating—both of them, that had interrupted Marty's tirade. Many years ago, he had been recovering from traumatic amputation of both legs. Today, however, the former patient turned trainer stood tall and moved well on his own bionic leg replacements. "Have I got something to show you! Take a look at this."

Jakob held up a pair of bionic limbs that looked like legs, but with considerable modifications. Nik had already seen them—he'd helped write up the justification and specifications, after all—but he watched as Glenn took a limb and examined it. It had the usual magnetic bearing at the knee, but the lower leg appeared slender, with a less pronounced heel and longer, more flexible toes.

"Those look almost like hands," Glenn said wonderingly.

"Got it in one. We're calling those 'tingers.' The whole structure is a 'foothand' although some of the techs shorten that to 'fands,'" Jakob told Glenn. "They're for use in zero-gee environments. I'm taking a job up in

O'Neill station with the construction crew for the *Clydesdale*, the third-generation Helicity-drive ship that will start a circuit of Mars and Ceres bases. Since I'll be operating in the absence of gravity most of the time, I don't really need feet—what I *do* need is an extra set of hands, or something like hands. These are modular and I can switch them out as needed. I've been practicing with them in the neutral buoyancy pool, although they support my weight just fine in full gee. They're a little awkward down here in the well, though—especially trying to find shoes. In orbit though? Four hands will be an advantage."

Nik took over at a nod. "We read about something like this in an old science fiction novel. Jakob was browsing my collection and called it to my attention. In the story, humans had been genetically altered to have four limbs that were essentially arms and hands. It seemed a bit excessive to me, but he convinced the developers that with modular bionics, he could easily swap out limbs for specific purposes."

"That's amazing," Glenn said. "No one should ever again question whether an amputee can be an effective contributor to operations in space."

"Hey, if you think this is something, take a look at what Vicky has over there." Jakob motioned to the other person who had come to talk with them in the social center.

Victoria was a short woman with natural legs, but rather obvious prosthetics replacing both of her arms. They were obvious because her left arm was artificial from the shoulder down and was bulky, more than twice the diameter of a flesh-and-blood arm. While her shoulders weren't completely asymmetric, it was clear that the bionic rebuild on that side extended into her shoulder and back. The right arm was only artificial from the elbow down, and ended not in fingers, but in many fine tools.

"These are my working arms," Victoria said, "and yes, I do have normal looking ones—for clubbing and dates. Unlike Jakob, though, I figured I'd actually wear mine and show you how they work." She held up the small prosthetic and demonstrated the powered drivers, wrenches, cutters, welders, and various tips that she could utilize in place of fingers. It could also divide in half to position tools at two different angles or serve as a clamp to work on any object in her grasp. "I have a bionic eye with telescopic and microscopic functions as well. I can trace a circuit, cut it, replace it, weld it, or even completely rewire it one-handed.

"As for the other hand…" She reached down and wrapped her left arm around Jakob's legs. He steadied himself with one hand on her shoulder as she lifted him off the ground. "This one's rigged for strength and leverage. My damage went all the way into the shoulder, so they replaced the shoulder socket and reinforced my collarbone and spine to give me additional leverage and increased lifting capacity. Between the two of these, I'm your ideal mechanic. I can lift a Moon buggy and perform all of the necessary repairs to put it back in service faster than the you can go find a jack just to get underneath."

"Shouldn't that be … 'on the one hand … on the other hand … on the gripping hand'?" Glenn asked, and was met by grins from Nik, Jakob, and Vic. Jen looked confused until Nik explained that it was a reference to a science fiction novel in which the aliens had three arms—

one large one for lifting, and two smaller ones on the opposite side for finer work.

"Thanks to you, they've both been reactivated to active duty," Nik told Glenn. "As he said, Jakob is going to O'Neill as part of the *Clydesdale* construction team. Vic's going to the Moon—for training. She won't be using that superstrength yet."

Victoria gave a wide grin. "I will when I go to Mars. It's at least a year until *Augeron* leaves, so I've got enough time to get trained up. In one-third gee, I'll be able to do absolutely anything the colony needs me to do. I plan to be the commander's number one technical specialist."

Nik and Glenn laughed.

"Hmm, I wonder who that commander might be?" Nik mused.

Victoria looked back and forth at the two of them grinning at her, and realization slowly dawned. "Awesome!"

The tour ended in the recreation center. It was the Steele Center's largest area dedicated to relaxation. The walls sported many plaques and portraits commemorating key developments in neuro-rehabilitation and prosthetics. Three portraits were separated from the rest and placed at the focal point of the room—Jack Steele, Marty Spruce, and Glenn. An interactive touch screen exhibit next to the portraits was currently playing a history of DARPA's bionic research from the leadership of Director Tony Tether and continuing on for many years with the development of the first fully articulated, neurally controlled "DEKA" arm.

Nik had been consulted on the content of the presentation, and he was a bit afraid of the reaction once it drew Glenn's attention. That particular loop ended with Nik talking about how his friend Shep was a shining example of someone who had gone through fire and come back to be the person he was always meant to be.

Nik stood by those words, even as he knew how much it would embarrass Shep. His friend had such a hard time with the concept of "hero."

"I'm just an ordinary guy in extraordinary situations."

"And that's what makes you a hero, hon," said Jen as she pulled him tighter.

ACKNOWLEDGEMENTS

※ ※ ※

In 1959, Dr. Jack Steele coined the term "bionic" to reference "bio-like" or "life-like" biologically inspired engineering.

Steele started off studying engineering in 1942, but the small matter of a war got in the way. After four years in the U.S. Army during World War II, he returned to college to study pre-medicine, and earned his M.D. in 1950. After a year as a teaching fellow, Steele returned to the military and served twenty years in the Air Force until retirement. He joined the Aerospace Medical Research Laboratory (AMRL) at Wright-Patterson Air Force Base in Dayton, Ohio; and in 1960, led a three-day symposium using his new term "bionics," to discuss uses of biology to solve engineering problems.

The AMRL helped prepare America's first astronauts, and also engaged in some of the first research to propose augmenting living organisms with artificial technology. The first mention of cybernetic organisms, or "cyborgs," was also in 1960, by Australian inventor Manfred Clynes and American scientist Nathan Kline, who proposed the integration of technology to assist in human exploration of space. The association of Steele's bionics and AMRLs research into cyborgs cemented the popular science fiction pairing of bionics with high-technology prosthetics, as exemplified by author and aviation expert Martin Caidin's 1972 novel *Cyborg*.

This has been a fun story to write. I hope many of my readers have heard of Caidin's book—or perhaps you've heard of the TV show *The Six Million Dollar Man*. The book and the series were quite influential in my choice of career. I entered graduate school in 1979, intending to study "bionics" only to find that the field didn't really exist. In 1982, I started a Ph.D. in physiology and pharmacology, and eventually specialized in Neuroscience. Computerized methods for studying the brain led to means to detect brain patterns in rats to study memory and detect behavioral choices based on memory. That led to more memory studies in rats, monkeys, and eventually humans. In 2019, I attended an annual conference in which the Defense Advanced Research Projects Agency reviewed progress across all of its funded research in neurotechnology. It was there that I met my first authentic bionic man, Johnny Matheny. Books, TV, movies all like to paint DARPA as the bad guy—but I'm here to tell you that they are truly good people doing good things. Johnny's advanced forearm and hand prosthetic were products of DARPA's Revolutionizing Prosthetics program under the direction of Colonel Geoffrey Ling, M.D. (US Army, retired) and Justin Sanchez, Ph.D. I looked around at the people attending that meeting, and realized that forty years after learning that "bionics" didn't exist the way I'd imagined it, these researchers and visionaries had created the field, after all, and DARPA was a major part of it.

Those two gentlemen were also program managers for the projects in which I participated, so my first acknowledgement is to Geoff and Justin at DARPA for seeing the potential in the science—and in me, as a not-so-young researcher who dreamed of turning science fiction into science. To my colleagues, including long-time mentor, collaborator and friend, Sam Deadwyler—it's been a wild ride and we finally made it. My one regret is no longer having long Friday afternoon conversations to daydream about "what's next?" To Mitch Riley and Brent Roeder, who represent my legacy in research, I give to you the Moon—take it and make it yours.

My publisher, Toni Weisskopf, and (former) editor, Tony Daniel, have been highly encouraging, reviewing the outline and early concepts for this book. Then, when it was all done, Toni sat me down and showed me how to make it better! This is a story I've wanted to tell for some time—my heartfelt thanks for the opportunity to do so.

Several authors have encouraged me in my development as a writer. Let's start with the classics referenced in the story: Robert Heinlein, Arthur C. Clarke, Isaac Asimov, and Martin Caidin, of course. More recent influences—and folks I've also had the honor to meet—include Lois McMaster Bujold, James Hogan, and Ben Bova. Several author friends have provided suggestions, guidance and even a sandbox of anthologies and collections to practice the writing craft—John Ringo, Tom Kratman, Mike Williamson, Sarah and Dan Hoyt, Chuck Gannon, Larry Correia, Les Johnson, Kevin J. Anderson, Chris Kennedy, Mark Wandrey, Kevin Steverson, Kevin Ikenberry, and Bill Webb. Several good friends who are "no-longer-newbie" authors from that sandbox also deserve special mention for their encouragement, notably Mike Massa, Kacey Ezell, and Chris Smith. Thanks for putting up with half-baked ideas and too much exposition! I owe you all a debt, as does every author who walks in the footprints of Those Who Have Gone Before.

For examples of how to do dictation and make it work for story writing, I thank Kevin J. Anderson, and particularly Martin Shoemaker. I shouldn't be surprised, but when it came time to "rewrite" the final chapters, I found it easier to pull out the voice recorder than to sit and write. For those who haven't tried it yet, more than ninety percent of this novel was dictated into a voice recorder and transcribed by software. It takes a lot of editing after the transcription—and Toni showed me that I need to be much more careful in the editing, since there is a tendency to repeat, but it's worth it to get the framework down and it allows me to "write" while driving—a very productive use of my time.

To Speaker Alpha, my team of first readers—I value your input, particularly on the half-finished novel when I was uncertain whether a certain character "worked." A lot of the early feedback got incorporated in the book. It is especially poignant that we lost member Rick Boatright before he got to see the finished product. He would have liked this one. He was excited when I told him what I was writing. Perhaps if it hadn't been so hard to write in 2020, it wouldn't have happened this way.

Coulda'.

Shoulda'.

Woulda'.

Nothing to be done about that now. Sorry, Rick, we'll miss you.

Likewise, our Cabal of Unlikely Suspects: Chris, KC, Bridget, Doc, Jeremy & Emily, Monalisa, Sandra, Casey, Greg, Mike, Eeps, Cathe, Tara & Brian, Scott & April, Joseph, and Vin . . . scientists and professionals, aspiring writers, and just plain good friends. We're not exactly a writer group, because we don't critique each other, but we do act as sounding board and companionship— something truly valuable in this time. They are my family-of-choice, brothers and sisters all.

For Nik Rao, thanks for letting me Tuckerize you (with a name change). It was supposed to be a brief appearance to set up the frustration and dark humor of Shepard's rehabilitation. Little did I know you wanted a bigger role! Your avatar kept whispering in my ear . . . and the stuff was *good*! Nik became the perfect way to shed light on Shepard's character, much the way Jen did.

There's been a lot of writing this year, some by myself, and a lot with my sister, co-author, and personal editor, Sandra Medlock. Thanks, San, you help me make it all look good. It's also a joy to write with you—even though this isn't one of those books, it helps a lot to bounce ideas off of you.

In support of that writing, my dear wife Ruann puts up with a lot, but she also fiercely protects my writing time— both that I get it done, but also that it doesn't spill over into interfering with work. As a professor, researcher, journal editor, graduate mentor, teacher, and writer, there are many overlapping demands on my time. She helps me keep it all straight. Besides that, she's the love of my life and makes me whole. Our two sons are fine young men, grown and out of the house. They are highly supportive and have put up with a lot of instances of me trying out story ideas and dialogue. Thanks, guys.

My mother, Marjorie Hampson, is my first reader and biggest fan. She reads even the earliest versions of everything I write—sometimes before I even give them to her! We share Kindle files, and she usually finds whatever I've loaded for travel editing or convention readings. She also finds the tough typos that we all miss. Thanks, Mom!

Sadly, we lost Dad a year ago. Leonard Hampson was an engineer and proud father. He was slightly disappointed that I studied biology instead of engineering, but *loved* the fact that I ended up in a heavily engineering-influenced field such as neurotech. He was proud of the books and stories Sandra and I'd written, even if SF wasn't his thing. He knew I was working on this book, but given 2020 . . . well, he didn't get to see much of it. I wish I could call him up just one more time to say "Hey Dad! It's finished! Let me tell you about it . . ." He was my hero and my role model and I miss him dearly.

To all of you readers. I couldn't (and I wouldn't) do this without you.

Robert E. Hampson
Winston-Salem, NC, November 2021

❉ ❉ ❉

Addendum. On August 8, 2023, the town of Lahaina, in which many scenes of this story are set, was overrun by wildfire. The town burned to the ground. I (obviously) have many fond memories of the Hawaiian Islands, and visit on a yearly basis. In October 2023 I talked with folks who had been there, or had friends and family there. The loss of life and property is tragic, but the people are strong. As of October, there are signs that the banyan tree has survived, making it the most fitting memorial to the strength and resilience of the residents. I am proud to have featured it so prominently in this story, and hope that it is a fitting tribute.

—REH, December 2023.

AUTHOR BIOGRAPHY

※ ※ ※

Internationally recognized physiologist and neuroscientist, Dr. Robert E. Hampson, leads the multi-university team that was first to demonstrate restoration of human memory function using the brain's own information codes. His forty-year scientific career has ranged from studying the effects of commonly abused drugs on memory, to the effects of space radiation on the brain. He is a popular speaker and advisor on memory and the brain, having been interviewed by BBC, CNN, NPR, BYU Radio, *Financial Times, MIT Technology Review*, and the *Wall Street Journal*. His work has also been featured in the documentary *Life 2.0* (S1E8, Mastering Memory).

Dr. Hampson is lead scientist for Braingrade, Inc., a company working to transform his research findings into a medical device to restore human memory function damaged by injury or disease. He is also a professor of physiology/pharmacology and neurology at Wake Forest University School of Medicine where he teaches regularly in the neuroscience and biomedical graduate curriculum. He developed and teaches a course on Communicating Science, in which young scientists practice writing for, and speaking to, the general public. His research has been funded by NIH, NSF, DARPA, Office of Naval Research, Air Force Office of Scientific Research, Army Research Office, and private foundations. He has reviewed for more than two dozen scientific journals, NIH, NASA, the Department of Defense, and is an associate editor for the *Journal of Neuroscience Methods*.

Also known in Science Fiction circles as "Speaker to

Lab Animals," Dr. Rob is a Hugo-nominated science writer with more than thirty essays, interviews, and talks on science for general audiences. As an SF author, he has published more than twenty-five short stories, coedited two anthologies which combine hard science and science fiction, authored one prior novel, and coauthored three novels (with another due out this year). With a combination of science and science fiction credentials, he has been a consultant to TV and game producers, defense contractors, and more than a dozen science fiction authors.

He is a well-regarded speaker and panelist at conventions spanning the range from science to science fiction and media, including LibertyCon, DragonCon, FenCon, and the Interstellar Research Group symposia. He is a member of SIGMA—the Science Fiction Think Tank— and the Science and Entertainment Exchange (a service of the National Academy of Sciences). His website is http://REHampson.com.

The Wellstone
TPB: 978-1-9821-2477-9 • $16.00 US / $22.00 CAN
MM: 978-1-9821-2588-2 • $8.99 US / $11.99 CAN

Humanity has conquered the Solar System, going so far as to vanquish death itself. But for the children of immortal parents, life remains a constant state of arrested development. With his complaints being treated as teenage whining, and his ability to inherit the throne, Prince Bascal Edward de Towaji Lutui and his fellow malcontents take to the far reaches of colonized space. The goal: to prove themselves a force to be reckoned with.

Lost in Transmission
TPB: 978-1-9821-2503-5 • $16.00 US / $22.00 CAN

Banished to the starship *Newhope*, now King Bascal and his fellow exiles face a bold future: to settle the worlds of Barnard's Star. The voyage will last a century, but with Queendom technology it's no problem to step into a fax machine and "print" a fresh, youthful version of yourself. But the paradise they seek is far from what they find, and death has returned with a vengeance.

To Crush the Moon
TPB: 978-1-9821-2524-0 • $16.00 US / $22.00 CAN
MM: 978-1-9821-9200-6 • $8.99 US / $11.99 CAN

Once the Queendom of Sol was a glowing monument to humankind's loftiest dreams. Ageless and immortal, its citizens lived in peaceful splendor. But as Sol buckled under the swell of an "immorbid" population, space itself literally ran out. Now a desperate mission has been launched: to literally crush the moon. Success will save billions, but failure will strand humanity between death and something unimaginably worse . . .

Antediluvian
HC: 978-1-4814-8431-2 • $25.00 US / $34.00 CAN
MM: 978-1-9821-2499-1 • $8.99 US / $11.99 CAN

What if all our Stone Age legends are true and older than we ever thought? It was a time when men and women struggled and innovated in a world of savage contrasts, preserved only in the oldest stories with no way to actually visit it. Until a daring inventor's discovery cracks the code embedded in the human genome.

Available in bookstores everywhere.
Or order ebooks online at www.baen.com.

THE FAMILY BUSINESS

TPB: 978-1-9821-2502-8 • $16.00 US / $22.00 CAN
PB: 978-1-9821-9199-3 • $8.99 US / $11.99 CAN

After a devastating war for humankind, the Visitors' willing human collaborators were left behind. Now, federal recovery agent Nathan Foster and his 14-year-old nephew Ben must hunt them down and bring them to justice.

"Kupari is a skilled tradesman, deftly creating characters that are easy to get invested in and easy to care for. You will cheer at their successes and commiserate with their failures. . . ." —*Warped Factor*

Trouble Walked In

TPB: 978-1-9821-9203-7 • $16.00 US / $22.00 CAN

Cassandra Blake, an employee for the Ascension Planetary Holdings Group has gone missing. When questions need answering on Nova Columbia, Detective Ezekiel "Easy" Novak is the man folks turn to. He gets results—one way or another.